BEST
SCIENCE FICTION
STORIES
OF THE YEAR
Seventh Annual Collection

Gardner Dozois was born and raised in Salem, Massachusetts, and has been writing and editing science fiction for over ten years. His short fiction has appeared in most of the leading SF magazines and anthologies, and he has been a Nebula Award finalist five times, a Hugo Award finalist four times, and a Jupiter Award finalist twice. He is the editor of a number of anthologies, among them *A Day in the Life, Future Power* (with Jack Dann), *Another World,* and *Beyond the Golden Age.* His most recent books are *Strangers,* a novel; *The Visible Man,* a collection of his short fiction; and *The Fiction of James Tiptree, Jr.,* a critical chapbook. He is also co-author, with George Alec Effinger, of the novel *Nightmare Blue,* and is currently at work on another novel. He is a member of the Science Fiction Writers of America, the SFWA Speakers' Bureau, and the Professional Advisory Committee to the Special Collections Department of the Paley Library at Temple University. Mr. Dozois lives in Philadelphia.

BEST SCIENCE FICTION STORIES OF THE YEAR

Seventh Annual Collection

Edited by

GARDNER DOZOIS

E.P. Dutton / New York

HOUSTON PUBLIC LIBRARY

The editor would like to thank the following people for their help and support:

Michael Swanwick, Jack Dann, Kirby McCauley, Virginia Kidd, Susan Casper, David G. Hartwell, Terry Carr, Art Saha, Alice Sheldon, Edward Bryant, George R. R. Martin, Pat LoBrutto, Howard Waldrop, Tom Monteleone, C. L. Grant, Gregory Benford, Don Benson, Gene Wolfe, Steve Roos, M. S. Wyeth, Jr., Karen Solen, Tom Dunne, Dennis Holler, Gloria R. Mosesson, Peter Weston, Roy Torgeson, Barry N. Malzberg, George H. Scithers, Rick Sternbach, Asenath Hammond-Sternbach, Adele Hull, Arnie Fenner, Pat Cadigan, A. A. Whyte, Charles C. Ryan, Jonathan Ostrowsky-Lantz, John M. Landsberg, Tom Whitehead and his staff from the Special Collections Department of the Paley Library at Temple University, Fred Fisher of the Hourglass SF bookstore in Philadelphia, and special thanks to my own editor, Jo Alford.

Acknowledgment is made for permission to print the following material:

"The Screwfly Solution" by Raccoona Sheldon. Copyright © 1977 by Alice B. Sheldon. First published in *Analog Science Fiction/Science Fact*, June 1977. Reprinted by permission of the author and the author's agent, Robert P. Mills, Ltd.

"In the Hall of the Martian Kings" by John Varley. Copyright © 1977 by Mercury Press, Inc. First published in *The Magazine of Fantasy and Science Fiction*, February 1977. Reprinted by permission of the author and the author's agent, Kirby McCauley.

"Particle Theory" by Edward Bryant. Copyright © 1977 by Condé Nast Publications, Inc. First published in *Analog Science Fiction/Science Fact*, February 1977. Reprinted by permission of the author.

"Bitterblooms" by George R. R. Martin. Copyright © 1977 by Baronet Publishing Company. First published in *Cosmos* 4, November 1977. Reprinted by permission of the author.

"Black as the Pit, From Pole to Pole" by Steven Utley and Howard Waldrop. Copyright © 1977 by Robert Silverberg. First published in *New Dimensions 7* (Harper & Row). Reprinted by permission of the authors.

"The House of Compassionate Sharers" by Michael Bishop. Copyright © 1977 by Baronet Publishing Company. First published in *Cosmos* 1, May 1977. Reprinted by permission of the author and the author's agent, Virginia Kidd.

"Stardance" by Spider Robinson and Jeanne Robinson. Copyright © 1977 by Condé Nast Publications, Inc. First published in *Analog Science Fiction/Science Fact*, March 1977. Reprinted by permission of the authors and the authors' agent, Kirby McCauley.

For information contact:
E.P. Dutton, 2 Park Avenue, New York, N.Y. 10016

Library of Congress Catalog Card Number: 77-190700

ISBN: 0-525-06496-6

Published simultaneously in Canada by
Clarke, Irwin & Company Limited, Toronto and Vancouver

Designed by Nicola Mazzella

10 9 8 7 6 5 4 3 2 1

First Edition

For
Rick Sternbach and Asenath Hammond-Sternbach

CONTENTS

INTRODUCTION
Summation: 1977

1977 will be remembered as the year the ceiling came off, finally and irrevocably. Any subsequent discussion of SF as an isolated category of literaure will now be hopelessly dated. For better or for worse, the days of insularity are over, and SF is now out in the light—the full, hot, bright, merciless spotlight of the modern media machine.

Certainly more SF and fantasy books were published in 1977 than ever before, and, even so, many publishers at year's end were talking about radically expanding their lines. More significantly, SF and fantasy books sold more copies this year, and several titles were staggering best sellers: J. R. R. Tolkien's *The Silmarillion* quickly ran through 700,000 copies (of a $10.95 edition!) and is reported to be the biggest-selling hardcover book of all time, excepting only the Bible; George Lucas's execrable *Star Wars* novelization was one of the hottest items in Ballantine's long history; Frank Herbert's *Children of Dune* and Terry Brooks's *The Sword of Shannara* made both hardcover and paperback bestseller lists; a $35 illustrated edition of Tolkien's *The Hobbit*, Stephen R. Donaldson's hardcover *Illearth* trilogy, and a number of other books all sold very well. As for big-money advances, new records were set: Reputedly, $250,000 was paid for Larry Niven's and Jerry Pournelle's *Lucifer's Hammer,* $3 million for a three-book package from Stephen King, and lots of high, five-figure advances went to other writers. There are now countless SF- and fantasy-oriented spinoff items such as art books, games, posters, and spoken-word records.

In short, 1977 was a boom year for SF, so big and flashy that the famous postwar boom of the Fifties pales into insignificance. Boom-and-bust cycles have been repeated several times in SF history, and I, myself, would not be surprised to see this boom ultimately crest and fall (although I suspect that it will last at least three or four years longer than the most conservative critics estimate, simply on momentum). However, I am not too dismayed. It has been pointed out, aptly I think, that every previous cycle of boom-and-bust has left the regular SF audience larger than it was before. No, I am more worried by another and more insidious danger, one that will grow even greater if the boom *doesn't* bust: the advent of the junk-food mentality.

A historically important fact about 1977 is that it unequivocally established that *SF is a moneymaker*; the message is suddenly bright and clear to people who previously had not even been aware of the genre's existence. The buttoned-down corporate accountants and PR experts will be moving in on us; the people who have turned much of book publishing into a sterile parade of manufactured bestsellers are the same kinds of people who eradicated America's former eating habits and plastered the country with fast-food chains. This is the junk-food mentality: Cut quality, cut costs, hype your product relentlessly, and sell in bulk. What will it do to SF?

Much of the extraordinary media attention SF received this year was generated by two big-budget SF movies that featured stunning visuals, superb production values, fast-and-furious action, and the best special effects ever put on the screen. Indeed, if the average, non-fan citizen thought about SF at all in 1977, chances are that it was in the context of 70mm Panavision and Dolby Sound.

Star Wars, George Lucas's action-packed fairy tale for grownups, was the most talked-about SF event since Stanley Kubrick's *2001* and is already the biggest boxoffice hit of all time. It became a cult item almost overnight and spawned an endless stream of *Star Wars* calendars, posters, games, comic books, light-swords, T-shirts, and other items. Another major SF film, Steven Spielberg's multimillion dollar UFO-believer movie, *Close Encounters of the Third Kind,* opened late in the year to huge crowds and is likely to be another big moneymaker.

Both movies are actually bad SF in most respects, full of scientific boners and logical inconsistencies. *Close Encounters* suffers from a Pollyanna cosmic ending that hung many viewers uneasily between catharsis and fits of giggling, and in the final analysis only the literally awesome special effects manage to save this silly movie from itself. *Star Wars* is redeemed only by Lucas's obvious affection for the pulp SF classics from which most of his material is drawn, and by the fact that his tongue is firmly planted in his cheek throughout. Even so, both films represent a welcome change from the run of dreary, pretentious, pseudo-profound SF movies of the last few years.

The long-term effects of the *Star Wars* phenomenon may be deleterious—it is likely to reestablish in the popular mind the very concept of SF as a literature concerned solely with Bug-Eyed Monsters and roaring blasters that most of us have been struggling to supplant. However, the optical techniques developed in the making of both movies are likely to remain important. For the first time, even the most grandiose of SF concepts—mile-long spaceships, mile-high cities, vast armadas battling in space—can be *shown* to an audience, visualized convincingly and realistically in motion and depth and color. Because of this, SF is suddenly the hottest theatrical property around, and that fact alone will have profound and far-reaching consequences on the field.

Ironically, the Science Fiction Writers of America finally abolished the Dramatic Presentation Nebula because of a dearth of worthwhile movies—about a month before the premiere of *Star Wars*.

In the magazine market, most successful from a commercial standpoint was *Isaac Asimov's Science Fiction Magazine*. Although the quality of the material there often varied wildly from issue to issue, and even from one story to the next, *IASFM* has been generally well received, and is presently selling about sixty thousand copies on the newsstand, with a subscription list of about thirty thousand. *IASFM* may be the only SF magazine in years able to compete successfully with *Analog* in terms of circulation. It will be going bimonthly in 1978, and Davis Publications is planning to launch a companion magazine: *Isaac Asimov's SF Adventure Magazine*, a large-format quarterly that editor George H. Scithers hopes will be "a new *Planet Stories*."

Cosmos, 1977's major new magazine, must be added to SF's unfortunately long list of worthwhile failures, right next to *Venture* and *Worlds Beyond*—it "suspended publication indefinitely" after its fourth issue. *Cosmos* was more daring and literarily more progressive than the somewhat conservative *IASFM*, although also uneven in quality; under editor David G. Hartwell it managed to publish several of the year's best stories and seemed to be selling decently when debts incurred by Baronet Publishing Company on behalf of its newly-launched movie magazine called *Bijou* forced both magazines under. *Cosmos's* inconclusive demise is especially frustrating as it leaves unresolved the decades-long debate as to whether or not a slick, large-format SF magazine can survive.

A hint of the answer to that old question was provided by the enormous commercial success of *Heavy Metal*, a large-format magazine from the publishers of *National Lampoon*. Although *Heavy Metal* consists primarily of strip cartoons and graphics in the "underground comix" tradition, it has run short SF pieces by Roger Zelazny, Harlan Ellison, James Tiptree, Jr., Richard A. Lupoff, and others, and seems to be getting a large cross-over audience. The success of *Heavy Metal* suggests to me that if *Cosmos* had replaced its essentially gray and unexciting cover art with jazzy pop underground illustrations —the type of artwork featured on the best rock album covers—it might have been able to tap some of the same audience without compromising its literary standards. The publishers of *Penthouse* are reputedly planning to bring out a slick, large-format SF magazine in the near future, so we may have more data on this whole question next year.

Galileo improved a good deal, particularly in cover art, although the bulk of the fiction still impressed me as mediocre. It is now reportedly selling about forty thousand copies per issue—not bad at all for a subscription-only magazine—and with time and more financial backing *Galileo* may well develop into a really viable professional market.

Also new this year was *Unearth*, a magazine devoted solely to "writers who [have] not yet made a sale." *Unearth* is a sincere little magazine, handsomely produced, and it features interesting columns and commentary by Harlan Ellison, Hal Clement, and others. Unfortunately, its fiction has not generally lived up to either the rest of the magazine or to the aggressive self-hype of *Unearth*'s editors; I'm not at all surprised, in fact, that most of the stories failed to find other markets, although some of them do show signs of promise.

Analog had a good year and published stories by Raccoona Sheldon, Edward Bryant, and Spider and Jeanne Robinson, which may well sweep all three Nebula short-fiction categories. But once again the magazine that was the most consistently superior in the overall quality of its short fiction was *The Magazine of Fantasy and Science Fiction*. Excellent material by Keith Roberts, John Varley, Avram Davidson, John Brunner, Hilbert Schenck, Tom Reamy, Robert Thurston, Woody Allen, and others, all appeared in *F&SF* this year.

Galaxy had another erratic year, skipping several issues and publishing the October issue in November without a cover date. John Varley's stories, the mainstay of *Galaxy* in 1976, were conspicuous by their absence. Toward the end of the year, *Galaxy* also lost its long-time editor, James F. Baen, and its two most popular columnists, Spider Robinson and Jerry Pournelle. Many writers and artists seem to be unofficially boycotting the magazine, and it remains to be seen whether or not new editor J. J. Pierce will be able to cope successfully with these and other problems.

Amazing and *Fantastic* managed to survive another year—how, I don't know.

It is significant that almost all of the worthwhile short fiction of 1977 was published in magazines; yet it is obviously much too early to speak of a magazine renaissance. None of the new magazines established itself with the sudden dramatic impact that marked the advent of *Galaxy* and *F&SF* in the early Fifties, nor has any of them yet succeeded in establishing the kind of pungent and clearly-defined editorial personality that distinguished those two great magazines in their heyday. Nevertheless, it is encouraging to see viable new titles, with the prospect of more new magazines to come.

On the other hand, the original anthology market was very weak this year, although there seemed to be more of them than ever—and perhaps there is a correlation in that as well. Terry Carr's *Universe 7* (Doubleday) was the best of the established anthology series this year and contains an excellent story by Fritz Leiber and good stuff by Carter Scholz, Gene Wolfe, Robert Chilson, and George Alec Effinger.

Robert Silverberg's *New Dimensions 7* (Harper & Row) features some first-rate work by Steven Utley and Howard Waldrop. A. A. Attanasio, Alex and Phyllis Eisenstein, and some others. But once again too large a proportion of the book is taken up by failed experimentation, and I begin to fear that *New Dimensions*—once the best of all the anthology series—is going into a slump similar to the one suffered by *Orbit* during its late middle years. Damon Knight's *Orbit 19* (Harper & Row) is less exciting than *Orbit 18*, although still comfortably better than the worst of its editions; good material here by Michael W. McClintock, John Varley, Kim Stanley Robinson, Felix C. Gotschalk, and Gene Wolfe.

Several of these series seemed to be in trouble. *Orbit*'s option was dropped by Harper & Row (although they will bring out a few volumes already in preparation), and if it is unable to find another publisher soon this longest-running of all anthology series may be doomed. *New Dimensions* also lost its paperback publisher this year, and has had considerable difficulty finding another. It may be that hardcover anthology series have become economically unsound in the face of rising production costs, skyrocketing cover prices, and the dwindling availability of opportunities for paperback publication.

Of the one-shot original anthologies, none pushed itself forward as really outstanding. Best of the lot were Edward Bryant's *2076: The American Tricentennial* (Pyramid) and George R. R. Martin's *New Voices in Science Fiction* (Macmillan).

1977 was a good year for novels, with a number of speculatively exciting and literarily ambitious books. Most of them were seriously flawed in one way or another, it's true, usually in plot structure; but even so, many of these "failures" were more interesting than last year's "successes." Unequivocally the best novel of the year was Frederik Pohl's *Gateway* (St. Martin's Press), followed closely by Algis Budrys's *Michaelmas* (Putnam)—which could have been one of the classics of the genre except for a disappointingly weak ending— and Gregory Benford's *In The Ocean of Night* (Dial Press). Other interesting novels included Michael Bishop's *Stolen Faces* (Harper & Row) and *A Little Knowledge* (Putnam), Philip K. Dick's *A Scanner Darkly* (Doubleday), Jack Dann's *Starhiker* (Harper & Row), Fritz Leiber's *Our Lady of Darkness* (Putnam), John Varley's *Ophiuchi Hotline* (Dial Press), C. J. Cherryh's *Hunter of Worlds* (DAW), and Cecelia Holland's *Floating Worlds* (Pocket Books).

Ballantine/Del Rey Books had most of the year's good short story collections: *The Best of Fredric Brown, The Best of Robert Bloch, The Best of Edmond Hamilton, The Best of Leigh Brackett*. A number of long-unavailable Sturgeon collections also came back into print all at once: *Sturgeon is Alive and Well* . . . (Pocket Books), *Caviar* (Ballantine), *E. Pluribus Unicorn* (Pocket Books), *Starshine* (Jove), and *Not Without Sorcery* (Ballantine). Also worthwhile were *Skirmish* (Putnam) by Clifford D. Simak and *Critical Mass* (Bantam) by Frederik Pohl and C. M. Kornbluth.

The best SF-oriented nonfiction book of the year, Damon Knight's *The Futurians* (John Day), is a fascinating, funny, and often poignant study of the closely knit fan group of the Thirties that gave us most of modern SF's best-known writers and editors; it is also one of the clearest delineations I've ever seen of the processes of mind and heart that turn the scruffy kids of today into the top-drawer professionals of tomorrow—highly recommended. Also by Knight, *Turning Points* (Harper & Row) is a massive collection of twenty-three critical articles about SF, an eclectic grab bag of a book. Its contents range widely between the inspired and the puerile, but it makes fascinating reading and certainly contains something to interest or outrage practically anybody. Still, at the $12.50 hardcover price, it is probably out of reach for most readers. Similar in nature, if not in tone, is *Science Fiction At Large* (Harper & Row), a collection of critical essays edited by Peter Nichols. His approach is less exuberant and serendipitous than Knight's, and his book is much more solemn and homogeneous in tone—but note the very strange piece by Philip K. Dick. Samuel R. Delany's collection of critical essays, *The Jewel-Hinged Jaw: Notes on the Language of Science Fiction* (Dragon Press) is probably too technical in its language and concerns to appeal to the casual reader, but Delany's trenchant arguments and generally well-founded conclusions give the book real value for the would-be SF writer.

One of the most handsome books of the year was Brian Ash's huge *Visual Encyclopedia of Science Fiction* (Harmony Books), which serves double duty as a history. Unfortunately, as in Ash's *Who's Who in Science Fiction* (Taplinger), the selection of material is so idiosyncratic (if not downright arbitrary) and the material itself so confusingly presented and riddled with factual errors that its value as a reference source is sharply lowered. Robert Scholes's and Eric S. Rabkin's *Science Fiction: History—Science—Vision* (Oxford University Press) is more staid than Ash's book, but a good deal better organized, and therefore more useful.

The 35th World Science Fiction Convention, inaptly named Suncon (it rained torrentially for the first three days), was held in Miami over the Labor Day weekend and had the smallest attendance (2,050) of any world convention since 1971. The 1976 Hugo Awards, presented at Suncon, were:

BEST NOVEL—*Where Late the Sweet Birds Sang* by Kate Wilhelm
BEST NOVELLA—"Houston, Houston, Do You Read?" by James Tiptree, Jr., and "By Any Other Name" by Spider Robinson (tie)
BEST NOVELETTE—"The Bicentennial Man" by Isaac Asimov
BEST SHORT STORY—"Tricentennial" by Joe Haldeman
BEST EDITOR—Ben Bova
BEST PROFESSIONAL ARTIST—Rick Sternbach
BEST FAN ARTIST—Phil Foglio
BEST FAN WRITER—Susan Wood and Richard E. Geis (tie)
BEST FANZINE—*Science Fiction Review*
JOHN W. CAMPBELL, JR., AWARD—C. J. Cherryh
GRAND MASTER OF FANTASY AWARD—Andre Norton

The 1976 Nebula Awards were:
BEST NOVEL—*Man Plus,* by Frederik Pohl
BEST NOVELLA—"Houston, Houston, Do You Read?" by James Tiptree, Jr.
BEST NOVELETTE—"The Bicentennial Man" by Isaac Asimov
BEST SHORT STORY—"A Crowd of Shadows" by Charles L. Grant
GRAND MASTER AWARD—Clifford D. Simak

The Third Annual World Fantasy Awards were:
BEST NOVEL—*Doctor Rat* by William Kotzwinkle
BEST SHORT FICTION—"There's A Long, Long Trail A-Winding" by Russell Kirk
BEST COLLECTION: *Frights* edited by Kirby McCauley
BEST ARTIST—Roger Dean
SPECIAL AWARD (Nonprofessional)—*Whispers* edited by Stuart Schiff
SPECIAL AWARD (Professional)—Alternate World Recordings
LIFE ACHIEVEMENT AWARD—Ray Bradbury.

SF lost two major talents this year, one a veteran who had been writing for almost fifty years, the other a relative newcomer at the start of what had promised to be a brilliant career.

Edmond Hamilton, born in Ohio in 1904, sold his first story to *Amazing* in 1928, only two years after the start of that first of all SF magazines. He quickly became one of the major figures in the era of "superscience" stories, earning the affectionate nickname of "World-Wrecker" Hamilton from his readers, because of the galaxy-spanning scale and headlong action of his fiction. Hamilton's books remained popular with the reading public, although his brand of SF would seem to go out of fashion, and he influenced more than one generation of upcoming SF writers. His many books include *The Star*

Kings (Berkley), *The City At World's End* (Fawcett Crest), and *The Valley of Creation* (Lancer); he lived long enough to see the publication of *The Best of Edmond Hamilton* (Del Rey Books), edited by his wife, writer Leigh Brackett.

Tom Reamy, born in Woodson, Texas, died at the age of 42. He had been a prominent figure in fandom since the late Fifties, editor of *Trumpet,* a major fanzine of its day, and several times a Hugo finalist. He later edited *Nickelodeon* and was one of the prime movers behind the 34th World Science Fiction Convention, MidAmeriCon. In 1973, he turned to writing and quickly established himself as one of the most popular of all the new SF writers. His story "Twilla" was a finalist for both Hugo and Nebula awards in 1975; he won the John W. Campbell, Jr., Award, and a Nebula Award in 1976 for his story "San Diego Lightfoot Sue." Putnam/Berkley will posthumously publish his novel *Blind Voices,* as well as a yet untitled collection of his short fiction.

Also dead in 1977 were Houston attorney Ben C. Ramey, who had two stories on the Nebula Final Ballot in 1968 under the pseudonym of H. H. Hollis; Raymond A. Palmer, long-time fan and editor of *Amazing* from 1938 to 1949; and Henry Hasse, author of the classic story "He Who Shrank."

Next year: boom or bust? Tune in and see!

Raccoona Sheldon is a pseudonym of Alice Sheldon, a semi-retired experimental psychologist who lives in McLean, Virginia; but Dr. Sheldon is perhaps better known under yet another of her pseudonyms: James Tiptree, Jr.

As Tiptree, Dr. Sheldon became one of the most acclaimed SF writers, won two Nebula and two Hugo awards, and published four very well-received books: three collections, Ten Thousand Light-Years from Home *(Ace);* Warm Worlds and Otherwise *(Ballantine); and* Star Songs of an Old Primate *(Del Rey Books); and a novel,* Up the Walls of the World *(Putnam). The search for the person behind the enigmatic Tiptree persona became one of the favorite literary parlor games of the Seventies, and from time to time self-appointed Tiptree experts would confidently announce that Tiptree was "really" Howard Hughes, or a CIA agent, or an AIM activist, or a worm rancher, or whatever. When the secret finally was revealed early in 1977, the subsequent debate and uproar sometimes obscured the fact that Alice Sheldon can write like a slumming angel under whatever name she chooses. The brilliant and chilling story at hand—unequivocally the best short story of the year —reaffirms her position at the very top of the SF pantheon.*

RACCOONA SHELDON

The Screwfly Solution

The young man sitting at 2° N, 75° W sent a casually venomous glance up at the nonfunctional shoofly *ventilador* and went on reading his letter. He was sweating heavily, stripped to his shorts in the hotbox of what passed for a hotel room in Cuyapán.

> *How do other wives* do *it? I stay busy-busy with the Ann Arbor grant review programs and the seminar, saying brightly "Oh yes, Alan is in Colombia setting up a biological pest control program, isn't it wonderful?" But inside I imagine you surrounded by nineteen-year-old raven-haired cooing beauties, every one panting with social dedication and filthy rich. And forty inches of bosom busting out of her delicate lingerie. I even figured it in centimeters, that's 101.6 centimeters of busting. Oh, darling, darling, do what you want only* come home safe.

Alan grinned fondly, briefly imagining the only body he longed for. His girl, his magic Anne. Then he got up to open the window another cautious notch. A long pale mournful face looked in—a goat. The room opened on the goatpen, the stench was vile. Air, anyway. He picked up the letter.

Everything is just about as you left it, except that the Peedsville horror seems to be getting worse. They're calling it the Sons of Adam cult now. Why can't they do something, even if it is a religion? The Red Cross has set up a refugee camp in Ashton, Georgia. Imagine, refugees in the U.S.A. I heard two little girls were carried out all slashed up. Oh, Alan.

Which reminds me, Barney came over with a wad of clippings he wants me to send you. I'm putting them in a separate envelope; I know what happens to very fat letters in foreign POs. He says, in case you don't get them, what do the following have in common? Peedsville, São Paulo, Phoenix, San Diego, Shanghai, New Delhi, Tripoli, Brisbane, Johannesburg and Lubbock, Texas. He says the hint is, remember where the Intertropical Convergence Zone is now. That makes no sense to me, maybe it will to your superior ecological brain. All I could see about the clippings was that they were fairly horrible accounts of murders or massacres of women. The worst was the New Delhi one, about "rafts of female corpses" in the river. The funniest (!) was the Texas Army officer who shot his wife, three daughters and his aunt, because God told him to clean the place up.

Barney's such an old dear, he's coming over Sunday to help me take off the downspout and see what's blocking it. He's dancing on air right now, since you left his spruce budworm-moth antipheromone program finally paid off. You know he tested over 2,000 compounds? Well, it seems that good old 2,097 really works. When I asked him what it does he just giggled, you know how shy he is with women. Anyway, it seems that a one-shot spray program will save the forests without harming a single other thing. Birds and people can eat it all day, he says.

Well sweetheart, that's all the news except Amy goes back to Chicago to school Sunday. The place will be a tomb, I'll miss her frightfully in spite of her being at the stage where I'm her worst enemy. The sullen sexy subteens, Angie says. Amy sends love to her Daddy. I send you my whole heart, all that words can't say.

Your Anne

Alan put the letter safely in his notefile and glanced over the rest of the thin packet of mail, refusing to let himself dream of home and Anne. Barney's "fat envelope" wasn't there. He threw himself on the rumpled bed, yanking off the lightcord a minute before the town generator went off for the night. In the darkness the list of places Barney had mentioned spread themselves around a misty globe that turned, troublingly, briefly in his mind. Something. . . .

But then the memory of the hideously parasitized children he had worked with at the clinic that day took possession of his thoughts. He set himself to considering the data he must collect. *Look for the vulnerable link in the behavioral chain*—how often Barney—Dr. Barnhard Braithwaite—had pounded it into his skull. Where was it, where? In the morning he would start work on bigger canefly cages. . . .

At that moment, five thousand miles north, Anne was writing:

Oh, darling, darling, your first three letters are here, they all came together. I knew you were writing. Forget what I said about swarthy heiresses, that was all a joke. My darling I know, I know . . . us. Those dreadful canefly larvae, those poor little kids. If you weren't my husband I'd think you were a saint or something. (I do anyway.)

I have your letters pinned up all over the house, makes it a lot less lonely. No real news here except things feel kind of quiet and spooky. Barney and I got the downspout out, it was full of a big rotted hoard of squirrel nuts. They must have been dropping them down the top. I'll put a wire over it. (Don't worry, I'll use a ladder this time.)

Barney's in an odd, grim mood. He's taking this Sons of Adam thing very seriously, it seems he's going to be on the investigation committee if that ever gets off the ground. The weird part is that nobody seems to be doing anything, as if it's just too big. Selina Peters has been printing some acid comments, like When one man kills his wife you call it murder, but when enough do it we call it a lifestyle. I think it's spreading, but nobody knows because the media have been asked to downplay it. Barney says it's being viewed as a form of contagious hysteria. He insisted I send you this ghastly interview. It's not *going to be published, of course. The quietness is worse, though, it's like something terrible was going on just out of sight. After reading Barney's thing I called up Pauline in San Diego to make sure she was all right. She sounded funny, as if she wasn't saying everything . . . my own sister. Just after she said things were great she suddenly asked if she could come and stay here a while next month. I said come right away, but she wants to sell her house first. I wish she'd hurry.*

Oh, the diesel car is okay now, it just needed its filter changed. I had to go out to Springfield to get one but Eddie installed it for only $2.50. He's going to bankrupt his garage.

In case you didn't guess, those places of Barney's are all about lati-

tude 30° N or S—the horse latitudes. When I said not exactly, he said remember the equatorial convergence zone shifts in winter, and to add in Libya, Osaka, and a place I forget—wait, Alice Springs, Australia. What has this to do with anything, I asked. He said, "Nothing—I hope." I leave it to you, great brains like Barney can be weird.

My dearest, here's all of me to all of you. Your letters make life possible. But don't feel you have to, I can tell how tired you must be. Just know we're together, always everywhere.

Your Anne

PS I had to open this to put Barney's thing in, it wasn't the secret police. Here it is. All love again. A.

In the goat-infested room where Alan read this, rain was drumming on the roof. He put the letter to his nose to catch the faint perfume once more, and folded it away. Then he pulled out the yellow flimsy Barney had sent and began to read, frowning.

PEEDSVILLE CULT/SONS OF ADAM SPECIAL. Statement by driver Sgt. Willard Mews, Globe Fork, Ark. We hit the roadblock about 80 miles west of Jacksonville. Major John Heinz of Ashton was expecting us, he gave us an escort of two riot vehicles headed by Capt. T. Parr. Major Heinz appeared shocked to see that the NIH medical team included two women doctors. He warned us in the strongest terms of the danger. So Dr. Patsy Putnam (Urbana, Ill.), the psychologist, decided to stay behind at the Army cordon. But Dr. Elaine Fay (Clinton, N.J.) insisted on going with us, saying she was the epi-something (epidemiologist).

We drove behind one of the riot cars at 30 mph for about an hour without seeing anything unusual. There were two big signs saying "SONS OF ADAM—LIBERATED ZONE." We passed some small pecan packing plants and a citrus processing plant. The men there looked at us but did not do anything unusual. I didn't see any children or women of course. Just outside Peedsville we stopped at a big barrier made of oil drums in front of a large citrus warehouse. This area is old, sort of a shantytown and trailer park. The new part of town with the shopping center and developments is about a mile further on. A warehouse worker with a shotgun came out and told us to wait for the Mayor. I don't think he saw Dr. Elaine Fay then, she was sitting sort of bent down in back.

Mayor Blount drove up in a police cruiser and our chief, Dr. Premack, explained our mission from the Surgeon General. Dr. Premack was very careful not to make any remarks insulting to the Mayor's religion. Mayor Blount agreed to let the party go on into Peedsville to take samples of the soil and water and so on and talk to the doctor who lives there. The mayor was about 6′ 2″, weight maybe 230 or 240, tanned, with grayish hair. He was smiling and chuckling in a friendly manner.

Then he looked inside the car and saw Dr. Elaine Fay and he blew up. He started yelling we had to all get the hell back. But Dr. Premack talked to him and cooled him down and finally the Mayor said Dr. Fay should go into the warehouse office and stay there with the door closed. I had to stay there too and see she didn't come out, and one of the Mayor's men would drive the party.

So the medical people and the Mayor and one of the riot vehicles went on into Peedsville and I took Dr. Fay back into the warehouse office and sat down. It was real hot and stuffy. Dr. Fay opened a window, but when I heard her trying to talk to an old man outside I told her she couldn't do that and closed the window. The old man went away. Then she wanted to talk to me but I told her I did not feel like conversing. I felt it was real wrong, her being there.

So then she started looking through the office files and reading papers there. I told her that was a bad idea, she shouldn't do that. She said the government expected her to investigate. She showed me a booklet or magazine they had there, it was called *Man Listens to God* by Reverend McIllhenny. They had a carton full in the office. I started reading it and Dr. Fay said she wanted to wash her hands. So I took her back along a kind of enclosed hallway beside the conveyor to where the toilet was. There were no doors or windows so I went back. After a while she called out that there was a cot back there, she was going to lie down. I figured that was all right because of the no windows, also I was glad to be rid of her company.

When I got to reading the book it was very intriguing. It was very deep thinking about how man is now on trial with God and if we fulfill our duty God will bless us with a real new life on Earth. The signs and portents show it. It wasn't like, you know, Sunday school stuff. It was deep.

After a while I heard some music and saw the soldiers from the other riot car were across the street by the gas tanks, sitting in the shade of some trees and kidding with the workers from the plant. One of them was playing a guitar, not electric, just plain. It looked so peaceful.

Then Mayor Blount drove up alone in the cruiser and came in. When he saw I was reading the book he smiled at me sort of fatherly, but he looked tense. He asked me where Dr. Fay was and I told him she was lying down in back. He said that was okay. Then he kind of sighed and went back down the hall, closing the door behind him. I sat and listened to the guitar man, trying to hear what he was singing. I felt really hungry, my lunch was in Dr. Premack's car.

After a while the door opened and Mayor Blount came back in. He looked terrible, his clothes were messed up and he had bloody scrape marks on his face. He didn't say anything, he just looked at me hard and fierce, like he might have been disoriented. I saw his zipper was open and there was blood on his clothing and also on his (private parts).

I didn't feel frightened, I felt something important had happened. I tried to get him to sit down. But he motioned me to follow him back down the hall, to where Dr. Fay was. "You must see," he said. He went into the toilet and I went into a kind of little room there, where the cot was. The light was fairly good, reflected off the tin roof from where the walls stopped. I saw Dr. Fay lying on the cot in a peaceful appearance. She was lying straight, her clothing was to some extent different but her legs were together. I was glad to see that. Her blouse was pulled up and I saw there was a cut or incision on her abdomen. The blood was coming out there, or it had been coming out there, like a mouth. It wasn't moving at this time. Also her throat was cut open.

I returned to the office. Mayor Blount was sitting down, looking very tired. He had cleaned himself off. He said, "I did it for you. Do you understand?"

He seemed like my father, I can't say it better than that. I realized he was under a terrible strain, he had taken a lot on himself for me. He went on to explain how Dr. Fay was very dangerous, she was what they call a cripto-female (crypto?), the most dangerous kind. He had exposed her and purified the situation. He was very straight-forward, I didn't feel confused at all, I knew he had done what was right.

We discussed the book, how man must purify himself and show God a clean world. He said some people raise the question of how can man reproduce without women but such people miss the point. The point is that as long as man depends on the old filthy animal way God won't help him. When man gets rid of his animal part, which is woman, this is the signal God is waiting. Then God will reveal the new true clean way, maybe angels will come bringing new souls, or maybe we will live forever, but it is not our place to speculate, only to obey. He said some men here had seen an Angel of the Lord. This was very deep, it seemed like it echoed inside me, I felt it was an inspiration.

Then the medical party drove up and I told Dr. Premack that Dr. Fay had been taken care of and sent away, and I got in the car to drive them out of the Liberated Zone. However four of the six soldiers from the roadblock refused to leave. Capt. Parr tried to argue them out of it but finally agreed they could stay to guard the oil-drum barrier.

I would have liked to stay too, the place was so peaceful, but they needed me to drive the car. If I had known there would be all this hassle I never would have done them the favor. I am not crazy and I have not done anything wrong and my lawyer will get me out. That is all I have to say.

In Cuyapán the hot afternoon rain had temporarily ceased. As Alan's fingers let go of Sgt. Willard Mews's wretched document he caught sight of pencil-scrawled words in the margin. Barney's spider hand. He squinted.

Man's religion and metaphysics are the voices of his glands. Schönweiser, 1878.

Who the devil Schönweiser was Alan didn't know, but he knew what Barney was conveying. This murderous crackpot religion of McWhosis was a symptom, not a cause. Barney believed something was physically affecting the Peedsville men, generating psychosis, and a local religious demagogue had sprung up to "explain" it.

Well, maybe. But cause or effect, Alan thought only of one thing: eight hundred miles from Peedsville to Ann Arzor. Anne should be safe. She *had* to be.

He threw himself on the lumpy cot, his mind going back exultantly to his work. At the cost of a million bites and cane-cuts he was pretty sure he'd found the weak link in the canefly cycle. The male mass-mating behavior, the comparative scarcity of ovulant females. It would be the screwfly solution all over again with the sexes reversed. Concentrate the pheromone, release sterilized females. Luckily the breeding populations were comparatively isolated. In a couple of seasons they ought to have it. Have to let them go on spraying poison meanwhile, of course; damn pity, it was slaughtering everything and getting in the water, and the caneflies had evolved to immunity anyway. But in a couple of seasons, maybe three, they could drop the canefly populations below reproductive viability. No more tormented human bodies with those stinking larvae in the nasal passages and brain. . . . He drifted off for a nap, grinning.

Up north, Anne was biting her lip in shame and pain.

Sweetheart, I shouldn't admit it but your wife is ~~scared~~ a bit jittery. Just female nerves or something, nothing to worry about. Everything is normal up here. It's so eerily normal, nothing in the papers, nothing anywhere except what I hear through Barney and Lillian. But Pauline's phone won't answer out in San Diego; the fifth day some strange man yelled at me and banged the phone down. Maybe she's sold her house—but why wouldn't she call?

Lillian's on some kind of Save-the-Women committee, like we were an endangered species, ha-ha—you know Lillian. It seems the Red

Cross has started setting up camps. But she says, after the first rush, only a trickle are coming out of what they call "the affected areas." Not many children, either, even little boys. And they have some airphotos around Lubbock showing what look like mass graves. Oh, Alan . . . so far it seems to be mostly spreading west, but something's happening in St. Louis, they're cut off. So many places seem to have just vanished from the news, I had a nightmare that there isn't a woman left alive down there. And nobody's doing anything. They talked about spraying with tranquillizers for a while and then that died out. What could it do? Somebody at the U.N. has proposed a convention on—you won't believe this—femicide. It sounds like a deodorant spray.

Excuse me, honey, I seem to be a little hysterical. George Searles came back from Georgia talking about God's Will—Searles the lifelong atheist. Alan, something crazy is happening.

But there aren't any facts. Nothing. The Surgeon General issued a report on the bodies of the Rahway Rip-Breast Team—I guess I didn't tell you about that. Anyway, they could find no pathology. Milton Baines wrote a letter saying in the present state of the art we can't distinguish the brain of a saint from a psychopathic killer, so how could they expect to find what they don't know how to look for?

Well, enough of these jitters. It'll be all over by the time you get back, just history. Everything's fine here, I fixed the car's muffler again. And Amy's coming home for the vacation, that'll get my mind off faraway problems.

Oh, something amusing to end with—Angie told me what Barney's enzyme does to the spruce budworm. It seems it blocks the male from turning around after he connects with the female, so he mates with her head instead. Like clockwork with a cog missing. There're going to be some pretty puzzled female spruceworms. Now why couldn't Barney tell me that? He really is such a sweet shy old dear. He's given me some stuff to put in, as usual. I didn't read it.

Now don't worry, my darling, everything's fine.

I love you, I love you so.

Always, all ways your Anne

Two weeks later in Cuyapán when Barney's enclosures slid out of the envelope, Alan didn't read them either. He stuffed them into the pocket of his bush jacket with a shaking hand and started bundling his notes together on the rickety table, with a scrawled note to Sister Dominique on top. The hell with the canefly, the hell with everything except that tremor in his Anne's firm handwriting. The hell with being five thousand miles away from his woman, his child, while some deadly madness raged. He crammed his meager belongings into his duffel. If he hurried he could catch the bus through to Bogotá and maybe make the Miami flight.

He made it, but in Miami he found the planes north jammed. He failed a quick standby; six hours to wait. Time to call Anne. When the call got through some difficulty he was unprepared for the rush of joy and relief that burst along the wires.

"Thank God—I can't believe it—Oh, Alan, my darling, are you really—I can't believe—"

He found he was repeating too, and all mixed up with the canefly data. They were both laughing hysterically when he finally hung up.

Six hours. He settled in a frayed plastic chair opposite Aerolineas Argentinas, his mind half back at the clinic, half on the throngs moving by him. Something was oddly different here, he perceived presently. Where was the decorative fauna he usually enjoyed in Miami, the parade of young girls in crotch-tight pastel jeans? The flounces, boots, wild hats and hairdos, and startling expanses of newly-tanned skin, the brilliant fabrics barely confining the bob of breasts and buttocks? Not here—but wait; looking closely, he glimpsed two young faces hidden under unbecoming parkas, their bodies draped in bulky, nondescript skirts. In fact, all down the long vista he could see the same thing: hooded ponchos, heaped-on clothes, and baggy pants, dull colors. A new style? No, he thought not. It seemed to him their movements suggested furtiveness, timidity. And they moved in groups. He watched a lone girl struggle to catch up with others ahead of her, apparently strangers. They accepted her wordlessly.

They're frightened, he thought. Afraid of attracting notice. Even that gray-haired matron in a pantsuit, resolutely leading a flock of kids, was glancing around nervously.

And at the Argentine desk opposite he saw another odd thing: two lines had a big sign over them, *Mujeres*. Women. They were crowded with the shapeless forms and very quiet.

The men seemed to be behaving normally; hurrying, lounging, griping, and joking in the lines as they kicked their luggage along. But Alan felt an undercurrent of tension, like an irritant in the air. Outside the line of storefronts behind him a few isolated men seemed to be handing out tracts. An airport attendant spoke to the nearest man; he merely shrugged and moved a few doors down.

To distract himself Alan picked up a *Miami Herald* from the next seat. It was surprisingly thin. The international news occupied him for a while; he had seen none for weeks. It too had a strange, empty quality, even the bad news seemed to have dried up. The African war which had been going on seemed to be over, or went unreported. A trade summit meeting was haggling over grain and steel prices. He

found himself at the obituary pages, columns of close-set type dominated by the photo of a defunct ex-senator. Then his eye fell on two
announcements at the bottom of the page. One was too flowery for
quick comprehension, but the other stated in bold plain type:

THE FORSETTE FUNERAL HOME REGRET-
FULLY ANNOUNCES
IT WILL NO LONGER ACCEPT FEMALE
CADAVERS

Slowly he folded the paper, staring at it numbly. On the back was
an item headed *Navigational Hazard Warning*, in the shipping news.
Without really taking it in, he read:

AP/NASSAU: The excursion liner *Carib Swallow* reached port under
tow today after striking an obstruction in the Gulf Stream off Cape
Hatteras. The obstruction was identified as part of a commercial
trawler's seine floated by female corpses. This confirms reports from
Florida and the Gulf of the use of such seines, some of them over
a mile in length. Similar reports coming from the Pacific coast and
as far away as Japan indicate a growing hazard to coastwise shipping.

Alan flung the thing into the trash receptacle and sat rubbing his
forehead and eyes. Thank God he had followed his impulse to come
home. He felt totally disoriented, as though he had landed by error
on another planet. Four and a half hours more to wait. . . . At
length he recalled the stuff from Barney he had thrust in his pocket,
and pulled it out and smoothed it.

The top item was from the *Ann Arbor News*. Dr. Lillian Dash, together with several hundred other members of her organization, had
been arrested for demonstrating without a permit in front of the White
House. They had started a fire in a garbage can, which was considered
particularly heinous. A number of women's groups had participated;
the total struck Alan as more like thousands than hundreds. Extraordinary security precautions were being taken despite the fact that the
President was out of town at the time.

The next item had to be Barney's acerbic humor.

UP/VATICAN CITY, 19 JUNE. Pope John IV today intimated that he
does not plan to comment officially on the so-called Pauline Purifica-
tion cults advocating the elimination of women as a means of justi-
fying man to God. A spokesman emphasized that the Church takes
no position on these cults but repudiates any doctrine involving a
"challenge" to or from God to reveal His further plans for man.
Cardinal Fazzoli, spokesman for the European Pauline movement, reaffirmed his view that the Scriptures define woman as merely

a temporary companion and instrument of Man. Women, he states, are nowhere defined as human, but merely as a transitional expedient or state. "The time of transition to full humanity is at hand," he concluded.

The next item was a thin-paper Xerox from a recent issue of *Science*:

SUMMARY REPORT OF THE AD HOC
EMERGENCY COMMITTEE ON FEMICIDE

The recent world-wide though localized outbreaks of femicide appear to represent a recurrence of similar outbreaks by groups or sects which are not uncommon in world history in times of psychic stress. In this case the root cause is undoubtedly the speed of social and technological change augmented by population pressure, and the spread and scope are aggravated by instantaneous world communications, thus exposing more susceptible persons. It is not viewed as a medical or epidemiological problem; no physical pathology has been found. Rather it is more akin to the various manias which swept Europe in the seventeenth century, e.g., the Dancing Manias; and like them, should run its course and disappear. The chiliastic cults which have sprung up around the affected areas appear to be unrelated, having in common only the idea that a new means of human reproduction will be revealed as a result of the "purifying" elimination of women.

We recommended that (1) inflammatory and sensational reporting be suspended; (2) refugee centers be set up and maintained for women escapees from the focal areas; (3) containment of affected areas by military cordon be continued and enforced; and (4) after a cooling-down period and the subsidence of the mania, qualified mental health teams and appropriate professional personnel go in to undertake rehabilitation.

SUMMARY OF THE MINORITY
REPORT OF THE AD HOC COMMITTEE

The nine members signing this report agree that there is no evidence for epidemiological contagion of femicide in the strict sense. *However*, the geographical relation of the focal areas of outbreak strongly suggests that they cannot be dismissed as purely psychosocial phenomena. The initial outbreaks have occurred around the globe near the 30th parallel, the area of principal atmospheric downflow of upper winds coming from the Intertropical Convergence Zone. An agent or condition in the upper equatorial atmosphere would thus be expected to reach ground level along the 30th parallel, with certain seasonal variations. One principal variation is that the downflow moves north over the East Asian continent during the late winter months, and those areas south of it (Arabia, Western India, parts of North Africa) have in fact been free of outbreaks until recently, when the downflow zone moved south. A similar downflow occurs in the Southern Hemisphere, and outbreaks have been reported along the 30th parallel running through Pretoria, and Alice Springs, Australia. (Information from Argentina is currently unavailable.)

This geographical correlation cannot be dismissed, and it is therefore urged that an intensified search for a physical cause be instituted. It is also urgently recommended that the rate of spread from known focal points be correlated with wind conditions. A watch for similar outbreaks along the secondary down-welling zones at 60° north and south should be kept.

(signed for the minority)
Barnhard Braithwaite

Alan grinned reminiscently at his old friend's name, which seemed to restore normalcy and stability to the world. It looked as if Barney was onto something, too, despite the prevalence of horses' asses. He frowned, puzzling it out.

Then his face slowly changed as he thought how it would be, going home to Anne. In a few short hours his arms would be around her, the tall, secretly beautiful body that had come to obsess him. Theirs had been a late-blooming love. They'd married, he supposed now, out of friendship, even out of friends' pressure. Everyone said they were made for each other, he big and chunky and blond, she willowy brunette; both shy, highly controlled, cerebral types. For the first few years the friendship had held, but sex hadn't been all that much. Conventional necessity. Politely reassuring each other, privately—he could say it now—disappointing.

But then, when Amy was a toddler, something had happened. A miraculous inner portal of sensuality had slowly opened to them, a liberation into their own secret unsuspected heaven of fully physical bliss . . . Jesus, but it had been a wrench when the Colombia thing had come up. Only their absolute sureness of each other had made him take it. And now, to be about to have her again, trebly desirable from the spice of separation—feeling-seeing-hearing-smelling-grasping. He shifted in his seat to conceal his body's excitement, half mesmerized by fantasy.

And Amy would be there, too; he grinned at the memory of that prepubescent little body plastered against him. She was going to be a handful, all right. His manhood understood Amy a lot better than her mother did; no cerebral phase for Amy. . . . But Anne, his exquisite shy one, with whom he'd found the way into the almost unendurable transports of the flesh. . . . First the conventional greeting, he thought; the news, the unspoken, savored, mounting excitement behind their eyes; the light touches; then the seeking of their own room, the falling clothes, the caresses, gentle at first—the flesh, the *nakedness*—the delicate teasing, the grasp, the first thrust—

A terrible alarm bell went off in his head. Exploded from his dream, he stared around, then finally down at his hands. *What was he doing with his open clasp-knife in his fist?*

Stunned, he felt for the last shreds of his fantasy and realized that the tactile images had not been of caresses, but of a frail neck strangling in his fist, the thrust had been the plunge of a blade seeking vitals. In his arms, legs, phantasms of striking and trampling, bones cracking. And Amy—

Oh God, Oh God—

Not sex, bloodlust.

That was what he had been dreaming. The sex was there, but it was driving some engine of death.

Numbly he put the knife away, thinking only over and over, it's got me. It's got me. Whatever it is, it's got me. *I can't go home.*

After an unknown time he got up and made his way to the United counter to turn in his ticket. The line was long. As he waited, his mind cleared a little. What could he do, here in Miami? Wouldn't it be better to get back to Ann Arbor and turn himself in to Barney? Barney could help him, if anyone could. Yes, that was best. But first he had to warn Anne.

The connection took even longer this time. When Anne finally answered he found himself blurting unintelligibly, it took a while to make her understand he wasn't talking about a plane delay.

"I tell you, I've caught it. Listen, Anne, for God's sake. If I should come to the house don't let me come near you. I mean it. I mean it. I'm going to the lab, but I might lose control and try to get to you. Is Barney there?"

"Yes, but darling—"

"Listen. Maybe he can fix me, maybe this'll wear off. But I'm not safe, Anne. Anne, I'd kill you, can you understand? Get a—get a weapon. I'll try not to come to the house. But if I do, don't let me get near you. Or Amy. It's a sickness, it's real. Treat me—treat me like a fucking wild animal. Anne, say you understand, say you'll do it."

They were both crying when he hung up.

He went shaking back to sit and wait. After a time his head seemed to clear a little more. *Doctor, try to think.* The first thing he thought of was to take the loathsome knife and throw it down a trash slot. As he did so he realized there was one more piece of Barney's material in his pocket. He uncrumpled it; it seemed to be a clipping from *Nature*.

At the top was Barney's scrawl: *Only guy making sense. U.K. infected now, Oslo, Copenhagen out of communication. Damfools still won't listen. Stay put.*

COMMUNICATION FROM
PROFESSOR IAN MACINTYRE, GLASGOW UNIV.

A potential difficulty for our species has always been implicit in the close linkage between the behavioural expression of aggression/predation and sexual reproduction in the male. This close linkage involves (a) many neuromuscular pathways which are utilized both in predatory and sexual pursuit: grasping, mounting, etc., and (b) similar states of adrenergic arousal which are activated in both. The same linkage is seen in the males of many other species; in some, the expression of aggression and copulation alternate or even coexist, an all-too-familiar example being the common house cat. Males of many species bite, claw, bruise, tread, or otherwise assault receptive females during the act of intercourse; indeed, in some species the male attack is necessary for female ovulation to occur.

In many if not all species it is the aggressive behaviour which appears first, and then changes to copulatory behaviour when the appropriate signal is presented (e.g., the three-tined stickleback and the European robin). Lacking the inhibiting signal, the male's fighting response continues and the female is attacked or driven off.

It seems therefore appropriate to speculate that the present crisis might be caused by some substance, perhaps at the viral or enzymatic level, which effects a failure of the switching or triggering function in the higher primates. (Note: Zoo gorillas and chimpanzees have recently been observed to attack or destroy their mates; rhesus not.) Such a dysfunction could be expressed by the failure of mating behaviour to modify or supervene over the aggressive/predatory response; i.e., sexual stimulation would produce attack only, the stimulation discharging itself through the destruction of the stimulating object.

In this connection it might be noted that exactly this condition is a commonplace of male functional pathology in those cases where murder occurs as a response to, and apparent completion of, sexual desire.

It should be emphasized that the aggression/copulation linkage discussed here is specific to the male; the female response (e.g., lordotic reflex) being of a different nature.

Alan sat holding the crumpled sheet a long time; the dry, stilted Scottish phrases seemed to help clear his head, despite the sense of brooding tension all around him. Well, if pollution or whatever had produced some substance, it could presumably be countered, filtered, neutralized. Very, very carefully, he let himself consider his life with Anne, his sexuality. Yes; much of their loveplay could be viewed as genitalized, sexually-gentled savagery. Play-predation. . . . He turned his mind quickly away. Some writer's phrase occurred to him: "The panic element in all sex." Who? Fritz Leiber? The violation of social distance, maybe; another threatening element. Whatever, it's our weak link, he thought. Our vulnerability. . . . The dreadful feeling of *rightness* he had experienced when he found himself knife in hand, fantasizing violence, came back to him. As though it was the right, the only way. Was that what Barney's budworms felt when they mated with their females wrong-end-to?

At long length, he became aware of body need and sought a toilet. The place was empty, except for what he took to be a heap of clothes blocking the door of the far stall. Then he saw the red-brown pool in which it lay, and the bluish mounds of bare, thin buttocks. He backed out, not breathing, and fled into the nearest crowd, knowing he was not the first to have done so.

Of course. Any sexual drive. Boys, men, too.

At the next washroom he watched to see men enter and leave normally before he ventured in.

Afterward he returned to sit, waiting, repeating over and over to himself: *Go to the lab. Don't go home. Go straight to the lab.* Three more hours; he sat numbly at 26° N, 81° W, breathing, breathing. . . .

Dear diary. Big scene tonite, Daddy came home!!! Only he acted so funny, he had the taxi wait and just held onto the doorway, he wouldn't touch me or let us come near him. (I mean funny weird, not funny ha-ha.) He said, I have something to tell you, this is getting worse not better. I'm going to sleep in the lab but I want you to get out, Anne, Anne, I can't trust myself any more. First thing in the morning you both get on the plane for Martha's and stay there. So I thought he had to be joking, I mean with the dance next week and Aunt Martha lives in Whitehorse where there's nothing nothing nothing. So I was yelling and Mother was yelling and Daddy was groaning. Go now! And then he started crying. Crying!!! So I realized, wow, this is serious, and I started to go over to him but Mother yanked me back and then I saw she had this big KNIFE!!! And she shoved me in back of her and started crying too Oh Alan, Oh Alan, like she was insane. So I said, Daddy, I'll never leave you, it felt like the perfect thing to say. And it was thrilling, he looked at me real sad and deep like I was a grown-up while Mother was treating me like I was a mere infant as usual. But Mother ruined it, raving Alan the child is mad, darling go. So he ran out the door yelling Be gone, Take the car, Get out before I come back.

Oh I forgot to say I was wearing what but my gooby green with my curltites still on, wouldn't you know of all the shitty luck, how could I have known such a beautiful scene was ahead we never know life's cruel whimsy. And mother is dragging out suitcases yelling Pack your things hurry! So she's going I guess but I am not repeat not going to spend the fall sitting in Aunt Martha's grain silo and lose the dance and all my summer credits. And Daddy was trying to communicate *with us, right? I think their relationship is obsolete. So when she goes upstairs I am splitting, I am going to go over to the lab and see Daddy.*

Oh PS Diane tore my yellow jeans she promised me I could use her pink ones Ha-ha that'll be the day.

I ripped that page out of Amy's diary when I heard the squad car coming. I never opened her diary before but when I found she'd gone I looked. . . . Oh, my darling girl. She went to him, my little girl, my poor little fool child. Maybe if I'd taken time to explain, maybe—

Excuse me, Barney. The stuff is wearing off, the shots they gave me. I didn't feel anything. I mean, I knew somebody's daughter went to see her father and he killed her. And cut his throat. But it didn't mean anything.

Alan's note, they gave me that but then they took it away. Why did they have to do that? His last handwriting, the last words he wrote before his hand picked up the, before he—

I remember it. *"Sudden and light as that, the bonds gave And we learned of finalities besides the grave.* The bonds of our humanity have broken, we are finished. I love—"

I'm all right, Barney, really. Who wrote that, Robert Frost? *The bonds gave.* . . . Oh, he said tell Barney: *The terrible rightness.* What does that mean?

You can't answer that, Barney dear. I'm just writing this to stay sane, I'll put it in your hidey-hole. Thank you, thank you, Barney dear. Even as blurry as I was, I knew it was you. All the time you were cutting off my hair and rubbing dirt on my face, I knew it was right because it was you. Barney, I never thought of you as those horrible words you said. You were always Dear Barney.

By the time the stuff wore off I had done everything you said, the gas, the groceries. Now I'm here in your cabin. With those clothes you made me put on I guess I do look like a boy, the gas man called me "Mister."

I still can't really realize, I have to stop myself from rushing back. But you saved my life, I know that. The first trip in I got a paper, I saw where they bombed the Apostle Islands refuge. And it had about those three women stealing the Air Force plane and bombing Dallas, too. Of course they shot them down, over the Gulf. Isn't it strange how we do nothing? Just get killed by ones and twos. Or more, now they've started on the refuges. . . . Like hypnotized rabbits. We're a toothless race.

Do you know I never said "we" meaning women before? "We" was always me and Alan, and Amy of course. Being killed selectively encourages group identification. . . . You see how sane-headed I am. But I still can't really realize.

My first trip in was for salt and kerosine. I went to that little Red Deer store and got my stuff from the old man in the back, as you told me—you see, I remembered! He called me "Boy," but I think maybe he suspects. He knows I'm staying at your cabin.

Anyway, some men and boys came in the front. They were all so *normal*, laughing and kidding. I just couldn't believe, Barney. In fact I started to go out past them when I heard one of them say, "Heinz saw an angel." An *angel*. So I stopped and listened. They said it was big and sparkly. Coming to see if man is carrying out God's Will, one of them said. And he said, Moosonee is now a liberated zone, and all up by Hudson Bay. I turned and got out the back, fast. The old man had heard them too. He said to me quietly, "I'll miss the kids."

Hudson Bay, Barney, that means it's coming from the north too, doesn't it? That must be about 60°.

But I have to go back once again, to get some fishhooks. I can't live on bread. Last week I found a deer some poacher had killed, just the head and legs. I made a stew. It was a doe. Her eyes; I wonder if mine look like that now.

I went to get the fishhooks today. It was bad, I can't ever go back. There were some men in front again, but they were different. Mean and tense. No boys. And there was a new sign out in front, I couldn't see it; maybe it says Liberated Zone too.

The old man gave me the hooks quick and whispered to me, "Boy, them woods'll be full of hunters next week." I almost ran out.

About a mile down the road a blue pickup started to chase me. I guess he wasn't from around there, I ran the VW into a logging draw and he roared on by. After a long while I drove out and came on back, but I left the car about a mile from here and hiked in. It's surprising how hard it is to pile enough brush to hide a yellow VW.

Barney, I can't stay here. I'm eating perch raw so nobody will see my smoke, but those hunters will be coming through. I'm going to move my sleeping bag out to the swamp by that big rock, I don't think many people go there.

Since the last lines I moved out. It feels safer. Oh, Barney, how did this *happen*?

Fast, that's how. Six months ago I was Dr. Anne Alstein. Now I'm a widow and bereaved mother, dirty and hungry, squatting in a swamp in mortal fear. Funny if I'm the last woman left alive on

Earth. I guess the last one around here, anyway. May be some holed out in the Himalayas, or sneaking through the wreck of New York City. How can we last?

We can't.

And I can't survive the winter here, Barney. It gets to 40° below. I'd have to have a fire, they'd see the smoke. Even if I worked my way south, the woods end in a couple hundred miles. I'd be potted like a duck. No. No use. Maybe somebody is trying something somewhere, but it won't reach here in time . . . and what do I have to live for?

No. I'll just make a good end, say up on that rock where I can see the stars. After I go back and leave this for you. I'll wait to see the beautiful color in the trees one last time.

Goodbye, dearest dearest Barney.

I know what I'll scratch for an epitaph.

HERE LIES THE SECOND MEANEST
PRIMATE ON EARTH.

I guess nobody will ever read this, unless I get the nerve and energy to take it back to Barney's. Probably I won't. Leave it in a Baggie, I have one here; maybe Barney will come and look. I'm up on the big rock now. The moon is going to rise soon, I'll do it then. Mosquitoes, be patient. You'll have all you want.

The thing I have to write down is that I saw an angel too. This morning. It was big and sparkly, like the man said; like a Christmas tree without the tree. But I knew it was real because the frogs stopped croaking and two bluejays gave alarm calls. That's important; it was *really there.*

I watched it, sitting under my rock. It didn't move much. It sort of bent over and picked up something, leaves or twigs, I couldn't see. Then it did something with them around its middle, like putting them into an invisible sample pocket.

Let me repeat—it was *there.* Barney, if you're reading this, THERE ARE THINGS HERE. And I think they've done whatever it is to us. Made us kill ourselves off.

Why? Well, it's a nice place, if it wasn't for people. How do you get rid of people? Bombs, death-rays—all very primitive. Leave a big mess. Destroy everything, craters, radioactivity, ruin the place.

This way there's no muss, no fuss. Just like what we did to the screwfly. Pinpoint the weak link, wait a bit while we do it for them. Only a few bones around; make good fertilizer.

Barney dear, goodbye. I saw it. It was there.

But it wasn't an angel.

I think I saw a real-estate agent.

It has become a cliché to speak of such-and-such a writer as "a rapidly rising star in the SF firmament," and yet no other phrase better describes John Varley. Varley appeared out of nowhere in 1975, and by the end of 1976 was recognized as the hottest new SF talent in years, generating more excitement in a shorter span of time than any writer since Zelazny. Last year he appeared in all of 1976's "Best of the Year" anthologies with a different story in each—a possibly unique distinction. Yet another story was on that year's Final Nebula Ballot, and he placed two stories on the Final Hugo Ballot as well. His first novel, Ophiuchi Hotline *(Dial Press), was one of the most-talked-about and controversial books of the year, arousing either intense admiration or loathing in the hearts of most critics. But his second novel has already been sold to Putnam/Berkley for a big, five-figure advance, and his career shows no signs of slowing down. His first short story collection,* Overdrawn at the Memory Bank, *is forthcoming from Dial Press and Dell.*

Here Varley takes us to Mars—not Burroughs's Mars, laced with canals, chockablock with giant green warriors, sword-wielding heroes, and beautiful egg-laying princesses, but rather the bleak, oxidized, apparently lifeless Mars of the Mariner probes—for a strange tale about the different kinds of rebirth: of humanity, of hope, of love—and of something else.

JOHN VARLEY

In the Hall of the Martian Kings

It took perseverance, alertness, and a willingness to break the rules to watch the sunrise in Tharsis Canyon. Matthew Crawford shivered in the dark, his suit heater turned to emergency setting, his eyes trained toward the east. He knew he had to be watchful. Yesterday he had missed it entirely, snatched away from him in the middle of a long, unavoidable yawn. His jaw muscles stretched, but he controlled it and kept his eyes firmly open.

And there it was. Like the lights in a theater after the show is over: just a quick brightening, a splash of localized bluish purple over the canyon rim, and he was surrounded by footlights. Day had come, the truncated Martian day that would never touch the blackness over his head.

This day, like the nine before it, illuminated a Tharsis radically changed from what it had been over the last sleepy ten thousand years. Wind erosion of rocks can create an infinity of shapes, but it never gets around to carving out a straight line or a perfect arc. The human encampment below him broke up the jagged lines of the rocks with regular angles and curves.

The camp was anything but orderly. No one would get the impression that any care had been taken in the haphazard arrangement of dome, lander, crawlers, crawler tracks, and scattered equipment. It had grown, as all human base camps seem to grow, without pattern. He was reminded of the footprints around Tranquillity Base, though on a much larger scale.

Tharsis Base sat on a wide ledge about halfway up from the uneven bottom of the Tharsis arm of the Great Rift Valley. The site had been chosen because it was a smooth area, allowing easy access up a gentle slope to the flat plains of the Tharsis Plateau, while at the same time only a kilometer from the valley floor. No one could agree which area was more worthy of study: plains or canyon. So this site had been chosen as a compromise. What it meant was that the exploring parties had to either climb up or go down, because there wasn't a damn thing worth seeing near the camp. Even the exposed layering and its areological records could not be seen without a half-kilometer crawler ride up to the point where Crawford had climbed to watch the sunrise.

He examined the dome as he walked back to camp. There was a figure hazily visible through the plastic. At this distance he would have been unable to tell who it was if it weren't for the black face. He saw her step up to the dome wall and wipe a clear circle to look through. She spotted his bright red suit and pointed at him. She was suited except for her helmet, which contained her radio. He knew he was in trouble. He saw her turn away and bend to the ground to pick up her helmet, so she could tell him what she thought of people who disobeyed her orders, when the dome shuddered like a jellyfish.

An alarm started in his helmet, flat and strangely soothing coming from the tiny speaker. He stood there for a moment as a perfect smoke ring of dust billowed up around the rim of the dome. Then he was running.

He watched the disaster unfold before his eyes, silent except for the rhythmic beat of the alarm bell in his ears. The dome was dancing and straining, trying to fly. The floor heaved up in the center, throwing the black woman to her knees. In another second the interior was a whirling snowstorm. He skidded on the sand and fell forward, got up in time to see the fiberglass ropes on the side nearest him snap free from the steel spikes anchoring the dome to the rock.

The dome now looked like some fantastic Christmas ornament, filled with snowflakes and the flashing red and blue lights of the emergency alarms. The top of the dome heaved over away from him, and the floor raised itself high in the air, held down by the unbroken anchors on the side farthest from him. There was a gush of snow and dust; then the floor settled slowly back to the ground. There was no motion now but the leisurely folding of the depressurized dome roof as it settled over the structures inside.

The crawler skidded to a stop, nearly rolling over, beside the deflated dome. Two pressure-suited figures got out. They started for the dome, hesitantly, in fits and starts. One grabbed the other's arm and pointed to the lander. The two of them changed course and scrambled up the rope ladder hanging over the side.

Crawford was the only one to look up when the lock started cycling. The two people almost tumbled over each other coming out of the lock. They wanted to *do* something, and quickly, but didn't know what. In the end, they just stood there silently twisting their hands and looking at the floor. One of them took off her helmet. She was a large woman in her thirties, with red hair shorn off close to the scalp.

"Matt, we got here as . . ." She stopped, realizing how obvious it was. "How's Lou?"

"Lou's not going to make it." He gestured to the bunk where a heavyset man lay breathing raggedly into a clear plastic mask. He was on pure oxygen. There was blood seeping from his ears and nose.

"Brain damage?"

Crawford nodded. He looked around at the other occupants of the room. There was the Surface Mission Commander, Mary Lang, the black woman he had seen inside the dome just before the blowout. She was sitting on the edge of Lou Prager's cot, her head cradled in her hands. In a way, she was a more shocking sight than Lou. No one who knew her would have thought she could be brought to this limp state of apathy. She had not moved for the last hour.

Sitting on the floor huddled in a blanket was Martin Ralston, the chemist. His shirt was bloody, and there was dried blood all over his face and hands from the nosebleed he'd only recently gotten under control, but his eyes were alert. He shivered, looking from Lang, his titular leader, to Crawford, the only one who seemed calm enough to deal with anything. He was a follower, reliable but unimaginative.

Crawford looked back to the newest arrivals. They were Lucy Stone McKillian, the redheaded ecologist, and Song Sue Lee, the exobiologist. They still stood numbly by the airlock, unable as yet to come to grips with the fact of fifteen dead men and women beneath the dome outside.

"What do they say on the *Burroughs*?" McKillian asked, tossing her helmet on the floor and squatting tiredly against the wall. The lander was not the most comfortable place to hold a meeting; all the couches were mounted horizontally since their purpose was cushioning the acceleration of landing and takeoff. With the ship sitting on its tail, this made ninety percent of the space in the lander useless. They were all gathered on the circular bulkhead at the rear of the life system, just forward of the fuel tank.

"We're waiting for a reply," Crawford said. "But I can sum up what they're going to say: not good. Unless one of you two has some experience in Mars-lander handling that you've been concealing from us."

Neither of them bothered to answer that. The radio in the nose sputtered, then clanged for their attention. Crawford looked over at Lang, who made no move to go answer it. He stood up and swarmed up the ladder to sit in the copilot's chair. He switched on the receiver.

"Commander Lang?"

"No, this is Crawford again. Commander Lang is . . . indisposed. She's busy with Lou, trying to do something."

"That's no use. The doctor says it's a miracle he's still breathing. If he wakes up at all, he won't be anything like you knew him. The telemetry shows nothing like the normal brain wave. Now I've got to talk to Commander Lang. Have her come up." The voice of Mission Commander Weinstein was accustomed to command, and about as emotional as a weather report.

"Sir, I'll ask her, but I don't think she'll come. This is still her operation, you know." He didn't give Weinstein time to reply to that. Weinstein had been trapped by his own seniority into commanding the *Edgar Rice Burroughs,* the orbital ship that got them to Mars and had been intended to get them back. Command of the *Podkayne,* the disposable lander that would make the lion's share of the headlines, had gone to Lang. There was little friendship between the two, especially when Weinstein fell to brooding about the very real financial benefits Lang stood to reap by being the first woman on Mars, rather than the lowly mission commander. He saw himself as another Michael Collins.

Crawford called down to Lang, who raised her head enough to mumble something.

"What'd she say?"

"She said take a message." McKillian had been crawling up the ladder as she said this. Now she reached him and said in a lower voice, "Matt, she's pretty broken up. You'd better take over for now."

"Right, I know." He turned back to the radio, and McKillian listened over his shoulder as Weinstein briefed them on the situation as he saw it. It pretty much jibed with Crawford's estimation, except at one crucial point. He signed off and they joined the other survivors.

He looked around at the faces of the others and decided it wasn't the time to speak of rescue possibilities. He didn't relish being a leader. He was hoping Lang would recover soon and take the burden from him. In the meantime he had to get them started on something.

He touched McKillian gently on the shoulder and motioned her to the lock.

"Let's go get them buried," he said. She squeezed her eyes shut tight, forcing out tears, then nodded.

It wasn't a pretty job. Halfway through it, Song came down the ladder with the body of Lou Prager.

"Let's go over what we've learned. First, now that Lou's dead there's very little chance of ever lifting off. That is, unless Mary thinks she can absorb everything she needs to know about piloting the *Podkayne* from those printouts Weinstein sent down. How about it, Mary?"

Mary Lang was lying sideways across the improvised cot that had recently held the *Podkayne* pilot, Lou Prager. Her head was nodding listlessly against the aluminum hull plate behind her, her chin was on her chest. Her eyes were half open.

Song had given her a sedative from the dead doctor's supplies on the advice of the medic aboard the *E.R.B.* It had enabled her to stop fighting so hard against the screaming panic she wanted to unleash. It hadn't improved her disposition. She had quit, she wasn't going to do anything for anybody.

When the blowout started, Lang had snapped on her helmet quickly. Then she had struggled against the blizzard and the undulating dome bottom, heading for the roofless framework where the other members of the expedition were sleeping. The blowout was over in ten seconds, and she then had the problem of coping with the collapsing roof, which promptly buried her in folds of clear plastic. It was far too much like one of those nightmares of running knee-deep in quicksand. She had to fight for every meter, but she made it.

She made it in time to see her shipmates of the last six months gasping soundlessly and spouting blood from all over their faces as they fought to get into their pressure suits. It was a hopeless task to choose which two or three to save in the time she had. She might have done better but for the freakish nature of her struggle to reach them; she was in shock and half believed it was only a nightmare. So she grabbed the nearest, who happened to be Doctor Ralston. He had nearly finished donning his suit; so she slapped his helmet on him and moved to the next one. It was Luther Nakamura, and he was not moving. Worse, he was only half suited. Pragmatically, she should have left him and moved on to save the ones who still had a chance. She knew it now but didn't like it any better than she had liked it then.

While she was stuffing Nakamura into his suit, Crawford arrived. He had walked over the folds of plastic until he reached the dormitory, then sliced through it with his laser normally used to vaporize rock samples.

And he had had time to think about the problem of whom to save. He went straight to Lou Prager and finished suiting him up. But it was already too late. He didn't know if it would have made any difference if Mary Lang had tried to save him first.

Now she lay on the bunk, her feet sprawled carelessly in front of her. She slowly shook her head back and forth.

"You sure?" Crawford prodded her, hoping to get a rise, a show of temper, *anything*.

"I'm sure," she mumbled. "You people know how long they trained Lou to fly this thing? And he almost cracked it up as it was. I . . . ah, nuts. It isn't possible."

"I refuse to accept that as a final answer," he said. "But in the meantime we should explore the possibilities if what Mary says is true."

Ralston laughed. It wasn't a bitter laugh; he sounded genuinely amused. Crawford plowed on.

"Here's what we know for sure. The *E.R.B.* is useless to us. Oh, they'll help us out with plenty of advice, maybe more than we want, but any rescue is out of the question."

"We know that," McKillian said. She was tired and sick from the sight of the faces of her dead friends. "What's the use of all this talk?"

"Wait a moment," Song broke in. "Why can't they . . . I mean they have plenty of time, don't they? They have to leave in six months, as I understand it, because of the orbital elements, but in that time . . ."

"Don't you know anything about spaceships?" McKillian shouted. Song went on, unperturbed.

"I do know enough to know the *Edgar* is not equipped for an atmosphere entry. My idea was, not to bring down the whole ship but only what's aboard the ship that we need. Which is a pilot. Might that be possible?"

Crawford ran his hands through his hair, wondering what to say. That possibility had been discussed, and was being studied. But it had to be classed as extremely remote.

"You're right," he said. "What we need is a pilot, and that pilot is Commander Weinstein. Which presents problems legally, if nothing else. He's the captain of a ship and should not leave it. That's what kept him on the *Edgar* in the first place. But he did have a lot of training on the lander simulator, back when he was so sure he'd be picked for the ground team. You know Winey, always the instinct to be the one-man show. So if he thought he could do it, he'd be down here in a minute to bail us out and grab the publicity. I understand they're trying to work out a heat-shield parachute system from one of the drop capsules that were supposed to ferry down supplies to us during the stay here. But it's very risky. You don't modify an aerodynamic design lightly, not one that's supposed to hit the atmosphere at ten thousand-plus kilometers. So I think we can rule that out. They'll keep working on it, but when it's done, Winey won't step into the damn thing. He wants to be a hero, but he wants to live to enjoy it, too."

There had been a brief lifting of spirits among Song, Ralston, and McKillian at the thought of a possible rescue. The more they thought about it, the less happy they looked. They all seemed to agree with Crawford's assessment.

"So we'll put that one in the Fairy Godmother file and forget about it. If it happens, fine. But we'd better plan on the assumption that it won't. As you may know, the *E.R.B.* and the *Podkayne* are the only ships in existence that can reach Mars and land on it. One other pair is in the congressional funding stage. Winey talked to Earth and thinks there'll be a speedup in the preliminary paperwork and the thing'll start building in a year. The launch was scheduled for five years from now, but it might get as much as a year's boost. It's a rescue mission now, easier to sell. But the design will need modification, if only to include five more seats to bring us all back. You can bet on there being more modifications when we send in our report on the blowout. So we'd better add another six months to the schedule."

McKillian had had enough. "Matt, what the hell are you talking about? Rescue mission? Damn it, you know as well as I that if they find us here, we'll be long dead. We'll probably be dead in another year."

"That's where you're wrong. We'll survive."

"How?"

"I don't have the faintest idea." He looked her straight in the eye as he said this. She almost didn't bother to answer, but curiosity got the best of her.

"Is this just a morale session? Thanks, but I don't need it. I'd rather face the situation as it is. Or do you really have something?"

"Both. I don't have anything concrete except to say that we'll survive the same way humans have always survived: by staying warm, by eating, by drinking. To that list we have to add 'by breathing.' That's a hard one, but other than that, we're no different than any other group of survivors in a tough spot. I don't know what we'll have to do, specifically, but I know we'll find the answers."

"Or die trying," Song said.

"Or die trying." He grinned at her. She at least had grasped the essence of the situation. Whether survival was possible or not, it was necessary to maintain the illusion that it was. Otherwise, you might as well cut your throat. You might as well not even be born, because life is an inevitably fatal struggle to survive.

"What about air?" McKillian asked, still unconvinced.

"I don't know," he told her cheerfully. "It's a tough problem, isn't it?"

"What about water?"

"Well, down in that valley there's a layer of permafrost about twenty meters down."

She laughed. "Wonderful. So that's what you want us to do? Dig down there and warm the ice with our pink little hands? It won't work, I tell you."

Crawford waited until she had run through a long list of reasons why they were doomed. Most of them made a great deal of sense. When she was through, he spoke softly.

"Lucy, listen to yourself."

"I'm just—"

"You're arguing on the side of death. Do you want to die? Are you so determined that you won't listen to someone who says you can live?"

She was quiet for a long time, then shuffled her feet awkwardly. She glanced at him, then at Song and Ralston. They were waiting, and she had to blush and smile slowly at them.

"You're right. What do we do first?"

"Just what we were doing. Taking stock of our situation. We need to make a list of what's available to us. We'll write it down on paper, but I can give you a general rundown." He counted off the points on his fingers.

"One, we have food for twenty people for three months. That comes to about a year for the five of us. With rationing, maybe a year and a half. That's assuming all the supply capsules reach us all right. In addition, the *Edgar* is going to clean the pantry to the bone and give us everything they can possibly spare and send it to us in the three spare capsules. That might come to two years or even three.

"Two, we have enough water to last us forever if the recyclers keep going. That'll be a problem, because our reactor will run out of power in two years. We'll need another power source, and maybe another water source.

"The oxygen problem is about the same. Two years at the outside. We'll have to find a way to conserve it a lot more than we're doing. Offhand, I don't know how. Song, do you have any ideas?"

She looked thoughtful, which produced two vertical punctuation marks between her slanted eyes.

"Possibly a culture of plants from the *Edgar*. If we could rig some way to grow plants in Martian sunlight and not have them killed by the ultraviolet. . . ."

McKillian looked horrified, as any good ecologist would.

"What about contamination?" she asked. "What do you think that sterilization was for before we landed? Do you want to louse up the entire ecological balance of Mars? No one would ever be sure if samples in the future were real Martian plants or mutated Earth stock."

"What ecological balance?" Song shot back. "You know as well as

I do that this trip has been nearly a zero. A few anaerobic bacteria, a patch of lichen, both barely distinguishable from Earth forms—"

"That's just what I mean. You import Earth forms now, and we'll never tell the difference."

"But it could be done, right? With the proper shielding so the plants won't be wiped out before they ever sprout, we could have a hydroponics plant functioning—"

"Oh, yes, it could be done. I can see three or four dodges right now. But you're not addressing the main question, which is—"

"Hold it," Crawford said. "I just wanted to know if you had any ideas." He was secretly pleased at the argument; it got them both thinking along the right lines, moved them from the deadly apathy they must guard against.

"I think this discussion has served its purpose, which was to convince everyone here that survival is possible." He glanced uneasily at Lang, still nodding, her eyes glassy as she saw her teammates die before her eyes.

"I just want to point out that instead of an expedition, we are now a colony. Not in the usual sense of planning to stay here forever, but all our planning will have to be geared to that fiction. What we're faced with is not a simple matter of stretching supplies until rescue comes. Stopgap measures are not likely to do us much good. The answers that will save us are the long-term ones, the sort of answers a colony would be looking for. About two years from now we're going to have to be in a position to survive with some sort of life-style that could support us forever. We'll have to fit into this environment where we can and adapt it to us where we can. For that, we're better off than most of the colonists of the past, at least for the short term. We have a large supply of everything a colony needs: food, water, tools, raw materials, energy, brains, and women. Without these things, no colony has much of a chance. All we lack is a regular resupply from the home country, but a really good group of colonists can get along without that. What do you say? Are you all with me?"

Something had caused Mary Lang's eyes to look up. It was a reflex by now, a survival reflex conditioned by a lifetime of fighting her way to the top. It took root in her again and pulled her erect on the bed, then to her feet. She fought off the effects of the drug and stood there, eyes bleary but aware.

"What makes you think that women are a natural resource, Crawford?" she said, slowly and deliberately.

"Why, what I meant was that without the morale uplift provided by members of the opposite sex, a colony will lack the push needed to make it."

"That's what you meant, all right. And you meant women, available to the *real* colonists as a reason to live. I've heard it before. That's a male-oriented way to look at it, Crawford." She was regain-

ing her stature as they watched, seeming to grow until she dominated the group with the intangible power that marks a leader. She
took a deep breath and came fully awake for the first time that day.

"We'll stop that sort of thinking right now. I'm the mission commander. I appreciate your taking over while I was . . . how did you
say it? Indisposed. But you should pay more attention to the social
aspects of our situation. If anyone is a commodity here, it's you and
Ralston, by virtue of your scarcity. There will be some thorny questions to resolve there, but for the meantime we will function as a unit,
under my command. We'll do all we can to minimize social competi-
tion among the women for the men. That's the way it must be. Clear?"

She was answered by quiet assent and nods of the head. She did
not acknowledge it but plowed right on.

"I wondered from the start why you were along, Crawford." She
was pacing slowly back and forth in the crowded space. The others
got out of her way almost without thinking, except for Ralston, who
still huddled under his blanket. "A historian? Sure, it's a fine idea, but
pretty impractical. I have to admit that I've been thinking of you as a
luxury, and about as useful as the nipples on a man's chest. But I was
wrong. All the NASA people were wrong. The Astronaut Corps fought
like crazy to keep you off this trip. Time enough for that on later
flights. We were blinded by our loyalty to the test-pilot philosophy
of space flight. We wanted as few scientists as possible and as many
astronauts as we could manage. We don't like to think of ourselves
as ferryboat pilots. I think we demonstrated during Apollo that we
could handle science jobs as well as anyone. We saw you as a kind of
insult, a slap in the face by the scientists in Houston to show us how
low our stock has fallen."

"If I might be able to—"

"Shut up. But we were wrong. I read in your résumé that you were
quite a student of survival. What's your honest assessment of our
chances?"

Crawford shrugged, uneasy at the question. He didn't know if it
was the right time to even postulate that they might fail.

"Tell me the truth."

"Pretty slim. Mostly the air problem. The people I've read about
never sank so low that they had to worry about where their next
breath was coming from."

"Have you ever heard of Apollo 13?"

He smiled at her. "Special circumstances. Short-term problems."

"You're right, of course. And in the only two other real space
emergencies since that time, all hands were lost." She turned and
scowled at each of them in turn.

"But we're *not* going to lose." She dared any of them to disagree,
and no one was about to. She relaxed and resumed her stroll around
the room. She turned to Crawford again.

"I can see I'll be drawing on your knowledge a lot in the years to come. What do you see as the next order of business?"

Crawford relaxed. The awful burden of responsibility, which he had never wanted, was gone. He was content to follow her lead.

"To tell you the truth, I was wondering what to say next. We have to make a thorough inventory. I guess we should start on that."

"That's fine, but there is an even more important order of business. We have to go out to the dome and find out what the hell caused the blowout. The damn thing should *not* have blown; it's the first of its type to do so. And from the *bottom*. But it did blow, and we should know why, or we're ignoring a fact about Mars that might still kill us. Let's do that first. Ralston, can you walk?"

When he nodded, she sealed her helmet and started into the lock. She turned and looked speculatively at Crawford.

"I swear, man, if you had touched me with a cattle prod you couldn't have got a bigger rise out of me than you did with what you said a few minutes ago. Do I dare ask?"

Crawford was not about to answer. He said, with a perfectly straight face, "Me? Maybe you should just assume I'm a chauvinist."

"We'll see, won't we?"

"What is that stuff?"

Song Sue Lee was on her knees, examining one of the hundreds of short, stiff spikes extruding from the ground. She tried to scratch her head but was frustrated by her helmet.

"It looks like plastic. But I have a strong feeling it's the higher life-form Lucy and I were looking for yesterday."

"And you're telling me those little spikes are what poked holes in the dome bottom? I'm not buying that."

Song straightened up, moving stiffly. They had all worked hard to empty out the collapsed dome and peel back the whole, bulky mess to reveal the ground it had covered. She was tired and stepped out of character for a moment to snap at Mary Lang.

"I didn't tell you that. We pulled the dome back and found spikes. It was your inference that they poked holes in the bottom."

"I'm sorry," Lang said quietly. "Go on with what you were saying."

"Well," Song admitted, "it wasn't a bad inference, at that. But the holes I saw were not punched through. They were eaten away." She waited for Lang to protest that the dome bottom was about as chemically inert as any plastic yet devised. But Lang had learned her lesson. And she had a talent for facing facts.

"So. We have a thing here that eats plastic. And seems to be made of plastic, into the bargain. Any ideas why it picked this particular spot to grow, and no other?"

"I have an idea on that," McKillian said. "I've had it in mind to do some studies around the dome to see if the altered moisture content we've been creating here had any effect on the spores in the soil. See, we've been here nine days, spouting out water vapor, carbon dioxide, and quite a bit of oxygen into the atmosphere. Not much, but maybe more than it seems, considering the low concentrations that are naturally available. We've altered the biome. Does anyone know where the exhaust air from the dome was expelled?"

Lang raised her eyebrows. "Yes, it was under the dome. The air we exhausted was warm, you see, and it was thought it could be put to use one last time before we let it go, to warm the floor of the dome and decrease heat loss."

"And the water vapor collected on the underside of the dome when it hit the cold air. Right. Do you get the picture?"

"I think so," Lang said. "It was so little water, though. You know we didn't want to waste it; we condensed it out until the air we exhausted was dry as a bone."

"For Earth, maybe. Here it was a torrential rainfall. It reached seeds or spores in the ground and triggered them to start growing. We're going to have to watch it when we use anything containing plastic. What does that include?"

Lang groaned. "All the airlock seals, for one thing." There were grimaces from all of them at the thought of that. "For another, a good part of our suits. Song, watch it, don't step on that thing. We don't know how powerful it is or if it'll eat the plastic in your boots, but we'd better play it safe. How about it, Ralston? Think you can find out how bad it is?"

"You mean identify the solvent these things use? Probably, if we can get some sort of workspace and I can get to my equipment."

"Mary," McKillian said, "it occurs to me that I'd better start looking for airborne spores. If there are some, it could mean that the airlock on the *Podkayne* is vulnerable. Even thirty meters off the ground."

"Right. Get on that. Since we're sleeping in it until we can find out what we can do on the ground, we'd best be sure it's safe. Meantime, we'll all sleep in our suits." There were helpless groans at this, but no protests. McKillian and Ralston headed for the pile of salvaged equipment, hoping to rescue enough to get started on their analyses. Song knelt again and started digging around one of the ten-centimeter spikes.

Crawford followed Lang back toward the *Podkayne*.

"Mary, I wanted . . . is it all right if I call you Mary?"

"I guess so. I don't think 'Commander Lang' would wear well over five years. But you'd better still *think* commander."

He considered it. "All right, Commander Mary." She punched him playfully. She had barely known him before the disaster. He had been a name on a roster and a sore spot in the estimation of the Astronaut Corps. But she had borne him no personal malice and now found herself beginning to like him.

"What's on your mind?"

"Ah, several things. But maybe it isn't my place to bring them up now. First, I want to say that if you're . . . ah, concerned, or doubtful of my support or loyalty because I took over command for a while . . . . earlier today, well . . ."

"Well?"

"I just wanted to tell you that I have no ambitions in that direction," he finished lamely.

She patted him on the back. "Sure, I know You forget, I read your dossier. It mentioned several interesting episodes that I'd like you to tell me about someday, from your 'soldier-of-fortune' days—"

"Hell, those were grossly overblown. I just happened to get into some scrapes and managed to get out of them."

"Still, it got you picked for this mission out of hundreds of applicants. The thinking was that you'd be a wild card, a man of action with proven survivability. Maybe it worked out. But the other thing I remember on your card was that you're not a leader. No, that you're a loner who'll cooperate with a group and be no discipline problem, but you work better alone. Want to strike out on your own?"

He smiled at her. "No, thanks. But what you said is right. I have no hankering to take charge of anything. But I do have some knowledge that might prove useful."

"And we'll use it. You just speak up, I'll be listening." She started to say something, then thought of something else. "Say, what are your ideas on a woman bossing this project? I've had to fight that all the way from my Air Force days. So if you have any objections you might as well tell me up front."

He was genuinely surprised. "You didn't take that crack seriously, did you? I might as well admit it. It was intentional, like that cattle prod you mentioned. You looked like you needed a kick in the ass."

"And thank you. But you didn't answer my question."

"Those who lead, lead," he said, simply. "I'll follow you as long as you keep leading."

"As long as it's in the direction you want?" She laughed and poked him in the ribs. "I see you as my Grand Vizier, the man who holds the arcane knowledge and advises the regent. I think I'll have to watch out for you. I know a little history, myself."

Crawford couldn't tell how serious she was. He shrugged it off.

"What I really wanted to talk to you about is this: You said you couldn't fly this ship. But you were not yourself, you were depressed and feeling hopeless. Does that still stand?"

"It stands. Come on up and I'll show you why."

In the pilot's cabin, Crawford was ready to believe her. Like all flying machines since the days of the windsock and open cockpit, this one was a mad confusion of dials, switches, and lights designed to awe anyone who knew nothing about it. He sat in the copilot's chair and listened to her.

"We had a backup pilot, of course. You may be surprised to learn that it wasn't me. It was Dorothy Cantrell, and she's dead. Now I know what everything does on this board, and I can cope with most of it easily. What I don't know, I could learn. Some of the systems are computer driven; give it the right program and it'll fly itself in space." She looked longingly at the controls, and Crawford realized that, like Weinstein, she didn't relish giving up the fun of flying to boss a gang of explorers. She was a former test pilot, and above all things she loved flying. She patted an array of hand controls on her right side. There were more like them on the left.

"This is what would kill us, Crawford. What's your first name? Matt. Matt, this baby is a flyer for the first forty thousand meters. It doesn't have the juice to orbit on the jets alone. The wings are folded up now. You probably didn't see them on the way in, but you saw the models. They're very light, supercritical, and designed for this atmosphere. Lou said it was like flying a bathtub, but it flew. And it's a *skill*, almost an art. Lou practiced for three years on the best simulators we could build and still had to rely on things you can't learn in a simulator. And he barely got us down in one piece. We didn't noise it around, but it was a *damn* close thing. Lou was young; so was Cantrell. They were both fresh from flying. They flew every day, they had the *feel* for it. They were tops." She slumped back into her chair. "I haven't flown anything but trainers for eight years."

Crawford didn't know if he should let it drop.

"But you were one of the best, everyone knows that. You still don't think you could do it?"

She threw up her hands. "How can I make you understand? This is nothing like anything I've ever flown. You might as well . . ." She groped for a comparison, trying to coax it out with gestures in the air. "Listen. Does the fact that someone can fly a biplane, maybe even be the best goddamn biplane pilot that ever was, does that mean they're qualified to fly a helicopter?"

"I don't know."

"It doesn't. Believe me."

"All right. But the fact remains that you're the closest thing on Mars to a pilot for the *Podkayne*. I think you should consider that when you're deciding what we should do." He shut up, afraid to sound like he was pushing her.

She narrowed her eyes and gazed at nothing.

"I have thought about it." She waited for a long time. "I think the chances are about a thousand to one against us if I try to fly it. But I'll do it, if we come to that. And that's *your* job. Showing me some better odds. If you can't, let me know."

Three weeks later, the Tharsis Canyon had been transformed into a child's garden of toys. Crawford had thought of no better way to describe it. Each of the plastic spikes had blossomed into a fanciful windmill, no two of them just alike. There were tiny ones, with the vanes parallel to the ground and no more than ten centimeters tall. There were derricks of spidery plastic struts that would not have looked too out of place on a Kansas farm. Some of them were five meters high. They came in all colors and many configurations, but all had vanes covered with a transparent film like cellophane, and all were spinning into colorful blurs in the stiff Martian breeze. Crawford thought of an industrial park built by gnomes. He could almost see them trudging through the spinning wheels.

Song had taken one apart as well as she could. She was still shaking her head in disbelief. She had not been able to excavate the long, insulated taproot, but she could infer how deep it went. It extended all the way to the layer of permafrost, twenty meters down.

The ground between the windmills was coated in shimmering plastic. This was the second part of the plants' ingenious solution to survival on Mars. The windmills utilized the energy in the wind, and the plastic coating on the ground was in reality two thin sheets of plastic with a space between for water to circulate. The water was heated by the sun then pumped down to the permafrost, melting a little more of it each time.

"There's still something missing from our picture," Song had told them the night before, when she delivered her summary of what she had learned. "Marty hasn't been able to find a mechanism that would permit these things to grow by ingesting sand and rock and turning it into plasticlike materials. So we assume there is a reservoir of something like crude oil down there, maybe frozen in with the water."

"Where would that have come from?" Lang had asked.

"You've heard of the long-period Martian seasonal theories? Well, part of it is more than a theory. The combination of the Martian polar inclination, the precessional cycle, and the eccentricity of the orbit produces seasons that are about twelve thousand years long. We're in the middle of winter, though we landed in the nominal 'summer.' It's been theorized that if there were any Martian life it would have adapted to these longer cycles. It hibernates in spores during the cold cycle, when the water and carbon dioxide freeze out at the poles, then comes out when enough ice melts to permit biological processes. We seem to have fooled these plants; they thought summer was here when the water vapor content went up around the camp."

"So what about the crude?" Ralston asked. He didn't completely believe that part of the model they had evolved. He was a laboratory chemist, specializing in inorganic compounds. The way these plants produced plastics without high heat, through purely catalytic interactions, had him confused and defensive. He wished the crazy windmills would go away.

"I think I can answer that," McKillian said. "These organisms barely scrape by in the best of times. The ones that have made it waste nothing. It stands to reason that any really ancient deposits of crude oil would have been exhausted in only a few of these cycles. So it must be that what we're thinking of as crude oil must be something a little different. It has to be the remains of the last generation."

"But how did the remains get so far below ground?" Ralston asked. "You'd expect them to be high up. The winds couldn't bury them that deep in only twelve thousand years."

"You're right," said McKillian. "I don't really know. But I have a theory. Since these plants waste nothing, why not conserve their bodies when they die? They sprouted from the ground; isn't it possible they could withdraw when things start to get tough again? They'd leave spores behind them as they retreated, distributing them all through the soil. That way, if the upper ones blew away or were sterilized by the ultraviolet, the ones just below them would still thrive when the right conditions returned. When they reached the permafrost, they'd decompose into this organic slush we've postulated, and . . . well, it does get a little involved, doesn't it?"

"Sounds all right to me," Lang assured her. "It'll do for a working theory. Now what about airborne spores?"

It turned out that they were safe from that imagined danger. There were spores in the air now, but they were not dangerous to the colonists. The plants attacked only certain kinds of plastics, and then only in certain stages of their lives. Since they were still changing, it bore watching, but the airlocks and suits were secure. The crew was enjoying the luxury of sleeping without their suits.

And there was much work to do. Most of the physical sort devolved on Crawford and, to some extent, on Lang. It threw them together a lot. The other three had to be free to pursue their researches, as it had been decided that only in knowing their environment would they stand a chance.

The two of them had managed to salvage most of the dome. Working with patching kits and lasers to cut the tough material, they had constructed a much smaller dome. They erected it on an outcropping of bare rock, rearranged the exhaust to prevent more condensation on the underside, and added more safety features. They now slept in a pressurized building inside the dome, and one of them stayed awake on watch at all times. In drills, they had come from a deep sleep to full pressure-integrity in thirty seconds. They were not going to get caught again.

Crawford looked away from the madly whirling rotors of the windmill farm. He was with the rest of the crew, sitting in the dome with his helmet off. That was as far as Lang would permit anyone to go except in the cramped sleeping quarters. Song Sue Lee was at the radio giving her report to the *Edgar Rice Burroughs*. In her hand was one of the pump modules she had dissected out of one of the plants. It consisted of a half-meter set of eight blades that turned freely on Teflon bearings. Below it were various tiny gears and the pump itself. She twirled it idly as she spoke.

"I don't really get it," Crawford admitted, talking quietly to Lucy McKillian. "What's so revolutionary about little windmills?"

"It's just a whole new area," McKillian whispered back. "Think about it. Back on Earth, nature never got around to inventing the wheel. I've sometimes wondered why not. There are limitations, of course, but it's such a good idea. Just look what *we've* done with it. But all motion in nature is confined to up and down, back and forth, in and out, or squeeze and relax. Nothing on Earth goes round and round, unless we built it. Think about it."

Crawford did, and began to see the novelty of it. He tried in vain to think of some mechanism in an animal or plant of earthly origin that turned and kept on turning forever. He could not.

Song finished her report and handed the mike to Lang. Before she could start, Weinstein came on the line.

"We've had a change in plan up here," he said, with no preface. "I hope this doesn't come as a shock. If you think about it, you'll see the logic in it. We're going back to Earth in seven days."

It didn't surprise them too much. The *Burroughs* had given them just about everything it could in the form of data and supplies. There was one more capsule load due; after that, its presence would only be a frustration to both groups. There was a great deal of irony in having two such powerful ships so close to each other and being so helpless to do anything concrete. It was telling on the crew of the *Burroughs*.

"We've recalculated everything based on the lower mass without the twenty of you and the six tons of samples we were allowing for. By using the fuel we would have ferried down to you for takeoff, we can make a faster orbit down toward Venus. The departure date for that orbit is seven days away. We'll rendezvous with a drone capsule full of supplies we hadn't counted on." And besides, Lang thought to herself, it's much more dramatic. *Plunging sunward on the chancy cometary orbit, their pantries stripped bare, heading for the fateful rendezvous. . . .*

"I'd like your comments," he went on. "This isn't absolutely final as yet."

They all looked at Lang. They were reassured to find her calm and unshaken.

"I think it's the best idea. One thing; you've given up on any thoughts of me flying the *Podkayne*?"

"No insult intended, Mary," Weinstein said, gently. "But, yes, we have. It's the opinion of the people Earthside that you couldn't do it. They've tried some experiments, coaching some very good pilots and putting them into the simulators. They can't do it, and we don't think you could, either."

"No need to sugarcoat it. I know it as well as anyone. But even a billion to one shot is better than nothing. I take it they think Crawford is right, that survival is at least theoretically possible?"

There was a long hesitation. "I guess that's correct. Mary, I'll be frank. I don't think it's possible. I hope I'm wrong, but I don't expect . . ."

"Thank you, Winey, for the encouraging words. You always did know what it takes to buck a person up. By the way, that other mission, the one where you were going to ride a meteorite down here to save our asses, that's scrubbed, too?"

The assembled crew smiled, and Song gave a high-pitched cheer. Weinstein was not the most popular man on Mars.

"Mary, I told you about that already," he complained. It was a gentle complaint, and, even more significant, he had not objected to the use of his nickname. He was being gentle with the condemned. "We worked on it around the clock. I even managed to get permission to turn over command temporarily. But the mock-ups they made Earthside didn't survive the re-entry. It was the best we could do. I couldn't risk the entire mission on a configuration the people back on Earth wouldn't certify."

"I know. I'll call you back tomorrow." She switched the set off and sat back on her heels. "I swear, if the Earthside tests on a roll of toilet paper didn't . . . he wouldn't . . ." She cut the air with her hands. "What am I saying? That's petty. I don't like him, but he's right." She stood up, puffing out her cheeks as she exhaled a pent-up breath.

"Come on, crew, we've got a lot of work."

They named their colony New Amsterdam, because of the windmills. The name of whirligig was the one that stuck on the Martian plants, though Crawford held out for a long time in favor of spinnakers.

They worked all day and tried their best to ignore the *Burroughs* overhead. The messages back and forth were short and to the point. Helpless as the mother ship was to render them more aid, they knew they would miss it when it was gone. So the day of departure was a stiff, determinedly nonchalant affair. They all made a big show of going to bed hours before the scheduled breakaway.

When he was sure the others were asleep, Crawford opened his eyes and looked around the darkened barracks. It wasn't much in the way of a home; they were crowded against each other on rough pads made of insulating material. The toilet facilities were behind a flimsy barrier against one wall, and smelled. But none of them would have wanted to sleep outside in the dome, even if Lang had allowed it.

The only light came from the illuminated dials that the guard was supposed to watch all night. There was no one sitting in front of them. Crawford assumed the guard had gone to sleep. He would have been upset, but there was no time. He had to suit up, and he welcomed the chance to sneak out. He began to furtively don his pressure suit.

As a historian, he felt he could not let such a moment slip by unobserved. Silly, but there it was. He had to be out there, watch it with his own eyes. It didn't matter if he never lived to tell about it, he must record it.

Someone sat up beside him. He froze, but it was too late. She rubbed her eyes and peered into the darkness.

"Matt?" she yawned. "What's . . . what is it? Is something—"

"Shh. I'm going out. Go back to sleep, Song."

"Um hmmm." She stretched, dug her knuckles fiercely into her eyes, and smoothed her hair back from her face. She was dressed in a loose-fitting bottom of a ship suit, a gray piece of dirty cloth that badly needed washing, as did all their clothes. For a moment, as he watched her shadow stretch and stand up, he wasn't interested in the *Burroughs*. He forced his mind away from her.

"I'm going with you," she whispered.

"All right. Don't wake the others."

Standing just outside the airlock was Mary Lang. She turned as they came out, and did not seem surprised.

"Were you the one on duty?" Crawford asked her.

"Yeah. I broke my own rule. But so did you two. Consider yourselves on report." She laughed and beckoned them over to her. They linked arms and stood staring up at the sky.

"How much longer?" Song asked, after some time had passed.

"Just a few minutes. Hold tight." Crawford looked over to Lang and thought he saw tears, but he couldn't be sure in the dark.

There was a tiny new star, brighter than all the rest, brighter than Phobos. It hurt to look at it but none of them looked away. It was the fusion drive of the *Edgar Rice Burroughs*, heading sunward, away from the long winter on Mars. It stayed on for long minutes, then sputtered and was lost. Though it was warm in the dome, Crawford was shivering. It was ten minutes before any of them felt like facing the barracks.

They crowded into the airlock, carefully not looking at each other's faces as they waited for the automatic machinery. The inner door opened and Lang pushed forward—and right back into the airlock. Crawford had a glimpse of Ralston and Lucy McKillian; then Mary shut the door.

"Some people have no poetry in their souls," Mary said.

"Or too much," Song giggled.

"You people want to take a walk around the dome with me? Maybe we could discuss ways of giving people a little privacy."

The inner lock door was pulled open, and there was McKillian, squinting into the bare bulb that lighted the lock while she held her shirt in front of her with one hand.

"Come on in," she said, stepping back. "We might as well talk about this." They entered, and McKillian turned on the light and sat down on her mattress. Ralston was blinking, nervously tucked into his pile of blankets. Since the day of the blowout he never seemed to be warm enough.

Having called for a discussion, McKillian proceeded to clam up. Song and Crawford sat on their bunks, and eventually as the silence stretched tighter, they all found themselves looking to Lang.

She started stripping out of her suit. "Well, I guess that takes care of that. So glad to hear all your comments. Lucy, if you were expecting some sort of reprimand, forget it. We'll take steps first thing in the morning to provide some sort of privacy for that, but, no matter what, we'll all be pretty close in the years to come. I think we should all relax. Any objections?" She was half out of her suit when she paused to scan them for comments. There were none. She stripped to her skin and reached for the light.

"In a way it's about time," she said, tossing her clothes in a corner. "The only thing to do with these clothes is burn them. We'll all smell better for it. Song, you take the watch." She flicked out the lights and reclined heavily on her mattress.

There was much rustling and squirming for the next few minutes as they got out of their clothes. Song brushed against Crawford in the dark and they murmured apologies. Then they all bedded down in their own bunks. It was several tense, miserable hours before anyone got to sleep.

The week following the departure of the *Burroughs* was one of hysterical overreaction by the New Amsterdamites. The atmosphere was forced and false; an eat-drink-and-be-merry feeling pervaded everything they did.

They built a separate shelter inside the dome, not really talking aloud about what it was for. But it did not lack for use. Productive work suffered as the five of them frantically ran through all the possible permutations of three women and two men. Animosities developed, flourished for a few hours, and dissolved in tearful reconciliations. Three ganged up on two, two on one, one declared war on all the other four. Ralston and Song announced an engagement, which lasted ten hours. Crawford nearly came to blows with Lang, aided by McKillian. McKillian renounced men forever and had a brief, tempestuous affair with Song. Then Song discovered McKillian with Ralston, and Crawford caught her on the rebound, only to be thrown over for Ralston.

Mary Lang let it work itself out, only interfering when it got violent. She herself was not immune to the frenzy but managed to stay aloof from most of it. She went to the shelter with whoever asked her, trying not to play favorites, and gently tried to prod them back to work. As she told McKillian toward the first of the week, "At least we're getting to know one another."

Things did settle down, as Lang had known they would. They entered their second week alone in virtually the same position they had started: no romantic entanglements firmly established. But they knew each other a lot better, were relaxed in the close company of each other, and were supported by a new framework of interlocking friendships. They were much closer to being a team. Rivalries never died out completely, but they no longer dominated the colony. Lang worked them harder than ever, making up for the lost time.

Crawford missed most of the interesting work, being more suited for the semiskilled manual labor that never seemed to be finished. So he and Lang had to learn about the new discoveries at the nightly briefings in the shelter. He remembered nothing about any animal life being discovered, and so when he saw something crawling through the whirligig garden, he dropped everything and started over to it.

At the edge of the garden he stopped, remembering the order from Lang to stay out unless collecting samples. He watched the thing—bug? turtle?—for a moment, satisfied himself that it wouldn't get too far away at its creeping pace, and hurried off to find Song.

"You've got to name it after me," he said as they hurried back to the garden. "That's my right, isn't it, as the discoverer?"

"Sure," Song said, peering along his pointed finger. "Just show me the damn thing and I'll immortalize you."

The thing was twenty centimeters long, almost round, and dome-shaped. It had a hard shell on top.

"I don't know quite what to do with it," Song admitted. "If it's the only one, I don't dare dissect it, and maybe I shouldn't even touch it."

"Don't worry, there's another over behind you." Now that they were looking for them, they quickly spied four of the creatures. Song took a sample bag from her pouch and held it open in front of the beast. It crawled halfway into the bag, then seemed to think something was wrong. It stopped, but Song nudged it in and picked it up. She peered at the underside and laughed in wonder.

"Wheels," she said. "The thing runs on wheels."

"I don't know where it came from," Song told the group that night. "I don't even quite believe in it. It'd make a nice educational toy for a child, though. I took it apart into twenty or thirty pieces, put it back together, and it still runs. It has a high-impact polystyrene carapace, nontoxic paint on the outside—"

"Not really polystyrene," Ralston interjected.

"—and I guess if you kept changing the batteries it would run forever. And it's *nearly* polystyrene, that's what you said."

"Were you serious about the batteries?" Lang asked.

"I'm not sure. Marty thinks there's a chemical metabolism in the upper part of the shell, which I haven't explored yet. But I can't really say if it's alive in the sense we use. I mean, it runs on *wheels*! It has three wheels, suited for sand, and something that's a cross between a rubber-band drive and a mainspring. Energy is stored in a coiled muscle and released slowly. I don't think it could travel more than a hundred meters. Unless it can re-coil the muscle, and I can't tell how that might be done."

"It sounds very specialized," McKillian said thoughtfully. "Maybe we should be looking for the niche it occupies. The way you describe it, it couldn't function without help from a symbiote. Maybe it fertilizes the plants, like bees, and the plants either donate or are robbed of the power to wind the spring. Did you look for some mechanism the bug could use to steal energy from the rotating gears in the whirligigs?"

"That's what I want to do in the morning," Song said. "Unless Mary will let us take a look tonight?" She said it hopefully, but without real expectation. Mary Lang shook her head decisively.

"It'll keep. It's *cold* out there, baby."

A new exploration of the whirligig garden the next day revealed several new species, including one more thing that might be an animal. It was a flying creature, the size of a fruit fly, that managed to glide from plant to plant when the wind was down by means of a freely rotating set of blades, like an autogiro.

Crawford and Lang hung around as the scientists looked things over. They were not anxious to get back to the task that had occupied them for the last two weeks: that of bringing the *Podkayne* to a horizontal position without wrecking her. The ship had been rigged with stabilizing cables soon after landing, and provision had been made in the plans to lay the ship on its side in the event of a really big windstorm. But the plans had envisioned a work force of twenty, working all day with a maze of pulleys and gears. It was slow work and could not be rushed. If the ship were to tumble and lose pressure, they didn't have a prayer.

So they welcomed an opportunity to tour fairyland. The place was even more bountiful than the last time Crawford had taken a look. There were thick vines that Song assured him were running with water, both hot and cold, and various other fluids. There were more of the tall variety of derrick, making the place look like a pastel oilfield.

They had little trouble finding where the matthews came from. They found dozens of twenty-centimeter lumps on the sides of the large derricks. They evidently grew from them like tumors and were released when they were ripe. What they were for was another matter. As well as they could discover, the "matthews" simply crawled in a straight line until their power ran out. If they were wound up again, they would crawl farther. There were dozens of them lying motionless in the sand within a hundred-meter radius of the garden.

Two weeks of research left them knowing no more. They had to abandon the matthews for the time, as another enigma had cropped up which demanded their attention.

This time Crawford was the last to know. He was called on the radio and found the group all squatted in a circle around a growth in the graveyard.

The graveyard, where they had buried their fifteen dead crewmates on the first day of the disaster, had sprouted with life during the week after the departure of the *Burroughs*. It was separated from the original site of the dome by three hundred meters of blowing sand. So McKillian assumed this second bloom was caused by the water in the bodies of the dead. What they couldn't figure out was why this patch should differ so radically from the first one.

There were whirligigs in the second patch, but they lacked the variety and disorder of the originals. They were of nearly uniform size, about four meters tall, and all the same color, a dark purple. They had pumped water for two weeks, then stopped. When Song examined them, she reported the bearings were frozen, dried out. They seemed to have lost the plasticizer that kept the structures fluid and living. The water in the pipes was frozen. Though she would not commit herself in the matter, she felt they were dead. In their place was a second network of pipes which wound around the derricks and spread transparent sheets of film to the sunlight, heating the water which circulated through them. The water was being pumped, but not by the now-familiar system of windmills. Spaced along each of the pipes were expansion-contraction pumps with valves very like those in a human heart.

The new marvel was a simple affair in the middle of that living petrochemical complex. It was a short plant that sprouted up half a meter, then extruded two stalks parallel to the ground. At the end of each stalk was a perfect globe, one gray, one blue. The blue one was much larger than the gray one.

Crawford looked at it briefly, then squatted down beside the rest, wondering what all the fuss was about. Everyone looked very solemn, almost scared.

"You called me over to see this?"

Lang looked over at him, and something in her face made him nervous.

"Look at it, Matt. Really look at it." So he did, feeling foolish, wondering what the joke was. He noticed a white patch near the top of the larger globe. It was streaked, like a glass marble with swirls of opaque material in it. It looked *very* familiar, he realized, with the hair on the back of his neck starting to stand up.

"It turns," Lang said quietly. "That's why Song noticed it. She came by here one day and it was in a different position than it had been."

"Let me guess," he said, much more calmly than he felt. "The little one goes around the big one, right?"

"Right. And the little one keeps one face turned to the big one. The big one rotates once in twenty-four hours. It has an axial tilt of twenty-three degrees."

"It's a . . . what's the word? Orrery. It's an orrery." Crawford had to stand up and shake his head to clear it.

"It's funny," Lang said, quietly. "I always thought it would be something flashy, or at least obvious. An alien artifact mixed in with caveman bones, or a spaceship entering the system. I guess I was thinking in terms of pottery shards and atom bombs."

"Well, that all sounds pretty ho-hum to me up against *this*," Song said. "Do you . . . do you *realize* . . . what are we talking about here? Evolution, or . . . or engineering? Is it the plants themselves that did this, or were they made to do it by whatever built them? Do you see what I'm talking about? I felt funny about those wheels for a long time. I just won't believe they'd evolve naturally."

"What do you mean?"

"I mean I think these plants we've been seeing were designed to be the way they are. They're *too* perfectly adapted, *too* ingenious to have just sprung up in response to the environment." Her eyes seemed to wander, and she stood up and gazed into the valley below them. It was as barren as anything that could be imagined: red and yellow and brown rock outcroppings and tumbled boulders. And in the foreground, the twirling colors of the whirligigs.

"But why this thing?" Crawford asked, pointing to the impossible artifact-plant. "Why a model of the Earth and Moon? And why right here, in the graveyard?"

"Because we were expected," Song said, still looking away from them. "They must have watched the Earth, during the last summer season. I don't know; maybe they even went there. If they did, they would have found men and women like us, hunting and living in caves. Building fires, using clubs, chipping arrowheads. You know more about it than I do, Matt."

"Who are *they*?" Ralston asked. "You think we're going to be meeting some Martians? People? I don't see how. I don't believe it."

"I'm afraid I'm skeptical, too," Lang said. "Surely there must be some other way to explain it."

"No! There's no other way. Oh, not people like us, maybe. Maybe we're seeing them right now, spinning like crazy." They all looked uneasily at the whirligigs. "But I think they're not here yet. I think we're going to see, over the next few years, increasing complexity in these plants and animals as they build up a biome here and get ready for the builders. Think about it. When summer comes, the conditions will be very different. The atmosphere will be almost as dense as ours, with about the same partial pressure of oxygen. By then, thousands of years from now, these early forms will have vanished. These things are adapted for low pressure, no oxygen, scarce water. The later ones will be adapted to an environment much like ours. And *that's* when we'll see the makers, when the stage is properly set." She sounded almost religious when she said it.

Lang stood up and shook Song's shoulder. Song came slowly back to them and sat down, still blinded by a private vision. Crawford had a glimpse of it himself, and it scared him. And a glimpse of something else, something that could be important but kept eluding him.

"Don't you see?" she went on, calmer now. "It's too pat, too much of a coincidence. This thing is like a . . . a headstone, a monument. It's growing right here in the graveyard, from the bodies of our friends. Can you believe in that as just a coincidence?"

Evidently no one could. But likewise, Crawford could see no reason why it should have happened the way it did.

It was painful to leave the mystery for later, but there was nothing to be done about it. They could not bring themselves to uproot the thing, even when five more like it sprouted in the graveyard. There was a new consensus among them to leave the Martian plants and animals alone. Like nervous atheists, most of them didn't believe Song's theories but had an uneasy feeling of trespassing when they went through the gardens. They felt subconsciously that it might be better to leave them alone in case they turned out to be private property.

And for six months, nothing really new cropped up among the whirligigs. Song was not surprised. She said it supported her theory that these plants were there only as caretakers to prepare the way for the less hardy, air-breathing varieties to come. They would warm the soil and bring the water closer to the surface, then disappear when their function was over.

The three scientists allowed their studies to slide as it became more important to provide for the needs of the moment. The dome material was weakening as the temporary patches lost strength, and so a new home was badly needed. They were dealing daily with slow leaks, any of which could become a major blowout.

The *Podkayne* was lowered to the ground, and sadly decommissioned. It was a bad day for Mary Lang, the worst since the day of the blowout. She saw it as a necessary but infamous thing to do to a proud flying machine. She brooded about it for a week, becoming short-tempered and almost unapproachable. Then she asked Crawford to join her in the private shelter. It was the first time she had asked any of the other four. They lay in each other's arms for an hour, and Lang quietly sobbed on his chest. Crawford was proud that she had chosen him for her companion when she could no longer maintain her tough, competent show of strength. In a way, it was a strong thing to do, to expose weakness to the one person among the four who might possibly be her rival for leadership. He did not betray the trust. In the end, she was comforting him.

After that day Lang was ruthless in gutting the old *Podkayne*. She supervised the ripping out of the motors to provide more living space, and only Crawford saw what it was costing her. They drained the fuel tanks and stored the fuel in every available container they could scrounge. It would be useful later for heating, and for recharging batteries. They managed to convert plastic packing crates into fuel containers by lining them with sheets of the double-walled material the whirligigs used to heat water. They were nervous at this vandalism, but had no other choice. They kept looking nervously at the graveyard as they ripped up meter-square sheets of it.

They ended up with a long cylindrical home, divided into two small sleeping rooms, a community room, and a laboratory-storehouse-workshop in the old fuel tank. Crawford and Lang spent the first night together in the "penthouse," the former cockpit, the only room with windows.

Lying there wide awake on the rough mattress, side by side in the warm air with Mary Lang, whose black leg was a crooked line of shadow lying across his body, looking up through the port at the sharp, unwinking stars—with nothing done yet about the problems of oxygen, food, and water for the years ahead and no assurance he would live out the night on a planet determined to kill him—Crawford realized he had never been happier in his life.

On a day exactly eight months after the disaster, two discoveries were made. One was in the whirligig garden and concerned a new plant that was bearing what might be fruit. They were clusters of grape-sized white balls, very hard and fairly heavy. The second discovery was made by Lucy McKillian and concerned the absence of an event that up to that time had been as regular as the full moon.

"I'm pregnant," she announced to them that night, causing Song to delay her examination of the white fruit.

It was not unexpected; Lang had been waiting for it to happen since the night the *Burroughs* left. But she had not worried about it. Now she must decide what to do.

"I was afraid that might happen," Crawford said. "What do we do, Mary?"

"Why don't you tell me what you think? You're the survival expert. Are babies a plus or a minus in our situation?"

"I'm afraid I have to say they're a liability. Lucy will be needing extra food during her pregnancy, and afterward, and it will be an extra mouth to feed. We can't afford the strain on our resources." Lang said nothing, waiting to hear from McKillian.

"Now wait a minute. What about all this line about 'colonists' you've been feeding us ever since we got stranded here? Who ever heard of a colony without babies? If we don't grow, we stagnate, right? We *have* to have children." She looked back and forth from Lang to Crawford, her face expressing formless doubts.

"We're in special circumstances, Lucy," Crawford explained. "Sure, I'd be all for it if we were better off. But we can't be sure we can even provide for ourselves, much less a child. I say we can't afford children until we're established."

"Do you want the child, Lucy?" Lang asked quietly.

McKillian didn't seem to know what she wanted. "No. I . . . but, yes. Yes, I guess I do." She looked at them, pleading for them to understand.

"Look, I've never had one, and never planned to. I'm thirty-four years old and never, never felt the lack. I've always wanted to go places, and you can't with a baby. But I never planned to become a colonist on Mars, either. I . . . things have changed, don't you see? I've been depressed." She looked around, and Song and Ralston were nodding sympathetically. Relieved to see that she was not the only one feeling the oppression, she went on, more strongly. "I think if I go another day like yesterday and the day before—and today—I'll end up screaming. It seems so pointless, collecting all that information, for what?"

"I agree with Lucy," Ralston said, surprisingly. Crawford had thought he would be the only one immune to the inevitable despair of the castaway. Ralston in his laboratory was the picture of carefree detachment, existing only to observe.

"So do I," Lang said, ending the discussion. But she explained her reasons to them.

"Look at it this way, Matt. No matter how we stretch our supplies, they won't take us through the next four years. We either find a way of getting what we need from what's around us, or we all die. And if we find a way to do it, then what does it matter how many of us there are? At the most, this will push our deadline a few weeks or a month closer, the day we have to be self-supporting."

"I hadn't thought of it that way," Crawford admitted.

"But that's not important. The important thing is what you said from the first, and I'm surprised you didn't see it. If we're a colony, we expand. By definition. Historian, what happened to colonies that failed to expand?"

"Don't rub it in."

"They died out. I know that much. People, we're not intrepid space explorers anymore. We're not the career men and women we set out to be. Like it or not, and I suggest we start liking it, we're pioneers trying to live in a hostile environment. The odds are very much against us, and we're not going to be here forever, but like Matt said, we'd better plan as if we were. Comment?"

There was none, until Song spoke up, thoughtfully.

"I think a baby around here would be fun. Two should be twice as much fun. I think I'll start. Come on, Marty."

"Hold on, honey," Lang said, dryly. "If you conceive now, I'll be forced to order you to abort. We have the chemicals for it, you know."

"That's discrimination."

"Maybe so. But just because we're colonists doesn't mean we have to behave like rabbits. A pregnant woman will have to be removed from the work force at the end of her term, and we can only afford one at a time. After Lucy has hers, then come ask me again. But watch Lucy carefully, dear. Have you really thought what it's going to take? Have you tried to visualize her getting into her pressure suit in six or seven months?"

From their expressions, it was plain that neither Song nor McKillian had thought of it.

"Right," Lang went on. "It'll be literal confinement for her, right here in the *Poddy*. Unless we can rig something for her, which I seriously doubt. Still want to go through with it, Lucy?"

"Can I have a while to think it over?"

"Sure. You have about two months. After that, the chemicals aren't safe."

"I'd advise you to do it," Crawford said. "I know my opinion means nothing after shooting my mouth off. I know I'm a fine one to talk; I won't be cooped up in here. But the colony needs it. We've all felt it: the lack of a direction or a drive to keep going. I think we'd get it back if you went through with this."

McKillian tapped her teeth thoughtfully with the tip of a finger.

"You're right," she said. "Your opinion *doesn't* mean anything." She slapped his knee delightedly when she saw him blush. "I think it's yours, by the way. And I think I'll go ahead and have it."

The penthouse seemed to have gone to Lang and Crawford as an unasked-for prerogative. It just became a habit, since they seemed to have developed a bond between them and none of the other three complained. Neither of the other women seemed to be suffering in any way. So Lang left it at that. What went on between the three of them was of no concern to her as long as it stayed happy.

Lang was leaning back in Crawford's arms, trying to decide if she wanted to make love again, when a gunshot rang out in the *Podkayne*.

She had given a lot of thought to the last emergency, which she still saw as partly a result of her lag in responding. This time she was through the door almost before the reverberations had died down, leaving Crawford to nurse the leg she had stepped on in her haste.

She was in time to see McKillian and Ralston hurrying into the lab at the back of the ship. There was a red light flashing, but she quickly saw it was not the worst it could be; the pressure light still glowed green. It was the smoke detector. The smoke was coming from the lab.

She took a deep breath and plunged in, only to collide with Ralston as he came out, dragging Song. Except for a dazed expression and a few cuts, Song seemed to be all right. Crawford and McKillian joined them as they laid her on the bunk.

"It was one of the fruit," she said, gasping for breath and coughing. "I was heating it in a beaker, turned away, and it blew. I guess it sort of stunned me. The next thing I knew, Marty was carrying me out here. Hey, I have to get back in there! There's another one . . . it could be dangerous, and the damage, I have to check on that—" She struggled to get up but Lang held her down.

"You take it easy. What's this about another one?"

"I had it clamped down, and the drill—did I turn it on, or not? I can't remember. I was after a core sample. You'd better take a look. If the drill hits whatever made the other one explode, it might go off."

"I'll get it," McKillian said, turning toward the lab.

"You'll stay right here," Lang barked. "We know there's not enough power in them to hurt the ship, but it could kill you if it hit you right. We stay right here until it goes off. The hell with the damage. And shut that door, quick!"

Before they could shut it they heard a whistling, like a teakettle coming to boil, then a rapid series of clangs. A tiny white ball came through the doorway and bounced off three walls. It moved almost faster than they could follow. It hit Crawford on the arm, then fell to the floor where it gradually skittered to a stop. The hissing died away, and Crawford picked it up. It was lighter than it had been. There was a pinhole drilled in one side. The pinhole was cold when he touched it with his fingers. Startled, thinking he was burned, he stuck his finger in his mouth, then sucked on it absently long after he knew the truth.

"These 'fruit' are full of compressed gas," he told them. "We have to open up another, carefully this time. I'm almost afraid to say what gas I think it is, but I have a hunch that our problems are solved."

By the time the rescue expedition arrived, no one was calling it that. There had been the little matter of a long, brutal war with the Palestinian Empire, and a growing conviction that the survivors of the First Expedition had not had any chance in the first place. There had been no time for luxuries like space travel beyond the moon and no billions of dollars to invest while the world's energy policies were being debated in the Arabian Desert with tactical nuclear weapons.

When the ship finally did show up, it was no longer a NASA ship. It was sponsored by the fledgling International Space Agency. Its crew came from all over Earth. Its drive was new, too, and a lot better than the old one. As usual, war had given research a kick in the pants. Its mission was to take up the Martian exploration where the first expedition had left off and, incidentally, to recover the remains of the twenty Americans for return to Earth.

The ship came down with an impressive show of flame and billowing sand, three kilometers from Tharsis Base.

The captain, an Indian named Singh, got his crew started on erecting the permanent buildings, then climbed into a crawler with three officers for the trip to Tharsis. It was almost exactly twelve Earth-years since the departure of the *Edgar Rice Burroughs.*

The *Podkayne* was barely visible behind a network of multicolored vines. The vines were tough enough to frustrate their efforts to push through and enter the old ship. But both lock doors were open, and sand had drifted in rippled waves through the opening. The stern of the ship was nearly buried.

Singh told his people to stop, and he stood back admiring the complexity of the life in such a barren place. There were whirligigs twenty meters tall scattered around him, with vanes broad as the wings of a cargo aircraft.

"We'll have to get cutting tools from the ship," he told his crew. "They're probably in there. What a place this is! I can see we're going to be busy." He walked along the edge of the dense growth, which now covered several acres. He came to a section where the predominant color was purple. It was strangely different from the rest of the garden. There were tall whirligig derricks but they were frozen, unmoving. And covering all the derricks was a translucent network of ten-centimeter-wide strips of plastic, which was thick enough to make an impenetrable barrier. It was like a cobweb made of flat, thin material instead of fibrous spider-silk. It bulged outward between all the crossbraces of the whirligigs.

"Hello, can you hear me now?"

Singh jumped, then turned around, looked at the three officers. They were looking as surprised as he was.

"Hello, hello, hello? No good on this one, Mary. Want me to try another channel?"

"Wait a moment. I can hear you. Where are you?"

"Hey, he hears me! Uh, that is, this is Song Sue Lee, and I'm right in front of you. If you look real hard into the webbing, you can just make me out. I'll wave my arms. See?"

Singh thought he saw some movement when he pressed his face to the translucent web. The web resisted his hands, pushing back like an inflated balloon.

"I think I see you." The enormity of it was just striking him. He kept his voice under tight control, as his officers rushed up around him, and managed not to stammer. "Are you well? Is there anything we can do?"

There was a pause. "Well, now that you mention it, you might have come on time. But that's water through the pipes, I guess. If you have some toys or something, it might be nice. The stories I've told little Billy of all the nice things you people were going to bring! There's going to be no living with him, let me tell you."

This was getting out of hand for Captain Singh.

"Ms. Song, how can we get in there with you?"

"Sorry. Go to your right about ten meters, where you see the steam coming from the web. There, see it?" They did, and as they looked, a section of the webbing was pulled open and a rush of warm air almost blew them over. Water condensed out of it in their faceplates, and suddenly they couldn't see very well.

"Hurry, hurry, step in! We can't keep it open too long." They groped their way in, scraping frost away with their hands. The web closed behind them, and they were standing in the center of a very complicated network made of single strands of the webbing material. Singh's pressure gauge read 30 millibars.

Another section opened up and they stepped through it. After three more gates were passed, the temperature and pressure were nearly Earth-normal. And they were standing beside a small oriental woman with skin tanned almost black. She had no clothes on, but seemed adequately dressed in a brilliant smile that dimpled her mouth and eyes. Her hair was streaked with gray. She would be—Singh stopped to consider—forty-one years old.

"This way," she said, beckoning them into a tunnel formed from more strips of plastic. They twisted around through a random maze, going through more gates that opened when they neared them, sometimes getting on their knees when the clearance lowered. They heard the sound of children's voices.

They reached what must have been the center of the maze and found the people everyone had given up on. Eighteen of them. The children became very quiet and stared solemnly at the new arrivals, while the other four adults . . .

The adults were standing separately around the space while tiny helicopters flew around them, wrapping them from head to toe in strips of webbing like human maypoles.

"Of course we don't know if we would have made it without the assist from the Martians," Mary Lang was saying, from her perch on an orange thing that might have been a toadstool. "Once we figured out what was happening here in the graveyard, there was no need to explore alternative ways of getting food, water, and oxygen. The need just never arose. We were provided for."

She raised her feet so a group of three gawking women from the ship could get by. They were letting them come through in groups of five every hour. They didn't dare open the outer egress more often than that, and Lang was wondering if it was too often. The place was crowded, and the kids were nervous. But better to have the crew satisfy their curiosity in here where we can watch them, she reasoned, than have them messing things up outside.

The inner nest was free-form. The New Amsterdamites had allowed it to stay pretty much the way the whirlibirds had built it, only taking down an obstruction here and there to allow humans to move around. It was a maze of gauzy walls and plastic struts, with clear plastic pipes running all over and carrying fluids of pale blue, pink, gold, and wine. Metal spigots from the *Podkayne* had been inserted in some of the pipes. McKillian was kept busy refilling glasses for the visitors who wanted to sample the antifreeze solution that was fifty percent ethanol. It was good stuff, Captain Singh reflected as he drained his third glass, and that was what he still couldn't understand.

He was having trouble framing the questions he wanted to ask, and he realized he'd had too much to drink. The spirit of celebration, the rejoicing at finding these people here past any hope; one could hardly stay aloof from it. But he refused a fourth drink regretfully.

"I can understand the drink," he said, carefully. "Ethanol is a simple compound and could fit into many different chemistries. But it's hard to believe that you've survived eating the food these plants produced for you."

"Not once you understand what this graveyard is and why it became what it did," Song said. She was sitting cross-legged on the floor nursing her youngest, Ethan.

"First you have to understand that all this you see," she waved around at the meters of hanging soft-sculpture, causing Ethan to nearly lose the nipple, "was designed to contain beings who are no more adapted to *this* Mars than we are. They need warmth, oxygen at fairly high pressures, and free water. It isn't here now, but it can be created by properly designed plants. They engineered these plants to be triggered by the first signs of free water and to start building places for them to live while they waited for full summer to come. When it does, this whole planet will bloom. Then we can step outside without wearing suits or carrying airberries."

"Yes, I see," Singh said. "And it's all very wonderful, almost too much to believe." He was distracted for a moment, looking up to the ceiling where the airberries—white spheres about the size of bowling balls—hung in clusters from the pipes that supplied them with high-pressure oxygen.

"I'd like to see that process from the start," he said. "Where you suit up for the outside, I mean."

"We were suiting up when you got here. It takes about half an hour; so we couldn't get out in time to meet you."

"How long are those . . . suits good for?"

"About a day," Crawford said. "You have to destroy them to get out of them. The plastic strips don't cut well, but there's another specialized animal that eats that type of plastic. It's recycled into the system. If you want to suit up, you just grab a whirlibird and hold onto its tail and throw it. It starts spinning as it flies, and wraps the end product around you. It takes some practice, but it works. The stuff sticks to itself, but not to us. So you spin several layers, letting each one dry, then hook up an airberry, and you're inflated and insulated."

"Marvelous," Singh said, truly impressed. He had seen the tiny whirlibirds weaving the suits, and the other ones, like small slugs, eating them away when the colonists saw they wouldn't need them. "But without some sort of exhaust, you wouldn't last long. How is that accomplished?"

"We use the breather valves from our old suits," McKillian said. "Either the plants that grow valves haven't come up yet or we haven't been smart enough to recognize them. And the insulation isn't perfect. We only go out in the hottest part of the day, and our hands and feet tend to get cold. But we manage."

Singh realize he had strayed from his original question.

"But what about the food? Surely it's too much to expect for these Martians to eat the same things we do. Wouldn't you think so?"

"We sure did, and we were lucky to have Marty Ralston along. He kept telling us the fruits in the graveyard were edible by humans. Fats, starches, proteins; all identical to the ones we brought along. The clue was in the orrery, of course."

Lang pointed to the twin globes in the middle of the room, still keeping perfect Earth-time.

"It was a beacon. We figured that out when we saw they grew only in the graveyard. But what was it telling us? We felt it meant that we were expected. Song felt that from the start, and we all came to agree with her. But we didn't realize just how much they had prepared for us until Marty started analyzing the fruits and nutrients here.

"Listen, these Martians—and I can see from your look that you still don't really believe in them, but you will if you stay here long enough—they know genetics. They really know it. We have a thousand theories about what they may be like, and I won't bore you with them yet, but this is one thing we do know. They can build anything they need, make a blueprint in DNA, encapsulate it in a spore and bury it, knowing exactly what will come up in forty thousand years. When it starts to get cold here and they know the cycle's drawing to an end, they seed the planet with the spores and . . . do something. Maybe they die, or maybe they have some other way of passing the time. But they know they'll return.

"We can't say how long they've been prepared for a visit from us. Maybe only this cycle; maybe twenty cycles ago. Anyway, at the last cycle they buried the kind of spores that would produce these little gismos." She tapped the blue ball representing the Earth with one foot.

"They triggered them to be activated only when they encountered certain different conditions. Maybe they knew exactly what it would be; maybe they only provided for a likely range of possibilities. Song thinks they've visited us, back in the Stone Age. In some ways it's easier to believe than the alternative. That way they'd know our genetic structure and what kinds of food we'd eat, and could prepare.

" 'Cause if they didn't visit us, they must have prepared other spores. Spores that would analyze new proteins and be able to duplicate them. Further than that, some of the plants might have been able to copy certain genetic material if they encountered any. Take a look at that pipe behind you." Singh turned and saw a pipe about as thick as his arm. It was flexible, and had a swelling in it that continuously pulsed in expansion and contraction.

"Take that bulge apart and you'd be amazed at the resemblance to a human heart. So there's another significant fact; this place started out with whirligigs, but later modified itself to use human heart pumps from the genetic information *taken from the bodies of the men and women we buried.*" She paused to let that sink in, then went on with a slightly bemused smile.

"The same thing for what we eat and drink. That liquor you drank, for instance. It's half alcohol, and that's probably what it would have been without the corpses. But the rest of it is very similar to hemoglobin. It's sort of like fermented blood. Human blood."

Singh was glad he had refused the fourth drink. One of his crew members quietly put his glass down.

"I've never eaten human flesh," Lang went on, "but I think I know what it must taste like. Those vines to your right; we strip off the outer part and eat the meat underneath. It tastes good. I wish we could cook it, but we have nothing to burn and couldn't risk it with the high oxygen count, anyway."

Singh and everyone else was silent for a while. He found he really was beginning to believe in the Martians. The theory seemed to cover a lot of otherwise inexplicable facts.

Mary Lang sighed, slapped her thighs, and stood up. Like all the others, she was nude and seemed totally at home with it. None of them had worn anything but a Martian pressure suit for eight years. She ran her hand lovingly over the gossamer wall, the wall that had provided her and her fellow colonists and their children protection from the cold and the thin air for so long. He was struck by her easy familiarity with what seemed to him outlandish surroundings. She looked at home. He couldn't imagine her anywhere else.

He looked at the children. One wide-eyed little girl of eight years was kneeling at his feet. As his eyes fell on her, she smiled tentatively and took his hand.

"Did you bring any bubblegum?" the girl asked.

He smiled at her. "No, honey, but maybe there's some in the ship." She seemed satisfied. She would wait to experience the wonders of earthly science.

"We were provided for," Mary Lang said, quietly. "They knew we were coming and they altered their plants to fit us in." She looked back to Singh. "It would have happened even without the blowout and the burials. The same sort of thing was happening around the

Podkayne, too, triggered by our waste; urine and feces and such. I don't know if it would have tasted quite as good in the food department, but it would have sustained life."

Singh stood up. He was moved, but did not trust himself to show it adequately. So he sounded rather abrupt, though polite.

"I suppose you'll be anxious to go to the ship," he said. "You're going to be a tremendous help. You know so much of what we were sent here to find out. And you'll be quite famous when you get back to Earth. Your back pay should add up to quite a sum."

There was a silence, then it was ripped apart by Lang's huge laugh. She was joined by the others, and the children, who didn't know what they were laughing about but enjoyed the break in the tension.

"Sorry, Captain. That was rude. But we're not going back."

Singh looked at each of the adults and saw no trace of doubt. And he was mildly surprised to find that the statement did not startle him.

"I won't take that as your final decision," he said. "As you know, we'll be here six months. If at the end of that time any of you want to go, you're still citizens of Earth."

"We are? You'll have to brief us on the political situation back there. We were United States citizens when we left. But it doesn't matter. You won't get any takers, though we appreciate the fact that you came. It's nice to know we weren't forgotten." She said it with total assurance, and the others were nodding. Singh was uncomfortably aware that the idea of a rescue mission had died out only a few years after the initial tragedy. He and his ship were here now only to explore.

Lang sat back down and patted the ground around her, ground that was covered in a multiple layer of the Martian pressure-tight web, the kind of web that would have been made only by warm-blooded, oxygen-breathing, water-economy beings who needed protection for their bodies until the full bloom of summer.

"We *like* it here. It's a good place to raise a family, not like Earth the last time I was there. And it couldn't be much better now, right after another war. And we can't leave, even if we wanted to." She flashed him a dazzling smile and patted the ground again.

"The Martians should be showing up any time now. And we aim to thank them."

*Writers often hold down a ragtag collection of jobs while waiting for
success to strike, but Edward Bryant's track record is odd even for a
writer. It includes stretches as disc jockey, radio newsman, and worker
in a stirrup buckle factory. Born in White Plains, New York, Bryant
now lives in Denver, Colorado, where he has taken over the management of the famous Milford Science Fiction Writers' Conference.
A full-time writer since 1969, Bryant quickly established himself as
one of the most prolific new short story writers of the Seventies,
appearing in anthologies, SF magazines, and other magazines such as*
Penthouse *and* National Lampoon. *His books include two critically
acclaimed collections,* Among the Dead *(Collier) and* Cinnabar *(Bantam); a novelization of a television script by Harlan Ellison,* Phoenix
Without Ashes *(Fawcett Gold Medal); and as editor,* 2076: The
American Tricentennial *(Pyramid), one of the better anthologies of the
year.*

*A well-received story, "The Hibakusha Gallery" (Penthouse), will
probably be on this year's Final Nebula Ballot. Attracting even more
attention and acclaim, however, is this novelette, another probable
Nebula finalist, a brilliant exploration of the interface between the
vast, inimical cosmos and one man's private reality.*

EDWARD BRYANT

Particle Theory

I see my shadow flung like black iron against the wall. My sundeck
blazes with untimely summer. Eliot was wrong; Frost, right.

Nanoseconds . . .

Death is as relativistic as any other apparent constant. I wonder:
Am I dying?

I thought it was a cliché with no underlying truth.

"Lives *do* flash in a compressed instant before dying eyes," said
Amanda. She poured me another glass of burgundy the color of her
hair. The fire highlighted both. "A psychologist named Noyes—" She
broke off and smiled at me. "You really want to hear this?"

"Sure." The fireplace light softened the taut planes of her face. I
saw a flicker of the gentler beauty she had possessed thirty years
before.

"Noyes catalogued testimonial evidence for death's-door phenomena
in the early Seventies. He termed it 'life review,' the second of three
clearly definable steps in the process of dying; like a movie, and not
necessarily linear."

I drink, I have a low threshold of intoxication, I ramble. "Why does it happen? How?" I didn't like the desperation in my voice. We were suddenly much further apart than the geography of the table separating us; I looked in Amanda's eyes for some memory of Lisa. "Life goes shooting off—or we recede from it—like Earth and an interstellar probe irrevocably severed. Mutual recession at light-speed, and the dark fills in the gap." I held my glass by the stem, rotated it, peered through the distorting bowl.

Pine logs crackled. Amanda turned her head and her eyes' image shattered in the flames.

The glare, the glare—

When I was thirty I made aggrieved noises because I'd screwed around for the past ten years and not accomplished nearly as much as I should. Lisa only laughed, which sent me into a transient rage and a longer-lasting sulk before I realized hers was the only appropriate response.

"Silly, silly," she said. "A watered-down Byronic character, full of self-pity and sloppy self-adulation." She blocked my exit from the kitchen and said millimeters from my face, "It's not as though you're waking up at thirty to discover that only fifty-six people have heard of you."

I stuttered over a weak retort.

"Fifty-seven?" She laughed; I laughed.

Then I was forty and went through the same pseudo-menopausal trauma. Admittedly, I hadn't done any work at all for nearly a year, and any *good* work for two. Lisa didn't laugh this time; she did what she could, which was mainly to stay out of my way while I alternately moped and raged around the coast house southwest of Portland. Royalties from the book I'd done on the fusion breakthrough kept us in groceries and mortgage payments.

"Listen, maybe if I'd go away for a while—" she said. "Maybe it would help for you to be alone." Temporary separations weren't alien to our marriage; we'd once figured that our relationship got measurably rockier if we spent more than about sixty percent of our time together. It had been a long winter and we were overdue; but then Lisa looked intently at my face and decided not to leave. Two months later I worked through the problems in my skull, and asked her for solitude. She knew me well—well enough to laugh again because she knew I was waking out of another mental hibernation.

She got into a jetliner on a gray winter day and headed east for my parents' old place in southern Colorado. The jetway for the flight was out of commission that afternoon, so the airline people had to roll out one of the old wheeled stairways. Just before she stepped into the cabin, Lisa paused and waved back from the head of the stairs; her dark hair curled about her face in the wind.

Two months later I'd roughed out most of the first draft for my initial book about the reproductive revolution. At least once a week I would call Lisa and she'd tell me about the photos she was taking river-running on an icy Colorado or Platte. Then I'd use her as a sounding board for speculations about ectogenesis, heterogynes, or the imminent emergence of an exploited human host-mother class.

"So what'll we do when you finish the first draft, Nick?"

"Maybe we'll take a leisurely month on the Trans-Canadian Railroad."

"Spring in the provinces . . ."

Then the initial draft was completed and so was Lisa's Colorado adventure. "Do you know how badly I want to see you?" she said.

"Almost as badly as I want to see you."

"Oh, no," she said. "Let me tell you—"

What she told me no doubt violated state and federal laws and probably telephone company tariffs as well. The frustration of only hearing her voice through the wire made me twine my legs like a contortionist.

"Nick, I'll book a flight out of Denver. I'll let you know."

I think she wanted to surprise me. Lisa didn't tell me when she booked the flight. The airline let me know.

And now I'm fifty-one. The pendulum has swung and I again bitterly resent not having achieved more. There is so much work left undone; should I live for centuries, I still could not complete it all. That, however, will not be a problem.

I am told that the goddamned level of acid phosphatase in my goddamned blood is elevated. How banal that single fact sounds, how sterile; and how self-pitying the phraseology. Can't I afford a luxurious tear, Lisa?

Lisa?

Death: I wish to determine my own time.

"Charming," I said much later. "End of the world."

My friend Denton, the young radio astronomer, said, "Christ almighty! Your damned jokes. How can you make a pun about this?"

"It keeps me from crying," I said quietly. "Wailing and breast-beating won't make a difference."

"Calm, so calm." She looked at me peculiarly.

"I've seen the enemy," I said. "I've had time to consider it."

Her face was thoughtful, eyes focused somewhere beyond this cluttered office. "*If* you're right," she said, "it could be the most fantastic event a scientist could observe and record." Her eyes refocused and met mine. "Or it might be the most frightening; a final horror."

"Choose one," I said.

"If I believed you at all."

"I'm dealing in speculations."

"Fantasies," she said.

"However you want to term it." I got up and moved to the door. "I don't think there's much time. You've never seen where I live. Come—" I hesitated, "—visit me if you care to. I'd like that—to have you there."

"Maybe," she said.

I should not have left the situation ambiguous.

I didn't know that in another hour, after I had left her office, pulled my car out of the Gamow Peak parking lot and driven down to the valley, Denton would settle herself behind the wheel of her sports car and gun it onto the Peak road. Tourists saw her go off the switchback. A Highway Department crew pried her loose from the embrace of Lotus and lodgepole.

When I got the news I grieved for her, wondering if this were the price of belief. I drove to the hospital and, because no next of kin had been found and Amanda intervened, the doctors let me stand beside the bed.

I had never seen such still features, never such stasis short of actual death. I waited an hour, seconds sweeping silently from the wall clock, until the urge to return home was overpowering.

I could wait no longer because daylight was coming and I would tell no one.

Toward the beginning:

I've tolerated doctors as individuals; as a class they terrify me. It's a dread like shark attacks or dying by fire. But eventually I made the appointment for an examination, drove to the sparkling white clinic on the appointed day and spent a surly half hour reading a year-old issue of *Popular Science* in the waiting room.

"Mr. Richmond?" the smiling nurse finally said. I followed her back to the examination room. "Doctor will be here in just a minute." She left. I sat apprehensively on the edge of the examination table. After two minutes I heard the rustling of my file being removed from the outside rack. Then the door opened.

"How's it going?" said my doctor. "I haven't seen you in a while."

"Can't complain," I said, reverting to accustomed medical ritual. "No flu so far this winter. The shot must have been soon enough."

Amanda watched me patiently. "You're not a hypochondriac. You don't need continual reassurance—or sleeping pills, anymore. You're not a medical groupie, God knows. So what is it?"

"Uh," I said. I spread my hands helplessly.

"Nicholas." Get-on-with-it-I'm-busy-today sharpness edged her voice.

"Don't imitate my maiden aunt."

"All right, *Nick*," she said. "What's wrong?"

"I'm having trouble urinating."

She jotted something down. Without looking up, "What kind of trouble?"

"Straining."

"For how long?"

"Six, maybe seven months. It's been a gradual thing."

"Anything else you've noticed?"

"Increased frequency."

"That's all?"

"Well," I said, "afterwards, I, uh, dribble."

She listed, as though by rote: "Pain, burning, urgency, hesitancy, change in stream of urine? Incontinence, change in size of stream, change in appearance of urine?"

"What?"

"Darker, lighter, cloudy, bloody discharge from penis, VD exposure, fever, night sweats?"

I answered with a variety of nods or monosyllables.

"Mmh." She continued to write on the pad, then snapped it shut. "Okay, Nick, would you get your clothes off?" And when I had stripped, "Please lie on the table. On your stomach."

"The greased finger?" I said. "Oh shit."

Amanda tore a disposable glove off the roll. It crackled as she put it on. "You think I get a thrill out of this?" She's been my GP for a long time.

When it was over and I sat gingerly and uncomfortably on the edge of the examining table, I said, "Well?"

Amanda again scribbled on a sheet. "I'm sending you to a urologist. He's just a couple of blocks away. I'll phone over. Try to get an appointment in—oh, inside of a week."

"Give me something better," I said, "or I'll go to the library and check out a handbook of symptoms."

She met my eyes with a candid blue gaze. "I want a specialist to check out the obstruction."

"You found something when you stuck your finger in?"

"Crude, Nicholas." She half smiled. "Your prostate is hard—stony. There could be a number of reasons."

"What John Wayne used to call the Big C?"

"Prostatic cancer," she said, "is relatively infrequent in a man of your age." She glanced down at my records. "Fifty."

"Fifty-one," I said, wanting to shift the tone, trying, failing. "You didn't send me a card on my birthday."

"But it's not impossible," Amanda said. She stood. "Come on up to the front desk. I want an appointment with you after the urology results come back." As always, she patted me on the shoulder as she followed me out of the examination room. But this time there was slightly too much tension in her fingers.

I was seeing grassy hummocks and marble slabs in my mind and didn't pay attention to my surroundings as I exited the waiting room.

"Nick?" A soft Oklahoma accent.

I turned back from the outer door, looked down, saw tousled hair. Jackie Denton, one of the bright young minds out at the Gamow Peak Observatory, held the well-thumbed copy of *Popular Science* loosely in her lap. She honked and snuffled into a deteriorating Kleenex. "Don't get too close. Probably doesn't matter at this point. Flu. You?" Her green irises were red-rimmed.

I fluttered my hands vaguely. "I had my shots."

"Yeah." She snuffled again. "I was going to call you later on from work. See the show last night?"

I must have looked blank.

"Some science writer," she said. "Rigel went supernova."

"Supernova," I repeated stupidly.

"Blam, you know? *Blooie.*" She illustrated with her hands and the magazine flipped into the carpet. "Not that you missed anything. It'll be around for a few weeks—biggest show in the skies."

A sudden ugly image of red-and-white aircraft warning lights merging in an actinic flare sprayed my retinas. I shook my head. After a moment I said, "First one in our galaxy in—how long? Three hundred and fifty years? I wish you'd called me."

"A little longer. Kepler's star was in 1604. Sorry about not calling —we were all a little busy, you know?"

"I can imagine. When did it happen?"

She bent to retrieve the magazine. "Just about midnight. Spooky. I was just coming off shift." She smiled. "Nothing like a little cosmic cataclysm to take my mind off jammed sinuses. Just as well; no sick leave tonight. That's why I'm here at the clinic. Kris says no excuses."

Krishnamurthi was the Gamow director. "You'll be going back up to the peak soon?" She nodded. "Tell Kris I'll be in to visit. I want to pick up a lot of material."

"For sure."

The nurse walked up to us. "Ms. Denton?"

"Mmph." She nodded and wiped her nose a final time. Struggling up from the soft chair, she said, "How come you didn't read about Rigel in the papers? It made every morning edition."

"I let my subscriptions lapse."

"But the TV news? The radio?"

"I didn't watch, and I don't have a radio in the car."

Before disappearing into the corridor to the examination rooms, she said, "That country house of yours must really be isolated."

The ice drips from the eaves as I drive up and park beside the garage. Unless the sky deceives me there is no new weather front moving in yet; no need to protect the car from another ten centimeters of fresh snow.

Sunset comes sooner at my house among the mountains; shadows stalk across the barren yard and suck heat from my skin. The peaks are, of course, deliberate barriers blocking off light and warmth from the coastal cities. Once I personified them as friendly giants, amiable *lummoxen* guarding us. No more. Now they are only mountains again, the Cascade Range.

For an instant I think I see a light flash on, but it is just a quick sunset reflection on a window. The house remains dark and silent. The poet from Seattle's been gone for three months. My coldness— her heat. I thought that transference would warm me. Instead she chilled. The note she left me in the vacant house was a sonnet about psychic frostbite.

My last eleven years have not been celibate, but sometimes they feel like it. Entropy ultimately overcomes all kinetic force.

Then I looked toward the twilight east and saw Rigel rising. Luna wouldn't be visible for a while, so the brightest object in the sky was the exploded star. It fixed me to this spot by my car with the intensity of an aircraft landing light. The white light that shone down on me had left the supernova five hundred years before (a detail to include in the inevitable article—a graphic illustration of interstellar distances never fails to awe readers).

Tonight, watching the 100 billion-degree baleful eye that was Rigel convulsed, I know *I* was awed. The cataclysm glared, brighter than any planet. I wondered whether Rigel—unlikely, I knew—had had a planetary system; whether guttering mountain ranges and boiling seas had preceded worlds frying. I wondered whether, five centuries before, intelligent beings had watched stunned as the stellar fire engulfed their skies. Had they time to rail at the injustice? There are 10 billion stars in our galaxy; only an estimated three stars go supernova per thousand years. Good odds: Rigel lost.

Almost hypnotized, I watched until I was abruptly rocked by the wind rising in the darkness. My fingers were stiff with cold. But as I started to enter the house I looked at the sky a final time. Terrifying Rigel, yes—but my eyes were captured by another phenomenon in the north. A spark of light burned brighter than the surrounding stars. At first I thought it was a passing aircraft, but its position remained stationary. Gradually, knowing the odds and unwilling to believe, I recognized the new supernova for what it was.

In five decades I've seen many things. Yet watching the sky I felt like I was a primitive, shivering in uncured furs. My teeth chattered from more than the cold. I wanted to hide from the universe. The door to my house was unlocked, which was lucky—I couldn't have fitted a key into the latch. Finally I stepped over the threshold. I turned on all the lights, denying the two stellar pyres burning in the sky.

My urologist turned out to be a dour black man named Sharpe who treated me, I suspected, like any of the other specimens that turned up in his laboratory. In his early thirties, he'd read several of my books. I appreciated his having absolutely no respect for his elders or for celebrities.

"You'll give me straight answers?" I said.

"Count on it."

He also gave me another of those damned urological fingers. When I was finally in a position to look back at him questioningly, he nodded slowly and said, "There's a nodule."

Then I got a series of blood tests for an enzyme called acid phosphatase. "Elevated," Sharpe said.

Finally, at the lab, I was to get the cystoscope, a shiny metal tube which would be run up my urethra. The biopsy forceps would be inserted through it. "Jesus, you're kidding." Sharpe shook his head. I said, "If the biopsy shows a malignancy . . ."

"I can't answer a silence."

"Come on," I said. "You've been straight until now. What are the chances of curing a malignancy?"

Sharpe had looked unhappy ever since I'd walked into his office. Now he looked unhappier. "Ain't my department," he said. "Depends on many factors."

"Just give me a simple figure."

"Maybe thirty percent. All bets are off if there's a metastasis." He met my eyes while he said that, then busied himself with the cystoscope. Local anesthetic or not, my penis burned like hell.

I had finally gotten through to Jackie Denton on a private line the night of the second supernova. "I thought last night was a madhouse," she said. "You should see us now. I've only got a minute."

"I just wanted to confirm what I was looking at," I said. "I saw the damn thing actually blow."

"You're ahead of everybody at Gamow. We were busily focusing on Rigel—" Electronic *wheeps* garbled the connection. "Nick, are you still there?"

"I think somebody wants the line. Just tell me a final thing: is it a full-fledged supernova?"

"Absolutely. As far as we can determine now, it's a genuine Type II."

"Sorry it couldn't be the biggest and best of all."

"Big enough," she said. "It's good enough. This time it's only about nine light-years away. Sirius A."

"Eight point seven light-years," I said automatically. "What's that going to mean?"

"Direct effects? Don't know. We're thinking about it." It sounded like her hand cupped the mouthpiece; then she came back on the line. "Listen, I've got to go. Kris is screaming for my head. Talk to you later."

"All right," I said. The connection broke. On the dead line I thought

I heard the 21-centimeter basic hydrogen hiss of the universe. Then the dial tone cut in and I hung up the receiver.

Amanda did not look at all happy. She riffled twice through what I guessed were my laboratory test results. "All right," I said from the patient's side of the wide walnut desk. "Tell me."

"Mr. Richmond? Nicholas Richmond?"

"Speaking?"

"This is Mrs. Kurnick, with TransWest Airways. I'm calling from Denver."

"Yes?"

"We obtained this number from a charge slip. A ticket was issued to Lisa Richmond—"

"My wife. I've been expecting her sometime this weekend. Did she ask you to phone ahead?"

"Mr. Richmond, that's not it. Our manifest shows your wife boarded our Flight 903, Denver to Portland, tonight."

"So? What is it? What's wrong? Is she sick?"

"I'm afraid there's been an accident."

Silence choked me. "How bad?" *The freezing began.*

"Our craft went down about ten miles northwest of Glenwood Springs, Colorado. The ground parties at the site say there are no survivors. I'm sorry, Mr. Richmond."

"No one?" I said. *"I mean—"*

"I'm truly sorry," said Mrs. Kurnick. *"If there's any change in the situation, we will be in touch immediately."*

Automatically I said, "Thank you."

I had the impression that Mrs. Kurnick wanted to say something else; but after a pause, she only said, "Good night."

On a snowy Colorado mountainside I died.

"The biopsy was malignant," Amanda said.

"Well," I said. "That's pretty bad." She nodded. "Tell me about my alternatives." *Ragged bits of metal slammed into the mountainside like teeth.*

My case was unusual only in a relative sense. Amanda told me that prostatic cancer is the penalty men pay for otherwise good health. If they avoid every other health hazard, twentieth-century men eventually get zapped by their prostates. In my case, the problem was about twenty years early; my bad luck. *Cooling metal snapped and sizzled in the snow, was silent.*

Assuming that the cancer hadn't already metastasized, there were several possibilities; but Amanda had, at this stage, little hope for either radiology or chemotherapy. She suggested a radical prostatectomy.

"I wouldn't suggest it if you didn't have a hell of a lot of valuable years left," she said. "It's not usually advised for older patients. But you're in generally good condition; you could handle it."

Nothing moved on the mountainside. "What all would come out?" I said.

"You already know the ramifications of 'radical.' "

I didn't mind so much the ligation of the spermatic tubes—I should have done that a long time before. At fifty-one I could handle sterilization with equanimity, but—

"Sexually dysfunctional?" I said. "Oh my God." I was aware of my voice starting to tighten. "I can't do that."

"You sure as hell can," said Amanda firmly. "How long have I known you?" She answered her own question. "A long time. I know you well enough to know that what counts isn't all tied up in your penis."

I shook my head silently.

"Listen, damn it, cancer death is worse."

"No," I said stubbornly. "Maybe. Is that the whole bill?"

It wasn't. Amanda reached my bladder's entry on the list. It would be excised as well.

"Tubes protruding from me?" I said. "*If* I live, I'll have to spend the rest of my life toting a plastic bag as a drain for my urine?"

Quietly she said, "You're making it too melodramatic."

"But am I right?"

After a pause. "Essentially, yes."

And all that was the essence of it; the *good* news, all assuming that the carcinoma cells wouldn't jar loose during surgery and migrate off to other organs. "No," I said. The goddamned, lousy, loathsome unfairness of it all slammed home. "Goddamn it, no. It's my choice; I won't live that way. If I just die, I'll be done with it."

"Nicholas! Cut the self-pity."

"Don't you think I'm entitled to some?"

"Be reasonable."

"You're supposed to comfort me," I said. "Not argue. You've taken all those death-and-dying courses. *You* be reasonable."

The muscles tightened around her mouth. "I'm giving you suggestions," said Amanda. "You can do with them as you damned well please." It had been years since I'd seen her angry.

We glared at each other for close to a minute. "Okay," I said. "I'm sorry."

She was not mollified. "Stay upset, even if it's whining. Get angry, be furious. I've watched you in a deep-freeze for a decade."

I recoiled internally. "I've survived. That's enough."

"No way. You've been sitting around for eleven years in suspended animation, waiting for someone to chip you free of the glacier. You've let people carom past, occasionally bouncing off you with no effect. Well, now it's not some*one* that's shoving you to the wall—it's some*thing*. Are you going to lie down for it? Lisa wouldn't have wanted that."

"Leave her out," I said.

"I can't. You're even more important to me because of her. She was my closest friend, remember?"

"Pay attention to her," Lisa had once said. "She's more sensible than either of us." Lisa had known about the affair; after all, Amanda had introduced us.

"I know." I felt disoriented; denial, resentment, numbness—the roller coaster clattered toward a final plunge.

"Nick, you've got a possibility for a healthy chunk of life left. I want you to have it, and if it takes using Lisa as a wedge, I will."

"I don't want to survive if it means crawling around as a piss-dripping cyborg eunuch." The roller coaster teetered on the brink.

Amanda regarded me for a long moment, then said earnestly, "There's an outside chance, a long shot. I heard from a friend there that the New Mexico Meson Physics Facility is scouting for a subject."

I scoured my memory. "Particle beam therapy?"

"Pions."

"It's chancy," I said.

"Are you arguing?" She smiled.

I smiled too. "No."

"Want to give it a try?"

My smile died. "I don't know. I'll think about it."

"That's encouragement enough," said Amanda. "I'll make some calls and see if the facility's as interested in you as I expect you'll be in them. Stick around home. I'll let you know."

"I haven't said yes. We'll let each other know." I didn't tell Amanda, but I left her office thinking only of death.

Melodramatic as it may sound, I went downtown to visit the hardware stores and look at their displays of pistols. After two hours, I tired of handling weapons. The steel seemed uniformly cold and distant.

When I returned home late that afternoon, there was a single message on my phone-answering machine:

"Nick, this is Jackie Denton. Sorry I haven't called for a while, but you know how it's been. I thought you'd like to know that Kris is going to have a press conference early in the week—probably Monday afternoon. I think he's worried because he hasn't come up with a good theory to cover the three Type II supernovas and the half-dozen standard novas that have occurred in the last few weeks. But then nobody I know has. We're all spending so much time awake nights, we're turning into vampires. I'll get back to you when I know the exact time of the conference. I think it must be about thirty seconds now, so I—" The tape ended.

I mused with winter bonfires in my mind as the machine rewound and reset. Three Type II supernovas? One is merely nature, I paraphrased. Two mean only coincidence. Three make a conspiracy.

Impulsively, I slowly dialed Denton's home number; there was no answer. Then the lines to Gamow Peak were all busy. It seemed logical to me that I needed Jackie Denton for more than being my sounding board, or for merely news about the press conference. I needed an extension of her friendship. I thought I'd like to borrow the magnum pistol I knew she kept in a locked desk drawer at her observatory office. I knew I could ask her a favor. She ordinarily used the pistol to blast targets on the peak's rocky flanks after work.

The irritating regularity of the busy signal brought me back to sanity. Just a second, I told myself. Richmond, what the hell are you proposing?

Nothing, was the answer. Not yet. Not . . . quite.

Later in the night, I opened the sliding glass door and disturbed the skiff of snow on the second-story deck. I shamelessly allowed myself the luxury of leaving the door partially open so that warm air would spill out around me while I watched the sky. The stars were intermittently visible between the towering banks of stratocumulus scudding over the Cascades. Even so, the three supernovas dominated the night. I drew imaginary lines with my eyes; connect the dots and solve the puzzle. How many enigmas can you find in this picture?

I reluctantly took my eyes away from the headline phenomena and searched for old standbys. I picked out the red dot of Mars.

Several years ago I'd had a cockamamie scheme that sent me to a Mesmerist—that's how she'd billed herself—down in Eugene. I'd been driving up the coast after covering an aerospace medical conference in Oakland. Somewhere around Crescent City, I capped a sea-bass dinner by getting blasted on prescribed pills and proscribed Scotch. Sometime during the evening, I remembered the computer-enhancement process JPL had used to sharpen the clarity of telemetered photos from such projects as the Mariner fly-bys and the Viking Mars lander. It seemed logical to me at the time that memories from the human computer could somehow be enhanced, brought into clarity through hypnosis. Truly stoned fantasies. But they somehow sufficed as rationale and incentive to wind up at Madame Guzmann's "Advice/Mesmerism/Health" establishment across the border in Oregon. Madame Guzmann had skin the color of her stained hardwood door; she made a point of looking and dressing the part of a stereotype we *gajos* would think of as Gypsy. The scarf and crystal ball strained the image. I think she was Vietnamese. At any rate, she convinced me she could hypnotize, and then she nudged me back through time.

Just before she ducked into the cabin, Lisa paused and waved back from the head of the stairs; her dark hair curled about her face in the wind.

I should have taken to heart the lesson of stasis; entropy is not so easily overcome.

What Madame Guzmann achieved was to freeze-frame that last

image of Lisa. Then she zoomed me in so close it was like standing beside Lisa. I sometimes still see it in my nightmares: Her eyes focus distantly. Her skin has the graininess of a newspaper photo. I look but cannot touch. I can speak but she will not answer. I shiver with the cold—

—and slid the glass door further open.

There! An eye opened in space. A glare burned as cold as a refrigerator light in a night kitchen. Mars seemed to disappear, swallowed in the glow from the nova distantly behind it. Another one, I thought. The new eye held me fascinated, pinned as securely as a child might fasten a new moth in the collection.

Nick?

Who is it?

Nick . . .

You're an auditory hallucination.

There on the deck the sound of laughter spiraled around me. I thought it would shake loose the snow from the trees. The mountain stillness vibrated.

The secret, Nick.

What secret?

You're old enough at fifty-one to decipher it.

Don't play with me.

Who's playing? Whatever time is left—

Yes?

You've spent eleven years now dreaming, drifting, letting others act on you.

I know.

Do you? Then act on that. Choose your actions. No lover can tell you more. Whatever time is left—

Shivering uncontrollably, I gripped the rail of the deck. A fleeting, pointillist portrait in black and white dissolved into the trees. From branch to branch, top bough to bottom, crusted snow broke and fell, gathering momentum. The trees shed their mantle. Powder swirled up to the deck and touched my face with stinging diamonds.

Eleven years was more than half what Rip van Winkle slept. "Damn it," I said. "Damn you." We prize our sleep. The grave rested peacefully among the trees. "Damn you," I said again, looking up at the sky.

On a snowy Oregon mountainside I was no longer dead.

And yes, Amanda. Yes.

After changing planes at Albuquerque, we flew into Los Alamos on a small feeder line called Ross Airlines. I'd never flown before on so ancient a DeHavilland Twin Otter, and I hoped never to again; I'd take a Greyhound out of Los Alamos first. The flight attendant and half the other sixteen passengers were throwing up in the turbulence as we approached the mountains. I hadn't expected the mountains. I'd assumed Los Alamos would lie in the same sort of southwestern scrub desert surrounding Albuquerque. Instead I found a small city nestled a couple of kilometers up a wooded mountainside.

The pilot's unruffled voice came on the cabin intercom to announce our imminent landing, the airport temperature, and the fact that Los Alamos has more PhD's per capita than any other American city. "Second only to Akademgorodok," I said, turning away from the window toward Amanda. The skin wrinkled around her closed eyes. She hadn't had to use her airsick bag. I had a feeling that despite old friendships, a colleague and husband who was willing to oversee the clinic, the urgency of helping a patient, and the desire to observe the exotic experiment, Amanda might be regretting accompanying me to what she'd termed "the meson factory."

The Twin Otter made a landing approach like a strafing run and then we were down. As we taxied across the apron I had a sudden sensation of déjà vu: the time a year ago when a friend had flown me north in a Cessna. The airport in Los Alamos looked much like the civil air terminal at Sea-Tac where I'd met the Seattle poet. It happened that we were both in line at the snack counter. I'd commented on her elaborate Haida-styled medallion. We took the same table and talked; it turned out she'd heard of me.

"I really admire your stuff," she said.

So much for my ideal poet using only precise images. Wry thought. She was—is—a first-rate poet. I rarely think of her as anything but "the poet from Seattle." Is that kind of depersonalization a symptom?

Amanda opened her eyes, smiled wanly, said, "I could use a doctor." The flight attendant cracked the door and thin New Mexican mountain air revived us both.

Most of the New Mexico Meson Physics Facility was buried beneath a mountain ridge. Being guest journalist as well as experimental subject, I think we were given a more exhaustive tour than would be offered most patients and their doctors. Everything I saw made me think of expensive sets for vintage science fiction movies: the interior of the main accelerator ring, glowing eggshell white and curving away like the space-station corridors in *2001;* the linac and booster areas; the straight-away tunnel to the meson medical channel; the five-meter bubble chamber looking like some sort of time machine.

I'd visited both FermiLab in Illinois and CERN in Geneva, so I had a general idea of what the facilities were all about. Still, I had a difficult time trying to explain to Amanda the *Alice in Wonderland* mazes that constituted high-energy particle physics. But then so did Delaney, the young woman who was the liaison biophysicist for my treatment. It became difficult sorting out the mesons, pions, hadrons, leptons, baryons, J's, fermions and quarks, and such quantum qualities as strangeness, color, baryonness, and charm. Especially charm, that ephemeral quality accounting for why certain types of radioactive decay should happen, but don't. I finally bogged down in the midst of quarks, antiquarks, charmed quarks, neoquarks and quarklets.

Some wag had set a sign on the visitors' reception desk in the administration center reading: "Charmed to meet you." "It's a joke, right?" said Amanda tentatively.

"It probably won't get any funnier," I said.

Delaney, who seemed to load every word with deadly earnestness, didn't laugh at all. "Some of the technicians think it's funny. I don't."

We rehashed the coming treatment endlessly. Optimistically I took notes for the book: *The primary problem with a radiological approach to the treatment of cancer is that hard radiation not only kills the cancerous cells, it also irradiates the surrounding healthy tissue. But in the mid-nineteen seventies, cancer researchers found a more promising tool: shaped beams of subatomic particles which can be selectively focused on the tissue of tumors.*

Delaney had perhaps two decades on Amanda; being younger seemed to give her a perverse satisfaction in playing the pedagogue. "Split atomic nuclei on a small scale—"

"Small?" said Amanda innocently.

"—smaller than a fission bomb. Much of the binding force of the nucleus is miraculously transmuted to matter."

"Miraculously?" said Amanda. I looked up at her from the easy cushion shot I was trying to line up on the green velvet. The three of us were playing rotation in the billiards annex of the NMMPF recreation lounge.

"Uh," said Delaney, the rhythm of her lecture broken. "Physics shorthand."

"Reality shorthand," I said, not looking up from the cue now. "Miracles are as exact a quality as charm."

Amanda chuckled. "That's all I wanted to know."

The miracle pertinent to my case was atomic glue, mesons, one of the fission-formed particles. More specifically, my miracle was the negatively charged pion, a subclass of meson. Electromagnetic fields could focus pions into a controllable beam and fire it into a particular target—me.

"There are no miracles in physics," said Delaney seriously. "I used the wrong term."

I missed my shot. A gentle stroke, and gently the cue ball rolled into the corner pocket, missing the eleven. I'd set things up nicely, if accidentally, for Amanda.

She assayed the table and smiled. "Don't come unglued."

"That's very good," I said. Atomic glue does become unstuck, thanks to pions' unique quality. When they collide and are captured by the nucleus of another atom, they reconvert to pure energy; a tiny nuclear explosion.

Amanda missed her shot too. The corner of Delaney's mouth curled in a small gesture of satisfaction. She leaned across the table, hands utterly steady. "Multiply pions, multiply target nuclei, and you have a controlled aggregate explosion releasing considerably more energy than the entering pion beam. *Hah!*"

She sank the eleven and twelve; then ran the table. Amanda and I exchanged glances. "Rack 'em up," said Delaney.

"Your turn," Amanda said to me.

In my case the NMMPF medical channel would fire a directed pion beam into my recalcitrant prostate. If all went as planned, the pions intercepting the atomic nuclei of my cancer cells would convert back into energy in a series of atomic flares. The cancer cells being more sensitive, tissue damage should be restricted, localized in my carcinogenic nodule.

Thinking of myself as a nuclear battlefield in miniature was wondrous. Thinking of myself as a new Stagg Field or an Oak Ridge was ridiculous.

Delaney turned out to be a pool shark *par excellence*. Winning was all-important and she won every time. I decided to interpret that as a positive omen.

"It's time," Amanda said.

"You needn't sound as though you're leading a condemned man to the electric chair." I tied the white medical smock securely about me, pulled on the slippers.

"I'm sorry. Are you worried?"

"Not so long as Delaney counts me as part of the effort toward a Nobel Prize."

"She's good." Her voice rang too hollow in the sterile tiled room. We walked together into the corridor.

"Me, I'm bucking for a Kalinga Prize," I said.

Amanda shook her head. Cloudy hair played about her face. "I'll just settle for a positive prognosis for my patient." Beyond the door, Delaney and two technicians with a gurney waited for me.

There is a state beyond indignity that defines being draped naked on my belly over a bench arrangement, with my rear spread and facing the medical channel. Rigidly clamped, a ceramic target tube opened a separate channel through my anus to the prostate. Monitoring equipment and shielding shut me in. I felt hot and vastly uncomfortable. Amanda had shot me full of chemicals, not all of whose names I'd recognized. Now dazed, I couldn't decide which of many discomforts was the most irritating.

"Good luck," Amanda had said. "It'll be over before you know it."
I'd felt a gentle pat on my flank.

I thought I heard the phasing-up whine of electrical equipment.
I could tell my mind was closing down for the duration; I couldn't
even remember how many billion electron-volts were about to route
a pion beam up my backside. I heard sounds I couldn't identify;
perhaps an enormous metal door grinding shut.

My brain swam free in a chemical river; I waited for something
to happen.

*I thought I heard machined ball bearings rattling down a chute; no,
particles screaming past the giant bending magnets into the medical
channel at 300,000 kilometers per second; flashing toward me through
the series of adjustable filters; slowing, slowing, losing energy as they
approach; then through the final tube and into my body. Inside . . .*

*The pion sails the inner atomic seas for a relativistically finite time.
Then the perspective inhabited by one is inhabited by two. The pion
drives toward the target nucleus. At a certain point the pion is no
longer a pion; what was temporarily matter transmutes back to energy.
The energy flares, expands, expends, and fades. Other explosions
detonate in the spaces within the patterns underlying larger patterns.*

Darkness and light interchange.

*The light coalesces into a ball; massive, hot, burning against the
darkness. Pierced, somehow stricken, the ball begins to collapse in
upon itself. Its internal temperature climbs to a critical level. At 600
million degrees, carbon nuclei fuse. Heavier elements form. When
the fuel is exhausted, the ball collapses further; again the temperature is driven upward; again heavier elements form and are in turn
consumed. The cycle repeats until the nuclear furnace manufactures
iron. No further nuclear reaction can be triggered; the heart's fire is
extinguished. Without the outward balance of fusion reaction, the ball
initiates the ultimate collapse. Heat reaches 100 billion degrees. Every
conceivable nuclear reaction is consummated.*

*The ball explodes in a final convulsive cataclysm. Its energy flares,
fades, is eaten by entropy. The time it took is no more than the time
it takes Sol-light to reach and illuminate the Earth.*

"How do you feel?" Amanda leaned into my field of vision, eclips-
ing the fluorescent rings overhead.

"Feel?" I seemed to be talking through a mouthful of cotton candy.

"Feel."

"Compared to what?" I said.

She smiled. "You're doing fine."

"I had one foot on the accelerator," I said.

She looked puzzled, then started to laugh. "It'll wear off soon." She
completed her transit and the lights shone back in my face.

"No hand on the brake," I mumbled. I began to giggle. Something pricked my arm.

I think Delaney wanted to keep me under observation in New Mexico until the anticipated ceremonies in Stockholm; I didn't have time for that. I suspected none of us did. Amanda began to worry about my moody silences; she ascribed them at first to my medication and then to the two weeks' tests Delaney and her colleagues were inflicting on me.

"To hell with this," I said. "We've got to get out of here." Amanda and I were alone in my room.

"What?"

"Give me a prognosis."

She smiled. "I think you may as well shoot for the Kalinga."

"Maybe." I quickly added, "I'm not a patient anymore; I'm an experimental subject."

"So? What do we do about it?"

We exited NMMPF under cover of darkness and struggled a half kilometer through brush to the highway. There we hitched a ride into town.

"This is crazy," said Amanda, picking thistle out of her sweater.

"It avoids a strong argument," I said as we neared the lights of Los Alamos.

The last bus of the day had left. I wanted to wait until morning. Over my protests, we flew out on Ross Airlines. "Doctor's orders," said Amanda, teeth tightly together, as the Twin Otter bumped onto the runway.

I dream of pions. I dream of colored balloons filled with hydrogen, igniting and flaming up in the night. I dream of Lisa's newsprint face. Her smile is both proud and sorrowful.

Amanda had her backlog of patients and enough to worry about, so I took my nightmares to Jackie Denton at the observatory. I told her of my hallucinations in the accelerator chamber. We stared at each other across the small office.

"I'm glad you're better, Nick, but—"

"That's not it," I said. "Remember how you hated my article about poetry glorifying the new technology? Too fanciful?" I launched into speculation, mixing with abandon pion beams, doctors, supernovas, irrational statistics, carcinogenic nodes, fire balloons, and gods.

"Gods?" she said. "*Gods?* Are you going to put that in your next column?"

I nodded.

She looked as though she were inspecting a newly found-out psychopath. "No one needs that in the press now, Nick. The whole planet's upset already. The possibility of nova radiation damaging the ozone layer, the potential for genetic damage, all that's got people spooked."

"It's only speculation."

She said, "You don't yell 'fire' in a crowded theater."

"Or in a crowded world?"

Her voice was unamused. "Not now."

"And if I'm right?" I felt weary. "What about it?"

"A supernova? No way. Sol simply doesn't have the mass."

"But a nova?" I said.

"Possibly," she said tightly. "But it shouldn't happen for a few billion years. Stellar evolution—"

"—is theory," I said. "*Shouldn't* isn't *won't*. Tonight look again at that awesome sky."

Denton said nothing.

"Could you accept a solar flare? A big one?"

I read the revulsion in her face and knew I should stop talking; but I didn't. "Do you believe in God? Any god?" She shook her head. I had to get it all out. "How about concentric universes, one within the next like Chinese carved ivory spheres?" Her face went white. "Pick a card," I said, "any card. A wild card."

"God damn you, shut up." On the edge of the desk, her knuckles were as white as her lips.

"Charming," I said, ignoring the incantatory power of words, forgetting what belief could cost. I do not think she deliberately drove her Lotus off the Peak road. I don't want to believe that. Surely she was coming to join me.

Maybe, she'd said.

Nightmares should be kept home. So here I stand on my sundeck at high noon for the Earth. No need to worry about destruction of the ozone layer and the consequent skin cancer. There will be no problem with mutational effects and genetic damage. I need not worry about deadlines or contractual commitments. I regret that no one will ever read my book about pion therapy.

All that—maybe.

The sun shines bright—The tune plays dirgelike in my head.

Perhaps I am wrong. The flare may subside. Maybe I am not dying. No matter.

I wish Amanda were with me now, or that I were at Jackie Denton's bedside, or even that I had time to walk to Lisa's grave among the pines. Now there is no time.

At least I've lived as long as I have now by choice.

That's the secret, Nick . . .

The glare illuminates the universe.

Born in Bayonne, New Jersey, George R. R. Martin has variously supported himself by directing professional chess tournaments, unloading trucks, sportswriting, and running the Tubs O'Fun at an amusement park. Presently he lives in Dubuque, Iowa, where he teaches journalism and creative writing at Clarke College. What he does best, however, is write—and he has done that well enough to make himself a Hugo winner, a mainstay of Analog *in recent years, and one of the most popular new writers of the Seventies. His books include the recently released novel* The Dying of the Light *(Simon & Schuster); two collections,* A Song for Lya *(Avon) and* Songs of Stars and Shadows *(Pocket Books); and an anthology,* New Voices in Science Fiction *(Macmillan).*

Here he spins a haunting tale of a young girl's coming-of-age on a bleak and frozen world where winter lasts for years, silent deadly shapes glide through ice-locked forests, and spring may come too late for things that bloom in snow and darkness. . . .

GEORGE R. R. MARTIN

Bitterblooms

When he finally died, Shawn found to her shame that she could not even bury him.

She had no proper digging tools, only her hands, the longknife strapped to her thigh, and the smaller blade in her boot. But it would not have mattered. Beneath its sparse covering of snow, the ground was frozen hard as rock. Shawn was sixteen, as her family counted years, and the ground had been frozen for half her lifetime. The season was deepwinter, and the world was cold.

Knowing the futility of it before she started, Shawn still tried to dig. She picked a spot a few meters from the rude lean-to she had built for their shelter, broke the thin crust of the snow and swept it away with her hands, and began to hack at the frozen earth with the smaller of her blades. But the ground was harder than her steel. The knife broke, and she looked at it helplessly, knowing how precious it had been, knowing what Creg would say. Then she began to claw at the unfeeling soil, weeping, until her hands ached and her tears froze within her mask. It was not right for her to leave him without burial; he had been father, brother, lover. He had always been kind to her, and she had always failed him. And now she could not even bury him.

Finally, not knowing what else to do, she kissed him one last time —there was ice in his beard and his hair, and his face was twisted unnaturally by the pain and the cold, but he was still family, after all—and toppled the lean-to across his body, hiding him within a rough bier of branches and snow. It was useless, she knew; vampires and windwolves would knock it apart easily to get at his flesh. But she could not abandon him without shelter of some kind.

She left him his skis and his big silverwood bow, its bowstring snapped by the cold. But she took his sword and his heavy fur cloak; it was little enough burden added to her pack. She had nursed him for almost a week after the vampire had left him wounded, and that long delay in the little lean-to had depleted most of their supplies. Now she hoped to travel light and fast. She strapped on her skis, standing next to the clumsy grave she had built him, and said her last farewell leaning on her poles. Then she set off over the snow, through the terrible silence of the deepwinter woods, toward home and fire and family. It was just past midday.

By dusk, Shawn knew that she would never make it.

She was calmer then, more rational. She had left her grief and her shame behind with his body, as she had been taught to do. The stillness and the cold were all around her, but the long hours of skiing had left her flushed and almost warm beneath her layers of leather and fur. Her thoughts had the brittle clarity of the ice that hung in long spears from the bare, twisted trees around her.

As darkness threw its cloak over the world, Shawn sought shelter in the lee of the greatest of those trees, a massive blackbark whose trunk was three meters across. She spread the fur cloak she had taken on a bare patch of ground and pulled her own woven cape over her like a blanket to shut out the rising wind. With her back to the trunk and her longknife drawn beneath her cape, just in case, she slept a brief, wary sleep, and woke in full night to contemplate her mistakes.

The stars were out; she could see them peeking through the bare black branches above her. The Ice Wagon dominated the sky, bringing cold into the world, as it had for as long as Shawn could remember. The driver's blue eyes glared down at her, mocking.

It had been the Ice Wagon that killed Lane, she thought bitterly. Not the vampire. The vampire had mauled him badly that night, when his bowstring broke as he tried to draw in their defense. But in another season, with Shawn nursing him, he would have lived. In deepwinter, he never had a chance. The cold crept in past all the defenses she had built for him, the cold drained away all his strength, all his ferocity. The cold left him a shrunken white thing, numb and pale, his lips tinged with blue. And now the driver of the Ice Wagon would claim his soul.

And hers too, she knew. She should have abandoned Lane to his fate. That was what Creg would have done, or Leila, any of them. There had never been any hope that he would live, not in deepwinter. Nothing lived in deepwinter. The trees grew stark and bare in deepwinter, the grass and the flowers perished, the animals all froze or went underground to sleep. Even the windwolves and the vampires grew lean and fierce, and many starved to death before the thaw.

As Shawn would starve.

They had already been running three days late when the vampire attacked them, and Lane had had them eating short rations. Afterward he had been so weak. He had finished his own food on the fourth day, and Shawn had started feeding him some of hers, never telling him. She had very little left now, and the safety of Carinhall was still nearly two weeks of hard travel away. In deepwinter, it might as well be two years.

Curled beneath her cape, Shawn briefly considered starting a fire. A fire would bring vampires—they could feel the heat three kilometers off. They would come stalking silently between the trees, gaunt black shadows taller than Lane had been, their loose skin flapping over skeletal limbs like dark cloaks, concealing the claws. Perhaps, if she lay in wait, she could take one by surprise. A full-grown vampire would feed her long enough to return to Carinhall. She played with the idea in the darkness, and only reluctantly put it aside. Vampires could run across the snow as fast as an arrow in flight, scarcely touching the ground, and it was virtually impossible to see them by night. But they could see her very well, by the heat she gave off. Lighting a fire would only guarantee her a quick and relatively painless death.

Shawn shivered and gripped the hilt of her longknife more tightly for reassurance. Every shadow suddenly seemed to have a vampire crouched within it, and in the keening of the wind she thought she could hear the flapping noise their skin made when they ran.

Then, louder and very real, another noise reached her ears; an angry high-pitched whistling like nothing Shawn had ever heard. And suddenly the black horizon was suffused with light, a flicker of ghostly blue radiance that outlined the naked bones of the forest and throbbed visibly against the sky. Shawn inhaled sharply, a draught of ice down her raw throat, and struggled to her feet, half afraid she was under attack. But there was nothing. The world was cold and black and dead; only the light lived, flickering dimly in the distance, beckoning, calling to her. She watched it for long minutes, thinking back on old Jon and the terrible stories he used to tell the children when they gathered round Carinhall's great hearth. *There are worse things than vampires*, he would tell them, and remembering, Shawn was suddenly a little girl again, sitting on the thick furs with her back to the fire, listening to Jon talk of ghosts and living shadows and cannibal families who lived in great castles built of bone.

As abruptly as it had come, the strange light faded and was gone, and with it went the high-pitched noise. Shawn had marked where it had shone, however. She took up her pack and fastened Lane's cloak about her for extra warmth, then began to don her skis. She was no child now, she told herself, and that light had been no ghost dance. Whatever it was, it might be her only chance. She took her poles in hand and set off toward it.

Night travel was dangerous in the extreme, she knew. Creg had told her that a hundred times, and Lane as well. In the darkness, in the scant starlight, it was easy to go astray, to break a ski or a leg or worse. And movement generated heat, heat that drew vampires from the deep of the woods. Better to lie low until dawn, when the nocturnal hunters had retired to their lairs; all of her training told her that, and all of her instincts. But it was deepwinter, and when she rested the cold bit through even the warmest of furs, and Lane was dead and she was hungry, and the light had been so close, so achingly close. So she followed it, going slowly, going carefully, and it seemed that this night she had a charm upon her. The terrain was all flatland, gentle to her, almost kind, and the snow cover was sparse enough so that neither root nor rock could surprise and trip her. No dark predators came gliding out of the night, and the only sound was the sound of her motion, the soft crackling of the snow crust beneath her skis.

The forest grew steadily thinner as she moved, and after an hour Shawn emerged from it entirely, into a wasteland of tumbled stone blocks and twisted, rusting metal. She knew what it was; she had seen other ruins before, where families had lived and died, and their halls and houses had gone all to rot. But never a ruin so extensive as this. The family that had lived here, however long ago, had been very great once; the shattered remains of their dwellings were more extensive than a hundred Carinhalls. She began to pick a careful path through the crumbling, snow-dusted masonry. Twice she came upon structures that were almost intact, and each time she considered seeking shelter within those ancient stone walls, but there was nothing in either of them that might have caused the light, so Shawn passed on after only a brief inspection. The river she came to soon thereafter stopped her for a slightly longer time; from the high bank where she paused, she could see the remains of two bridges that had once spanned the narrow channel, but both of them had fallen long ago. The river was frozen over, however, so she had no trouble crossing it. In deepwinter the ice was thick and solid and there was no danger of her falling through.

As she climbed painstakingly up the far bank, Shawn came upon the flower.

It was a very small thing, its thick black stem emerging from between two rocks low on the river bank. She might never have seen it in the night, but her pole dislodged one of the ice-covered stones as she struggled up the slope, and the noise made her glance down to where it grew.

It startled her so that she took both poles in one hand and with the other fumbled in the deepest recesses of her clothing, so that she might risk a flame. The match gave a short, intense light. But it was enough; Shawn saw.

A flower, tiny, so tiny, with four blue petals, each the same pale blue shade that Lane's lips had been just before he died. A flower, here, alive, growing in the eighth year of deepwinter when all the world was dead.

They would never believe her, Shawn thought, not unless she brought the truth with her, back to Carinhall. She freed herself from her skis and tried to pick the flower. It was futile, as futile as her effort to bury Lane. The stem was as strong as metal wire. She struggled with it for several minutes, and fought to keep from crying when it would not come. Creg would call her a liar, a dreamer, all the things he always called her.

She did not cry, though, finally. She left the flower where it grew, and climbed to the top of the river ridge. There she paused.

Beneath her, going on and on for meters, was a wide empty field. Snow stood in great drifts in some places, and in others there was only bare, flat stone, naked to the wind and the cold. In the center of the field was the strangest building Shawn had ever seen, a great fat teardrop of a building that squatted like an animal in the starlight on three black legs. The legs were bent beneath it, flexed and rimed over with ice at their joints, as if the beast had been about to leap straight up into the sky. And legs and building both were covered with flowers.

There were flowers everywhere, Shawn saw when she took her eyes off the squat building long enough to look. They sprouted, singly and in clusters, from every little crack in the field, with snow and ice all around them, making dark islands of life in the pure white stillness of deepwinter.

Shawn walked through them, closer to the building, until she stood next to one of the legs and reached up to touch its joint wonderingly with a gloved hand. It was all metal, metal and ice and flowers, like the building itself. Where each of the legs rested, the stone beneath had broken and fractured in a hundred places, as if shattered by some great blow, and vines grew from the crevices, twisting black vines that crawled around the flanks of the structure like the webs of a summer-spinner. The flowers burst from the vines, and now that she stood up close, Shawn saw that they were not like her little river bloom at all. There were blossoms of many colors, some as big as her head, growing in wild profusion everywhere, as if they did not realize that it was deepwinter, when they should be black and dead.

She was walking around the building, looking for an entrance, when a noise made her turn her head toward the ridge.

A thin shadow flickered briefly against the snow, then seemed to vanish. Shawn trembled and retreated quickly, putting the nearest of the tall legs to her back, and then she dropped everything and Lane's sword was in her left hand and her own longknife in her right, and she stood cursing herself for that match, that stupid, stupid match, and listening for the *flap-flap-flap* of death on taloned feet.

It was too dark, she realized, and her hand shook, and even as it did the shape rushed upon her from the side. Her longknife flashed at it, stabbing, slicing, but cut only the skincloak, and then the vampire gave a shriek of triumph and Shawn was buffeted to the ground and she knew she was bleeding. There was a weight on her chest, and something black and leathery settled across her eyes, and she tried to knife it and that was when she realized that her blade was gone. She screamed.

Then the vampire screamed, and the side of Shawn's head exploded in pain, and she had blood in her eyes, and she was choking on blood, and blood and blood, and nothing more. . . .

It was blue, all blue; hazy, shifting blue. A pale blue, dancing, dancing, like the ghost light that had flickered on the sky. A soft blue, like the little flower, the impossible blossom by the riverbank. A cold blue, like the eyes of the Ice Wagon's black driver, like Lane's lips when last she kissed them. Blue, blue, and it moved and would not be still. Everything was blurred, unreal. There was only blue. For a long time, only blue.

Then music. But it was blurred music, blue music somehow, strange and high and fleeting, very sad, lonely, a bit erotic. It was a lullaby, like old Tesenya used to sing when Shawn was very little, before she grew weak and sick and Creg put her out to die. It had been so long since Shawn had heard such a song; all the music she knew was Creg on his harp, and Rys on her guitar. She found herself relaxing, floating, all her limbs turned to water, lazy water, though it was deep-winter and she knew she should be ice.

Soft hands began to touch her, lifting her head, pulling off her facemask so the blue warm brushed her naked cheeks, then drifting lower, lower, loosening her clothes, stripping her of furs and cloth and leather, off with her belt and off with her jerkin and off with her pants. Her skin tingled. She was floating, floating. Everything was warm, so warm, and the hands fluttered here and there and they were so gentle, like old mother Tesenya had been, like her sister Leila was sometimes, like Devin. Like Lane, she thought, and it was a pleasant thought, comforting and arousing at the same time, and Shawn held close to it. She was with Lane, she was safe and warm and . . . and she remembered his face, the blue in his lips, the ice in his beard where his breath had frozen, the pain burned into him, twisting his features like a mask. She remembered, and suddenly she was drowning in the blue, choking on the blue, struggling, screaming.

The hands lifted her and a stranger's voice muttered something low and soothing in a language she did not understand. A cup was pressed to Shawn's lips. She opened her mouth to scream again, but instead she was drinking. It was hot and sweet and fragrant, full of spices, and some of them were very familiar, but others she could not place at all. Tea, she thought, and her hands took it from the other hands as she gulped it down.

She was in a small dim room, propped up on a bed of pillows, and her clothes were piled next to her and the air was full of blue mist from a burning stick. A woman knelt beside her, dressed in bright tatters of many different colors, and gray eyes regarded her calmly from beneath the thickest, wildest hair that Shawn had ever seen. "You . . . who . . . ," Shawn said.

The woman stroked her brow with a pale soft hand. "Carin," she said clearly.

Shawn nodded, slowly, wondering who the woman was, and how she knew the family.

"Carinhall," the woman said, and her eyes seemed amused and a bit sad. "Lin and Eris and Caith. I remember them, little girl. Beth, Voice Carin, how hard she was. And Kaya and Dale and Shawn."

"Shawn. I'm Shawn. That's me. But Creg is Voice Carin . . ."

The woman smiled faintly, and continued to stroke Shawn's brow. The skin of her hand was very soft. Shawn had never felt anything so soft. "Shawn is my lover," the woman said. "Every tenth year, at Gathering."

Shawn blinked at her, confused. She was beginning to remember. The light in the forest, the flowers, the vampire. "Where am I?" she asked.

"You are everywhere you never dreamed of being, little Carin," the woman said, and she laughed at herself.

The walls of the room shone like dark metal, Shawn noticed. "The building," she blurted, "the building on legs, with all the flowers . . ."

"Yes," the woman said.

"Do you . . . who are you? Did you make the light? I was in the forest, and Lane was dead and I was nearly out of food, and I saw a light, a blue . . ."

"That was my light, Carin child, as I came down from the sky. I was far away, oh yes, far away in lands you never heard of, but I came back." The woman stood up suddenly, and whirled around and around, and the gaudy cloth she wore flapped and shimmered, and she was wreathed in pale blue smoke. "I am the witch they warn you of in Carinhall, child," she yelled, exulting, and she whirled and whirled until finally, dizzy, she collapsed again beside Shawn's bed.

No one had ever warned Shawn of a witch. She was more puzzled than afraid. "You killed the vampire," she said. "How did you . . ."

"I am magic," the woman said. "I am magic and I can do magic things and I will live forever. And so will you, Carin child, Shawn, when I teach you. You can travel with me, and I will teach you all the magics and tell you stories, and we can be lovers. You are my lover already, you know, you've always been, at Gathering. Shawn, Shawn." She smiled.

"No," Shawn said. "That was some other person."

"You're tired, child. The vampire hurt you, and you don't remember. But you will remember, you will." She stood up and moved across the room, snuffing out the burning stick with her fingertips, quieting the music. When her back was turned, her hair fell nearly to her waist, and all of it was curls and tangles; wild restless hair, tossing as she moved like the waves on the distant sea. Shawn had seen the sea once, years ago, before deepwinter came. She remembered.

The woman faded the dim lights somehow, and turned back to Shawn in darkness. "Rest now. I took away your pain with my magics, but it may come back. Call me if it does. I have other magics."

Shawn did feel drowsy. "Yes," she murmured, unresisting. But when the woman moved to leave, Shawn called out to her again. "Wait," she said. "Your family, mother. Tell me who you are."

The woman stood framed in yellow light, a silhouette without features. "My family is very great, child. My sisters are Lilith and Marcyan and Erika Stormjones and Lamiya-Bailis and Deirdre d'Allerane. Kleronomas and Stephen Cobalt Northstar and Tomo and Walberg were all brothers to me, and fathers. Our house is up past the Ice Wagon, and my name, my name is Morgan." And then she was gone, and the door closed behind her, and Shawn was left to sleep.

Morgan, she thought as she slept. Morganmorganmorgan. The name drifted through her dreams like smoke.

She was very little, and she was watching the fire in the hearth at Carinhall, watching the flames lick and tease at the big black logs, smelling the sweet fragrances of thistlewood, and nearby someone was telling a story. Not Jon, no, this was before Jon had become storyteller, this was long ago. It was Tesenya, so very old, her face wrinkled, and she was talking in her tired voice so full of music, her lullaby voice, and all the children listened. Her stories had been different from Jon's. His were always about fighting, wars and vendettas and monsters, chock-full with blood and knives and impassioned oaths sworn by a father's corpse. Tesenya was quieter. She told of a group of travelers, six of family Alynne, who were lost in the wild one year during the season of freeze. They chanced upon a huge hall built all of metal and the family within welcomed them with a great feast. So the travelers ate and drank, and just as they were wiping their lips to go, another banquet was served, and thus it went. The Alynnes stayed and stayed, for the food was richer and more delightful than any they had ever tasted, and the more they ate of it, the hungrier they grew. Besides, deepwinter had set in outside the metal hall. Finally, when thaw came many years later, others of family Alynne went searching for the six wanderers. They found them dead in the forest. They had put off their good warm furs and dressed in flimsies, their steel had gone all to rust, and each of them had starved. For the name of the metal hall was Morganhall, Tesenya told the children, and the family who lived there was the family named Liar, whose food is empty stuff made of dreams and air.

Shawn woke naked and shivering.

Her clothes were still piled next to her bed. She dressed quickly, first pulling on her undergarments, and over them a heavy blackwool shift, and over that her leathers, pants and belt and jerkin, then her coat of fur with its hood, and finally the capes, her own of child's cloth and Lane's cloak. Last of all was her facemask; she pulled the taut leather down over her head and laced it closed beneath her chin, and then she was safe from deepwinter winds and stranger's touches both. Shawn found her weapons thrown carelessly in a corner with her boots. When Lane's sword was in her hand and her longknife back in its familiar sheath, she felt complete again. She stepped outside determined to find skis and exit.

Morgan met her with laughter bright and brittle, in a chamber of glass and shining silver metal. She stood framed against the largest window Shawn had ever seen, a sheet of pure clean glass taller than a man and wider than Carinhall's great hearth, even more flawless than the mirrors of family Terhis, who were famed for their glass-blowers and lensmakers. Beyond the glass it was midday; the cool blue midday of deepwinter. Shawn saw the field of stone and snow and flowers, and beyond it the low ridge that she had climbed, and beyond that the frozen river winding through the ruins.

"You look so fierce and angry," Morgan said, when her silly laughter had stopped. She had been threading her wild hair with wisps of cloth and gems on silver clips that sparkled when she moved. "Come, Carin child, take off your furs again. The cold can't touch us here, and if it does we can leave it. There are other lands, you know." She walked across the room.

Shawn had let the point of her sword droop toward the floor; now she jerked it up again. "Stay away," she warned. Her voice sounded hoarse and strange.

"I am not afraid of you, Shawn," Morgan said. "Not you, my Shawn, my lover." She moved around the sword easily, and took off the scarf she wore, a gossamer of gray spidersilk set with tiny crimson jewels, to drape it around Shawn's neck. "See, I know what you are thinking," she said, pointing to the jewels. One by one, they were changing color; fire became blood, blood crusted and turned brown,

brown faded to black. "You are frightened of me, nothing more. No anger. You would never hurt me." She tied the scarf neatly under Shawn's facemask and smiled.

Shawn stared at the gems with horror. "How did you do that?" she demanded, backing off uncertainly.

"With magic," Morgan said. She spun on her heels and danced back to the window. "Morgan is full of magic."

"You are full of lies," Shawn said. "I know about the six Alynnes. I'm not going to eat here and starve to death. Where are my skis?"

Morgan seemed not to hear her; the older woman's eyes were clouded, wistful. "Have you ever seen Alynne House in summer, child? It's very beautiful. The sun comes up over the redstone tower, and sinks every night into Jamei's Lake. Do you know it, Shawn?"

"No," Shawn said boldly, "and you don't either. What do you talk about Alynne House for, you said your family lived on the Ice Wagon, and they all had names I never heard of, Kleraberus and things like that."

"Kleronomas," Morgan said, giggling. She raised her hand to her mouth to still herself, and chewed on a finger idly while her gray eyes shone. All her fingers were ringed with bright metal. "You should see my brother Kleronomas, child. He is half of metal and half of flesh, and his eyes are bright as glass, and he knows more than all the Voices who've ever spoken for Carinhall."

"He does not," Shawn said. "You're lying again!"

"He *does*," Morgan said. Her hand fell and she looked cross. "He's magic. We all are. Erika died, but she wakes up to live again and again and again. Stephen was a warrior, he killed a billion families, more than you can count, and Celia found a lot of secret places that no one had ever found before. My family all does magic things." Her expression grew suddenly sly. "I killed the vampire, didn't I? How do you think I did that?"

"With a knife!" Shawn said fiercely. But beneath her mask she flushed. Morgan *had* killed the vampire; that meant there was a debt. And she had drawn steel! She flinched under Creg's imagined fury, and dropped the sword to clatter on the floor. All at once she was very confused.

Morgan's voice was gentle. "But you had a longknife *and* a sword, and you couldn't kill the vampire, could you, child? No." She came across the room. "You are mine, Shawn Carin, you are my lover and my daughter and my sister. You have to learn to trust. I have much to teach you. Here." She took Shawn by the hand and led her to the window. "Stand here. Wait, Shawn, wait and watch, and I will show you more of Morgan's magics." At the far wall, smiling, she did something with her rings to a panel of bright metal and square dim lights.

Watching, Shawn grew suddenly afraid.

Beneath her feet, the floor began to shake, and a sound assaulted her, a high whining shriek that stabbed at her ears through the leather mask, until she clapped her gloved hands on either side of her head to shut it out. Even then she could hear it, like a vibration in her bones. Her teeth ached, and she was aware of a sudden shooting pain up in her left temple, and that was not the worst of it.

For outside, where everything had been cold and bright and still, a somber blue light was shifting and dancing and staining all the world. The snowdrifts were a pale blue, and the plumes of frozen powder that blew from each of them were paler still, and blue shadows came and went upon the river ridge where none had been before. And Shawn could see the light reflected even on the river itself, and on the ruins that stood desolate and broken upon the farther crest. Morgan was giggling behind her, and then everything in the window began to blur, until there was nothing to be seen at all, only colors, colors bright and dark running together, like pieces of a rainbow melting in some vast stewpot. Shawn did not budge from where she stood, but her hand fell to the hilt of her longknife, and despite herself she trembled.

"Look, Carin child!" Morgan shouted, over the terrible whine. Shawn could barely hear her. "We've jumped up into the sky now, away from all that cold. I told you, Shawn. We're going to ride the Ice Wagon now." And she did something to the wall again, and the noise vanished, and the colors were gone. Beyond the glass was sky.

Shawn cried out in fear. She could see nothing except darkness and stars, stars everywhere, more than she had ever seen before. And she knew she was lost. Lane had taught her all the stars, so she could use them for a guide, find her way from anywhere to anywhere, but these stars were wrong, were *different*. She could not find the Ice Wagon, or the Ghost Skier, or even Lara Carin with her windwolves. She could find nothing familiar; only stars, stars that leered at her like a million eyes, red and white and blue and yellow, and none of them would ever blink.

Morgan was standing behind her. "Are we in the Ice Wagon?" Shawn asked in a small voice.

"Yes."

Shawn trembled, threw away her knife so that it bounded noisily off a metal wall, and turned to face her host. "Then we're dead, and the driver is taking our souls off to the frozen waste," she said. She did not cry. She had not wanted to be dead, especially not in deepwinter, but at least she would see Lane again.

Morgan began to undo the scarf she had fastened round Shawn's neck. The stones were black and frightening. "No, Shawn Carin," she said evenly. "We are not dead. Live here with me, child, and you will never die. You'll see." She pulled off the scarf and started unlacing the thongs of Shawn's facemask. When it was loose, she pulled it up and off the girl's head, tossing it casually to the floor.

"You're pretty, Shawn. You have always been pretty, though. I re-member, all those years ago. I remember."

"I'm not pretty," Shawn said. "I'm too soft, and I'm too weak, and Creg says I'm skinny and my face is all pushed in. And I'm not . . ."

Morgan shushed her with a touch to her lips, and then unfastened her neck clasp. Lane's battered cloak slipped from her shoulders. Her own cape followed, and then her coat was off, and Morgan's fingers moved down to the laces of her jerkin.

"No," Shawn said, suddenly shying away. Her back pressed up against the great window, and she felt the awful night laying its weight upon her. "I can't, Morgan. I'm Carin, and you're not family, I *can't*."

"Gathering," Morgan whispered. "Pretend this is Gathering, Shawn. You've always been my lover during the Gathering."

Shawn's throat was dry. "But it *isn't* Gathering," she insisted. She had seen one Gathering, down by the sea, when forty families came together to trade news and goods and love. But that had been years before her blood, so no one had taken her; she was not yet a woman, and thus untouchable. "It *isn't* Gathering," she repeated, close to tears.

Morgan giggled. "Very well. I am no Carin, but I am Morgan full-of-magic. I can make it Gathering." She darted across the room on bare feet, and thrust her rings against the wall once more, and moved them this way and that, in a strange pattern. Then she called out, "Look! Turn and look." Shawn, confused, glanced back at the win-dow.

Under the double suns of highsummer, the world was bright and green. Sailing ships moved languidly on the slow-flowing waters of the river, and Shawn could see the bright reflections of the twin suns bobbing and rolling in their wake, balls of soft yellow butter afloat upon the blue. Even the sky seemed sweet and buttery; white clouds moved like the stately schooners of family Crien, and nowhere could a star be seen. The far shore was dotted by houses, houses small as a road shelter and greater than even Carinhall, towers as tall and sleek as the wind-carved rocks in the Broken Mountains. And here and there and all among them people moved; lithe, swarthy folk strange to Shawn, and people of the families too, all mingling together. The stone field was free of snow and ice, but there were metal buildings everywhere, some larger than Morganhall, many smaller, each with its distinctive markings, and every one of them squatting on three legs. Between the buildings were the tents and stalls of the families, with their sigils and their banners. And mats, the gaily colored lovers' mats. Shawn saw people coupling, and felt Morgan's hand resting lightly on her shoulder.

"Do you know what you are seeing, Carin child?" Morgan whis-pered.

Shawn turned back to her with fear and wonder in her eyes. "It is a Gathering."

Morgan smiled. "You see," she said. "It is Gathering, and I claim you. Celebrate with me." And her fingers moved to the buckle on Shawn's belt, and Shawn did not resist.

Within the metal walls of Morganhall, seasons turned to hours turned to years turned to days turned to months turned to weeks turned to seasons once again. Time had no sense. When Shawn awoke, on a shaggy fur that Morgan had spread beneath the window, high-summer had turned back into deepwinter, and the families, ships, and Gathering were gone. Dawn came earlier than it should have, and Morgan seemed annoyed, so she made it dusk; the season was freeze, with its ominous chill, and where the stars of sunrise had shown, now gray clouds raced across a copper-colored sky. They ate while the copper turned to black. Morgan served mushrooms and crunchy summer greens, dark bread dripping with honey and butter, creamed spice-tea, and thick cuts of red meat floating in blood, and afterward there was flavored ice with nuts, and finally a tall hot drink with nine layers, each a different color with a different taste. They sipped the drink from glasses of impossibly thin crystal, and it made Shawn's head ache. And she began to cry, because the food had seemed real and all of it was good, but she was afraid that if she ate any more of it she would starve to death. Morgan laughed at her and slipped away and returned with dried leathery strips of vampire meat; she told Shawn to keep it in her pack and munch on it whenever she felt hungry.

Shawn kept the meat for a long time, but never ate from it.

At first she tried to keep track of the days by counting the meals they ate, and how many times they slept, but soon the changing scenes outside the window and the random nature of life in Morganhall confused her past any hope of understanding. She worried about it for weeks—or perhaps only for days—and then she ceased to worry. Morgan could make time do anything she pleased, so there was no sense in Shawn caring about it.

Several times Shawn asked to leave, but Morgan would have none of it. She only laughed and did some great magic that made Shawn forget about everything. Morgan took her blades away one night when she was asleep, and all her furs and leathers too, and afterward Shawn was forced to dress as Morgan wanted her to dress, in clouds of colored silk and fantastic tatters, or in nothing at all. She was angry and upset at first, but later she grew used to it. Her old clothing would have been much too hot inside Morganhall, anyway.

Morgan gave her gifts. Bags of spice that smelled of summer. A windwolf fashioned of pale blue glass. A metal mask that let Shawn see in the dark. Scented oils for her bath, and bottles of a slow golden liquor that brought her forgetfulness when her mind was troubled. A mirror, the finest mirror that had ever been. Books that Shawn could not read. A bracelet set with small red stones that drank in light all day and glowed by night. Cubes that played exotic music when Shawn warmed them with her hand. Boots woven of metal that were so light and flexible she could crumple them up in the palm of one hand. Metal miniatures of men and women and all manner of demons.

Morgan told her stories. Each gift she gave to Shawn had a story that went with it, a tale of where it came from and who had made it and how it had come here. Morgan told them all. There were tales for each of her relatives as well; indomitable Kleronomas who drove across the sky hunting for knowledge, Celia Marcyan the ever-curious and her ship *Shadow Chaser*, Erika Stormjones whose family cut her up with knives that she might live again, savage Stephen Cobalt Northstar, melancholy Tomo, bright Dierdre d'Allerane and her grim ghostly twin. Those stories Morgan told with magic. There was a place in one wall with a small square slot in it, and Morgan would go there and insert a flat metallic box, and then all the lights would go out and Morgan's dead relatives would live again, bright phantoms who walked and talked and dripped blood when they were hurt. Shawn thought they were real until the day when Deirdre first wept for her slain children, and Shawn ran to comfort her and found they could not touch. It was not until afterward that Morgan told her Deirdre and the others were only spirits, called down by her magic.

Morgan told her many things. Morgan was her teacher as well as her lover, and she was nearly as patient as Lane had been, though much more prone to wander and lose interest. She gave Shawn a beautiful twelve-stringed guitar and began to teach her to play it, and she taught her to read a little, and she taught her a few of the simpler magics, so Shawn could move easily around the ship. That was another thing that Morgan taught her; Morganhall was no building after all, but a ship, a sky-ship that could flex its metal legs and leap from star to star. Morgan told her about the planets, lands out by those far-off stars, and said that all the gifts she had given Shawn had come from out there, from beyond the Ice Wagon; the mask and mirror were from Jamison's World, the books and cubes from Avalon, the bracelet from High Kavalaan, the oils from Braque, the spices from Rhiannon and Tara and Old Poseidon, the boots from Bastion, the figurines from Chul Damien, the golden liquor from a land so far away that even Morgan did not know its name. Only the fine glass windwolf had been made here, on Shawn's world, Morgan said. The windwolf had always been one of Shawn's favorites, but now she found she did not like it half so well as she had thought she did. The others were so much more exciting. Shawn had always wanted to travel, to visit distant families in wild distant climes, to gaze on seas and mountains. But she had been too young, and when she finally reached her womanhood, Creg would not let her go; she was too slow, he said, too timid, too irresponsible. Her life would be spent at home, where she could put her meager talents to better use for Carinhall. Even the fateful trip that had led her here had been a fluke; Lane had insisted, and Lane alone of all the others was strong enough to stand up to Creg, Voice Carin.

Morgan took her traveling, though, on sails between the stars. When blue fire flickered against the icy landscape of deepwinter and the sound rose up out of nowhere, higher and higher, Shawn would rush eagerly to the window, where she would wait with mounting impatience for the colors to clear. Morgan gave her all the mountains and all the seas she could dream of, and more. Through the flawless glass Shawn saw the lands from all the stories; Old Poseidon with its weathered docks and its fleets of silver ships, the meadows of Rhiannon, the vaulting black steel towers of ai-Emerel, High Kavalaan's windswept plains and rugged hills, the island-cities of Port Jamison and Jolostar on Jamison's World. Shawn learned about cities from Morgan, and suddenly the ruins by the river seemed different in her eyes. She learned about other ways of living as well, about arcologies and holdfasts and brotherhoods, about bond companies and slavery and armies. Family Carin no longer seemed the beginning and the end of human loyalties.

Of all the places they sailed to, they came to Avalon most often, and Shawn learned to love it best. On Avalon the landing field was always full of other wanderers, and Shawn could watch ships come and go on wands of pale blue light. And in the distance she could see the buildings of the Academy of Human Knowledge, where Kleronomas had deposited all his secrets so that they might be held in trust for Morgan's family. Those jagged glass towers filled Shawn with a longing that was almost a hurt, but a hurt that she somehow craved.

Sometimes—on several of the worlds, but most particularly on Avalon—it seemed to Shawn that some stranger was about to board their ship. She would watch them come, striding purposefully across the field, their destination clear from every step. They never came aboard, though, much to her disappointment. There was never anyone to touch or talk to except Morgan. Shawn suspected that Morgan magicked the would-be visitors away, or else lured them to their doom. She could not quite make up her mind which; Morgan was so moody that it might be both. One dinnertime she remembered Jon's story of the cannibal hall, and looked down with horror at the red meat they were eating. She ate only vegetables that meal, and for several meals thereafter, until she finally decided that she was being childish. Shawn considered asking Morgan about the strangers who approached and vanished, but she was afraid. She remembered Creg, whose temper was awful if you asked him the wrong question. And if the older woman were really killing those who tried to board her ship, it would not be wise to mention it to her. When Shawn was just a child, Creg had beaten her savagely for asking why old Tesenya had to go outside and die.

Other questions Shawn did ask, only to find that Morgan would not answer. Morgan would not talk about her own origins, or the source of their food, or the magic that flew the ship. Twice Shawn asked to learn the spells that moved them from star to star, and both times Morgan refused with anger in her voice. She had other secrets from Shawn as well. There were rooms that would not open to Shawn, things that she was not allowed to touch, other things that Morgan would not even talk about. From time to time Morgan would disappear for what seemed like days, and Shawn would wander about desolately, with nothing outside the window to occupy her but steady, unwinking stars. On those occasions Morgan would be somber and secretive when she returned, but only for a few hours, after which she would return to normal.

For Morgan, though, normal was different than for other people.

She would dance about the ship endlessly, singing to herself, sometimes with Shawn as a dancing partner and sometimes alone. She would converse with herself in a musical tongue that Shawn did not know. She would be alternately as serious as a wise old mother, and three times as knowledgeable as a Voice, and as giddy and giggly as a child of one season. Sometimes Morgan seemed to know just who Shawn was, and sometimes she insisted on confusing her with that other Shawn Carin who had loved her during Gatherings. She was very patient and very impetuous; she was unlike anyone that Shawn had met before. "You're silly," Shawn told her once. "You wouldn't be so silly if you lived in Carinhall. Silly people die, you know, and they hurt their families. Everyone has to be useful, and you're not useful. Creg would make you be useful. You're lucky that you aren't a Carin."

Morgan had only caressed her, and gazed at her from sad gray eyes. "Poor Shawn," she'd whispered. "They've been so hard to you. But the Carins were always hard. Alynne House was different, child. You should have been born an Alynne." And after that she would say no more of it.

Shawn squandered her days in wonder and her nights in love, and she thought of Carinhall less and less, and gradually she found that she had come to care for Morgan as if she were family. And more, she had come to trust her.

Until the day she learned about the bitterblooms.

Shawn woke up one morning to find that the window was full of stars, and Morgan had vanished. That usually meant a long, boring wait, but this time Shawn was still eating the food that Morgan had left out for her when the older woman returned with her hands full of pale blue flowers.

She was so eager; Shawn had never seen her so eager. She made Shawn leave her breakfast half-eaten, and come across the room to the fur rug by the window, so that she could wind the flowers in Shawn's hair. "I saw while you were sleeping, child," she said happily as she worked, "your hair has grown long. It used to be so short, chopped off and ugly, but you've been here long enough and now it's better, long like mine. The bitterblooms will make it best of all."

"Bitterblooms?" Shawn asked, curious. "Is that what you call them? I never knew."

"Yes, child," Morgan replied, still fussing and arranging. Shawn had her back to her, so she could not see her face. "The little blue ones are the bitterblooms. They flower even in the bitterest cold, so that's why they call them that. Originally they came from a world named Ymir, very far off, where they have winters nearly as long and cold as we do. The other flowers are from Ymir too, the ones that grow on the vines around the ship. Those are called frost-flowers. Deepwinter is always so bleak, so I planted them to make everything look nicer." She took Shawn by the shoulder and turned her around. "Go and get your mirror and see for yourself, Carin child."

"It's over there," Shawn answered, and she darted around Morgan to get it. Her bare foot came down in something cold and wet. She flinched from it and made a noise; there was a puddle on the rug.

Shawn frowned. She stood very still and looked at Morgan. The woman had not removed her boots. They dripped.

And behind Morgan, there was nothing to be seen but blackness and unfamiliar stars. Shawn was afraid; something was very wrong. Morgan was looking at her uneasily.

She wet her lips, then smiled shyly, and went to get the mirror.

Morgan magicked the stars away before she went to sleep; it was night outside their window, but a gentle night far from the frozen rigor of deepwinter. Leafy trees swayed in the wind on the perimeter of their landing field, and a moon overhead made everything bright and beautiful. A good safe world to sleep on, Morgan said.

Shawn did not sleep. She sat across the room from Morgan, staring at the moon. For the first time since she had come to Morganhall, she was using her mind like a Carin. Lane would have been proud of her; Creg would only have asked what took her so long.

Morgan had returned with a handful of bitterblooms and boots wet with snow. But outside had been nothing, only the emptiness that Morgan said filled the space between the stars.

Morgan said that the light Shawn had seen in the forest had been the fires of her ship as it landed. But the thick vines of the frost-flowers grew in and around and over the legs of that ship, and they had been growing for years.

Morgan would not let her go outside. Morgan showed her everything through the great window. But Shawn could not remember seeing any window when she had been *outside* Morganhall. And if the window was a window, where were the vines that should have crept across it, the deepwinter frost that should have covered it?

For the name of the metal hall was Morganhall, Tesenya told the children, and the family who lived there was the family named Liar, whose food is empty stuff made of dreams and air.

Shawn arose in the lie of moonlight and went to where she kept the gifts that Morgan had given her. She looked at them each in turn and lifted the heaviest of them, the glass windwolf. It was a large sculpture, hefty enough so that Shawn used two hands to lift it, one hand on the creature's snarling snout, the other around its tail. "Morgan!" she shouted.

Morgan sat up drowsily, and smiled. "Shawn," she murmured. "Shawn child. What are you doing with your windwolf?"

Shawn advanced and lifted the glass animal high above her head. "You lied to me. We've never gone anywhere. We're still in the ruined city, and it's still deepwinter."

Morgan's face was somber. "You don't know what you're saying." She got shakily to her feet. "Are you going to hit me with that thing, child? I'm not afraid of it. Once you held a sword on me, and I wasn't afraid of you then, either. I am Morgan, full-of-magic. You cannot hurt me, Shawn."

"I want to leave," Shawn said. "Bring me my blades and my clothing, my old clothing. I'm going back to Carinhall. I am a woman of Carin, not a child. You've made a child of me. Bring me food too."

Morgan giggled. "So serious. And if I don't?"

"If you don't," Shawn said, "then I'll throw this right through your window." She hefted the windwolf for emphasis.

"No," Morgan said. Her expression was unreadable. "You don't want to do that, child."

"I *will*," Shawn said. "Unless you do as I say."

"You don't want to leave me, Shawn Carin, no you don't. We're lovers, remember. We're family. I can do magics for you." Her voice trembled. "Put that down, child. I'll show you things I never showed you before. There are so many places we can go together, so many stories I can tell you. Put that down." She was pleading.

Shawn could sense triumph; oddly enough, there were tears in her eyes. "Why are you so afraid?" she demanded angrily. "You can fix a broken window with your magic, can't you? Even I can fix a broken window, and Creg says I'm hardly good for anythnig at all." The tears were rolling down her naked cheeks now, but silently, silently. "It's warm outside, you can see that, and there's moonlight to work by, and even a city. You could hire a glazier. I don't see why you are so afraid. It isn't as if it were deepwinter out there, with cold and ice, vampires gliding through the dark. It isn't like that."

"No," Morgan said. "No."

"No," Shawn echoed. "Bring me my things."

Morgan did not move. "It wasn't all lies. It wasn't. If you stay with me, you'll live for a long time. I think it's the food, but it's true. A lot of it was true, Shawn. I didn't mean to lie to you. I wanted it to be best, the way it was for me at first. You just have to pretend, you know. Forget that the ship can't move. It's better that way." Her voice sounded young, frightened; she was a woman, and she begged like a little girl, in a little girl's voice. "Don't break the window. The window is the most magic thing. It can take us anywhere, almost. Please, *please*, don't break it, Shawn. Don't."

Morgan was shaking. The fluttering rags she wore seemed faded and shabby suddenly, and her rings did not sparkle. She was just a crazy old woman. Shawn lowered the heavy glass windowlf. "I want my clothing, and my sword, and my skis. And food. Lots and lots of food. Bring it to me and maybe I won't break your window, liar. Do you hear me?"

And Morgan, no logner full of magic, nodded and did as she was told. Shawn watched her in silence. They never spoke again.

Shawn returned to Carinhall and grew old.

Her return was a sensation. She had been missing for more than a standard year, she discovered, and everyone had presumed that both she and Lane were dead. Creg refused to believe her story at first, and the others followed his lead, until Shawn produced a handful of bitterblooms that she had picked from her hair. Even then, Creg could not accept the more fanciful parts of her tale. "Illusions," he snorted, "every bit of it illusion. Tesenya told it true. If you went back, your magic ship would be gone, with no sign that it had ever been there. Believe me, Shawn." But it was never clear to her whether Creg truly believed himself. He issued orders, and no man or woman of family Carin ever went that way again.

Things were different at Carinhall after Shawn's return. The family was smaller. Lane's was not the only face she missed at the meal table. Food had grown very short while she had been away, and Creg, as was the custom, had sent the weakest and most useless out to die. Jon was among the missing. Leila was gone too, Leila who had been so young and strong. A vampire had taken her three months ago. But not everything was sadness. Deepwinter was ending. And, on a more personal level, Shawn found that her position in the family had changed. Now even Creg treated her with a rough respect. A year later, when thaw was well under way, she bore her first child and was accepted as an equal into the councils of Carinhall. Shawn named her daughter Lane.

She settled easily into family life. When it was time for her to choose a permanent profession, she asked to be a trader, and was surprised to find that Creg did not speak against her choice. Rys took her as apprentice, and after three years she got an assignment of her own. Her work kept her on the road a great deal. When she was home in Carinhall, however, Shawn found to her surprise that she had become the favored family storyteller. The children said she knew the best stories of anyone. Creg, ever practical, said that her fancies set the children a bad example and had no proper lesson to them. But by that time he was very sick, a victim of highsummer fever, and his opposition carried little weight. He died soon after, and Devin became Voice, a gentler and more moderate Voice than Creg. Family Carin had a generation of peace while he spoke for Carinhall, and their numbers increased from forty to nearly one hundred.

Shawn was frequently his lover. Her reading had improved a great deal by then, through long study, and Devin once yielded to her whim and showed her the secret library of the Voices, where each Voice for untold centuries had kept a journal detailing the events of his service. As Shawn had suspected, one of the thicker volumes was called *The Book of Beth, Voice Carin*. It was about sixty years old.

Lane was the first of nine children for Shawn. Six of them lived, two fathered by family and four that she brought back with her from Gathering. Devin honored her for bringing so much fresh blood into Carinhall, and later another Voice would name her for exceptional prowess as a trader. She traveled widely, met many families, saw waterfalls and volcanoes as well as seas and mountains, sailed halfway around the world on a Crien schooner. She had many lovers and much esteem. Jannis followed Devin as Voice, but she had a bitter, unhappy time of it, and when she passed, the mothers and fathers of family Carin offered the position to Shawn. She turned it down. It would not have made her happy. Despite everything she had done, she was not a happy person.

She remembered too much, and sometimes she could not sleep very well at night.

During the fourth deepwinter of her life, the family numbered two hundred and thirty-seven, fully a hundred of them children. But game was scarce, even in the third year after freeze, and Shawn could see the hard cold times approaching. The Voice was a kind woman who found it hard to make the decisions that had to be made, but Shawn knew what was coming. She was the second eldest of those in Carinhall. One night she stole some food—just enough, two weeks' traveling supply—and a pair of skis, left Carinhall at dawn, and spared the Voice the giving of the order.

She was not so fast as she had been when she was young. The journey took closer to three weeks than two, and she was lean and weak when she finally entered the ruined city.

But the ship was just as she had left it.

Extremes of heat and cold had cracked the stone of the spacefield over the years, and the alien flowers had taken advantage of every little opening. The stone was dotted with bitterblooms, and the frost-flower vines that twined around the ship were twice as thick as Shawn remembered them. The big brightly colored blossoms stirred faintly in the wind.

Nothing else moved.

She circled the ship three times, waiting for a door to open, waiting for someone to see her and appear. But if the metal noticed her presence, it gave no sign. On the far side of the ship, you can't see it from outside, Shawn found something she hadn't seen before—writing, faded but still legible, obscured only by ice and flowers. She used her longknife to shatter the ice and cut the vines, so she might read. It said:

MORGAN LE FAY
Registry: Avalon 476 3319

Shawn smiled. So even her name had been a lie. Well, it did not matter now. She cupped her gloved hands together over her mouth. "Morgan," she shouted. "It's Shawn." The wind whipped her words away from her. "Let me in, Morgan. Lie to me, Morgan full-of-magic. I'm sorry. Lie to me and make me believe."

There was no answer. Shawn dug herself a hollow in the snow and sat down to wait. She was tired and hungry, and dusk was close at hand. Already she could see the driver's ice blue eyes staring through the wispy clouds of twilight.

When at last she slept, she dreamt of Avalon.

This modern myth—brilliantly assembled by its two young authors from the brightly colored shards of other dreams—must be added to the small and exclusive list of successful SF pastiches, alongside Brian Aldiss's Nebula-winning "The Saliva Tree," Fritz Leiber's "The Night He Cried," and Philip José Farmer's Lord Tyger *(Signet). "Black as the Pit" is dedicated to Mary Wollstonecraft Shelley, Edgar Allan Poe, Herman Melville, Jules Verne, Edgar Rice Burroughs, H. P. Lovecraft, and Philip José Farmer, and with good reason—but like all such stories, this one works because it weaves from disparate elements a beauty, wonder, pathos, and joy entirely its own, a vision and a dreaming world that otherwise never would have been. . . .*

Steven Utley and Howard Waldrop are two of the best known of a large regional group of SF writers from Texas. Their last collaboration, "Custer's Last Jump," was reprinted in the sixth annual Best Science Fiction Stories of the Year *and was a strong contender for the 1976 Nebula Award.*

STEVEN UTLEY and HOWARD WALDROP

Black as the Pit, from Pole to Pole

I

In an early American spring, the following circular was sent to learned men, scholars, explorers, and members of the Congress. It was later reprinted by various newspapers and magazines, both in the United States and abroad.

St. Louis, Missouri Territory, North America
April 10, 1818

I declare that the earth is hollow; habitable within; containing a number of solid concentric spheres; one within the other, and that it is open at the pole twelve or sixteen degrees. I pledge my life in support of this truth, and am ready to explore the hollow if the world will support and aid me in the undertaking. John Cleves Symmes of Ohio, Late Captain of Infantry.

N.B. I have ready for the press a treatise on the principles of Matter, wherein I show proofs on the above proposition, account for various phenomena, and disclose Dr. Darwin's "Golden Secret."

My terms are the patronage of this and the new world; I dedicate to my wife and her ten children.

I select Dr. S. L. Mitchel, Sir H. Davy, and Baron Alexander Von Humboldt as my protectors. I ask 100 brave companions, well-equipped to start from Siberia, in the fall season, with reindeer and sledges, on the ice of the frozen sea; I engage we find a warm and rich land, stocked with thrifty vegetables and animals, if not men, on reaching one degree northward of latitude 82; we will return in the succeeding spring. J.C.S.

From the Introduction to *Frankenstein; or, The Modern Prometheus,* revised edition, 1831, by Mary Wollstonecraft Shelley:

Many and long were the conversations between Lord Byron and Shelley, to which I was a devout but nearly silent listener. During one of these, various philosophical doctrines were discussed, and among others the nature of the principle of life, and whether there was any possibility of its ever being discovered and communicated. They talked of the experiments of Dr. Darwin (I speak not of what the Doctor really did, or said that he did, but, as more to my purpose, of what was then spoken of as having been done by him) who preserved a piece of vermicelli in a glass case, 'til by some extraordinary means it began to move with a voluntary motion. Not thus, after all, would life be given. Perhaps a corpse would be reanimated; galvanism had given token of such things; perhaps the component parts of a creature might be manufactured, brought together and imbued with vital warmth. . . .

It ends here.
The creature's legs buckled. His knees crunched through the crust as he went down. The death's-head face turned toward the sky. The wind swept across the ice cap, gathering up and flinging cold dust into his eyes.
The giant, the monster, the golem closed his fine-veined eyelids and fell sideways. He could go no farther. He was numb and exhausted. He pressed his face down into the snow, and his thin, black lips began to shape the words of an unvoiced prayer:
It ends here, Victor Frankenstein. I am too weary to go on. Too weary even to cremate myself. Wherever you are now, whether passed into Heaven, Hell, or that nothingness from which you summoned me, look upon me with pity and compassion now. I had no choice. It ends here. At the top of the world, where no one shall ever come to remark on the passing of this nameless, forsaken wretch. It ends here, and the world is rid of me. Once again, Victor, I beseech you. Forgive me for my wicked machinations. Even as I forgave you yours.

He waited for death, his ears throbbing with the ever-slowing beat of his handseled heart. Sports of blackness began to erupt in his head and spread, overtaking and overwhelming the astonishingly vivid assortment of memories which flickered through his mind. Such a pretty little boy. I will not eat you, do not scream. Be quiet, please. I mean you no harm. Please. I want to be your friend. Hush now. Hush. Hush. I didn't know that he would break so easily. There is open sea not far from where I sprawl in the snow, awaiting death. The sea is the mother of all life. Save mine. The young man's name was Felix, and he drove me away. I could have crushed his skull with a single casual swat with the back of my hand. And I let him drive me away. Such a pretty little boy. Such a pretty little boy. Why was I not made pretty? Tell me now, Frankenstein. It is important that I know. Do I have a soul? Felix. Felix. I will be with you on your wedding night. I will be with you. Do I have a *soul*, Victor Frankenstein?

He suddenly pushed himself up on his elbows and shook ice from his eyelids. He could see the sea before him, but it was too bright to gaze upon. It seemed to burn like molten gold, and it was as though the very maw of Hell were opening to receive him.

He collapsed, burying his face in the snow, and lay there whimpering, no strength left now, no sensation in his legs and hands. *Do I have a soul?* he demanded a final time, just as he felt himself sliding, sliding, about to take the plunge into oblivion. There was time enough for a second question. *If so, where will it go?* And then there was no time at all.

He had not felt so disoriented since the night of his first awakening. He sat up painfully and glared around in confusion. Then tears streamed from his eyes and froze upon his cheeks, and he shrieked with rage and frustration.

"Fiend! Monster! *Damn you!*"

He struggled to his feet and tottered wildly, flailing the air with his mismatched fists. And he kept screaming.

"*This* is the full horror of your great achievement! Death won't have me, Frankenstein! Hell spews me forth! *You made me better than you thought!*"

His thickly wrapped legs, aching with the slow return of circulation, began to pump stiffly, driving him across the ice. He kicked up clouds of cold snow dust. Then glass-sliver pain filled his lungs, and his mad run slowed to a walk. Fury spun and eddied in his guts, hotter by far than the fire in his chest, but it was fury commingled with sorrow. He sat down abruptly, put his face into his hands, and sobbed.

Death had rejected him again.

At the instant of his birth on a long-ago, almost forgotten midnight, he had drawn his first puzzled breath, and Death had bowed to Life for the first time, had permitted a mere man to pry its fingers from the abandoned bones and flesh of the kirk yard and the charnel house.

Death had never reclaimed that which had been taken from it. Time and again, Death had chosen not to terminate his comfortless existence.

I was never ill, Frankenstein. I survived fire and exposure. I sustained injuries which would have killed or at least incapacitated even the hardiest of human beings. Even you could not kill me, you who gave me life. That should make you proud. You shot me at point-blank range after I killed your beautiful Elizabeth. You couldn't kill me, though. Perhaps nothing can kill me.

His sobbing subsided. He sat in the snow and dully rolled the bitter thought over and over in his mind. Perhaps nothing can kill me. Perhaps *nothing* can kill me. When Victor Frankenstein had shot him, the ball struck him low in the left side of the back and emerged a couple of inches above and to the right of the incongruous navel. The impact had knocked him from the sill of the château window through which he had been making an escape. Doubled up on the ground beneath the window, he had heard Frankenstein's howl of anguish over the murdered Elizabeth. Then, clutching his abdomen, he had lurched away into the night.

The bleeding had ceased within minutes. The wounds were closed by the following morning and, at the end of a week's time, were no more than moon-shaped, moon-colored scars. He had wondered about his regenerative powers but briefly, however, for his enraged creator was breathing down his neck in hot, vengeful pursuit. There had been no time for idle speculation during the trek across Europe, across Siberia, into the windswept Arctic.

He pushed his tongue out and licked his frostbitten lips. Words started to rumble up from the deep chest, then lost all life of their own, and emerged dull sounding and flat. "You cheated me, Victor Frankenstein. In every way, you cheated me."

He paused, listening. The wind moaned like the breath of some immense frost-god wrapped in unpleasant dreams. Muffled thunder rolled across the ice from the direction of the now-leaden sea.

"I owe you nothing, Victor. *Nothing.*"

He got to his feet again and began moving toward the edge of the ice. Plucking bits of ice from his face and hair, his mind bubbling and frothing, he was suddenly stopped in his tracks by a particularly vicious gust of wind. His eyes filled with salt water. The cold cut through his parka, flesh, and bone, and he cried out in pure animal misery. He sucked on his frozen fingers and tried to stamp warmth back into his limbs. In the sky, its bottom half under the horizon, the heatless, useless sun mocked him. He snarled at it, shook his fist at it, turned his back on it.

And could not believe what he saw before him.

Hanging between the northern edge of the world and the zenith was a second, smaller sun.

II

In the year 1818, *Frankenstein; or, The Modern Prometheus* was published. Mary Shelley was twenty-one years old.

John Cleves Symmes, late of the Ohio Infantry, published his treatise about the hollow earth. He was a war hero and a Missouri storekeeper. He was thirty-eight years old.

Herman Melville would not be born for another year.

Jeremiah N. Reynolds was attending Ohio University but would soon become a doctor and a scientist. He would also fall under the spell of Symmes.

Edgar Allan Poe, nine years old, was living with his foster parents.

Percy Shelley, Lord Byron, and Dr. Polidori sailed as often as possible in the sloop *Ariel* on Lake Como.

In New Bedford, Massachusetts, young Arthur Gordon Pym sailed around the harbor in his sloop, also christened *Ariel*. His one burning desire was to go to sea.

In the South Sea, Mocha Dick, the great white whale, was an age no man could know or guess. Mocha Dick was not aware of aging, nor of the passing of time. It knew only of the sounding deeps and, infrequently, of the men who stuck harpoons into it until it turned on them and broke apart their vessels.

Victor Frankenstein's patchwork man was similarly unaware of the passing of time. The creature did not know how long he had slept in the ice at the top of the world, nor was he able to mark time within earth.

It became subtly warmer as the mysterious second sun rose in time with the ice cap's apparent northerly drift. The creature kept telling himself that what he saw was impossible, that there could be no second sun, that it was merely an illusion, a reflected image of the sun he had always known, a clever optical trick of some sort. But he was too miserable to ponder the phenomenon for very long at a time.

He subsisted on the dried meat which he had carried with him from Siberia in the pouch of his parka. He had little strength for exercise, and the circulation of his vital fluids often slowed to the point where he was only semiconscious. His eyes began playing other tricks on him. The horizon started to rise before him, to warp around him outrageously, curving upward and away in every direction, as though he had been carried over the lip of an enormous bowl and was slowly, lazily sliding toward its bottom. He could account for none of it.

He was dozing, frozen, in the shelter of an ice block when a shudder passed through the mass beneath him. He blinked, vaguely aware of something being wrong, and then he was snapped fully awake by the sight and *sound* of a gigantic blossom of spray at the edge of the sea. The thunder of crumbling ice brought him up on hands and knees. He stared, fascinated, as the eruption of water hung in the air for a long moment before falling, very slowly, very massively, back into the sea.

Then panic replaced fascination. He realized what was happening.

The ice was breaking up. He spun, the motion consuming years, took two steps and sank, howling, into snow suddenly turned to quicksand. He fell and scrambled up in time to see an ice ridge explode into powder. The shelf on which he stood pitched crazily as it started to slide down the parent mass's new face. The scraping walls of the fissure shook the air with the sound of a million tormented, screaming things. Dwarfed to insignificance by the forces at play around him, the giant was hurled flat. The breath left his lungs painfully.

He pushed himself up on elbows and sucked the cold, cutting air back into his tormented chest. The world beyond his clenched fists seemed to sag, then dropped out of sight. A moment later, clouds of freezing seawater geysered from the abyss as the shelf settled and rolled, stabilizing itself.

The creature turned and crawled away from the chasm. He kept moving until he was at the approximate center of the new iceberg. He squatted there, alternately shaking and going numb with terror.

He had seen the abyss open inches from him.

He had looked down the throat of the death he had wanted.

He had felt no temptation.

He cursed life for its tenacity. He cursed, again, the man whose explorations into the secrets of life had made it impossible for him to simply lie down, sleep, and let the Arctic cold take him.

He could not help but brood over his immunity to death. What would have happened, he wondered, had he been precipitated into the fissure when the shelf broke off? Surely he would have been smeared to thin porridge between the sliding, scraping masses. But—

There was another rumble behind him. He turned his head and saw a large section of the berg drop out of sight into the sea.

It doesn't matter, he reflected as he dug into his parka for a piece of meat. The ice is going to melt, and I will be hurled into the sea. I wonder if I can drown.

He did not relish the prospect of finding out.

His virtually somnambulistic existence resumed. He ate his dried meat, melted snow in his mouth to slake his thirst, and fully regained consciousness only when the berg shook him awake with the crash and roar of its disintegration. The sun he had known all of his life, the one which he could not think of as other than the *real* sun, at last disappeared behind him, while the strange second sun now seemed fixed unwaveringly at zenith. The horizon was still rising, rolling up the sky until it appeared behind occasional cloud masses and, sometimes, above them. It was as though the world were trying to double over on itself and enfold him.

He amused himself with that image between naps. Nothing was

strange to him anymore, not the stationary sun, not the horizonless vista. He was alive, trapped on a melting iceberg. He was in Hell.

It was only when he began to make out the outlines of a coast in the sky that he experienced a renewed sense of wonder. In the time which followed, a time of unending noon, of less sleep and more terror as the berg's mass diminished, the sight of that concave, stood-on-edge land filled him with awe and a flickering sort of hope which even hunger, physical misery, and fear could not dispel.

He was alive, but merely being alive was not enough. It had never been enough.

He was alive, and here, sweeping down out of the sky, rolling itself out toward him in open invitation was . . . what?

He stood at the center of his iceberg and looked at his hands. He thought of the scars on his body, the proofs of his synthesis, and he thought:

What *was* my purpose, Victor Frankenstein? Did you have some kind of destiny planned for me when you gave me life? Had you not rejected me at the moment of my birth, had you accepted responsibility for my being in the world, would there have been some sort of fulfillment, some use, for me in the world of men?

The berg shivered underfoot for a second, and he cried out, went to his knees, hugged a block of ice desperately. The dark land mass swam in the air. When the tremor had subsided, he laughed shakily and got to his feet. His head spun, grew light, filled with stars and explosions. He reached for the ice block in an effort to steady himself but fell anyway and lay in the snow thinking.

Thinking, This is no natural land before me, Frankenstein, and perhaps there are no men here.

Thinking, I could be free of men here, free of everything.

Thinking, This is going to be *my* land, Frankenstein.

Thinking, This is no natural land, and I am no natural man.

Thinking.

The berg had begun crunching its way through drifting sheets of pack ice when the creature spotted something else which stood out against the brilliant whiteness of the frozen sea. He watched the thing for a long time, noting that it did not move, before he was able to discern the sticklike fingers of broken masts and the tracery of rigging. It looked like some forgotten, bedraggled toy, tossed aside by a bored child.

The ship was very old. Its sides had been crushed in at the waterline, and the ice-sheathed debris of its rigging and lesser masts sat upon the hulk like a stand of dead, gray trees. A tattered flag hung from the stern, frozen solid, looking to be fashioned from thick glass.

When his iceberg had finally slowed to an imperceptible crawl in the midst of the pack, the creature cautiously made his way down to the sheet and walked to the ship. When he had come close enough, he called out in his ragged voice. There was no answer. He had not expected one.

Below decks, he found unused stores and armaments, along with three iron-hard corpses. There were flint, frozen biscuits, and salt pork, kegs of frozen water and liquor. There was a wealth of cold-climate clothing and lockers packed with brittle charts and strange instruments.

He took what he could carry. From the several armaments lockers, he selected a long, double-edged dagger, a heavy cutlass and scabbard, a blunderbuss, and a brace of pistols to supplement the one he had carried throughout his Siberian trek. There had been two pistols originally—he had stolen the set before leaving Europe and had used them on a number of occasions to get what he needed in the way of supplies from terrified Siberian peasants. One of the pistols had been missing after his departure from the whaling vessel. He supposed that it had fallen from his belt when he leaped from the ship to the ice.

There was enough powder in several discarded barrels to fill a small keg. He found shot in a metal box and filled the pouch of his parka.

He did not bother himself with thoughts about the dead men or their vanished comrades. Whoever they had been, they had left in a hurry, and they had left him their goods. He was still cold, tired, and hungry, but the warm clothing was now his, and he could rest in the shelter of the derelict. He had hardtack and meat and the means to make fire. And he had weapons.

He returned to the deck for a moment and contemplated the upward-curving landscape ahead.

In this world, perhaps, there are no men.

He waved the cutlass, wearily jubilant, and, for the first time in his life, he began to feel truly free.

III

John Cleves Symmes published a novel in 1820, under the name Adam Seaborn. Its title was *Symzonia: A Voyage of Discovery*, and it made extensive use of Symmes's theories about the hollow world and the polar openings. In the novel, Captain Seaborn and his crew journeyed to the inner world, where they discovered many strange plants and animals and encountered a Utopian race. The explorers eventually emerged from the interior and returned to known waters. They became rich as traders, exchanging Symzonian goods for cacao and copra.

In 1826, James McBride wrote a book entitled *Symmes' Theory of*

Concentric Spheres. Meanwhile, Congress was trying to raise money to finance an expedition to the North Pole, largely to find out whether or not there were indeed openings at the northern verge.

Symmes traveled about the United States lecturing on his theory and raising funds from private donors in order to finance his proposed expedition to the north. The Russian government offered to outfit an expedition to the Pole if Symmes would meet the party at St. Petersburg, but the American did not have the fare for the oceanic crossing. He continued to range throughout the Midwest and New England, lecturing and raising money. His disciple, Jeremiah N. Reynolds, accompanied him during the last years of his life.

During his winter lecture tour of 1828, Symmes fell ill and returned to Hamilton, Ohio, where he died on May 29, 1829.

The ice pack eventually yielded to snow-covered tundra, spotted here and there with patches of moss and lichens. In a matter of a long while, he entered a land marked by ragged growths of tough grass and stunted, wind-twisted trees. There was small game here, mainly rodents of a kind he did not recognize. They appeared to have no fear of him. Killing them was easy.

Larger game animals began to show themselves as he put still more distance between the ice-bound sea and himself. He supplemented his diet of biscuits, salt pork, and rodents with venison. He walked unafraid, until he saw a distant pack of wolves chase down something which looked like an elk. But wolves and elk alike looked far too large, even from where he observed them, to be the ones he had known in Europe.

After that, he kept his firearms cleaned, loaded, and primed at all times, and he carried his cutlass like a cane. When he slept he slept ringed by fires. For all of his apprehensions, he had only one near-fatal encounter.

He had crested a hillock, on the trail of giant elk, when he saw several dozen enormous beasts grazing some distance away. The animals looked somewhat like pictures of elephants he had seen, but he recalled that elephants were not covered with shaggy reddish-brown hair, that their tusks were straighter and shorter than the impressively curved tusks of these woolly beasts.

The creature pondered the unlikelihood of his blunderbuss bringing down one of the beasts and decided to skirt the herd in the direction of a thicket.

He was almost in the shadow of the ugly trees when he heard a bellow and a crash. A massive, shaggy thing as large as a coach charged him, mowing down several small trees as it burst from the thicket. Frankenstein's man dropped his blunderbuss and cutlass and hurled himself to one side as his attacker thundered past, long head down, long horn out. The beast did not turn. It galloped straight past and disappeared over the hillock. In the thicket something coughed.

Retrieving his weapons, the creature decided to skirt the thicket.

Below the ice and snow, beyond the pine forests that were the domain of strange and yet familiar mammals, beyond glaciers and a ring of mountains were the swampy lowlands. The bottom of the bowl-shaped continent turned out to be a realm of mist and semigloom, of frequent warm rains and lush growth. Cinder cones and hot springs dotted the landscape.

It was a realm of giants, too, of beasts grander and of more appalling aspect than any which the creature had previously thought possible.

He saw swamp-dwelling monsters six times larger than the largest of the odd woolly elephants. Their broad black backs broke the surface of fetid pools like smooth islets, and their serpentine necks rose and fell rhythmically as they nosed through the bottom muck, scooping up masses of soft plants, then came up to let gravity drag the mouthfuls down those incredibly long throats.

He saw a hump-backed quadruped festooned with alternating rows of triangular plates of bone along its spine. Wicked-looking spikes were clustered near the tip of the thing's muscular tail. It munched ferns and placidly regarded him as he circled it, awed, curious, and properly respectful.

He saw small flying animals which, despite their wedge-shaped heads, reminded him irresistibly of bats. There were awkward birds with tooth-filled beaks here, insects as big as rats, horse-sized lizards with ribbed sails sprouting along their spines, dog-sized salamanders with glistening polychromatic skin and three eyes. He could not set his boot down without crushing some form of life underfoot. Parasites infested him, and it was only by bathing frequently in the hot springs that he could relieve himself of his unwanted guests. Clouds of large dragonflies and other, less readily named winged things exploded from the undergrowth constantly as he slogged across the marshy continental basin, driven by the compulsion to explore and establish the boundaries of *his* world. There was life everywhere in the lowlands.

And there was the striding horror that attacked him, a hissing, snapping reptile with a cavernous maw and sharklike teeth as long as his fingers. It was the lord of the realm. When it espied the wandering patchwork man, it roared out its authority and charged, uprooting saplings and small tree ferns with its huge hind feet.

The creature stood his ground and pointed the blunderbuss. Flint struck steel, the pan flared, and, with a boom and an echo which stilled the jungle for miles, the charge caught the predator full in its lowered face.

The reptile reared and shrieked as the viscid wreckage of its eyes dribbled from its jowls and dewlap. Lowering its head again, it charged blindly and blundered past its intended victim into the forest, where it was soon lost from sight, if not from hearing.

The creature quickly but carefully reloaded the blunderbuss and resumed his trek. A short while later, one of the blinded monster's lesser cousins, a man-sized biped with needlelike teeth and skeletal fingers, attacked. The blunderbuss blew it to pieces.

He got away from the twitching fragments as quickly as he could and watched from a distance as at least half a dozen medium-large bipeds and sail-backed lizards converged unerringly upon the spot. He turned his back on the ensuing free-for-all and, cradling the blunderbuss in his arms, looked longingly at the ice-topped mountains encircling the basin.

He had found the cold highlands infinitely more to his liking. He could not comprehend mountain-big reptiles who did nothing but eat. He was tired of being bitten and stung by insects, sick to death of mud and mist and the stench of decaying vegetation. He was, he frankly admitted to himself, not at all willing to cope with the basin's large predators on a moment-to-moment basis. The beasts of the highlands had been odd but recognizable, like parodies of the forms of that other world, the world of men.

He chuckled mirthlessly, and when he spoke, his voice sounded alien, out of place, amid the unceasing cacophony of the basin denizens' grunting, bellowing, shrilling, croaking, screeching, chittering.

What he said was, "We are all parodies here!"

It was extremely easy to become lost in the lowlands. The mists rose and fell in accordance with a logic all their own. He walked, keeping the peaks before him whenever he could see them, trusting in his sense of direction when he could not. Encounters with predatory reptiles came to seem commonplace. His blunderbuss was capable of eviscerating the lesser flesh-eating bipeds, and the cutlass was good for lopping off heads and limbs. He could outrun the darting but quickly winded sail-backed lizards. He made very wide detours around the prowling titans.

And he got lost.

He began to notice many holes in the ground as he blundered through the land of mist. He supposed that these might lead back to the world of men, but he did not care to find out. He knew where he wanted to be. He would be more than glad to let the basin's carnivorous lords have their murky realm, just as he was happy to leave men to their own world.

He finally came to a cave-pocked escarpment. Two great rivers emptied noisily into hollows at the base of the towering formation.

The basalt mass rose into the mists, higher than he could see. It was isolated from his yearned-for mountains. There was no point in attempting to scale it.

He ranged back and forth across the base of the escarpment for some time, from one river to the other. He ate the eggs of the flying reptiles who made their nests on the cliff face. He slept in the caves. He sulked.

At last, he began to explore the caves which honeycombed the escarpment.

IV

Jeremiah N. Reynolds stood at the aft rail of the *Annawan* as she slid from the harbor into the vast Atlantic, windy already in October, and cold. But the *Annawan* was bound for much colder waters: those of the Antarctic.

To starboard was the *Annawan*'s sister, the *Seraph*. Together, they would cross the Atlantic along its length and sail into the summer waters of the breaking ice pack. Reynolds hoped to find Symmes's southern polar opening. He was not to have much luck.

The *Annawan* and *Seraph* expedition got as far as 62° South—far south indeed, but Antarctica had already been penetrated as deeply as 63°45′ by Palmer in 1820. A landing party was sent out toward the Pole, or, as Reynolds hoped, toward the southern verge. Symmes had thought that the concavities toward the interior world would be located at or just above latitude 82°. Reynolds and his party had come so close, but bad weather forced them to wait, and then supplies ran low. The party was rescued just in time. The expedition headed northward before the Antarctic winter could close on them.

It was while Reynolds was with his ill-fated landing party that John Cleves Symmes died in Ohio, but Reynolds was not to learn this for nearly a year. Off the coast of Chile, the *Seraph*'s crew mutinied, put Reynolds and the officers ashore, and took off for a life of piracy.

Jeremiah N. Reynolds devoted the next three or four years to various South Seas expeditions, to whaling, to botanical and zoological studies in the Pacific. He continued to defend Symmes's theories and traveled about the United States to gain support, as Symmes had done before him, for a gigantic assault upon the interior world.

The creature went down.

He lost his way a second time and could only wander aimlessly through the caves, and he went down.

Into another world.

Into the world containing the great open sea, fed by the two great rivers that drained into hollows beneath the great escarpment. This second interior world was illuminated by electrical discharges and filled with constant thunder. There was a fringe of land populated by a few small animals and sparse, blighted plants.

The creature could not find his way back up to the basin. He had no choice but to pass through the world of the great open sea, into a third interior world.

There was a fourth world, a fifth, a sixth, and probably more which were not in line with his burrowing course. He moved constantly, eating what he could find, amazed and appalled by the extremes represented by the various worlds. He caught himself dreaming of the sun and moon, of days and night, But, if he ever felt the old stirrings of loneliness now, he did not admit as much to himself. Good or bad, he told himself, these worlds were his to claim if he chose to do so. He did not need companionship.

Even so, even so, he left his mark for others to see.

There was an ape in one of the interior worlds. It was the largest ape that had ever lived in or on the earth, and, though it was an outsider to all of the ape tribes in its cavernous habitat, it ruled over them like some human monarch. It came and went freely from band to band. What it wanted, it took. This ranged from simple backrubs to sexual favors. While it was at one of the females in a given band, the erstwhile dominant males would go off to bite mushroom stalks or shake trees or do some other displacement activity. Had they interfered, the great ape would have killed them.

Frankenstein's creature tripped over the ape as the latter slept in a tangle of dead plant stalks.

The patchwork man lost the third finger on his left hand.

The great ape lost its life, its hide, and some of its meat. A pack of lesser pongids came across the carcass after the victor had departed. They gave the place a wide berth thereafter, for they reasoned among themselves—dimly, of course—that no animal had done this. No animal could have skinned the great ape that way. Something new and more terrible stalked the world now, something too dangerous, too wild, for them to understand.

They heard from other tribes that the thing which had taken the skin carried it over its shoulders. The thing looked much like a hairless ape. It made the lightning flames with its hands and placed meat in the fire before eating it.

They would nervously look behind themselves for generations to come, fearing the new thing infinitely more than they had ever feared the great ape whose skin it had taken.

V

The Franklin expedition set out for the North Pole in the summer of 1844. Sir John Franklin took with him two ships, the *Erebus* and the

Terror. These were powerful, three-masted vessels with steam screws. They were made to conquer the Arctic.

The Franklin expedition was lost with all 129 members. The Arctic was the scene of a search for survivors for more than forty years afterward. During the course of these rescue missions, more of the north was mapped than had previously been dreamed possible.

In the 1860s, an American lived for several years among the Esquimaux to the north and west of Hudson Bay. He continually troubled them with questions, perhaps in the hope of learning something of the last days of the Franklin expedition.

He finally came to a village in which the storyteller, an old woman, told him of a number of white men who had pulled a boat across the ice. The American plied the storyteller with questions and soon realized that she was not talking about survivors of the Franklin expedition of fifteen years before. She was recounting the story of some survivors of one of Frobisher's voyages, three hundred years before, in search of the Northwest Passage.

The creature fought his way through other lands, and somewhere he passed by the middle of the earth and never knew it.

The next world he conquered, for human beings lived there.

VI

Some Navaho, all of the Hopi, and the Pueblo Indians of the American Southwest each have a legend about the Under-Earth People, their gods.

The legends all begin:

It was dark under the earth, and the people who lived there wanted to come up. So they came up through the holes in the ground, and they found this new world with the sun in the sky. They went back down and returned with their uncles and their cousins. Then, when they all got here, they made us.

In the center of the villages are *kivas*, underground structures in which religious ceremonies are held. In the center of the floor of each kiva is a well going far down out of sight. It is from the wells that the first men are said to have come to the outside world.

The memory of the Hopi may be better than that of the Esquimaux. The Hopi remember further back than Frobisher. If you ask them, they will tell of Esteban, the black slave of Cabeza de Vaca. They will tell of the corn circle they made when Coronado came, and of the fight in the clouds of the highest pueblo, and how many had to jump to their deaths when the village was set afire by the Spaniards.

But, mostly, the Hopi remember Esteban, the second outsider whom they ever saw. Esteban was tall and black. He had thick lips, and he loved to eat chili peppers, they will tell you.

That was 1538.

And in the center of each pueblo is a kiva, where the first men came from inside the earth.

He saw them first as they paddled animal-hide boats through the quietness of a calm lake where he drank. They were indistinct blobs of men, difficult to see in the perpetual twilight of this new interior world. But they were men.

The creature withdrew into the shadows beneath the grayish, soft-barked trees and watched thoughtfully as the men paddled past and vanished into the gloom.

Men. Men *here*. In *his* world. *How?* He weighed the blunderbuss in his hands. Could mere men have fought their way this far into the earth? Even with ships in which to cross the Arctic sea, even with firearms and warm clothing and the strength of numbers, could poor, weak human beings do what he had done? How could there be men here? How? Were they native to this subterranean world? He shrugged in his ape-hide cloak, and a frown creased his broad forehead.

I know what to expect of men. I will leave this place and go. . . .

Where? Back to the cavern of the apes? Back to the land of heat and molten rock? Back to the great open sea?

No, he thought, then said the word aloud: "No." The inner world belongs to me. All of it. I won't share it with men. He made a careful check of his firearms, shouldered the blunderbuss, and set out to find these human beings.

He tried to remain alert and wary as he walked, for there were dangers other than men in this world. Once, from a safe distance, he had seen a vaguely bearlike beast tearing at a carcass. Another time, he had watched as an obviously large flying reptile, larger by far than the delicate horrors he had observed in the basin, glided past, a black silhouette against the swirling gray murk overhead. Yet another time, he had happened upon the spoor of a four-footed animal whose claw-tipped paws left impressions six inches wide. Only a fool would not have been cautious here. But, still, his mind wandered.

I could attack these men, he told himself. I have weapons, and I have my great strength. And I cannot die by ordinary means. I would have the element of surprise in my favor, too. I could charge into their camp and wipe them out easily. And then, once again, I would be free to come and go as I please. If I do not kill them now, when the odds favor me, they'll find out about me eventually, and then I'll have to fight them anyway. They will not tolerate my existence once they know.

But . . . He stopped, perplexed by a sudden thought. But what if these men are different from those I knew before? Idiotic notion! Don't delude yourself. You know what men are like. They hate you on sight. You don't belong with men. You aren't a man, and you have no place among men. But what if . . . ?

He had eaten several times and slept twice when he finally located a squalid village built on the shore of a deep inlet. From a vantage point among the trees, the creature could see that the village consisted of perhaps two dozen lodges, crudely fashioned of poles and hides. He saw women smoking fish on racks and chewing animal skins to soften them while the men repaired their ungainly boats at the water's edge. Naked children ran among the lodges, chasing dogs and small piglike animals.

The men, he noted, were armed mainly with spears, though a very few also had what appeared to be iron swords of primitive design at their sides. He smiled grimly, envisioning the psychological impact his blunderbuss's discharge might have upon such poorly armed opponents.

He was thinking about tactics when a long, low craft hove into view at the mouth of the inlet and sped toward the beach. The men on the shore shouted and waved. The women put aside their skins, and the children raced a yelping horde of dogs to the water's edge. As soon as the canoe had been beached, its passengers—about ten men—were mobbed. The sounds were jubilant. The sounds were of welcome. In his place of hiding, Frankenstein's man unexpectedly found himself sick at heart.

Now, whispered a part of himself. Creep down now, and begin killing them while their attention is diverted.

He regarded the blunderbuss in his hands. At close range, it could probably kill two or three people at once, and possibly maim others. He felt the pistols digging into his skin where his belt held them against his abdomen. He closed his eyes and saw heads and bellies splitting open as he strode through the village swinging the cutlass in devastating arcs. He saw all of the villagers dead and mutilated on the ground before him. The palms of his hands started to itch. Kill them off.

A celebration was getting under way in the village. Eyes still closed, the creature listened to the thin, shrill laughter, to the bursts of song. Something twisted a knife in his heart, and he knew that he was helpless to do anything to these people.

He wanted to go down into the village. He wanted to be with these people. He wanted to be of them. He had not known that he was so painfully lonely. I still want people, he bleakly admitted to himself. Frankenstein made me a fool. I am a monster who wants friends. I want to have a place among men. It isn't right that I should be so alone.

Cold reason attempted to assert itself. *These people will kill you if they have the chance. They don't need you. They don't want you. Your own creator turned his back on you. Frankenstein put his curse on you. Frankenstein made you what you are, and that is all you can be. A monster. An abomination in the eyes of men. A—*

Frankenstein is dead.

His work lives on.

Frankenstein has no power over me now. I control my own life.

He was on his feet, walking into the village, and, within himself, there were still screams. *Will you throw your life away so easily? Will you—*

I want people. I want friends. I want what other men have.

Bearlike in his shaggy cloak of ape skin, he entered the village.

If Victor Frankenstein had made him a monster, the blunderbuss made him a god.

The men who had arrived in the long boat were obviously home from a fairly successful raiding trip. A quantity of goods had been heaped at the approximate center of the village. Nearby was a smaller pile of grislier trophies: severed heads, hands, feet, and genitals. The villagers had started drinking from earthen vessels, and many of them were already inebriated.

But one of the children spotted the creature as he stepped out of the shadows. A cry of alarm went up. The women and youngsters scattered. The men lurched forward with spears and swords at the ready.

The creature had stopped dead in his tracks as soon as the commotion began. Now he swung the blunderbuss up and around. He blew a patch of sod as big around as his head from the ground in front of the warriors, then watched, immensely gratified, as the spears and swords slipped, one and two at a time, from trembling hands.

"We are going to be friends," he said. And laughed with wicked delight. "Oh, Victor, were you but here!"

The creature had just had an inspired thought.

Before eighteen months had passed in the outer world, the creature was the leader of the largest war party ever seen in the interior. His firearms, coupled with his demonic appearance, guaranteed him godhood, for the barbarians who lived on the shores of the great lake were a deeply superstitious lot. They dared not incur his wrath. Their petty animosities were forgotten or at least ignored, as he conquered village after village, impressing the inhabitants into his service.

With three hundred warriors at his back, he finally left the lake and followed a lazily winding river until he came to the first of the city-states. It was called Karac in the harsh tongue of the innerworld, and it was almost magnificent after the rude villages of the lake dwellers. Karac sent an army of five hundred men to deal with the savages howling around the walls. The creature routed Karac's army, slept, and marched into the city.

Ipks fell next, then Kaerten, Sandten, Makar, until only Brasandokar, largest of the city-states, held against him by the might of its naval forces.

Against that city the creature took with him not only his mob of warriors but also the armies of his conquered city-states, ripe for revenge. They had been under the domination of Brasandokar for a long time, and they wanted its blood. Under the creature, they got it. Two thousand men attacked in the dim twilight, from the land, from the great river. They swarmed over the gates and walls, they swept the docks and quays. Flames lit the air as the raiders ran through the stone-paved streets. They plundered, and Frankenstein's man ravaged with them.

He stopped them only when he saw the woman.

Her name was Megan, and she was the second daughter of the War Leader of Brasandokar. The creature looked up from his pillaging and saw her in the window of a low tower toward which the invaders were sweeping. He stopped the rapine and went to the tower and escorted her down. He could not say why he did this. He knew that not even the woman whom his accursed creator had begun to fashion for him had moved him so much. Megan had stood in the tower window, her head turned to the side, listening to the battle raging below. Brave? Foolish?

It took him a moment after he found her in the tower to realize that she was blind. He placed her small, pale hand upon his arm and silently led her down the stairs. Together, they entered the courtyard, and his panting, blood-spattered men parted to let him pass, and all that he could think was, I have found my destiny.

Glow-lamps fashioned from luminous weed hung everywhere. The city-state of Brasandokar seemed laid out for a masked ball, but there were still embers to be found in the fire-gutted buildings, and the streets were still full of the stench of drying blood. Widows sat in doorways and sang songs of mourning. The sounds of their grief were punctuated by shouts and hammerings.

In the tower where he had first seen her, the creature sat across from Megan. She toyed restlessly with his gift, a black jewel taken from the coffers of Sandten.

I have never before seen such a beautiful woman, he thought. And then that dark and seething part of himself which had once urged the extermination of the villagers said, Fool, fool . . . He shook his head angrily. No. Not this time. Not a fool. Not a monster. A man. An emperor. A god.

A god in love for the first time in his life.

"Sir," said the Lady Megan, setting the jewel aside.

"Yes?"

"I ask you not to go on with this suit."

There was a mocking laugh inside his head. He shuddered and ground his teeth together. "Do I offend you?" he asked, and his voice sounded thick and strange.

"You are a conqueror, sir, and Brasandokar is yours to do with as you please. Your power is unlimited. A word from you, and your armies—"

"I am finished with this city, Lady Megan. I am finished with my armies. Brasandokar will show no sign of having been invaded within a matter of . . ." He trailed off helplessly. There were no weeks in a timeless world.

She nodded slightly. "I hear people working outside. But I hear wives crying for their husbands, too. My father is still abed with his wounds, and my brother-in-law is still dead. You are still a conqueror. I cannot consider your suit. Take me as is your right, but—"

"No."

Lady Megan turned her blind eyes in the direction of his voice. "You may be thought a weak king otherwise, sir."

He rose to his full height and began pacing back and forth across the room. Not much of an emperor after all, he thought bitterly. Certainly not much of a god.

"Why do you not take me?" Lady Megan asked quietly.

Because. Because. "Because I am in love with you. I don't want to take you against your will. Because I am very ugly."

Because I am a monster. Life without soul. A golem. A travesty. Thing. It. Creature. He stopped pacing and stood by the window from which she had listened to the sack of Brasandokar. At his orders his followers labored alongside the cizitens to repair the damage inflicted upon the city. His empire would bear few scars.

Ashes in my mouth. Shall I leave now? Take away their god, and these people will soon go back to their squabbles and raids. And where can a god go now? Yes. Downriver. To the great flat river beyond Brasandokar. Into new worlds. Into old hells.

He started when he felt her hands upon his back. He turned and looked down at her, and she reached up as far as she could to run her fingers across his face and neck.

"Yes," Lady Megan said. "You are very ugly. All scars and seams." She touched his hands. "You are mismatched. Mismatched also is your heart. You have the heart of a child in the body of a beast."

"Shall I leave you, Lady Megan?"

She backed away and went unerringly to her seat. "I do not love you."

"I know."

"But, perhaps, I could come to love you."

VII

Edgar Allan Poe's first published story, "MS Found in a Bottle," was about Symmes's Hole, although Poe did not know it at the time. It wasn't until 1836, while editing Arthur Gordon Pym's manuscript, that Poe came across one of Jeremiah N. Reynolds's speeches to the

U.S. House of Representatives urging them to outfit an expedition to the South Seas. In the same issue which carried the opening installment of Pym's memoirs, Poe had an article defending both Reynolds and the theories of the late Captain Symmes.

A year after the publication of *The Narrative of Arthur Gordon Pym,* Reynolds published his book on whaling in the South Pacific, memoirs of his days as expedition scientist aboard the *Annawan.* In this book, he gave the first complete accounts of the savage white whale, Mocha Dick, who terrorized whaling fleets for half a century.

Poe and Reynolds never met.

They were married in Brasandokar. The creature had to wear his wedding signet on his little finger, since his ring finger had been bitten off by the great ape. After the ceremony, he took his Lady Megan to the tallest tower in the city and gently turned her face up so that her dead eyes peered into the murk.

"There should be stars there," he told her, "and the moon. Lights in the air. A gift to you, were I able to make it so."

"It sounds as if it would be wonderful to see."

If only I could make it so.

Sex was difficult for them, owing to the way he had been made. They managed nonetheless, and Lady Megan bore him a stillborn son. She was heartbroken, but he did not blame her. He cursed himself, his creator, the whole uncaring universe; and his own words to Victor Frankenstein came back to haunt him: "I shall be with you on your wedding night."

Frankenstein would always be with him, though he was long since dead.

In what would have been, in the outer world, the third year of their love, Kaerten revolted. Within Brasandokar, there was dissent: his generals wanted him to launch an all-out attack and raze Kaerten to the ground.

He stood in his tower and spoke to them.

"You would be as I once was. You would kill and go on killing. Otherwise, all this land would have been empty with my rage. Do you understand? I would not have stopped until everyone was dead. Then my men and I would have turned on each other. I have come to know a stillness in my soul. It came when I stopped killing. We can do the same as a people."

Still they pressed for war. The armies were restless. An example needed to be made of Kaerten, lest the other cities regard his inaction as a mark of weakness. Already, conspiracies were being hatched in Karac, in Ipks, in Makar. Brasandokar itself was not without troublemakers.

"If you want so badly to kill," he finally snarled, "come to me. I'll give you all the killing you can stomach!"

Then he stomped away to his chambers.

Lady Megan took his giant hand in both of hers and kissed it. "They will learn," she said soothingly. "You'll show them. But, for now, they can't stand that you've taught yourself not to kill."

He remained pessimistic.

"War! War! War!"

He felt Megan shiver alongside him. He drew her closer and hugged her gently, protectively. Her head rested upon his shoulder, and her hand lay upon his pale, scarred chest.

In the courtyard below, the army continued to chant. "War! War! War! War!"

He had left his bed at one point to look down upon them. Many of his original followers were in the crowd. He had shaken his fist at them.

"I'm afraid now," Megan confessed. "I remember listening at my window in my father's house when you took the city. I was frightened then, but I was curious, too. I didn't quite know what to expect, even when you came in and escorted me down. Now I'm afraid, really afraid. These men were your friends."

"Hush. Try to sleep. I've sent word to my officers. I'll make them disperse the soldiers. Or, if worse comes to worst, I'll call on the units that are still loyal to me."

He kissed her forehead and lay back, trying to shut out the chant. Let the army level Kaerten. Let the empire shudder at my wrath. But leave me in peace.

The chant abruptly broke off into a bedlam of yells punctuated by the clang of swords. The creature rolled away from the Lady Megan and sprang to the window in time to see his personal guards go down before the mob. Shrieks and curses began to filter up from the floors below.

Lady Megan sat up in bed and said, quietly, "It's happened, hasn't it?"

He made no reply as he pulled on his breeches and cloak, then went to an ornately carved wooden cabinet.

"What are you going to do?" she asked when she heard the rattle of his cutlass in its scabbard. There was a rising note of terror in her voice now.

"They still fear the firearms," he growled as he began loading the pistol. There was just enough powder and shot to arm each of the weapons, including the blunderbuss. He tossed the keg and the tin box aside, thrust the pistols and a dagger into his belt, and cradled the blunberbuss in the crook of his arm. The sounds of battle were closer. Too close.

"Stay here until I return. Bolt—"

The door bulged inward as something heavy was slammed against it on the other side. Lady Megan screamed. The creature held the muzzle of the blunderbuss a foot away from the door and fired. Within the confines of his bedchamber, the roar of the discharge hurt his eardrums, but it failed to completely drown out cries of agony.

A spear poked through one of the several holes he had blown in the door. He grabbed it away and thrust the barrel of a pistol through the hole. A second spear snaked through another hole and jabbed him in the wrist. A third stabbed him shallowly in the left side. He roared with fury and emptied his pistols into the attackers. When he had run out of firearms, he stepped back, stooped, and picked up the spear he had previously snatched.

Then the door came off its hinges and fell into the room, followed by the heavy iron bench which had battered it down. The creature impaled the first man through the door. A sword nicked him across the forearm as he whipped the cutlass out of its scabbard, catching the swordsman in the sternum. Assassins spilled into the room, stumbling over the bench and the corpses, losing hands and arms and the tops of skulls, falling and creating greater obstacles for those behind. A blade drove through his side, snapping ribs. A spear slid under his sword arm, into his belly. Another sword went into his thigh. He howled. And swung the cutlass, grunting as something crunched beneath the blade. There was no end to them. They kept coming, more than he could count, faster than he could kill them. He swung the cutlass and missed, and someone stabbed him in the groin. He swung and missed again, and someone caught him on the cheek with the flat of a blade. He swung and missed and dropped the cutlass, and something hot and sharp pierced him high in the chest, and he went down. They had killed him for the time being.

Flanked by his bodyguards, he lumbered through the streets of one of his cities. The Lady Megan, second daughter of the War Leader of Brasandokar, rode at his side in a litter borne by four strong men who panted and grumbled as they tried to match his long stride. From time to time, he would glance at the woman and smile fleetingly. She did not love him, but she had told him that she might come to love him. That was enough for now, he kept telling himself.

His people, on the other hand, would probably never learn to love him. He had their respect and their obedience. But they could not love what they feared. Their children ran away at the sight of him, and the hubbub of the marketplace diminished noticeably as he passed through. Nevertheless, he enjoyed touring the city afoot, and he was happy that Lady Megan had agreed to accompany him. He paused occasionally to describe things to her. The luster of jewels from Sandten. The patterns in cloth woven in Ipks. The iridescent scales of strange fish hauled up from the river's bottom. He took her by the quays and told her of an incredible motley of vessels, skin-hulled canoes, sail-less galleys, freight barges, flatboats, and rafts.

And one rose on the docks to confront him, and that one was Victor Frankenstein, a pale corpse with opaque eyes, frostbitten cheeks, and ice beaded on the fur of his parka.

I am waiting for you to join me, Frankenstein said. His voice was the same one which had lurked in the creature's head, calling him fool, urging him to commit monstrous deeds.

I see you at last, the creature replied.

Frankenstein looked past him to Lady Megan. You will lose everything, he told the creature, not taking his eyes from the beautiful blind woman. Even as I lost everything. We two are joined at the soul, monster, and our destinies run parallel to each other.

You're dead, Frankenstein, and I am free. Go back to the grave.

Not alone, demon. Not alone. Frankeinstein laughed shrilly and, without taking a step, reached forward, his arm elongating night-marishly, his hand darting past the creature's head toward Lady Megan's face.

Yes! Alone! He tore Victor Frankenstein to pieces on the spot, then led Lady Megan back to ther tower.

The top of Megan's head came to his breastbone. She had long, fine hair of a light, almost silvery hue. Her flesh was pale, the color of subtly tinted porcelain. She had small, pointed breasts, a firm, delicately rounded belly, and slim hips. She was not much more than a girl when he married her, but she knew about sexual technique—there was no premium set on virginity in Brasandokar—and she did not mock him for his virtually total ignorance of such matters. She was the first woman he had ever seen naked.

And after their first clumsy copulation, Victor Frankenstein materialized at the foot of the bed to regard him scornfully. Megan seemed oblivious to the apparition.

Even in this respect you are a travesty, said Frankenstein, pointing at the creature's flaccid penis. You remove the beauty from all human functions.

The sin is with my maker.

The sin is that you have broken the promise you made at my deathbed. You live on, monster.

I have little choice in the matter. The creature rolled from the bed to drive the ghost away, but his knee buckled as soon as he put his weight on it, and he went sprawling on the floor. Pain exploded in his head, his torso, his limbs. He lay upon his face and gasped for breath. The earth closed in and smothered him.

It took him forever to claw his way up to the surface. The closer he got, the worse the pain became. The taste of blood was in his mouth. He moaned, raised his head, and dully looked around at the carnage. Nothing made any sense. A splintered door, knocked from its hinges. An iron bench. A litter of weapons. Blood everywhere. He dropped his head back into his hands and puzzled together the things he had seen.

Megan. Lady Megan. Where was the Lady Megan?

Horror began to gnaw within him. He dragged himself forward across the floor until he reached the corner of the bed, pushed himself up on hands and knees. Looked. Looked. Looked. Looked.

Until the sight of the bloody meat on the bed doubled him up on the floor. Until he saw only a huge swimming red ocean before him. Until he heard himself scream in animal pain and loss.

They heard him in the streets below, heard a sound like all of the demons in whom they half believed set loose at once, and some of them unsheathed swords and made as though to return to the tower in which they had slain the conqueror, his woman, his few supporters. They stopped when they saw him at his window.

"I'll show you war!" he howled, and a metal bench crashed into their midst. Cries and moans filled the courtyard. He disappeared from the window. Moments later, a heavy cabinet sailed through the window and shattered on the pavement. It was followed by chairs, a wardrobe, the bodies of warriors.

Then he came down with his cutlass in his hand, and they broke and ran in the face of his fury, casting away their weapons, trampling those who fell. He flew at their backs, his wounds forgotten. He drove them before him, killing all whom he could reach.

He raged the breadth of Brasandokar. He demolished booths and slaughtered penned animals in the marketplace. He overturned braziers and kicked over tables laden with goods. He smashed open casks of liquor and heaved a disemboweled soldier into a public well. He grabbed a torch and set fires everywhere, and the city's burning began to light the cavern sky for miles around. He dragged people from their homes and butchered them in the gutters.

At last, he staggered to the docks, dazed, exhausted, in shock. Lowering himself onto a raft, he cut it loose and entered the current. Behind him, Brasandokar blazed, and he was tiredly certain that he had destroyed it for all time. He shook his fist at the flames.

"No scars on the face of my empire!" he shouted, but there was no feeling of triumph in his heart. Megan was still dead. Megan was dead.

Screaming, crying, he fell to the bottom of the raft. It drifted toward the great flat river where men did not go.

The creature awoke just before the river entered a low, dark cavern.

How long he had drifted to this, he did not know, nor could he tell how long and how far he traveled through the cave. The river flowed smoothly. The raft sometimes nudged an invisible bank, sometimes floated aft-foremost along the water. The walls of the cavern sometimes glowed with the balefire of mushroom clusters, sometimes with a wonder of animals shining on the ceiling like moving stalactites.

More often than not, though, there was the darkness, impenetrable before and behind.

From one hell to another I go, he thought, dipping up a handful of water from the river. The water was cooler now, but were not underground streams always cool? Had he not lived in caves before, hunted by men, despised by all natural things, and had not the underground waters been cool then? He could hardly remember but decided that the matter was unimportant anyway.

What is important is that this river leads somewhere, away from the lands of men, where I can be free of their greeds, their fears. I am warm in my cloak. My wounds heal. I still have my cutlass. I am still free. He curled up on the raft and tried to ignore the first pangs of hunger. The top of Lady Megan's head comes to my breastbone. She has long, fine hair of a light, almost silvery hue. Her flesh is . . .

He eventually noticed the river's current slowing and its bed becoming wider and shallower. He peered into the gloom and, from the corner of his eye, saw the movement of light. He turned his head. The light vanished. The waters lay black around him.

The light reappeared in front of the raft. He stared into the water. There were small movements below: a series of dots undulated, darted away, returned. He put his hand into the water. The dots flashed away into the depths. He kept his hand in the water.

Presently, the dots snaked into sight again. He lunged, felt contact, and squeezed. Something struggled in his hand. He hauled his long arm up and over and smashed its heavy burden against the deck. The thing tried to flop away. He slammed it against the deck a second time, and it lay still. Its glow faded swiftly.

He looked around and saw more of the dots moving in the water. There was a noisy splash behind the raft. The lights winked out.

Soon the raft entered another lighted place. The light was from bracket mushrooms halfway up the walls of the cavern. The creature poled close to the bank and, as he passed, snapped off a piece of fungus. Some of its luminescence came off on his hand.

He poled back to the middle of the river, then knelt to examine the thing he had dragged from the water. It was a salamander, perhaps three feet long. Along its dorsal side was the row of phosphorescent dots that had given it over to death. The skull was flat and arrowheadlike.

He ate it happily. With his hunger quelled, he took more notice of his surroundings. The walls of the cavern were gradually curving away to the sides. The bracket mushrooms grew more thickly as he drifted farther, and the waters frequently parted where fish broke the surface. The river grew shallower, though there were places where his pole could not touch bottom. He let the weakening current carry him past these places. He wondered what might dwell at the bottoms of those deep places.

He was poling the raft forward at one point when he heard the sloshing of a large thing ahead. The water stretched flat and unbroken before him. Nothing moved below the surface. Something had frightened away the salamanders and fish. There was another splashing noise. He raised the pole like a harpoon and waited, but nothing happened. Gradually, the dotted lines reappeared in the water.

In a little while, the sides of the river slid out of sight. There was almost no current. Overhead were faint smudgy patches of light, arcing out forever before and to either side of him. Here, he thought, was the end of the great river. A vast subterranean lake. Perhaps it drained into other worlds. Perhaps it opened up to the exterior. He shrugged, willing to accept anything, and lay down on the deck to rest.

He was awakened by soft, dry rain pelting his face. He opened his eyes and, for the first time in many years, thought he saw the stars. But underground? And rain? In a cave?

The creature sat up and shook his head to clear it. This was a rain such as men had never seen. Tiny luminous things bounced off the deck of the raft. Fish swirled and turned in the water and flopped onto the deck in attempts to get the things.

He reached into his hair and drew out a pupal case, then looked up again, blinking against the cascade. From the dimly lit ceiling was falling a faintly glowing snow, and tiny winged shapes fluttered beneath the ceiling.

The creature rolled the pupal case in his hand. The worms were hatching, and the fish were going crazy with gluttony. He scooped up and killed the larger fish that flopped onto the raft, brushed piles of insect cases into the water, and left the rain of pupal cases as unexpectedly as he had entered it. As he started to eat one of his fish, he heard splashes of panic behind him as something large wallowed through the feeding schools. He could see nothing.

But, later, he was sure that he saw lazy white shapes swim past at a distance.

VIII

The dark-haired little man was dying, in delirium.

Two ward heelers had gotten him drunk that election day in Baltimore, Maryland, and taken him from place to place and had him vote under assumed names. It was common practice to gather up drunks and derelicts to swell the election rolls.

Neither of the two men knew who it was that they dragged, moaning and stumbling, between them. The man was Edgar Allan Poe, but Poe so far gone into the abyss that even the few friends he had would not have recognized him. Opium and alcohol had done their work on a mind already broken by a life of tragic accidents.

They left Poe in a doorway when the polls closed. He was found there by a policeman and taken to a small hospital. He burned with fever, he tossed in his bed, he mumbled. The hospital staff could not keep him quiet.

Early the next morning, Edgar Allan Poe stiffened and sat up in bed.

"Reynolds!" he said. "Reynolds!"

And lay back and died.

Have you no name, sir? the Lady Megan asked.

I have been called Demon, the creature replied. And worse, he added to himself. My soldiers call me the Bear, or the Ape, or the Shatterer.

But a *name*, she persisted, a real name. I cannot call you Bear or Ape.

Victor Frankenstein did not christen me.

Who was Vitter Frang—? She shook her head, unable to utter the odd syllables. Who was he? She? A friend, a god?

He told her. She looked horrified, then disappeared.

He lay on the raft and felt tears on his face. He had been crying in his sleep.

He heard their raucous cries long before he saw them. The high, worm-lit cavern ceiling sloped down before him, brightening ahead. The sounds grew louder as he drifted toward the sloping roof, and he glimpsed indistinct white shapes in the water from time to time.

He stripped the rope from one end of the pole and sharpened it with his dagger. It would make a crude but lethal spear.

White shapes awaited his coming. They screamed at him and began piling into the water on either side of his raft. They were as tall as men, with large beaks, webbed feet, and the merest vestiges of wings.

Behind them was a circle of brighter light. He bellowed his challenge at the things splashing around him and poled forward. They were too heavy to climb onto the raft, but they managed to slow his advance by massing in his path. He stabbed at them with the pole until he felt the raft crunch against the bottom. Then he leaped into the calf-deep water and sloshed toward the circle of light, swinging the pole like a club, beating a path through a cawing mass of white feathers and beaks. The light was a cool white circle ahead: the mouth of a tunnel. Eggs cracked under his feet, young birds squirmed and died as he passed.

One of the giant birds rose to block his path. A shock ran up his arm as he broke the improvised spear over its skull. Leaping over the carcass, he dashed toward the light, into the tunnel. Into a world of nightmare-polished stone of deepest ebony.

A wave of white horrors pursued him. He ran through corridors chiseled out of the rock by something far older than human beings. He glimpsed carvings on the walls and sculptures which no human hand had made, but he did not slow his feet until he had emerged into the light of a large central opening. Tunnels yawned to right and left. Above the opening was a grayish sheet of ice. It arched to form a dome. The floor of the chamber was littered with the rubble which must once have formed the roof.

The creature heard the vengeful white birds screeching at his back and plunged into one of the tunnels to find himself at the foot of a spiral ramp. It was cold there, and it had the smell of dust and antiquity. It had the smell of tumble-down churches he had seen, of dark mold and dead leaves on the forest floor. He shivered in spite of himself as he began to ascend.

He came out in a hall of glass cases and strode, wondering, past incomprehensible displays and strange machinery. Here were strangely curved hand tools, levers, and wheels in riotous profusion, brassy colors, iron, gold, silver. In one case was a curve-bladed cutting tool like a halberd-pike. The creature banged on the glass with the stump of his pole to no effect. He put his arms around the case and toppled it, and one pane broke with a peculiarly metallic crash.

It was followed by a dim, echoing sound. A gong was being struck somewhere.

The creature pulled the pike-ax from its mountings and examined it. It was made entirely of metal. It was curiously balanced. It had never been designed to be hefted by a being with hands. He was pleased with it, nonetheless, and when the first of the white birds burst into the hall and charged him, he sheared its head off with a casual swing. The gong continued to clang, and the sound was everywhere now. He ran. The decapitated bird thrashed on the floor. Its angry, squawking breathren flowed into the room.

It was in a second ascending tunnel that he first saw the beings that the clangor had summoned. Shapes out of nightmare; sight beyond reason. They were paralleling his course through the tunnel. There were few of them at first, but each time he came to a lighted connecting tunnel, there were more, blocking the paths so that he could not turn aside. Their voices piped and echoed through the halls and tunnels, and he saw tentacles, cilia, myriad dim eyes as he ran.

He turned a corner, and three of the things stood in his way, their pikes raised, their bodies hunched as low as barrel-thick cones could be lowered.

His halberd chopped into the nearest of the things just below its bunched eyestalks and cilia. The top of the cone described a green-bleeding arc and ricocheted off the wall, and the trunk toppled forward, the pike slipping from tentacles. Five sets of leathery wings, like the thin arms of a starfish, began to beat and buzz spasmodically.

The creature did not pause with that ax stroke but stepped closer and caught the second cone with his backswing. The blade stuck in the trunk. It swung its pike at his head.

He dived to the floor as the halberd whistled past, grabbed the base, and heaved. The thing went backward into the third cone. Both fell into a struggling heap. He threw himself upon them, seized bunches of eyestalks in his hands, and ripped them free. The cones' high, distressed pipings ceased when he opened the trunks with a pike. It was like splitting melons.

Then he was on his way once more, his feet slippery with green ichor. More pipings sounded ahead, commingled with the raucous voices of the great white birds.

Twice he turned aside when the cones blocked his way. The third time, he realized that they were desperate to keep him out of the interconnecting tunnels. Were they guarding something? Their ruler? Their children?

He was on another group before they knew it. Piping screams of warning came too late to save the first two guards in his path. He was through them before they recovered. The pipings behind him rose in pitch and volume as he raced through the tunnel. He saw movement ahead: there was a room at the end, and two cones were slashing the air with their pikes, warning him away. Behind them, a third cone seized a wheel with its tentacles and turned it. A panel began to slide from the ceiling and close off the room.

He yelled and leaped. The cones dropped their pikes and fled. He watched them go, then looked around at the chamber. At the far side of the room was a huge metal door, studded with bolts, leading . . . where? Into darker recesses? Hell? A weapons room, a nursery? The machinery in the room gave him no clue.

The creature abruptly noted a thick, sickening smell which overlay the place's scent of antiquity. The odor seemed to be coming through cracks in that gigantic door. He stepped nearer and heard a sloshing, rolling sound, as if a putrefying carcass of vast size were being dragged. He raised his halberd.

Two cones appeared to one side. They saw him approaching the door and started to hoot and honk, their tentacles and cilia beating, their wings buzzing, their eyestalks writhing, as though imploring him to stay away from the portal. Whatever lay beyond the door, they obviously did not want him to see it. He sought only escape. Perhaps it lay there.

One of the cones threw a flask at him but missed. There was a pop and an explosion as the vial hit the wall, and fire spread an orange tongue across the floor.

For an instant, the creature felt panic, then saw that the fire separated him from the two cones but not from a panel of levers and dials set in the wall next to the door. He seized levers and threw his weight upon them. Nothing happened. He tried other levers. Nothing. The helpless cones wailed with terror.

And the room began to shake.

The door through which he had come reopened. Past the snakes of flame, he saw masses of the cones pour in from the tunnel. One threw a small hatchet at him. It smashed dials near his hand. Far, far below, tremors rocked some gigantic machinery. The huge door groaned, the groan rising to a shriek of protesting metal, and slowly, ponderously, opened. It swung away on huge rollers and hinges, and a smell of death and rotting things filled the room.

The creature, huddled to one side, poised to leap through the flames, through the door to safety, stared in horror as something oozed from the opening. It flowed out forever, skirting the flames behind which he stood, moving faster and faster until it reached the hindmost of the cones now trying to escape through side tunnels. There was a greasy sucking sound, and a cone disappeared into the mass. Other cones screamed. Some fluttered their wings, rose from the floor, circled, banged into the walls like blinded canaries. They fell, and sticky edges of the gelatinous horror covered them.

There was an explosion somewhere below, and the floor sagged, cracked, yawned open. The oozing thing rippled and twisted, then slid into the fissure. As it fell from sight, another mass emerged through the door, skirted both fire and fissure, and squeezed its bulk into one of the tunnels. Screams and whistles ended in mid-note. A third horror came through, then a fourth, a fifth. The earth trembled, and a seam ran from the hole in the floor to the wall and upward. Dust sifted down from the ceiling.

The creature, driven back by the fire, saw the crack open. It reached the roof of the chamber and stopped, a forty-five-degree slash up the wall. He bounded forward, squeezed himself into the rent, and started making his way up, away from the flames, away from the shapeless nightmares from behind the great portal. The pike hampered him, but he refused to abandon it.

He climbed through the ceiling and found himself in another circular chamber. The place shook and rocked, a bedlam of moving things, shrieks, and groans in the air and in the earth. Smoke billowed up from below. Piping cones swept past him and paid him no attention. He ran with them, into tunnels that led upward. Always upward. He passed machinery noisily tearing itself to pieces. He passed the flightless white birds and did not bother to wonder whether they had invaded the tunnels en masse to find him or were merely some sort of livestock maintained by the cones.

Once, he saw a cone run past the mouth of a side tunnel. Pseudopodia shot out of the tunnel, snared it, and pulled it back out of sight. Once, the earth heaved and smashed him to the floor.

Upward. Always upward.

Upward, into the sunlight.

The creature followed some of the birds through a rent into a light-filled tunnel whose ceiling had fallen in. Clouds of ash fell all around. In the distance, a volcano sputtered and spat. There was a sound of continuous thunder in the air, and of masses of ice breaking up, of water turning to steam, of the earth sundering.

He screamed as the white hot ash touched him. The birds squawked as if on fire beneath the deadly rain. The snow steamed. He hurled himself down and rolled in the snow, trying to escape, and as he rolled, he heard a roar that drowned out everything else. His ears turned his eyes in the direction of the roar. He gasped.

A crack had opened in the world. It ran straight and true across the ice cap, and down the crack came a wall of water. Roiling and seething, the waters swept past with the speed of a tornado.

He thought of the spewing volcano and of the unbridled energy which would be released when the cold water met the magma. He picked himself up, the halberd still clasped in his fist, and slogged away. The ash swirled about his head, blinding him, and covered him from head to foot.

There was a sound like the universe breaking. A giant hand struck him from behind and threw him headlong into the steaming snows. Broken white birds tumbled past. He was rolled and carried by the sound. Steam, slivers of ice, and hot ash blew in a gale. New furies of cinders fell on him.

He picked himself up and ran. For the sea, for water, for relief from the falling hellish rain which scoured his skin. It lay ahead, a troubled line of gray against the white tongues of the land. The crack through which the cataract ran pointed like the finger of God to escape from the ash. He ran, covered with hot dust. He ran, and, overhead, birds appeared, disturbed from some ethereal rookery or nest, giving voice to harsh echoing cries as they made their way through the burning air. He ran, and the flightless birds from the caverns below fled with him. He ran, and the ghost of Victor Frankenstein uncoiled in his head, a serpent rising to sink its fangs into him.

Welcome to the Pit, Frankenstein said. And laughed. And the white ash continued to fall.

IX

Herman Melville published *Moby Dick; or, The White Whale* in 1851, to generally scathing notices. Less than 4,000 copies of the novel were sold during the next three and one-half decades; it was not until 1921 that the book began to receive plaudits, and by 1921, Melville had been dead for thirty years.

The cataract worked terror on the land through which it tore. The white banks gave way and caved in. Behind was a mountain-sized wall of steam, at the heart of which could be seen the reddish glow of the volcano's maw.

Looking like a snowman built by crazy children, the creature came at last to the coast. Two miles to his left was the mouth of the crack. Most of the waddling white birds had struck out for the torrent at once, drawn by the lure of cold water. There was no doubt in his mind that the current had swept them back toward the depths below.

It must close, he thought, watching as hillocks of ice bobbed and shattered in the cataract. It must close, or the sea will fill the interior of the earth. He imagined the dark waters rushing through the tunnels of the underground city, engorging the great river, backing up to flood Brasandokar, Sandten, to the cavern of the great apes, to the cavern of magma. Another explosion, another cataclysm. The world bursting open like a ripe fruit. Good riddance to it all.

He turned and began to run around the headland, away from the roaring river. After a time, its roar diminished noticeably. He sat down on the ice, exhausted, and stared out to sea, oblivious even to the cinders which continued to fall. He could go no farther.

Welcome to the Pit, Frankenstein said again.

Go away, he thought wearily, burning with the torment of the white ash.

This is where it ends, said Frankenstein. Feel the heat of the ash, demon. Listen to the thunder of water rushing to meet magma. Hell, demon. Hell. You are home.

The creature peered into the darkness gathering over the sea. On the waters was a canoe. It was being carried toward the cataract.

He clambered to his feet, picked up the halberd, and stumbled to the edge of the sea. Two figures could be seen in the canoe, one seated in the prow, the other aft. As the canoe drew nearer, he saw that the men looked haggard, listless, and did nothing to try to alter their course. The one in the prow seemed more active, turning his face to stare at the creature on the shore.

The canoe crunched nose-first against the shore, spun in the current, rocking and heaving as it cartwheeled through the choppy waters.

The creature swung the pike-ax high over his head, out over the water, and snagged a gunwale. The ice beneath his feet threatened to crumble as he strained backward, drawing the unwieldly vessel with him, fighting the craft's weight and momentum and the pull of the current. He growled inarticulately, feeling pain in his shoulder sockets, the corded muscles of his back and legs. Wounds in his thighs opened and seeped blood.

But the long canoe came out of the water, onto the shelf.

The man at the bow was too stunned to resist. He could only stare, wide-eyed. Then the creature grabbed him and hurled him onto the ice. The man landed heavily and did not move.

The man in the stern called out feebly, his voice barely more than a croak, as the creature dragged the canoe farther inland. Ice dust lifted as the shelf shuddered and cracked, letting chunks of itself swirl away toward the cataract.

When he had gained safety, the creature wrenched the halberd from the gunwale. The man in the stern waved an oar, weakly menacing. The pike clove him from pate to clavicle.

There was a dead black man in the bottom of the canoe. He pulled out both corpses, laid the halberd in the boat, and started dragging it across the ice cap, away from the cataract, away from the ash and heat. Victor Frankenstein appeared at his side, keeping pace.

You can still kill after all, Frankenstein noted with satisfaction.

Yes. I can still kill.

Where now, demon? Hell is not to your liking?

There isn't room here for both of us, Victor.

Birds passed overhead on their way out to sea. *Tekeli-li*, they screamed. *Tekeli-li.*

X

Late in June 1863, Professor Otto Lidenbrock of the University of Hamburg, arrived with his nephew Axel and a guide on the rim of the Icelandic volcano Sneffel. They descended into the crater, determined to reach the interior of the earth by way of a chimney on the crater floor.

A Frenchman edited Axel Lidenbrock's subsequent account of the expedition, and it appeared in *Hetzell's Young People's Magazine for Education and Recreation* in 1864.

In New England, seventeen-year-old Abner Perry read geology and paleontology texts and tinkered together curious little inventions in the attic of his father's house.

He sculled the canoe for a long time. Even this far out, he could not rest, for the current still nibbled gently at the boat. If he rested, he might lose ground. Somehow, he had to keep paddling until he outran the pull of the waterfall to the center of the earth.

The ragged curtain of fire and ash in the air had begun to settle.

The air seemed full of dust. The sun hung on the horizon like a sinking ship. It was dim and the color of blood.

He turned his gaze toward the prow and saw what he at first took to be a similarly blood-red island. A calved ice cake, perhaps, like the one which had borne him into the earth—how many years before?

Then the island sank from sight, to reemerge a hundred yards off the port gunwale. Twin corkscrews of foam rose and fell. The creature watched in awe.

The whale went under with hardly a ripple, as smoothly as a surgeon's blade slides under the skin. For a few seconds, the sea was flat, like glass, with only a few dimples as ash sifted onto it.

The whale broke the sea into a million liquid mirrors as it breached. It was huge, huge, and it stood in the air like a trout fighting to free itself of a hook. Its eyes were tiny in comparison with its bulk, and took in the world to each side: on this, the calm sea; on that, one of the hated boats. But the boat did not pursue. A single creature stood in it.

The whale was white, white as land ice, marbled with patches like sooted snow. Its redness came from the setting sun. To the monster, the patchwork being in the boat, it was the biggest thing in the universe. It stood apart from heaven and earth. In its side were innumerable harpoons and lances, tangled lines, all covered with barnacles, unlike the whale's smooth white skin. It hung in the air like a heavy cloud, then slowly, so slowly, went back into the ocean.

The creature's heart leaped with it, and he danced in the stern of the boat.

"Free!" he yelled as the whale breached a second time, farther away. "Free! Free! Free!"

He watched, smiling, until the great whale was lost to sight. It seemed to him that God had passed through this part of the world and found it good.

A long twilight began as the sun slipped behind the horizon. The creature sculled with the sweeps, ignoring the Antarctic cold which was finally displacing the heat of the recent cataclysm. He was bound northward for the lands of men.

The stars came out slowly. Above, the twin smudges of the Magellanic Clouds shone dimly. They had lighted the way for sailors for three hundred years. They would light his.

He rowed happily, willing, for the moment, to accept whatever lay ahead. And Victor Frankenstein sat in the prow, frowning. And could say nothing.

Not enough science fiction is concerned with what it means *to be human, with the subtle properties of mind and heart and spirit that distinguish us from the intricate clockwork mechanisms around us. A notable exception is the following fine study of empathy, sacrifice, loathing, and love by Michael Bishop, perhaps the best of all the new SF writers, author of* Stolen Faces *(Harper & Row),* A Little Knowledge *(Putnam),* Beneath Shattered Moons *(DAW), and* A Funeral for the Eyes of Fire *(Ballantine).*

MICHAEL BISHOP

The House of Compassionate Sharers

And he was there, and it was not far enough, not yet, for the earth hung overhead like a rotten fruit, blue with mold, crawling, wrinkling, purulent and alive—Damon Knight, "Masks"

In the Port Iranani Galenshall I awoke in the room Diderits liked to call the "Black Pavilion." I was an engine, a system, a series of myoelectric and neuromechanical components, and The Accident responsible for this clean and enamel-hard enfleshing lay two full D-years in the past. This morning was an anniversary of sorts. I ought by now to have adjusted. And I had. I had reached an absolute accommodation with myself. Narcissistic, one could say. And that was the trouble.

"Dorian? Dorian Lorca?"

The voice belonged to KommGalen Diderits, wet and breathy even though it came from a small metal speaker to which the sable curtains of the dome were attached. I stared up into the ring of curtains.

"Dorian, it's Target Day. Will you answer me, please?"

"I'm here, my galen. Where else would I be?" I stood up, listening to the almost musical ratcheting that I make when I move, a sound like the concatenation of tiny bells or the purring of a stope-car. The sound is conveyed through the tempered porcelain plates, metal vertebrae, and osteoid polymers holding me together, and no one else can hear it.

"Rumer's here, Dorian. Are you ready for her to come in?"

"If I agreed, I suppose I'm ready."

"Dammit, Dorian, don't feel you're bound by *honor* to see her! We've spent the last several brace-weeks preparing you for a resumption of normal human contact." Diderits began to enumerate: "Chameleodrene treatments . . . hologramic substitution . . . stimulus-response therapy. . . . You ought to want Rumer to come in to you, Dorian."

Ought. My brain was—is—my own, but the body Diderits and the other kommgalens had given me had "instincts" and "tropisms" peculiar to itself, ones whose templates had a mechanical rather than a biological origin. What I ought to feel, in human terms, and what I in fact felt, as the inhabitant of a total prosthesis, were as dissimilar as blood and oil.

"Do you *want* her to come in, Dorian?"

"All right. I do." And I did. After all the biochemical and psychiatric preparation, I wanted to see what my reaction would be. Still sluggish from some drug, I had no exact idea how Rumer's presence would affect me.

At a parting of the pavilion's draperies, only two or three meters from my couch, appeared Rumer Montieth, my wife. Her garment of overlapping latex scales, glossy black in color, was a hauberk designed to reveal only her hands, face, and hair. The way Rumer was dressed was one of Diderits's deceits, or "preparations": I was supposed to see my wife as little different from myself, a creature as intricately assembled and synapsed as the engine I had become. But the hands, the face, the hair—nothing could disguise their unaugmented humanity, and revulsion swept over me like a tide.

"Dorian?" And her voice—wet, breath-driven, expelled between parted lips.

I turned away from her, "No," I told the speaker overhead. "It hasn't worked, my galen. Every part of me cries out against this."

Diderits said nothing. Was he still out there? Or was he trying to give Rumer and me a privacy I didn't want?

"Disassemble me," I urged him. "Link me to the control systems of a delta-state vessel and let me go out from Diroste for good. You don't want a zombot among you, Diderits—an unhappy anproz. Damn you all, you're torturing me!"

"And you, us," Rumer said quietly. I faced her. "As you're very aware, Dorian, as you're very aware. . . . Take my hand."

"No." I didn't shrink away; I merely refused.

"Here. Take it."

Fighting my own disgust, I seized her hand, twisted it over, showed her its back. "Look."

"I *see* it, Dor." I was hurting her.

"Surfaces, that's all you see. Look at this growth, this wen." I pinched the growth. "Do you see that, Rumer? That's sebum, fatty matter. And the smell, if only you could—"

She drew back, and I tried to quell a mental nausea almost as profound as my regret. . . . To go out from Diroste seemed to be the only answer. Around me I wanted machinery—thrumming, inorganic machinery—and the sterile, actinic emptiness of outer space. I wanted to be the probeship *Dorian Lorca*. It hardly seemed a step down from my position as "prince consort" to the Governor of Diroste.

"Let me out," Rumer commanded the head of the Port Iranani Galenshall, and Diderits released her from the "Black Pavilion."

Then I was alone again in one of the few private chambers of a surgical complex given over to adapting Civi Korps personnel to our leprotic little planet's fume-filled mine shafts. The Galenshall was also devoted to patching up these civkis after their implanted respirators had atrophied, almost beyond saving, the muscles of their chests and lungs.

Including administrative personnel, Kommfleet officials, and the Civi Korps laborers in the mines, in the year I'm writing of there were over a half million people on Diroste. Diderits was responsible for the health of all of them not assigned to the outlying territories. Had I not been the husband of Diroste's first Governor, he might well have let me die along with the seventeen "expendables" on tour with me in the Fetneh District when the roof of the Haft Paykar diggings fell in on us. Rumer, however, made Diderits's duty clear to him, and I am as I am because the resources were at hand in Port Iranani, and Diderits saw fit to obey his Governor.

Alone in my pavilion, I lifted a hand to my face and heard a caroling of minute, copper bells. . . .

Nearly a month later I observed Rumer, Diderits, and a stranger by closed-circuit television as they sat in one of the Galenshall's wide conference rooms. The stranger was a woman, bald but for a scalp-lock, who wore gold silk pantaloons that gave her the appearance of a clown, and a corrugated green jacket that somehow reversed this impression. Even on my monitor I could see the thick sunlight pouring into their room.

"This is Wardress Kefa," Rumer informed me.

I greeted her through a microphone and tested the cosmetic work of Diderits's associates by trying to smile for her.

"She's from Earth, Dor, and she's here because KommGalen Diderits and I asked her to come."

"Forty-six lights," I murmured, probably inaudibly. I was touched and angry at the same time. To be constantly the focus of your friends' attentions, especially when they have more urgent matters to see to, can lead to either a corrosive cynicism or a humility just as crippling.

"We want you to go back with her on *Nizami*," Diderits said, "when it leaves Port Iranani tomorrow night."

"Why?"

"Wardress Kefa came all this way," Rumer responded, "because we wanted to talk to her. As a final stage in your therapy she's convinced us that you ought to visit her . . . her establishment there. And if this fails, Dorian, I give you up; if that's what you want, I relinquish you."

Today Rumer was wearing a yellow sarong, a tasseled gold shawl, and a nun's hood of yellow and orange stripes. When she spoke she averted her eyes from the conference room's monitor and looked out its high windows instead. At a distance, I could appreciate the spare aesthetics of her profile.

"Establishment? What sort of establishment?" I studied the tiny wardress, but her appearance volunteered nothing.

"The House of Compassionate Sharers," Diderits began. "It's located in Earth's western hemisphere, on the North American continent, nearly two hundred kilometers southwest of the gutted Urban Nucleus of Denver. It can be reached from Manitou Port by 'rail."

"Good. I shouldn't have any trouble finding it. But what is it, this mysterious house?"

Wardress Kefa spoke for the first time: "I would prefer that you learn its nature and its purposes from me, Mr. Lorca, when we have arrived safely under its several roofs."

"Is it a brothel?" This question fell among my three interlocutors like a heavy stone.

"No," Rumer said after a careful five-count. "It's a unique sort of clinic for the treatment of unique disorders." She glanced at the wardress, concerned that she had revealed too much.

"Some would call it a brothel," Wardress Kefa admitted huskily. "Earth has become a haven of misfits and opportunists, a crossroads of Glatik Komm influence and trade. The House, I must confess, wouldn't prosper if it catered only to those who suffer from rare dissociations of feeling. Therefore a few—a very few—of those who come to us are kommthors rich in power and exacting in their tastes. But these people are exceptions, Governor Montieth, KommGalen Diderits; they represent an uneasy compromise we must make in order to carry out the work for which the House was originally envisioned and built."

A moment later Rumer announced, "You're going, Dor. You're going tomorrow night. Diderits and I, well, we'll see you in three E-months." That said, she gathered in her cloak with both hands and rearranged it on her shoulders. Then she left the room.

"Goodbye, Dorian," Diderits said, standing.

Wardress Kefa fixed upon the camera conveying her picture to me a keen glance made more disconcerting by her small, naked face. "Tomorrow, then."

"Tomorrow," I agreed. I watched my monitor as the galen and the curious-looking wardress exited the conference room together. In the room's high windows Diroste's sun sang a cappella in the lemon sky.

They gave me a private berth on *Nizami*. I used my "nights," since sleep no longer meant anything to me, to prowl through those nacelles of shipboard machinery not forbidden to passengers. Although I wasn't permitted in the forward command module, I did have access to the computer-ringed observation turret and two or three corridors of auxiliary equipment necessary to the maintenance of a continuous probe-field. In these places I secreted myself and thought seriously about the likelihood of an encephalic/neural linkage with one of Kommfleet's interstellar frigates.

My body was a trial. Diderits had long ago informed me that it—that *I*—was still "sexually viable," but this was something I hadn't yet put to the test, nor did I wish to. Tyrannized by morbidly vivid images of human viscera, human excreta, human decay, I had been rebuilt of metal, porcelain, and plastic *as if* from the very substances—skin, bone, hair, cartilage—that these inorganic materials derided. I was a contradiction, a quasi-immortal masquerading as one of the ephemera who had saved me from their own short-lived lot. Still another paradox was the fact that my aversion to the organic was itself a human (i.e., an organic) emotion. That was why I so fervently wanted out. For over a year and a half on Diroste I had hoped that Rumer and the others would see their mistake and exile me, not only from themselves, but from the body that was a deadly daily reminder of my total estrangement.

But Rumer was adamant in her love, and I had been a prisoner in the Port Iranani Galenshall—with but one chilling respite—ever since the Haft Paykar explosion and cave-in. Now I was being given into the hands of a new wardress, and as I sat amid the enamel-encased engines of *Nizami* I couldn't help wondering what sort of prison the House of Compassionate Sharers must be. . . .

Among the passengers of a monorail car bound outward from Manitou Port, Wardress Kefa in the window seat beside me, I sat tense and stiff. Anthrophobia. Lorca, I told myself repeatedly, you must exercise self-control. Amazingly, I did. From Manitou Port we rode the sleek underslung bullet of our car through rugged, sparsely populated terrain toward Wolf Run Summit, and I controlled myself.

"You've never been 'home' before?" Wardress Kefa asked me.

"No. Earth isn't home. I was born on GK-world Dai-Han, Wardress. And as a young man I was sent as an administrative colonist to Diroste, where—"

"Where you were born again," Wardress Kefa interrupted. "Nevertheless, this is where we began."

The shadows of the mountains slid across the wraparound glass of our car, and the imposing white pylons of the monorail system flashed past us like the legs of giants. Yes. Like huge, naked cyborgs hiding among the mountains' aspens and pines.

"Where I met Rumer Montieth, I was going to say; where I eventually got married and settled down to the life of a bureaucrat who happens to be married to power. You anticipate me, Wardress." I didn't add that now Earth and Diroste were equally alien to me, that the probeship *Nizami* had bid fair to assume first place among my loyalties.

A 'rail from Wolf Run came sweeping past us toward Manitou Port. The sight pleased me; the vibratory hum of the passing 'rail lingered sympathetically in my hearing, and I refused to talk, even though the wardress clearly wanted to draw me out about my former life. I was surrounded and beset. Surely this woman had all she needed to know of my past from Diderits and my wife. My annoyance grew.

"You're very silent, Mr. Lorca."

"I have no innate hatred of silences."

"Nor do I, Mr. Lorca—unless they're empty ones."

Hands in lap, humming bioelectrically, inaudibly, I looked at my tiny guardian with disdain. "There are some," I told her, "who are unable to engage in a silence without stripping it of its unspoken cargo of significance."

To my surprise the woman laughed heartily. "That certainly isn't true of you, is it?" Then, a wry expression playing on her lips, she shifted her gaze to the hurtling countryside and said nothing else until it came time to disembark at Wolf Run Summit.

Wolf Run was a resort frequented principally by Kommfleet officers and members of the administrative hierarchy stationed in Port Manitou. Civi Korps personnel had built quaint, gingerbread châteaus among the trees and engineered two of the slopes above the hamlet for year-round skiing. "Many of these people," Wardress Kefa explained, indicating a crowd of men and women beneath the deck of Wolf Run's main lodge, "work inside Shays Mountain, near the light-probe port, in facilities built originally for satellite tracking and missile-launch detection. Now they monitor the display boards for Kommfleet orbiters and shuttles; they program the cruising and descent lanes of these vehicles. Others are demographic and wildlife managers, bent on resettling Earth as efficiently as it may be done. Tedious work, Mr. Lorca. They come here to play." We passed below the lodge on a path of unglazed vitrifoam. Two or three of Wolf Run's bundled visitors stared at me, presumably because I was in my tunic sleeves and conspicuously undaunted by the spring cold. Or maybe their stares were for my guardian. . . .

"How many of these people are customers of yours, Wardress?"

"That isn't something I can divulge." But she glanced back over her shoulder as if she had recognized someone.

"What do they find at your establishment they can't find in Manitou Port?"

"I don't know, Mr. Lorca; I'm not a mind reader."

To reach the House of Compassionate Sharers from Wolf Run, we had to go on foot down a narrow path worked reverently into the flank of the mountain. It was very nearly a two-hour hike. I couldn't believe the distance or Wardress Kefa's stamina. Swinging her arms, jolting herself on stiff legs, she went down the mountain with a will. And in all the way we walked we met no other hikers.

At last we reached a clearing giving us an open view of a steep, pine-peopled glen: a grotto that fell away beneath us and led our eyes to an expanse of smooth white sky. But the wardress pointed directly down into the foliage.

"There," she said. "The House of Compassionate Sharers."

I saw nothing but afternoon sunlight on the aspens, boulders huddled in the mulch cover and swaying tunnels among the trees. Squinting, I finally made out a geodesic structure built from the very materials of the woods. Like an upland sleight, a wavering mirage, the House slipped in and out of my vision, blending, emerging, melting again. It was a series of irregular domes as hard to hold as water vapor—but after several redwinged blackbirds flew noisily across the plane of its highest turret, the House remained for me in stark relief; it had shed its invisibility.

"It's more noticeable," Wardress Kefa said, "when its external shutters have been cranked aside. Then the House sparkles like a dragon's eye. The windows are stained glass."

"I'd like to see that. Now it appears camouflaged."

"That's deliberate, Mr. Lorca. Come."

When we were all the way down, I could see of what colossal size the House really was: it reared up through the pine needles and displayed its interlocking polygons to the sky. Strange to think that no one in a passing helicraft was ever likely to catch sight of it. . . .

Wardress Kefa led me up a series of plank stairs, spoke once at the door, and introduced me into an antechamber so clean and military that I thought "barracks" rather than "bawdyhouse." The ceiling and walls were honeycombed, and the natural flooring was redolent of the outdoors. My guardian disappeared, returned without her coat, and escorted me into a much smaller room shaped like a tapered well. By means of a wooden hand-crank she opened the shutters, and varicolored light filtered in upon us through the room's slant-set windows. On elevated cushions that snapped and rustled each time we moved, we sat facing each other.

"What now?" I asked the wardress.

"Just listen. The Sharers have come to the House of their own volition, Mr. Lorca; most lived and worked on extrakomm worlds toward Glaktik Center before being approached for duty here. The ones who are here accepted the invitation. They came to offer their presence to people very like yourself."

"Me? Are they misconceived machines?"

"I'm not going to answer that. Let me just say that the variety of services the Sharers offer is surprisingly wide. As I've told you, for some visitants the Sharers are simply a convenient means of satisfying exotically aberrant tastes. For others they're a way back to the larger community. We take whoever comes to us for help, Mr. Lorca, in order that the Sharers not remain idle nor the House vacant."

"So long as whoever comes is wealthy and influential?"

She paused before speaking. "That's true enough. But the matter's out of my hands, Mr. Lorca. I'm an employee of Glaktik Komm, chosen for my empathetic abilities. I don't make policy. I don't own title to the House."

"But you *are* its madam. Its 'wardress,' rather."

"True. For the last twenty-two years. I'm the first and only wardress to have served here, Mr. Lorca, and I love the Sharers. I love their devotion to the fragile mentalities who visit them. Even so, despite the time I've lived among them, I still don't pretend to understand the source of their transcendent concern. That's what I wanted to tell you."

"You think me a 'fragile mentality'?"

"I'm sorry—but you're here, Mr. Lorca, and you certainly aren't fragile of *limb*, are you?" The wardress laughed. "I also wanted to ask you to . . . well, to restrain your crueler impulses when the treatment itself begins."

I stood up and moved away from the little woman. How had I borne her presence for as long as I had?"

"Please don't take my request amiss. It isn't *specifically* personal, Mr. Lorca. I make it of everyone who comes to the House of Compassionate Sharers. Restraint is an unwritten corollary of the only three rules we have here. Will you hear them?"

I made a noise of compliance.

"First, that you do not leave the session chamber once you've entered it. Second, that you come forth immediately upon my summoning you. . . ."

"And third?"

"That you do not kill the Sharer."

All the myriad disgusts I had been suppressing for seven or eight hours were now perched atop the ladder of my patience, and, rung by painful rung, I had to step them back down. Must a rule be made to prevent a visitant from murdering the partner he had bought? Incredible. The wardress herself was just perceptibly sweating, and I noticed too how grotesquely distended her earlobes were.

"Is there a room in this establishment for a wealthy and influential patron? A private room?"

"Of course," she said. "I'll show you."

It had a full-length mirror. I undressed and stood in front of it. Only during my first "period of adjustment" on Diroste had I spent much time looking at what I had become. Later, back in the Port Iranani Galenshall, Diderits had denied me any sort of reflective surface at all—looking glasses, darkened windows, even metal spoons.

The waxen perfection of my features ridiculed the ones another Dorian Lorca had possessed before the Haft Paykar incident. Cosmetic mockery. Faintly corpselike, speciously paradigmatic, I was both more than I was supposed to be and less.

In Wardress Kefa's House the less seemed preeminent. I ran a finger down the inside of my right arm, scrutinizing the track of one of the intubated veins through which circulated a serum that Diderits called hematocybin: an efficient, "low-maintenance" blood substitute, combative of both fatigue and infection, which requires changing only once every six D-months. With a proper supply of hematocybin and a plastic recirculator I can do the job myself, standing up. That night, however, the ridge of my vein, mirrored only an arm's length away, was more horror than miracle. I stepped away from the looking glass and closed my eyes.

Later that evening Wardress Kefa came to me with a candle and a brocaded dressing gown. She made me put on the gown in front of her, and I complied. Then, the robe's rich and symbolic embroidery on my back, I followed her out of my first-floor chamber to a rustic stairwell seemingly connective to all the rooms in the House.

The dome contained countless smaller domes and five or six primitive staircases, at least. Not a single other person was about. Lit flickeringly by Wardress Kefa's taper as we climbed one of these sets of stairs, the House's mid-interior put me in mind of an Escheresque drawing in which verticals and horizontals become hopelessly confused, and a figure who from one perspective seems to be going up a series of steps, from another seems to be coming down them. Presently the wardress and I stood on a landing above this topsy-turvy well of stairs (though there were still more stairs above us), and, looking down, I experienced an unsettling reversal of perspectives. Vertigo. Why hadn't Diderits, against so human a susceptibility, implanted tiny gyrostabilizers in my head? I clutched a railing and held on.

"You can't fall," Wardress Kefa told me. "It's an illusion. A whim of the architects."

"Is it an illusion behind this door?"

"Oh, the Sharer's real enough, Mr. Lorca. Please. Go on in." She touched my face and left me, taking her candle with her.

After hesitating a moment I went through the door to my assignation, and the door locked of itself. I stood with my hand on the butterfly shape of the knob and felt the night working in me and the room. The only light came from the stove-bed on the opposite wall, for the fitted polygons overhead were still blanked out by their shutters and no candles shone here. Instead, reddish embers glowed behind an isinglass window beneath the stove-bed, strewn with quilts, on which my Sharer awaited me.

Outside, the wind played harp music in the trees.

I was trembling rhythmically, as when Rumer had come to me in the "Black Pavilion." Even though my eyes adjusted rapidly, automatically, to the dark, it was still difficult to see. Temporizing, I surveyed the dome. In its high central vault hung a cage in which, disturbed by my entrance, a bird hopped skittishly about. The cage swayed on its tether.

Go on, I told myself.

I advanced toward the dais and leaned over the unmoving Sharer who lay there. With a hand on either side of the creature's head, I braced myself. The figure beneath me moved, moved weakly, and I drew back. But because the Sharer didn't stir again, I reassumed my previous stance: the posture of either a lover or a man called upon to identify a disfigured corpse. But identification was impossible; the embers under the bed gave too feeble a sheen. In the chamber's darkness even a lover's kiss would have fallen clumsily. . . .

"I'm going to touch you," I said. "Will you let me do that?"

The Sharer lay still.

Then, willing all of my senses into the cushion of synthetic flesh at my forefinger's tip, I touched the Sharer's face.

Hard, and smooth, and cool.

I moved my finger from side to side; and the hardness, smoothness, coolness continued to flow into my pressuring fingertip. It was like touching the pate of a death's-head, the cranial cap of a human being: bone rather than metal. My finger distinguished between these two possibilities, deciding on bone; and, half panicked, I concluded that I had traced an arc on the skull of an intelligent being who wore his every bone on the outside, like an armor of calcium. Could that be? If so, how could this organism—this entity, this *thing*—express compassion?

I lifted my finger away from the Sharer. Its tip hummed with a pressure now relieved and emanated a faint warmth.

A death's-head come to life. . . .

Maybe I laughed. In any case, I pulled myself onto the platform and straddled the Sharer. I kept my eyes closed, though not tightly. It didn't seem that I was straddling a skeleton.

"Sharer," I whispered. "Sharer, I don't know you yet."

Gently, I let my thumbs find the creature's eyes, the sockets in the smooth exoskeleton, and both thumbs returned to me a hardness and a coldness that were unquestionably metallic in origin. Moreover, the Sharer didn't flinch—even though I'd anticipated that probing his eyes, no matter how gently, would provoke at least an involuntary pulling away. Instead, the Sharer lay still and tractable under my hands.

And why not? I thought. *Your eyes are nothing but two pieces of sophisticated optical machinery. . . .*

It was true. Two artificial, light-sensing, image-integrating units gazed up at me from the sockets near which my thumbs probed, and

I realized that even in this darkness my Sharer, its vision mechanically augmented beyond my own, could *see* my blind face staring down in a futile attempt to create an image out of the information my hands had supplied me. I opened my eyes and held them open. I could see only shadows, but my thumbs could *feel* the cold metal rings that held the Sharer's photosensitive units so firmly in its skull.

"An animatronic construct," I said, rocking back on my heels. "A soulless robot. Move your head if I'm right."

The Sharer continued motionless.

"All right. You're a sentient creature whose eyes have been replaced with an artificial system. What about that? Lord, are we brothers then?"

I had a sudden hunch that the Sharer was very old, a senescent being owing its life to prosthetics, transplants, and imitative organs of laminated silicone. Its life, I was certain, had been *extended* by these contrivances, not saved. I asked the Sharer about my feeling, and very, very slowly it moved the helmetlike skull housing its artificial eyes and its aged, compassionate mind. Uncharitably, I then believed myself the victim of a deception, whether the Sharer's or Wardress Kefa's I couldn't say. Here, after all, was a creature who had chosen to prolong its organic condition rather than to escape it, and it had willingly made use of the same materials and methods Diderits had brought into play to save me.

"You might have died," I told it. "Go too far, Sharer—go too far with these contrivances and you may forfeit suicide as an option."

Then, leaning forward again, saying, "I'm still not through, I still don't know you," I let my hands come down the Sharer's bony face to its throat. Here a shield of cartilage graded upward into its jaw and downward into the plastically silken skin covering the remainder of its body, internalizing all but the defiantly naked skull of the Sharer's skeletal structure. A death's-head with the body of a man. . . .

That was all I could take. I rose from the stove-bed and, cinching my dressing gown tightly about my waist, crossed to the other side of the chamber. There was no furniture in the room but the stove-bed (if that qualified), and I had to content myself with sitting in a lotus position on the floor. I sat that way all night, staving off dreams.

Diderits had said that I needed to dream. If I didn't dream, he warned, I'd be risking hallucinations and eventual madness; in the Port Iranani Galenshall he'd seen to it that drugs were administered to me every two days and my sleep period monitored by an ARC machine and a team of electroencephalographers. But my dreams were almost always nightmares, descents into klieg-lit charnel houses, and I infinitely preferred the risk of going psychotic. There was always the chance someone would take pity and disassemble me, piece by loving piece. Besides, I had lasted two E-weeks now on nothing but grudging catnaps, and so far I still had gray matter upstairs instead of scrambled eggs. . . .

I crossed my fingers.

A long time after I'd sat down, Wardress Kefa threw open the door. It was morning. I could tell because the newly canted shutters outside our room admitted a singular roaring of light. The entire chamber was illumined, and I saw crimson wall hangings, a mosaic of red and purple stones on the section of the floor, and a tumble of scarlet quilts. The bird in the suspended cage was a redwinged blackbird.

"Where is it from?"

"You could use a more appropriate pronoun."

"*He? She?* Which is the more appropriate, Wardress Kefa?"

"Assume the Sharer masculine, Mr. Lorca."

"My sexual proclivities have never run that way, I'm afraid."

"Your sexual proclivities," the wardress told me stingingly, "enter into this only if you persist in thinking of the House as a brothel rather than a clinic and the Sharers as whores rather than therapists!"

"Last night I heard two or three people clomping up the stairs in their boots, that and a woman's raucous laughter."

"A visitant, Mr. Lorca, *not* a Sharer."

"I didn't think she was a Sharer. But it's difficult to believe I'm in a 'clinic' when that sort of noise disrupts my midnight meditations, Wardress."

"I've explained that. It can't be helped."

"All right, all right. Where is *he* from, this 'therapist' of mine?"

"An interior star. But where he's from is of no consequence in your treatment. I matched him to your needs, as I see them, and soon you'll be going back to him."

"Why? To spend another night sitting on the floor?"

"You won't do that again, Mr. Lorca. And you needn't worry. Your reaction wasn't an uncommon one for a newcomer to the House."

"Revulsion?" I cried. "Revulsion's therapeutic?"

"I don't think you were as put off as you believe."

"Oh? Why not?"

"Because you talked to the Sharer. You addressed him directly, not once but several times. Many visitants never get that far during their first session, Mr. Lorca."

"Talked to him?" I said dubiously. "Maybe. Before I found out what he was."

"Ah. Before you found out what he was." In her heavy green jacket and swishy pantaloons the tiny woman turned about and departed the well of the sitting room.

I stared bemusedly after her for a long time.

Three nights after my first "session," the night of my conversation with Wardress Kefa, I entered the Sharer's chamber again. Everything was as it had been, except that the dome's shutters were open and moonlight coated the mosaic work on the floor. The Sharer awaited me in the same recumbent, unmoving posture, and inside its cage the redwinged blackbird set one of its perches to rocking back and forth.

Perversely, I had decided not to talk to the Sharer this time—but I did approach the stove-bed and lean over him. *Hello,* I thought, and the word very nearly came out. I straddled the Sharer and studied him in the stained moonlight. He looked just as my sense of touch had led me to conclude previously . . . like a skull, oddly flattened and beveled, with the body of a man. But despite the chemical embers glowing beneath his dais the Sharer's body had no warmth, and to know him more fully I resumed tracing a finger over his alien parts.

I discovered that at every conceivable pressure point a tiny scar existed, or the tip of an implanted electrode, and that miniature canals into which wires had been sunk veined his inner arms and legs. Just beneath his sternum a concave disk about eight centimeters across, containing neither instruments nor any other surface features, had been set into the Sharer's chest like a stainless-steel brooch. It seemed to hum under the pressure of my finger as I drew my nail silently around the disk's circumference. What was it for? What did it mean? Again, I almost spoke.

I rolled toward the wall and lay stretched out beside the unmoving Sharer. Maybe he *couldn't* move. On my last visit he had moved his dimly phosphorescent head for me, of course, but that only feebly, and maybe his immobility was the result of some cybergamic dysfunction. I had to find out. My resolve not to speak deserted me, and I propped myself up on my elbow.

"Sharer . . . Sharer, can you move?"

The head turned toward me slightly, signaling . . . well, what?

"Can you get off this platform? Try. Get off this dais under your own power."

To my surprise the Sharer nudged a quilt to the floor and in a moment stood facing me. Moonlight glinted from the photosensitive units serving the creature as eyes and gave his bent, elongated body the appearance of a piece of Inhodlef Era statuary, primitive work from the extrakomm world of Glaparcus.

"Good," I praised the Sharer, "very good. Can you tell me what you're supposed to share with me? I'm not sure we have as much in common as our wardress seems to think."

The Sharer extended both arms toward me and opened his tightly closed fists. In the cups of his palms he held two items I hadn't discovered during my tactile examination of him. I accepted these from the Sharer. One was a small metal disk, the other a thin metal cylinder. Looking them over, I found that the disk reminded me of the larger, mirrorlike bowl set in the alien's chest, while the cylinder seemed to be a kind of penlight.

Absently, I pulled my thumb over the head of the penlight; a ridged metal sheath followed the motion of my thumb, uncovering a point of ghostly red light stretching away into the cylinder seemingly deeper than the penlight itself. I pointed this instrument at the wall, at our bedding, at the Sharer himself—but it emitted no beam. When I turned the penlight on my wrist, the results were predictably similar: not even a faint red shadow appeared along the edge of my arm. Nothing. The cylinder's light existed internally, a beam continuously transmitted and retransmitted between the penlight's two poles. Pulling back the sheath on the instrument's head had in no way interrupted the operation of its self-regenerating circuit.

I stared wonderingly into the hollow of redness, then looked up. "Sharer, what's this thing for?"

The Sharer reached out and took from my other hand the disk I had so far ignored. Then he placed this small circle of metal in the smooth declivity of the larger disk in his chest, where it apparently adhered—for I could no longer see it. That done, the Sharer stood distressingly immobile, even more like a statue than he had seemed a moment before, one arm frozen across his body and his hand stilled at the edge of the sunken plate in which the smaller disk had just adhered. He looked dead and self-commemorating.

"Lord!" I exclaimed. "What've you done, Sharer? Turned yourself off? That's right, isn't it?"

The Sharer neither answered nor moved.

Suddenly I felt sickeningly weary, opiate-weary, and I knew that I wouldn't be able to stay on the dais with this puzzle-piece being from an anonymous sun standing over me like a dark angel from my racial subconscious. I thought briefly of manhandling the Sharer across the room, but didn't have the will to touch this catatonically rigid being, this sculpture of metal and bone, and so dismissed the idea. Nor was it likely that Wardress Kefa would help me, even if I tried to summon her with murderous poundings and cries—a bitterly amusing prospect. Wellaway, another night propped against the chamber's far wall, keeping sleep at bay. . . .

Is this what you wanted me to experience, Rumer? The frustration of trying to piece together my own "therapy"? I looked up through one of the dome's unstained polygons in lethargic search of the constellation Auriga. Then I realized that I wouldn't recognize it even if it happened to lie within my line of sight. Ah, Rumer, Rumer . . .

"You're certainly a pretty one," I told the Sharer. Then I pointed the penlight at his chest, drew back the sheath on its head, and spoke a single onomatopoeic word: *"Bang."*

Instantly a beam of light sang between the instrument in my hand and the plate in the Sharer's chest. The beam died at once (I had registered only its shattering brightness, not its color), but the disk continued to glow with a residual illumination.

The Sharer dropped his frozen arm and assumed a posture more limber, more suggestive of life. He looked . . . expectant.

I could only stare. Then I turned the penlight over in my hands, pointed it again at the Sharer, and waited for another coursing of light. To no purpose. The instrument still burned internally, but it wouldn't relume the alien's inset disk, which, in any case, continued to glow dimly. Things were all at once interesting again. I gestured with the penlight.

"You've rejoined the living, haven't you?"

The Sharer acknowledged this with a slight turn of the head.

"Forgive me, Sharer, but I don't want to spend another night sitting on the floor. If you can move again, how about over there?" I pointed at the opposite wall. "I don't want you hovering over me."

Oddly, he obeyed. But he did so oddly, without turning around. He cruised backward as if on invisible coasters—his legs moving a little, yes, but not enough to propel him so smoothly, so quickly, across the chamber. Once against the far wall, the Sharer settled into the motionless but expectant posture he had assumed after his "activation" by the penlight. I could see that he still had some degree of control over his own movements, for his long fingers curled and uncurled and his skull nodded eerily in the halo of moonlight pocketing him. Even so, I realized that he had truly moved only at my voice command and my simultaneous gesturing with the penlight. And what did *that* mean?

. . . Well, that the Sharer had relinquished control of his body to the man-machine Dorian Lorca, retaining for himself just those meaningless reflexes and stirrings that convince the manipulated of their own autonomy. It was an awesome prostitution, even if Wardress Kefa would have frowned to hear me say so. Momentarily I rejoiced in it, for it seemed to free me from the demands of an artificial eroticism, from the need to figure through what was expected of me. The Sharer would obey my simplest wrist-turning, my briefest word; all I had to do was *use* the control he had literally handed to me.

This virtually unlimited power, I thought then, was a therapy whose value Rumer would understand only too well. This was a harsh assessment, but, penlight in hand, I felt that I too was a kind of marionette. . . .

Insofar as I could, I tried to come to grips with the physics of the Sharer's operation. First, the disk-within-a-disk on his chest apparently broke the connections ordinarily allowing him to exercise the senile powers that were still his. And, second, the penlight's beam restored and amplified these powers but delivered them into the hands of the speaker of imperatives who wielded the penlight. I recalled that in Earth's lunar probeship yards were crews of animatronic laborers programmed for fitting and welding. A single trained supervisor could direct from fifteen to twenty receiver-equipped laborers with one penlight and a microphone—

"Sharer," I commanded, blanking out this reverie, pointing the pen-light, "go there. . . . No, no, not like that. Lift your feet. March for me. . . . That's right, a *goosestep*."

While Wardress Kefa's third rule rattled in the back of my mind like a challenge, for the next several hours I toyed with the Sharer. After the marching I set him to calisthenics and interpretative dance, and he obeyed, moving more gracefully than I would have imagined possible. Here—then there—then back again. All he lacked was Beethoven's piano sonatas for an accompaniment.

At intervals I rested, but always the fascination of the penlight drew me back, almost against my will, and I once again played puppetmaster.

"Enough, Sharer, enough." The sky had a curdled quality suggestive of dawn. Catching sight of the cage overhead, I was taken by an irresistible impulse. I pointed the penlight at the cage and commanded, "Up, Sharer. Up, up, up."

The Sharer floated up from the floor and glided effortlessly toward the vault of the dome: a beautiful, aerial walk. Without benefit of hawsers or scaffolds or wings the Sharer levitated. Hovering over the stove-bed he had been made to surrender, hovering over everything in the room, he reached the cage and swung before it with his hands touching the scrolled ironwork on its little door. I dropped my own hands and watched him. So tightly was I gripping the penlight, however, that my knuckles must have resembled the caps of four tiny bleached skulls.

A great deal of time went by, the Sharer poised in the gelid air awaiting some word from me.

Morning began coming in the room's polygonal windows.

"Take the bird out," I ordered the Sharer, moving my penlight. "Take the bird out of the cage and kill it." This command, sadistically heartfelt, seemed to me a foolproof, indirect way of striking back at Rumer, Diderits, the wardress, and the Third Rule of the House of Compassionate Sharers. More than anything, against all reason, I wanted the redwinged blackbird dead. And I wanted the Sharer to kill it.

Dawn made clear the cancerous encroachment of age in the Sharer's legs and hands, as well as the full horror of his cybergamically rigged death's-head. He looked like he had been unjustly hanged. And when his hands went up to the cage, instead of opening its door the Sharer lifted the entire contraption off the hook fastening it to its tether and then accidentally lost his grip on the cage.

I watched the cage fall—land on its side—bounce again. The Sharer stared down with his bulging, silver-ringed eyes, his hands still spread wide to accommodate the fallen cage.

"Mr. Lorca." Wardress Kefa was knocking at the door. "Mr. Lorca, what's going on, please?"

I arose from the stove-bed, tossed my quilt aside, straightened my heavy robe. The wardress knocked again. I looked at the Sharer swaying in the half-light like a sword or a pendulum, an instrument of severance. The night had gone faster than I liked.

Again, the purposeful knocking.

"Coming," I barked.

In the dented cage there was a flutter of crimson, a stillness, and then another bit of melancholy flapping. I hurled my penlight across the room. When it struck the wall, the Sharer rocked back and forth for a moment without descending so much as a centimeter. The knocking continued.

"You have the key, Wardress. Open the door."

She did, and stood on its threshold taking stock of the games we had played. Her eyes were bright but devoid of censure, and I swept past her wordlessly, burning with shame and bravado.

I slept that day—all that day—for the first time since leaving my own world. And I dreamed. I dreamed that I was connected to a mechanism pistoning away on the edge of the Haft Paykar diggings, siphoning deadly gases out of the shafts and perversely recirculating them through the pump with which I shared a symbiomechanic linkage. Amid a series of surreal turquoise sunsets and intermittent gusts of sand, this pistoning went on, and on, and on. When I awoke I lifted my hands to my face, intending to scar it with my nails. But a moment later, as I had known it would, the mirror in my chamber returned me a perfect, unperturbed Dorian Lorca. . . .

"May I come in?"

"I'm the guest here, Wardress. So I suppose you may."

She entered and, quickly intuiting my mood, walked to the other side of the chamber. "You slept, didn't you? And you dreamed?"

I said nothing.

"You dreamed, didn't you?"

"A nightmare, Wardress. A long and repetitious nightmare, notable only for being different from the ones I had on Diroste."

"A start, though. You weren't monitored during your sleep, after all, and even if your dream *was* a nightmare, Mr. Lorca, I believe you've managed to survive it. Good. All to the good."

I went to the only window in the room, a hexagonal pane of dark blue through which it was impossible to see anything. "Did you get him down?"

"Yes. And restored the birdcage to its place." Her tiny feet made pacing sounds on the hardwood. "The bird was unharmed."

"Wardress, what's all this about? Why have you paired me with . . . with this particular Sharer?" I turned around. "What's the point?"

"You're not estranged from your wife only, Mr. Lorca, You're—"

"I know that. I've *known* that."

"And I know that you know it. Give me a degree of credit. . . .

You also know," she resumed, "that you're estranged from yourself, body and soul at variance—"

"Of course, damn it! And the argument between them's been stamped into every pseudo-organ and circuit I can lay claim to!"

"Please, Mr. Lorca, I'm trying to explain. This interior 'argument' you're so aware of . . . it's really a metaphor for an attitude you involuntarily adopted after Diderits performed his operations. And a metaphor can be taken apart and explained."

"Like a machine."

"If you like." She began pacing again. "To take inventory you have to surmount that which is to be inventoried. You go outside, Mr. Lorca, in order to come back in." She halted and fixed me with a colorless, lopsided smile.

"All of that," I began cautiously, "is clear to me. 'Know thyself,' saith Diderits and the ancient Greeks. . . . Well, if anything, my knowledge has *increased* my uneasiness about not only others, but the very phenomena permitting us to spawn." I had an image of crimson-gilled fish firing upcurrent in a roiling, untidy barrage. "What I know hasn't cured anything, Wardress."

"No. That's why we've had you come here. To extend the limits of your knowledge and to involve you in relationships demanding a recognition of others as well as self."

"As with the Sharer I left hanging up in the air?"

"Yes. Distance is advisable at first, perhaps inevitable. You needn't feel guilty. In a night or two you'll be going back to him, and then we'll just have to see."

"Is this the only Sharer I'm going to be . . . working with?"

"I don't know. It depends on the sort of progress you make."

But for Wardress Kefa, the Sharer in the crimson dome, and the noisy, midnight visitants I had never seen, there were times when I believed myself the only occupant of the House. The thought of such isolation, although not unwelcome, was an anchoritic fantasy: I knew that breathing in the chambers next to mine, going about the arcane business of the lives they had bartered away, were humanoid creatures difficult to imagine; harder still, once lodged in the mind, to put out of it. To what number and variety of beings had Wardress Kefa indentured her love? . . .

I had no chance to ask this question. We heard an insistent clomping on the steps outside the House and then muffled voices in the antechamber.

"Who's that?"

The wardress put up her hand to silence me and opened the door to my room. "A moment," she called. "I'll be with you in a moment." But her husky voice didn't carry very well, and whoever had entered the House set about methodically knocking on doors and clomping from apartment to apartment, all the while bellowing the wardress's name. "I'd better go talk with them," she told me apologetically.

"But who is it?"

"Someone voice-coded for entrance, Mr. Lorca. Nothing to worry about." And she went into the corridor, giving me a scent of spruce needles and a vision of solidly hewn rafters before the door swung to.

But I got up and followed the wardress. Outside I found her face to face with two imposing persons who looked exactly alike in spite of their being one a man and the other a woman. Their faces had the same lantern-jawed mournfulness, their eyes a hooded look under prominent brows. They wore filigreed pea jackets, ski leggings, and fur-lined caps bearing the interpenetrating-galaxies insignia of Glaktik Komm. I judged them to be in their late thirties, E-standard, but they both had the domineering, glad-handing air of high-ranking veterans in the bureaucratic establishment, people who appreciate their position just to the extent that their position can be exploited. I knew. I had once been an official of the same stamp.

The man, having been caught in mid-bellow, was now trying to laugh. "Ah, Wardress, Wardress."

"I didn't expect you this evening," she told the two of them.

"We were granted a proficiency leave for completing the Salous blueprint in advance of schedule," the woman explained, "and so caught a late 'rail from Manitou Port to take advantage of the leave. We hiked down in the dark." Along with her eyebrows she lifted a hand lantern for our inspection.

"We *took* a proficiency leave," the man said, "even if we *were* here last week. And we deserved it too." He went on to tell us that "Salous" dealt with reclaiming the remnants of aboriginal populations and pooling them for something called integrative therapy. "The Great Plains will soon be our bordello, Wardress. There, you see: you and the Orhas are in the same business . . . at least until we're assigned to stage-manage something more prosaic." He clapped his gloved hands together and looked at me. "You're new, aren't you? Who are you going to?"

"Pardon me," the wardress interjected wearily. "Who do *you* want tonight?"

The man looked at his partner with a mixture of curiosity and concern. "Cleva?"

"The mouthless one," Cleva responded at once. "Drugged, preferably."

"Come with me, Orhas," the wardress directed. She led them first to her own apartment and then into the House's mid-interior, where the three of them disappeared from my sight. I could hear them climbing one of the sets of stairs.

Shortly thereafter the wardress returned to my room.

"They're twins?"

"In a manner of speaking, Mr. Lorca. Actually they're clonemates:

Cleva and Cleirach Orha, specialists in Holosyncretic Management. They do abstract computer planning involving indigenous and alien populations, which is why they know of the House at all and have an authorization to come here."

"Do they always appear here together? Go upstairs together?"

The wardress's silence clearly meant yes.

"That's a bit kinky, isn't it?"

She gave me an angry look whose implications immediately silenced me. I started to apologize, but she said: "The Orhas are the only visitants to the House who arrive together, Mr. Lorca. Since they share a common upbringing, the same genetic material, and identical biochemistries, it isn't surprising that their sexual preferences should coincide. In Manitou Port, I'm told, is a third clonemate who was permitted to marry, and her I've never seen, either here or in Wolf Run Summit. It seems there's a *degree* of variety even among clonal siblings."

"Do these two come often?"

"You heard them in the House several days ago."

"They have frequent leaves then?"

"Last time was an overnighter. They returned to Manitou Port in the morning, Mr. Lorca. Just now they were trying to tell me that they intend to be here for a few days."

"For treatment," I said.

"You know better. You're baiting me, Mr. Lorca." She had taken her graying scalplock into her fingers and was holding its fan of hair against her right cheek. In this posture, despite her preoccupation with the arrival of the Orhas, she looked very old and very innocent.

"Who is the 'mouthless one,' Wardress?"

"Goodnight, Mr. Lorca. I only returned to tell you goodnight." And with no other word she left.

It was the longest I had permitted myself to talk with her since our first afternoon in the House, the longest I had been in her presence since our claustrophobic 'rail ride from Manitou Port. Even the Orhas, bundled to the gills, as vulgar as sleek bullfrogs, hadn't struck me as altogether insufferable.

Wearing neither coat nor cap, I took a walk through the glens below the House, touching each wind-shaken tree as I came to it and trying to conjure out of the darkness a viable memory of Rumer's smile. . . .

"Sex as weapon," I told my Sharer, who sat propped on the stove-bed amid ten or twelve quilts of scarlet and off-scarlet. "As prince consort to the Governor of Diroste, that was the only weapon I had access to. . . . Rumer employed me as an emissary, Sharer, an espionage agent, a protocol officer, whatever state business required. I received visiting representatives of Glaktik Komm, mediated disputes in the Port Iranani business community, and went on biannual inspection tours of the Fetneh and Furak district mines. I did a little of everything, Sharer."

As I paced, the Sharer observed me with a macabre, but somehow not unsettling penetration. The hollow of his chest was exposed, and, as I passed him, an occasional metallic wink caught the corner of my eye.

I told him the story of my involvement with a minor official in Port Iranani's department of immigration, a young woman whom I had never called by anything but her maternal surname, Humay. There had been others besides this woman, but Humay's story was the one I chose to tell. Why? Because alone among my ostensible "lovers," Humay I had never lain with. I had never chosen to.

Instead, to her intense bewilderment, I gave Humay ceremonial pendants, bracelets, ear-pieces, brooches, necklaces, and die-cut cameos of gold on silver, all from the collection of Rumer Montieth, Governor of Diroste—anything, in short, distinctive enough to be recognizable to my wife at a glance. Then, at those state functions requiring Rumer's attendance upon a visiting dignitary, I arranged for Humay to be present; sometimes I accompanied her myself, sometimes I found her an escort among the unbonded young men assigned to me as aides. Always I insured that Rumer should see Humay, if not in a reception line then in the promenade of the formal recessional. Afterward I asked Humay, who never seemed to have even a naïve insight into the purposes of my game, to hand back whatever piece of jewelry I had given her for ornament, and she did so. Then I returned the jewelry to Rumer's sandalwood box before my wife could verify what her eyes had earlier that evening tried to tell her. Everything I did was designed to create a false impression of my relationship with Humay, and I wanted my dishonesty in the matter to be conspicuous.

Finally, dismissing Humay for good, I gave her a cameo of Rumer's that had been crafted in the Furak District. I learned later that she had flung this cameo at an aide of mine who entered the offices of her department on a matter having nothing to do with her. She created a disturbance, several times raising my name. Ultimately (in two days' time), she was disciplined by a transfer to the frontier outpost of Yagme, the administrative center of the Furak District, and I never saw her again.

"Later, Sharer, when I dreamed of Humay, I saw her as a woman with mother-of-pearl flesh and ruby eyes. In my dreams she *became* the pieces of jewelry with which I'd tried to incite my wife's sexual jealousy—blunting it even as I incited it."

The Sharer regarded me with hard but sympathetic eyes.

Why? I asked him. Why had I dreamed of Humay as if she were an expensive clockwork mechanism, gilded, beset with gemstones, invulnerably enameled? And why had I so fiercely desired Rumer's jealousy?

The Sharer's silence invited confession.

After the Haft Paykar incident (I went on, pacing), after Diderits had fitted me with a total prosthesis, my nightmares often centered on the young woman who'd been exiled to Yagme. Although in Port Iranani I hadn't once touched Humay in an erotic way, in my monitored nightmares I regularly descended into either a charnel catacomb or a half-fallen quarry—it was impossible to know which—and there forced myself, without success, on the bejeweled automaton she had become. In every instance Humay waited for me underground; in every instance she turned me back with coruscating laughter. Its echoes always drove me upward to the light, and in the midst of nightmare I realized that I wanted Humay far less than I did residency in the secret, subterranean places she had made her own. The klieg lights that invariably directed my descent always followed me back out, too, so that Humay was always left kilometers below exulting in the dark. . . .

My Sharer got up and took a turn around the room, a single quilt draped over his shoulders and clutched loosely together at his chest. This was the first time since I had been coming to him that he had moved so far of his own volition, and I sat down to watch. Did he understand me at all? I had spoken to him as if his understanding were presupposed, a certainty—but beyond a hopeful *feeling* that my words meant something to him I'd had no evidence at all, not even a testimonial from Wardress Kefa. All of the Sharer's "reactions" were really nothing but projections of my own ambiguous hopes.

When he at last returned to me, he extended both hideously canaled arms and opened his fists. In them, the disk and the penlight. It was an offering, a compassionate, selfless offering, and for a moment I stared at his open hands in perplexity. What did they want of me, this Sharer, Wardress Kefa, the people who had sent me here? How was I supposed to buy either their forebearance or my freedom? By choosing power over impotency? By manipulation? . . . But these were altogether different questions, and I hesitated.

The Sharer then placed the small disk in the larger one beneath his sternum. Then, as before, a thousand esoteric connections severed, he froze. In the hand still extended toward me, the penlight glittering faintly and threatened to slip from his insensible grasp. I took it carefully from the Sharer's fingers, pulled back the sheath on its head, and gazed into its red-lit hollow. I released the sheath and pointed the penlight at the disk in his chest.

If I pulled the sheath back again, he would become little more than a fully integrated, *external* prosthesis—as much at my disposal as the hands holding the penlight.

"No," I said. "Not this time." And I flipped the penlight across the chamber, out of the way of temptation. Then, using my fingernails, I pried the small disk out of its electromagnetic moorings above the Sharer's heart.

He was restored to himself.
As was I to myself. As was I.

A day later, early in the afternoon, I ran into the Orhas in the House's mid-interior. They were coming unaccompanied out of a lofty, seemingly sideways-canted door as I stood peering upward from the access corridor. Man and woman together, mirror images ratcheting down a Moebius strip of stairs, the Orhas held my attention until it was too late for me to slip away unseen.

"The new visitant," Cleirach Orha informed his sister when he reached the bottom step. "We've seen you before."

"Briefly," I agreed. "The night you arrived from Manitou Port for your proficiency leave."

"What a good memory you have," Cleva Orha said. "We also saw you the day *you* arrived from Manitou Port. You and the wardress were just setting out from Wolf Run Summit together. Cleirach and I were beneath the ski lodge, watching."

"You wore no coat," her clonemate said in explanation of their interest.

They both stared at me curiously. Neither was I wearing a coat in the well of the House of Compassionate Sharers—even though the temperature inside hovered only a few degrees above freezing and we could see our breaths before us like the ghosts of ghosts. . . . I was a queer one, wasn't I? My silence made them nervous and brazen.

"No coat," Cleva Orha repeated, "and the day cold enough to fur your spittle. 'Look at that one,' Cleirach told me; 'thinks he's a polar bear.' We laughed about that, studling. We laughed heartily."

I nodded, nothing more. A coppery taste of bile, such as I hadn't experienced for several days, flooded my mouth, and I wanted to escape the Orhas' warty good humor. They were intelligent people, otherwise they would never have been cloned, but face to face with their flawed skins and their loud, insinuative sexuality I began to feel my newfound stores of tolerance overbalancing like a tower of blocks. It was a bitter test, this meeting below the stairs, and one I was on the edge of failing.

"We seem to be the only ones in the House this month," the woman volunteered. "Last month the wardress was gone, the Sharers had a holiday, and Cleirach and I had to content ourselves with incestuous buggery in Manitou Port."

"Cleva!" the man protested, laughing.

"It's true." She turned to me. "It's true, studling. And that little she-goat—Kefa, I mean—won't even tell us why the Closed sign was out for so long. Delights in mystery, that one."

"That's right," Cleirach went on. "She's an exasperating woman. She begrudges you your privileges. You have to tread lightly on her patience. Sometimes you'd like to take *her* into a chamber and find out what makes her tick. A bit of exploratory surgery, hey-la!" Saying this, he showed me his trilling tongue.

"She's a maso-ascetic, Brother."

"I don't know. There are many mansions in this House, Cleva, several of which she's refused to let us enter. Why?" He raised his eyebrows suggestively, as Cleva had done the night she lifted her hand lantern for our notice. The expressions were the same.

Cleva Orha appealed to me as a disinterested third party: "What do you think, studling? Is Wardress Scalplock at bed and at bone with one of her Sharers? Or does she lie by herself, maso-ascetically, under a hide of untanned elk hair? What do you think?"

"I haven't really thought about it." Containing my anger, I tried to leave. "Excuse me, Orha-clones."

"Wait, wait, wait," the woman said mincingly, half-humorously. "You know our names and a telling bit of our background. That puts you up, studling. We won't have that. You can't go without giving us a name."

Resenting the necessity, I told them my name.

"From where?" Cleirach Orha asked.

"Colony World GK-ll. We call it Diroste."

Brother and sister exchanged a glance of sudden enlightenment, after which Cleva raised her thin eyebrows and spoke in a mocking rhythm: "Ah ha, the mystery solved. Out and back our wardress went and therefore closed her House."

"Welcome, Mr. Lorca. Welcome."

"We're going up to Wolf Run for an after-bout of toddies and P-nol. What about you? Would you like to go? The climb wouldn't be anything to a warm-blooded studling like you. Look, Cleirach. Biceps unbundled and his sinuses still clear."

In spite of the compliment I declined.

"Who have *you* been with?" Cleirach Orha wanted to know. He bent forward conspiratorially. "We've been with a native of an extra-komm world called Trope. That's the local name. Anyhow, there's not another such being inside of a hundred light-years, Mr. Lorca."

"It's the face that intrigues us," Cleva Orha explained, saving me from an immediate reply to her brother's question. And then she reached out, touched my arm, and ran a finger down my arm to my hand. "Look. Not even a goose bump. Cleirach, you and I are suffering the shems and trivs, and our earnest Mr. Lorca's standing here bare-boned."

Brother was annoyed by this analysis. There was something he wanted to know, and Cleva's non sequiturs weren't advancing his case. Seeing that he was going to ask me again, I rummaged about for an answer that was neither informative nor tactless.

Cleva Orha, meanwhile, was peering intently at her fingertips. Then she looked at my arm, again at her fingers, and a second time at my arm. Finally she locked eyes with me and studied my face as if for some clue to the source of my reticence.

Ah, I thought numbly, she's recognized me for what I am. . . .

"Mr. Lorca can't tell you who he's been with, Cleirach," Cleva Orha told her clonemate, "because he's not a visitant to the House at all and he doesn't choose to violate the confidences of those who are."

Dumbfounded, I said nothing.

Cleva put her hand on her brother's back and guided him past me into the House's antechamber. Over her shoulder she bid me good afternoon in a toneless voice. Then the Orha-clones very deliberately let themselves out the front door and began the long climb to Wolf Run Summit.

What had happened? It took me a moment to figure it out. Cleva Orha had recognized me as a human-machine and from this recognition drawn a logical but mistaken inference: She believed me, like the "mouthless one" from Trope, a slave of the House. . . .

During my next tryst with my Sharer I spoke for an hour, two hours, maybe more, of Rumer's infuriating patience, her dignity, her serene ardor. I had moved her—maneuvered her—to the expression of these qualities by my own hollow commitment to Humay and the others before Humay who had engaged me only physically. Under my wife's attentions, however, I preened sullenly, demanding more than Rumer —than any woman in Rumer's position—had it in her power to give. My needs, I wanted her to know, my needs were as urgent and as real as Diroste's.

And at the end of one of these vague encounters Rumer seemed both to concede the legitimacy of my demands and to decry their intemperance by removing a warm pendant from her throat and placing it like an accusation in my palm.

"A week later," I told the Sharer, "was the inspection tour of the diggings at Haft Paykar."

These things spoken, I did something I had never done before in the wardress's House: I went to sleep under the hands of my Sharer. My dreams were dreams rather than nightmares, and clarified ones at that, shot through with light and accompanied from afar by a peaceful funneling of sand. The images that came to me were haloed arms and legs orchestrated within a series of shifting yellow, yellow-orange, and subtly red disks. The purr of running sand behind these movements conferred upon them the benediction of mortality, and that, I felt, was good.

I awoke in a blast of icy air and found myself alone. The door to the Sharer's apartment was standing open on the shaft of the stairwell, and I heard faint, angry voices coming across the emptiness between. Disoriented, I lay on my stove-bed staring toward the door, a square of shadow feeding its chill into the room.

"Dorian!" a husky voice called. *"Dorian!"*

Wardress Kefa's voice, diluted by distance and fear. A door opened, and her voice hailed me again, this time with more clarity. Then the door slammed shut, and every sound in the House took on a smothered quality, as if mumbled through cold, semiporous wood.

I got up, dragging my bedding with me, and reached the narrow porch on the stairwell with a clear head. Thin starlight filtered through the unshuttered windows in the ceiling. Nevertheless, looking from stairway to stairway to stairway inside the House, I had no idea behind which door the wardress now must be.

Because there existed no connecting stairs among the staggered landings of the House, my only option was to go down. I took the steps two at a time, very nearly plunging.

At the bottom I found my Sharer with both hands clenched about the outer stair rail. He was trembling. In fact, his chest and arms were quivering so violently that he seemed about to shake himself apart. I put my hands on his shoulders and tightened my grip until the tremors wracking him threatened to wrack my systems, too. Who would come apart first?"

"Go upstairs," I told the Sharer. "Get the hell upstairs."

I heard the wardress call my name again. Although by now she had squeezed some of the fear out of her voice, her summons was still distance-muffled and impossible to pinpoint.

The Sharer either couldn't or wouldn't obey me. I coaxed him, cursed him, goaded him, tried to turn him around so that he was heading back up the steps. Nothing availed. The wardress, summoning me, had inadvertently called the Sharer out as my proxy, and he now had no intention of giving back to me the role he'd just usurped. The beautifully faired planes of his skull turned toward me, bringing with them the stainless-steel rings of his eyes. These were the only parts of his body that didn't tremble, but they were helpless to countermand the agues shaking him. As inhuman and unmoving as they were, the Sharer's features still managed to convey stark, unpitiable entreaty. . . .

I sank to my knees, felt about the insides of the Sharer's legs, and took the penlight and the disk from the two pocketlike incisions tailored to these instruments. Then I stood and used them.

"Find Wardress Kefa for me, Sharer," I commanded, gesturing with the penlight at the windows overhead. "Find her."

And the Sharer floated up from the steps through the mid-interior of the House. In the crepuscular starlight, rocking a bit, he seemed to pass through a knot of curving stairs into an open space where he was all at once brightly visible.

"Point to the door," I said, jabbing the penlight uncertainly at several different landings around the well. "Show me the one."

My words echoed, and the Sharer, legs dangling, inscribed a slow half-circle in the air. Then he pointed toward one of the nearly hidden doorways.

I stalked across the well, found a likely-seeming set of stairs, and climbed them with no notion at all of what was expected of me.

Wardress Kefa didn't call out again, but I heard the same faint, somewhat slurred voices that I'd heard upon waking and knew that they belonged to the Orhas. A burst of muted female laughter, twice repeated, convinced me of this, and I hesitated on the landing.

"All right," I told my Sharer quietly, turning him around with a turn of the wrist, "go on home."

Dropping through the torus of a lower set of stairs, he found the porch in front of our chamber and settled upon it like a clumsily handled puppet. And why not? I was a clumsy puppetmaster. Because there seemed to be nothing else I could do, I slid the penlight into a pocket of my dressing gown and knocked on the Orhas' door.

"Come in," Cleva Orha said. "By all means, Sharer Lorca, come in."

I entered and found myself in a room whose surfaces were all burnished as if with beeswax. The timbers shone. Whereas in the other chambers I had seen nearly all the joists and rafters were rough-hewn, here they were smooth and splinterless. The scent of sandalwood pervaded the air, and opposite the door was a carven screen blocking my view of the chamber's stove-bed. A tall wooden lamp illuminated the furnishings and the three people arrayed around the lamp's border of light like iconic statues.

"Welcome," Cleirach Orha said. "Your invitation was from the wardress, however, not us." He wore only a pair of silk pantaloons drawn together at the waist with a cord, and his right forearm was under Wardress Kefa's chin, restraining her movement without quite cutting off her wind.

His disheveled clonemate, in a dressing gown very much like mine, sat crosslegged on a cushion and toyed with a wooden stiletto waxed as the beams of the chamber were waxed. Her eyes were too wide, too lustrous, as were her brother's, and I knew this was the result of too much placenol in combination with too much Wolf Run small-malt in combination with the Orhas' innate meanness. The woman was drugged, and drunk, and, in consequence of these things, malicious to a turn. Cleirach didn't appear quite so far gone as his sister, but all he had to do to strangle the wardress, I understood, was raise the edge of his forearm into her trachea. I felt again the familiar sensation of being out of my element, gill-less in a sluice of stinging saltwater. . . .

"Wardress Kefa—" I began.

"She's all right," Cleva Orha assured me. "Perfectly all right." She tilted her head so that she was gazing at me out of her right eye alone, and then barked a hoarse, deranged-sounding laugh.

"Let the wardress go," I told her clonemate.

Amazingly, Cleirach Orha looked intimidated. "Mr. Lorca's an anproz," he reminded Cleva. "That little letter opener you're cleaning your nails with, it's not going to mean anything to him."

"Then let her go, Cleirach. Let her go."

Cleirach released the wardress, who, massaging her throat with both hands, ran to the stove-bed. She halted beside the carven screen and beckoned me with a doll-like hand. "Mr. Lorca . . . Mr. Lorca, please . . . will you see to him first? I beg you."

"I'm going back to Wolf Run Summit," Cleirach informed his sister, and he slipped on a night jacket, gathered up his clothes, and left the room. Cleva Orha remained seated on her cushion, her head tilted back as if she were tasting a bitter potion from a heavy metal goblet.

Glancing doubtfully at her, I went to the wardress. Then I stepped around the wooden divider to see her Sharer.

The Tropeman lying there was a slender creature, almost slight. There was a ridge of flesh where his mouth ought to be, and his eyes were an organic variety of crystal, uncanny and depthful stones. One of these brandy-colored stones had been dislodged in its socket by Cleva's "letter opener"; and although the Orhas had failed to pry the eye completely loose, the Tropeman's face was streaked with blood from their efforts. The streaks ran down into the bedding under his narrow, fragile head and gave him the look of an aborigine in war paint. Lacking external genitalia, his sexless body was spread-eagled atop the quilts so that the burn marks on his legs and lower abdomen cried out for notice as plangently as did his face.

"Sweet light, sweet light," the wardress chanted softly, over and over again, and I found her locked in my arms, hugging me tightly above her beloved, butchered ward, this Sharer from another star.

"He's not dead," Cleva Orha said from her cushion. "The rules . . . the rules say not to kill 'em, and we go by the rules, Brother and I."

"What can I do, Wardress Kefa?" I whispered, holding her. "What do you want me to do?"

Slumped against me, the wardress repeated her consoling chant and held me about the waist. So, fearful that this being with eyes like precious gems would bleed to death as we delayed, each of us undoubtedly ashamed of our delay, we delayed—and I held the wardress, pressed her head to my chest, gave her a warmth I hadn't before believed in me. And she returned this warmth in undiluted measure.

Wardress Kefa, I realized, was herself a Compassionate Sharer; she was as much a Sharer as the bleeding Tropeman on the stove-bed or that obedient creature whose electrode-studded body and luminous death's-head had seemed to mock the efficient, mechanical deadness in myself—a deadness that, in turning away from Rumer, I had made a god of. In the face of this realization my disgust with the Orhas was transfigured into something very unlike disgust: a mode of perception, maybe; a means of adapting. An answer had been revealed to me, and, without its being either easy or uncomplicated, it was still, somehow, very simple: I, too, was a Compassionate Sharer. Monster, machine, anproz, the designation didn't matter any longer. Wherever I might go,

I was forevermore a ward of this tiny woman's House—my fate, inescapable and sure.

The wardress broke free of my embrace and knelt beside the Tropeman. She tore a piece of cloth from the bottom of her tunic. Wiping the blood from the Sharer's face, she said, "I heard him calling me while I was downstairs, Mr. Lorca. Encephalogoi. 'Brain words,' you know. And I came up here as quickly as I could. Cleirach took me aside. All I could do was shout for you. Then, not even that."

Her hands touched the Sharer's burns, hovered over the wounded eye, moved about with a knowledge the wardress herself seemed unaware of.

"We couldn't get it all the way out," Cleva Orha laughed. "Wouldn't come. Cleirach tried and tried."

I found the cloned woman's pea jacket, leggings, and tunic. Then I took her by the elbow and led her down the stairs to her brother. She reviled me tenderly as we descended, but otherwise didn't protest.

"You," she predicted once we were down, ". . . you we'll never get."

She was right. It was a long time before I returned to the House of Compassionate Sharers, and, in any case, upon learning of their sadistic abuse of one of the wards of the House, the authorities in Manitou Port denied the Orhas any future access to it. A Sharer, after all, was an expensive commodity.

But I did return. After going back to Diroste and living with Rumer the remaining forty-two years of her life, I applied to the House as a novitiate. I am here now. In fact as well as in metaphor, I am today one of the Sharers.

My brain cells die, of course, and there's nothing anyone can do to stop utterly the depredations of time—but my body seems to be that of a middle-aged man and I still move inside it with ease. Visitants seek comfort from me, as once, against my will, I sought comfort here; and I try to give it to them . . . even to the ones who have only a muddled understanding of what a Sharer really is. My battles aren't really with these unhappy people; they're with the advance columns of my senility (I don't like to admit this) and the shock troops of my memory, which is still excessively good. . . .

Wardress Kefa has been dead seventeen years, Diderits twenty-three, and Rumer two. That's how I keep score now. Death has also carried off the gem-eyed Tropeman and the Sharer who drew the essential Dorian Lorca out of the prosthetic rind he had mistaken for himself.

I intend to be here a while longer yet. I have recently been given a chamber into which the light sifts with a painful white brilliance reminiscent of the sands of Diroste or the snows of Wolf Run Summit. This is all to the good. Either way, you see, I die at home. . . .

Husband and wife writing teams have always been something of a specialty in SF: C. L. Moore and Henry Kuttner, Walt and Leigh Richmond, Joan and Vernor Vinge, Leigh Brackett and Edmond Hamilton. To this list of famous collaborators must now be added the names of the authors of the powerful story that follows.

Spider Robinson started writing at the beginning of the decade, and quickly established himself as one of Analog's *most popular contributors with his series of stories about Callahan's Bar, recently collected as* Callahan's Crosstime Saloon *(Ace). He won the John W. Campbell, Jr., Award in 1974, and a Hugo Award in 1977 for his novella "By Any Other Name," an expanded version of which was released as the novel* Telempath *(Berkley). His most recent project is an anthology series* The Best of All Possible Worlds, *upcoming from Ace.*

Jeanne Robinson, a professional dancer, dance teacher, and choreographer, has been dancing for over twenty years. She studied at the Boston Conservatory of Music and Dance, the Toronto Dance Theater and at the Martha Graham School in New York. She is presently the director of Valley Dance Experience, a combination dance school and performing company in Nova Scotia, where the Robinsons live. "Stardance" is her first published story.

A novel version of "Stardance" is forthcoming next year from Dial Press and Dell.

SPIDER ROBINSON and
JEANNE ROBINSON

Stardance

I can't really say that I knew her, certainly not the way Seroff knew Isadora. All I know of her childhood and adolescence are the anecdotes she chanced to relate in my hearing—just enough to make me certain that all three of the contradictory biographies on the current best-seller list are fictional. All I know of her adult life are the hours she spent in my presence and on my monitors—more than enough to tell me that every newspaper account I've seen is fictional. Carrington probably believed he knew her better than I, and in a limited sense he was correct—but he would never have written of it, and now he is dead.

But I was her video man since the days when you touched the camera with your hands, and I knew her backstage: a type of relationship like no other on Earth or off it. I don't believe it can be described to anyone not of the profession—you might think of it as somewhere between co-workers and combat buddies. I was with her the day she came to Skyfac, terrified and determined, to stake her life upon a dream. I watched her work and worked with her for that whole two months, through endless rehearsals, and I have saved every tape and they are not for sale.

And, of course, I saw the Stardance. I was there; I taped it.

I guess I can tell you some things about her.

To begin with, it was not, as Cahill's *Shara* and Von Derski's *Dance Unbound: The Creation of New Modern* suggest, a lifelong fascination with space and space travel that led her to become the race's first zero-gravity dancer. Space was a means to her, not an end, and its vast empty immensity scared her at first. Nor was it, as Melberg's hard-cover tabloid *The Real Shara Drummond* claims, because she lacked the talent to make it as a dancer on Earth. If you think free-fall dancing is easier than conventional dance, you try it. Don't forget your dropsickness bag.

But there is a grain of truth in Melberg's slander, as there is in all the best slanders. She could *not* make it on Earth—but not through lack of talent.

I first saw her in Toronto in July of 1984. I headed Toronto Dance Theater's video department at that time, and I hated every minute of it. I hated everything in those days. The schedule that day called for spending the entire afternoon taping students, a waste of time and tape which I hated more than anything except the phone company. I hadn't seen the year's new crop yet and was not eager to. I love to watch dance done well—the efforts of a tyro are usually as pleasing to me as a first-year violin student in the next apartment is to you.

My leg was bothering me even more than usual as I walked into the studio. Norrey saw my face and left a group of young hopefuls to come over. "Charlie. . . ?"

"I know, I know. They're tender fledglings, Charlie, with egos as fragile as an Easter egg in December. Don't bite them, Charlie. Don't even bark at them if you can help it, Charlie."

She smiled. "Something like that. Leg?"

"Leg."

Norrey Drummond is a dancer who gets away with looking like a woman because she's small. There's about a hundred and fifteen pounds of her, and most of it is heart. She stands about five-four, and is perfectly capable of seeming to tower over the tallest student. She has more energy than the North American Grid and uses it as efficiently as a vane pump (have you ever studied the principle of a standard piston-type pump? Go look up the principle of a vane pump. I wonder what the original conception of *that* notion must have been like, as an emotional experience). There's a signaturelike uniqueness to her dance, the only reason I can see why she got so few of the really juicy parts in company productions until modern gave way to new modern. I liked her because she didn't pity me.

"It's not only the leg," I admitted. "I hate to see the tender fledglings butcher your choreography."

"Then you needn't worry. The piece you're taping today is by . . . one of the students."

"Oh, fine. I knew I should have called in sick." She made a face. "What's the catch?"

"Eh?"

"Why did the funny thing happen to your voice just as you got to 'one of my students'?"

She blushed. "Damnit, she's my sister."

My eyebrows rose. "She must be good then."

"Why thank you, Charlie."

"Bullshit. I give compliments right-handed or not at all—I'm not talking about heredity. I mean that you're so hopelessly ethical you'd bend over backward to avoid nepotism. For you to give your own sister a feature like that, she must be *terrific*."

"Charlie, she is," Norrey said simply.

"We'll see. What's her name?"

"Shara." Norrey pointed her out, and I understood the rest of the catch. Shara Drummond was ten years younger than her sister—and seven inches taller, with thirty or forty more pounds. I noted absently that she was stunningly beautiful, but it didn't deter my dismay—in her best years, Sophia Loren could never have become a modern dancer. Where Norrey was small, Shara was big, and where Norrey was big, Shara was bigger. If I'd seen her on the street I might have whistled appreciatively—but in the studio I frowned.

"My God, Norrey, she's enormous."

"Mother's second husband was a football player," she said mournfully. "She's awfully good."

"If she *is* good, that *is* awful. Poor girl. Well, what do you want me to do?"

"What makes you think I want you to do anything?"

"You're still standing here."

"Oh. I guess I am. Well . . . have lunch with us, Charlie?"

"Why?" I knew perfectly well why, but I expected a polite lie.

Not from Norrey Drummond. "Because you two have something in common, I think."

I paid her honesty the compliment of not wincing. "I suppose we do."

"Then you will?"

"Right after the session."

She twinkled and was gone. In a remarkably short time she had organized the studio full of wandering, chattering young people into something that resembled a dance ensemble if you squinted. They warmed up during the twenty minutes it took me to set up and check out my equipment. I positioned one camera in front of them, one behind, and kept one in my hands for walk-around close-up work. I never triggered it.

There's a game you play in your mind. Every time someone catches or is brought to your attention, you begin making guesses about them. You try to extrapolate their character and habits from their appearance. Him? Surly, disorganized—leaves the cap off the toothpaste and drinks boilermakers. Her? Art student type, probably uses a diaphragm and writes letters in a stylized calligraphy of her own invention. Them? They look like schoolteachers from Miami, probably here to see what snow looks like, attend a convention. Sometimes I come pretty close. I don't know how I typecast Shara Drummond, in those first twenty minutes. The moment she began to dance, all preconceptions left my mind. She became something elemental, something unknowable, a living bridge between our world and the one the Muses live in.

I know, on an intellectual and academic level, all there is to know about dance, and I could not categorize or classify or even really comprehend the dance she danced that afternoon. I saw it, I even appreciated it, but I was not equipped to understand it. My camera dangled from the end of my arm, next to my jaw. Dancers speak of their "center," the place their motion centers around, often quite near the physical center of gravity. You strive to "dance from your center" and the "contraction-and-release" idea which underlies much of modern dance depends on the center for its focus of energy. Shara's center seemed to move about the room under its own power, trailing limbs that attached to it by choice rather than necessity. What's the word for the outermost part of the sun, the part that still shows in an eclipse? Corona? That's what her limbs were: four lengthy tongues of flame that followed the center in its eccentric, whirling orbit, writhing fluidly around its surface. That the lower two frequently contacted the floor seemed coincidental—indeed the other two touched the floor nearly as regularly.

There were other students dancing. I know this because the two automatic videocameras, unlike me, did their job and recorded the piece as a whole. It was called *Birthing* and depicted the formation of a galaxy that ended up resembling Andromeda. It was only vaguely accurate, literally, but it wasn't intended to be. Symbolically, it felt like the birth of a galaxy.

In retrospect. At the time I was aware only of the galaxy's heart: Shara. Students occluded her from time to time, and I simply never noticed. It hurt to watch her.

If you know anything about dance, this must all sound horrid to you. A dance about a *nebula*? I know, I know. It's a ridiculous notion. And it worked. In the most gut-level, cellular way it worked—save only that Shara was too good for those around her. She did not belong in that eager crew of awkward, half-trained apprentices. It was like listening to the late Stephen Wonder trying to work with a pick-up band in a Montreal bar.

But that wasn't what hurt.

Le Maintenant was shabby, but the food was good and the house brand of grass was excellent. Show a Diner's Club card in there and they'd show you a galley full of dirty dishes. It's gone now. Norrey and Shara declined a toke, but in my line of work it helps. Besides, I needed a few hits. How to tell a lovely lady her dearest dream is hopeless?

I didn't need to ask Shara to know that her dearest dream was to dance. More: to dance professionally. I have often speculated on the motives of the professional artist. Some seek the narcissistic assurance that others will actually pay cash to watch or hear them. Some are so incompetent or disorganized that they can support themselves in no other way. Some have a message which they feel needs expressing. I suppose most artists combine elements of all three. This is no complaint—what they do for us is necessary. We should be grateful that there *are* motives.

But Shara was one of the rare ones. She danced because she needed to. She needed to say things which could be said in no other way, and she needed to take her meaning and her living from the saying of them. Anything else would have demeaned and devalued the essential statement of her dance. I know this, from watching that one dance.

Between toking up and keeping my mouth full and then toking again (a mild amount to offset the slight down that eating brings), it was over half an hour before I was required to say anything beyond an occasional grunted response to the luncheon chatter of the ladies. As the coffee arrived, Shara looked me square in the eye and said, "Do you talk, Charlie?"

She was Norrey's sister, all right.

"Only inanities."

"No such thing. Inane people, maybe."

"Do you enjoy dancing, Miss Drummond?"

She answered seriously. "Define 'enjoy.' "

I opened my mouth and closed it, perhaps three times. You try it.

"And for God's sake tell me why you're so intent on not talking to me. You've got me worried."

"Shara!" Norrey looked dismayed.

"Hush. I want to know."

I took a crack at it. "Shara, before he died I had the privilege of meeting Bertram Ross. I had just seen him dance. A producer who knew and liked me took me backstage, the way you take a kid to see Santa Claus. I had expected him to look even older offstage, at rest. He looked younger, as if that incredible motion of his was barely in check. He talked to me. After a while I stopped opening my mouth, because nothing ever came out."

She waited, expecting more. Only gradually did she comprehend the compliment and its dimension. I had assumed it would be obvious. Most artists *expect* to be complimented. When she did twig, she did not blush or simper. She did not cock her head and say, "Oh, come on." She did not say, "You flatter me." She did not look away.

She nodded slowly and said, "Thank you, Charlie. That's worth a lot more than idle chatter." There was a suggestion of sadness in her smile, as if we shared a bitter joke.

"You're welcome."

"For heaven's sake, Norrey, what are you looking so upset about?"

The cat now had Norrey's tongue.

"She's disappointed in me," I said. "I said the wrong thing."

"That was the wrong thing?"

"It should have been, 'Miss Drummond, I think you ought to give up dancing.' "

"It should have been, '*Shara*, I think you ought' . . . *what?*"

"Charlie," Norrey began.

"I was supposed to tell you that we can't all be professional dancers, that they also surf who only sand and wade. Shara, I was supposed to tell you to dump the dance—before it dumps you."

In my need to be honest with her, I had been more brutal than was necessary, I thought. I was to learn that bluntness never dismayed Shara. She demanded it.

"Why you?" was all she said.

"We're inhabiting the same vessel, you and I. We've both got an itch that our bodies just won't let us scratch."

Her eyes softened. "What's your itch?"

"The same as yours."

"Eh?"

"The man was supposed to come and fix the phone on Thursday. My roommate Karen and I had an all-day rehearsal. We left a note. Mister telephone man, we had to go out, and we sure couldn't call you, heh heh. Please get the key from the concierge and come on in; the phone's in the bedroom. The phone man never showed up. They never do." My hands seemed to be shaking. "We came home up the back stairs from the alley. The phone was still dead, but I never thought to take down the note on the front door. I got sick the next morning. Cramps. Vomiting. Karen and I were just friends, but she stayed home to take care of me. I suppose on a Friday night the note seemed even more plausible. He slipped the lock with a piece of plastic, and Karen came out of the kitchen as he was unplugging the stereo. He was so indignant he shot her. Twice. The noise scared him; by the time I got there he was halfway out the door. He just had time to put a slug through my hip joint, and then he was gone. They never got him. They never even came to fix the phone." My hands were under control now. "Karen was a damned good dancer, but I was better. In my head, I still am."

Her eyes were round. "You're not Charlie . . . Charles *Armstead*."

I nodded.

"Oh my God. So *that's* where you went."

I was shocked by how she looked. It brought me back from the cold and windy border of self-pity. I began a little to pity her. I should have guessed the depth of her empathy. And in the way that really mattered, we were too damned alike—we *did* share the same bitter joke. I wondered why I had wanted to shock her.

"They couldn't repair the joint?" she asked softly.

"I can walk splendidly. Given a strong enough motivation, I can even run short distances. I can't dance worth a damn."

"So you became a video man."

"Three years ago. People who know both video and dance are about as common as garter belts these days. Oh, they've been taping dance since the Seventies—with the imagination of a network news camera-man. If you film a stage play with two cameras in the orchestra pit, is it a movie?"

"You do for dance what the movie camera did for drama?"

"Pretty fair analogy. Where it breaks down is that dance is more analogous to music than to drama. You can't stop and start it, or go back and retake a scene that didn't go in the can right, or reverse the chronology to get a tidy shooting schedule. The event happens and you record it. What I am is what the record industry pays top dollars for —a mixman with savvy enough to know which ax is wailing at the moment and mike it high—and the sense to have given the heaviest dudes the best mikes. There are a few others like me. I'm the best."

She took it the way she had the compliment to herself—at face value. Usually when I say things like that, I don't give a damn what reaction I get, or I'm being salty and hoping for outrage. But I was pleased at her acceptance, pleased enough to bother me. A faint irritation made me go brutal again, *knowing* it wouldn't work. "So what all this leads to is that Norrey was hoping I'd suggest some similar form of sublimation for you. Because I'll make it in dance before you will."

She stubborned up. "I don't buy that, Charlie. I know what you're talking about, I'm not a fool, but I think I can beat it."

"Sure you will. *You're too damned big, lady.* You've got tits like both halves of a prize honeydew melon and an ass that any actress in Hollywood would sell her parents for, and in modern dance that makes you d-e-d dead, you haven't got a chance. Beat it? You'll beat your head in first. How'm I doing, Norrey?"

"For Christ's sake, Charlie!"

I softened. I can't work Norrey into a tantrum—I like her too much. "I'm sorry, hon. My leg's giving me the mischief, and I'm stinkin' mad.

She *ought* to make it—and she won't. She's your sister, and so it saddens you. Well, I'm a total stranger, and it enrages me."

"How do you think it makes me feel?" Shara blazed, startling us both. I hadn't known she had so much voice. "So you want me to pack it in and rent me a camera, huh, Charlie? Or maybe sell apples outside the studio?" A ripple ran up her jaw. "Well, I will be damned by all the gods in Southern California before I'll pack it in. God gave me the large economy size, but there is not a surplus pound on it and it fits me like a glove and I can, by Jesus, *dance* it and I will. You may be right—I may beat my head in first. But I will get it done." She took a deep breath. "Now I thank you for your kind intentions, Char . . . Mister Armst . . . oh shit." The tears came and she left hastily, spilling a quarter-cup of cold coffee on Norrey's lap.

"Charlie," Norrey said through clenched teeth, "why do I like you so much?"

"Dancers are dumb." I gave her my handkerchief.

"Oh." She patted at her lap a while. "How come you like me?"

"Video men are smart."

"Oh."

I spent the afternoon in my apartment reviewing the footage I'd shot that morning, and the more I watched, the madder I got.

Dance requires intense motivation at an extraordinarily early age— a blind devotion, a gamble on the as-yet-unrealized potentials of heredity and nutrition. You can begin, say, classical ballet training at age six—and at fourteen find yourself broad-shouldered, the years of total effort utterly wasted. Shara had set her sights on modern dance —and found out too late that God had dealt her the body of a woman.

She was not fat—you have seen her. She was tall, big-boned tall, and on that great frame was built a rich, ripely female body. As I ran and reran the tapes of *Birthing*, the pain grew in me until I even forgot the ever-present aching of my own leg. It was like watching a supremely gifted basketball player who stood four feet tall.

To make it in modern dance, it is essential to get into a company. You cannot be seen unless you are visible. Norrey had told me, on the walk back to the studio, of Shara's efforts to get into a company—and I could have predicted nearly every word.

"Merce *Cunningham* saw her dance, Charlie. Martha Graham saw her dance, just before she died. Both of them praised her warmly, for her choreography as much as for her technique. Neither offered her a position. I'm not even sure I blame them—I can sort of understand."

Norrey could understand all right. It was her own defect magnified a hundredfold: uniqueness. A company member must be capable of excellent solo work—but she must also be able to blend into group effort, in ensemble work. Shara's very uniqueness made her virtually useless as a company member. She could not help but draw the eye.

And once drawn, the male eye at least would never leave. Modern dancers must sometimes work nude these days, and it is therefore meet that they have the body of a fourteen-year-old boy. We may have ladies dancing with few or no clothes on up here, but by God it is Art. An actress or a musician or a singer or a painter may be lushly endowed, deliciously rounded—but a dancer must be nearly as sexless as a high-fashion model. Perhaps God knows why. Shara could not have purged her dance of her sexuality even if she had been interested in trying, and as I watched her dance on my monitor and in my mind's eye, I knew she was not.

Why did her genius have to lie in the only occupation besides model and nun in which sexiness is a liability? It broke my heart, by empathic analogy.

"It's no good at all, is it?"

I whirled and barked, "Dammit, you made me bite my tongue."

"I'm sorry." She came from the doorway into my living room. "Norrey told me how to find the place. The door was ajar."

"I forgot to shut it when I came home."

"You leave it open?"

"I've learned the lesson of history. No junkie, no matter how strung out he is, will enter an apartment with the door ajar and the radio on. Obviously there's someone home. And you're right, it's no damn good at all. Sit down."

She sat on the couch. Her hair was down now, and I liked it better that way. I shut off the monitor and popped the tape, tossing it on a shelf.

"I came to apologize. I shouldn't have blown up at you at lunch. You were trying to help me."

"You had it coming. I imagine by now you've built up quite a head of steam."

"Five years' worth. I figured I'd start in the States instead of Canada. Go farther faster. Now I'm back in Toronto and I don't think I'm going to make it here either. You're right, Mr. Armstead—I'm too damned big. Amazons don't dance."

"It's still Charlie. Listen, something I want to ask you. That last gesture, at the end of *Birthing*—what was that? I thought it was a beckoning; Norrey says it was a farewell; and now that I've run the tape it looks like a yearning, a reaching out."

"Then it worked."

"Pardon?"

"It seemed to me that the birth of a galaxy called for all three. They're so close together in spirit it seemed silly to give each a separate movement."

"Mmm." Worse and worse. Suppose Einstein had aphasia. "Why couldn't you have been a rotten dancer? That'd just be irony. This," I pointed to the tape, "is high tragedy."

"Aren't you going to tell me I can still dance for myself?"

"No. For you that'd be worse than not dancing at all."

"My god, you're perceptive. Or am I that easy to read?"

I shrugged.

"Oh Charlie," she burst out, "what am I going to do?"

"You'd better not ask me that." My voice sounded funny.

"Why not?"

"Because I'm already two-thirds in love with you. And because you're not in love with me and never will be. And so that is the sort of question you shouldn't ask me."

It jolted her a little, but she recovered quickly. Her eyes softened, and she shook her head slowly. "You even know why I'm not, don't you?"

"And why you won't be."

I was terribly afraid she was going to say, "Charlie, I'm sorry." But she surprised me again. What she said was, "I can count on the fingers of one foot the number of grown-up men I've ever met. I'm grateful for you. I guess ironic tragedies come in pairs?"

"Sometimes."

"Well, now all I have to do is figure out what to do with my life. That should kill the weekend."

"Will you continue your classes?"

"Might as well. It's never a waste of time to study. Norrey's teaching me things."

All of a sudden my mind started to percolate. Man is a rational animal, right? Right? "What if I had a better idea?"

"If you've got another idea, it's better. Speak."

"Do you have to have an audience? I mean, does it have to be *live*?"

"What do you mean?"

"Maybe there's a back way in. Home video machines are starting to sell—once people understood they could collect old movies and such like they do records, it was just a matter of making it cheap enough for the traffic to bear. It's just about there—you know, TDT's already thinking of entering the market, and the Graham company has."

"So?"

"So suppose we go freelance? You and me? You dance it and I'll tape it: a straight business deal. I've got a few connections, and maybe I can get more. I could name you ten acts in the music business right now that never go on tour—just record and record. Why don't you bypass the structure of the dance companies and take a chance on the public? Maybe word of mouth could. . . ."

Her face was beginning to light up like a jack-o'-lantern. "Charlie, do you think it could work? Do you really think so?"

"I don't think it has a snowball's chance." I crossed the room, opened up the beer fridge, took out the snowball I keep there in the summer, and tossed it at her. She caught it, but just barely, and when she realized what it was, she burst out laughing. "I've got just enough faith in the idea to quit working for TDT and put my time into it. I'll invest my time, my tape, my equipment, and my savings. Ante up."

She tried to get sober, but the snowball froze her fingers and she broke up again. "A snowball in July. You madman. Count me in. I've got a little money saved. And . . . and I guess I don't have much choice, do I?"

"I guess not."

The next three years were some of the most exciting years of my life, of both our lives. While I watched and taped, Shara transformed herself from a potentially great dancer into something truly awesome. She did something I'm not sure I can explain.

She became dance's analogy of the jazzman.

Dance was, for Shara, self-expression, pure and simple, first, last, and always. Once she freed herself of the attempt to fit into the world of company dance, she came to regard choreography, per se, as an *obstacle* to her self-expression, as a preprogramed rut, inexorable as a script and as limiting. And so she devalued it.

A jazzman may blow *Night in Tunisia* for a dozen consecutive nights, and each evening will be a different experience, as he interprets and reinterprets the melody according to his mood of the moment. Total unity of artist and his art: spontaneous creation. The melodic starting point distinguishes the result from pure anarchy.

In just this way Shara devalued preperformance choreography to a starting point, a framework on which to build whatever the moment demanded, and then jammed around it. She learned in those three busy years to dismantle the interface between herself and her dance. Dancers have always tended to sneer at improv dancing, even while they practiced it in the studio, for the looseness it gave. They failed to see that *planned* improv, improv around a theme fully thought out in advance, was the natural next step in dance. Shara took the step. You must be very, very good to get away with that much freedom. She was good enough.

There's no point in detailing our professional fortunes over those three years. We worked hard, we made some magnificent tapes, and we couldn't sell them for paperweights. A home video cassette industry indeed formed—and they knew as much about modern dance as the record industry knew about the blues when *they* started. The big outfits wanted credentials, and the little outfits wanted cheap talent. Finally we even got desperate enough to try the schlock houses—and learned what we already knew. They didn't have the distribution, the prestige, or the technical specs for the critics to pay any attention to them. Word-of-mouth advertising is like a gene pool—if it isn't a certain minimum size to start with, it doesn't get anywhere. "Spider" John Koerner is an incredibly talented musician and songwriter who has been making and selling his own records since 1972. How many of you have ever heard of him?

In May of 1987 I opened my mailbox in the lobby and found the letter from VisuEnt, Inc., terminating our option with deepest sorrow and no severance. I went straight over to Shara's apartment, and my leg felt like the bone marrow had been replaced with thermite and ignited. It was a very long walk.

She was working on *Weight Is a Verb* when I got there. Converting her big living room into a studio had cost time, energy, skull-sweat, and a fat bribe to the landlord, but it was cheaper than renting time in a studio, considering the sets we wanted. It looked like high mountain country that day, and I hung my hat on a fake alder when I entered.

She flashed me a smile and kept moving, building up to greater and greater leaps. She looked like the most beautiful mountain goat I ever saw. I was in a foul mood and I wanted to kill the music (McLaughlin and Miles together, leaping some themselves), but I never could interrupt Shara when she was dancing. She built it gradually, with directional counterpoint, until she seemed to hurl herself into the air, stay there until she was damned good and ready, and then hurl herself down again. Sometimes she rolled when she hit and sometimes she landed on her hands, and always the energy of falling was transmuted into something instead of being absorbed. It was total energy output, and by the time she was done I had calmed down enough to be almost philosophical about our mutual professional ruin.

She ended up collapsed in upon herself, head bowed, exquisitely humbled in her attempt to defy gravity. I couldn't help applauding. It felt corny, but I couldn't help it.

"Thank you, Charlie."

"I'll be damned. Weight *is* a verb. I thought you were crazy when you told me the title."

"It's one of the strongest verbs in dance—and you can make it do *anything*."

"Almost anything."

"Eh?"

"VisuEnt gave us our contract back."

"Oh." Nothing showed in her eyes, but I knew what was behind them. "Well, who's next on the list?"

"There is no one left on the list."

"*Oh*." This time it showed. "Oh."

"We should have remembered. Great artists are never honored in their own lifetime. What we ought to do is drop dead—then we'd be all set."

In my way I was trying to be strong for her, and she knew it and tried to be strong for me.

"Maybe what we should do is go into death insurance, for artists," she said. "We pay the client premiums against a controlling interest in his estate, and we insure that he'll die."

"We can't lose. And if he becomes famous in his lifetime he can buy out."

"Terrific. Let's stop this before I laugh myself to death."

"Yeah."

She was silent for a long time. My own mind was racing efficiently, but the transmission seemed to be blown—it wouldn't *go* anywhere. Finally she got up and turned off the music machine, which had been whining softly ever since the tape ended. It made a loud *click*.

"Norrey's got some land on Prince Edward Island," she said, not meeting my eyes. "There's a house."

I tried to head her off with the punchline from the old joke about the kid shoveling out the elephant cage in the circus whose father offers to take him back and set him up with a decent job. "What? And leave show business?"

"Screw show business," she said softly. "If I went out to PEI now, maybe I could get the land cleared and plowed in time to get a garden in." Her expression changed. "How about you?"

"Me? I'll be okay. TDT asked me to come back."

"That was six months ago."

"They asked again. Last week."

"And you said no. Moron."

"Maybe so, maybe so."

"The whole damn thing was a waste of time. All that time. All that energy. All that work. I might as well have been farming in PEI—by now the soil'd be starting to bear well. What a waste, Charlie, what a stinking waste."

"No, I don't think so, Shara. It sounds glib to say that 'nothing is wasted,' but—well, it's like that dance you just did. Maybe you can't beat gravity—but it surely is a beautiful thing to *try*."

"Yeah, I know. Remember the Light Brigade. Remember the Alamo. They tried." She laughed, a bitter laugh.

"Yes, and so did Jesus of Nazareth. Did you do it for material reward, or because it needed doing? If nothing, else, we now have several hundred thousand feet of the most magnificent dance recordings on tape, commercial value zero, real value incalculable, and by me that is no waste. It's over now, and we'll both go do the next thing, but it was *not a waste*." I discovered that I was shouting, and stopped.

She closed her mouth. After a while she tried a smile. "You're right, Charlie. It wasn't waste. I'm a better dancer than I ever was."

"Damn right. You've transcended choreography."

She smiled ruefully. "Yeah. Even Norrey thinks it's a dead end."

"It is *not* a dead end. There's more to poetry than haiku and sonnets. Dancers don't *have* to be robots, delivering memorized lines with their bodies."

"They do if they want to make a living."

"We'll try again in a few years. Maybe they'll be ready then."

"Sure. Let me get us some drinks."

I slept with her that night, for the first and last time. In the morning I broke down the set in the living room while she packed. I promised to write. I promised to come and visit when I could. I carried her bags down to the car and stowed them inside. I kissed her and waved goodbye. I went looking for a drink, and at four o'clock the next morning a mugger decided I looked drunk enough, and I broke his jaw, his nose, and two ribs and then sat down on him and cried. On Monday morning I showed up at the studio with my hat in my hand and a mouth like a bus-station ashtray and crawled back into my old job. Norrey didn't ask any questions. What with rising food prices, I gave up eating anything but bourbon, and in six months I was fired. It went like that for a long time.

I never did write to her. I kept getting bogged down after "Dear Shara . . ."

When I got to the point of selling my video equipment for booze, a relay clicked somewhere and I took stock of myself. The stuff was all the life I had left, and so I went to the local AlAnon instead of the pawn shop and got sober. After a while my soul got numb, and I stopped flinching when I woke up. A hundred times I began to wipe the tapes I still had of Shara—she had copies of her own—but in the end I could not. From time to time I wondered how *she* was doing, and I could not bear to find out. If Norrey heard anything, she didn't tell me about it. She even tried to get me my job back a third time, but it was hopeless. Reputation can be a terrible thing once you've blown it. I was lucky to land a job with an educational TV station in New Brunswick.

It was a long couple of years.

Vidphones were coming out by 1990 and I had breadboarded one of my own without the knowledge or consent of the phone company, which I still hated more than anything. When the peanut bulb I had replaced the damned bell with started glowing softly on and off one evening in June, I put the receiver on the audio pickup and energized the tube, in case the caller was also equipped. "Hello?"

She was. When Shara's face appeared, I got a cold cube of fear in the pit of my stomach, because I had quit seeing her face everywhere when I quit drinking, and I had been thinking lately of hitting the sauce again. When I blinked and she was still there, I felt a little better and tried to speak. It didn't work.

"Hello, Charlie. It's been a long time."

The second time it worked. "Seems like yesterday. Somebody else's yesterday."

"Yes, it does. It took me *days* to find you. Norrey's in Paris, and no one else knew where you'd gone."

"Yeah. How's farming?"

"I . . . I've put that away, Charlie. It's even more creative than dancing, but it's not the same."

"Then what *are* you doing?"

"Working."

"Dancing?"

"Yes. Charlie, I need you. I mean, I have a job for you. I need your cameras and your eye."

"Never mind the qualifications. Any kind of need will do. *Where are you?* When's the next plane there? Which cameras do I pack?"

"New York, an hour from now, and none of them. I didn't mean 'your cameras' literally—unless you're using GLX-5000s and a Hamilton Board lately."

I whistled. It hurt my mouth. "Not on my budget. Besides, I'm old-fashioned—I like to hold 'em with my hands."

"For this job you'll use a Hamilton, and it'll be a twenty input Masterchrome, brand new."

"You grew poppies on that farm? Or just struck diamonds with the roto-tiller?"

"You'll be getting paid by Bryce Carrington."

I blinked.

"Now will you catch that plane so I can tell you about it? The New Age, ask for the Presidential Suite."

"The hell with the plane, I'll walk. Quicker." I hung up.

According to the *Time* magazine in my dentist's waiting room, Bryce Carrington was the genius who had become a multimillionaire by convincing a number of giants of industry to underwrite Skyfac, the great orbiting complex that kicked the bottom out of the crystals market. As I recalled the story, some rare poliolike disease had wasted both his legs and put him in a wheelchair. But the legs had lost strength, not function—in lessened gravity, they worked well enough. So he created Skyfac, establishing mining crews on Luna to supply it with cheap raw materials, and lived in orbit under reduced gravity. His picture made him look like a reasonably successful author (as opposed to writer). Other than that I knew nothing about him. I paid little attention to news and none at all to space news.

The New Age was *the* hotel in New York in those days, built on the ruins of the Sheraton. Ultraefficient security, bulletproof windows, carpet thicker than the outside air, and a lobby of an architectural persuasion that John D. MacDonald once called "Early Dental Plate." It stank of money. I was glad I'd made the effort to locate a necktie, and I wished I'd shined my shoes. An incredible man blocked my way as I came in through the airlock. He moved and was built like the toughest, fastest bouncer I ever saw, and he dressed and acted like God's butler. He said his name was Perry. He asked if he could help me, as though he didn't think so.

"Yes, Perry. Would you mind lifting up one of your feet?"

"Why?"

"I'll bet twenty dollars you've shined your soles."

Half his mouth smiled, and he didn't move an inch. "Who did you wish to see?"

"Shara Drummond."

"Not registered."

"The Presidential Suite."

"Oh." Light dawned. "Mister Carrington's lady. You should have said so. Wait here, please." While he phoned to verify that I was expected, keeping his eye on me and his hand near his pocket, I swallowed my heart and rearranged my face. It took some time. So that was how it was. All right then. That was how it was.

Perry came back and gave me the little button-transmitter that would let me walk the corridors of the New Age without being cut down by automatic laser-fire, and explained carefully that it would blow a largish hole in me if I attempted to leave the building without returning it. From his manner I gathered that I had just skipped four grades in social standing. I thanked him, though I'm damned if I know why.

I followed the green fluorescent arrows that appeared on the bulbless ceiling, and came after a long and scenic walk to the Presidential Suite. Shara was waiting at the door, in something like an angel's pajamas. It made all that big body look delicate. "Hello, Charlie."

I was jovial and hearty. "Hi, babe. Swell joint. How've you been keeping yourself?"

"I haven't been."

"Well, how's Carrington been keeping you, then?" Steady, boy.

"Come in Charlie."

I went in. It looked like where the Queen stayed when she was in town, and I'm sure she enjoyed it. You could have landed an airplane in the living room without waking anyone in the bedroom. It had two pianos. Only one fireplace, barely big enough to barbecue a buffalo—you have to scrimp somewhere, I guess. Roger Kellaway was on the quadio, and for a wild moment I thought he was actually in the suite, playing some unseen third piano. So this was how it was.

"Can I get you something, Charlie?"

"Oh, sure. Hash oil, Tangier Supreme. Dom Perignon for the pipe."

Without cracking a smile she went to a cabinet, which looked like a midget cathedral, and produced precisely what I had ordered. I kept my own features impassive and lit up. The bubbles tickled my throat, and the rush was exquisite. I felt myself relaxing, and when we had passed the narghile's mouthpiece a few times I felt her relax. We looked at each other then—really looked at each other—then at the room around us and then at each other again. Simultaneously we roared with laughter, a laughter that blew all the wealth out of the room and let in richness. Her laugh was the same whooping, braying belly laugh I remembered so well, an un-self-conscious and lusty laugh, and it reassured me tremendously. I was so relieved I couldn't stop laughing myself, and that kept *her* going, and just as we might have stopped she pursed her lips and blew a stuttered arpeggio. There's an old recording called the *Spike Jones Laughing Record*, where the tuba player tries to play "The Flight of the Bumblebee" and falls down laughing, and the whole band breaks up and horse-laughs for a full two minutes, and every time they run out of air the tuba player tries another flutter and roars and they all break up again, and once when Shara was blue I bet her ten dollars that she couldn't listen to that record without at least giggling and I won. When I understood now that she was quoting it, I shuddered and dissolved into great whoops of new laughter, and a minute later we had reached the stage where we literally laughed ourselves out of our chairs and lay on the floor in agonies of mirth, weakly pounding the floor and howling. I take that laugh out of my memory now and then and rerun it—but not often, for such records deteriorate drastically with play.

At last we dopplered back down to panting grins, and I helped her to her feet.

"What a perfectly dreadful place," I said, still chuckling.

She glanced around and shuddered. "Oh God, it *is*, Charlie. It must be awful to need this much front."

"For a horrid while I thought *you* did."

She sobered and met my eyes. "Charlie, I wish I could resent that. In a way I do need it."

My eyes narrowed. "Just what do you mean?"

"I need Bryce Carrington."

"This time you can trot out the qualifiers. *How* do you need him?"

"I need his money," she cried.

How can you relax and tense up at the same time? "Oh, *damn* it, Shara! Is *that* how you're going to get to dance? Buy your way in? What does a critic go for, these days?"

"Charlie, stop it. I need Carrington to get seen. He's going to rent me a hall, that's all."

"If that's all, let's get out of the dump right now. I can bor . . . get enough cash to rent you any hall in the world, and I'm just as willing to risk my money."

"Can you get me Skyfac?"

"*Uh?*"

I couldn't for the life of me imagine why she proposed to go to Skyfac to dance. Why not Antarctica?

"Shara, you know even less about space than I do, but you must know that a satellite broadcast doesn't have to be made from a satellite?"

"Idiot. It's the setting I want."

I thought about it. "Moon'd be better, visually. Mountains. Light. Contrast."

"The visual aspect is secondary. I don't want one-sixth gee, Charlie. I want zero gravity."

My mouth hung open.

"And I want you to be my video man."

God, she was a rare one. What I needed then was to sit there with my mouth open and think for several minutes. She let me do just that, waiting patiently for me to work it all out.

"Weight isn't a verb anymore, Charlie," she said finally. "That dance ended on the assertion that you can't beat gravity—you said so yourself. Well, that statement is incorrect—obsolete. The dance of the twenty-first century will have to acknowledge that."

"And it's just what you need to make it. A new kind of dance for a new kind of dancer. Unique. It'll catch the public eye, and you should have the field entirely to yourself for years. I like it, Shara. I like it. But can you pull it off?"

"I thought about what you said: that you can't beat gravity but it's beautiful to try. It stayed in my head for months, and then one day I was visiting a neighbor with a TV and I saw newsreels of the crew working on Skyfac Two. I was up all night thinking, and the next morning came up to the States and got a job in Skyfac One. I've been up there for nearly a year, getting next to Carrington. I can do it, Charlie, I can make it work." There was a ripple in her jaw that I had seen before—when she told me off in Le Maintenant. It was a ripple of determination.

Still I frowned. "With Carrington's backing."

Her eyes left mine. "There's no such thing as a free lunch."

"What does he charge?"

She failed to answer, for long enough to answer me. In that instant, I began believing in God again, for the first time in years, just to be able to hate Him.

But I kept my mouth shut. She was old enough to manage her own finances. The price of a dream gets higher every year. Hell, I'd half expected it from the moment she'd called me.

But only half.

"Charlie, don't just sit there with your face all knotted up. Say something. Cuss me out, call me a whore, *something*."

"Nuts. You be your own conscience, I have trouble enough being my own. You want to dance, you've got a patron. So now you've got a video man."

I hadn't intended to say that last sentence at all.

Strangely, it almost seemed to disappoint her at first. But then she relaxed and smiled. "Thank you, Charlie. Can you get out of whatever you're doing right away?"

"I'm working for an educational station in Shediac. I even got to shoot some dance footage. A dancing bear from the London Zoo. The amazing thing was how well he danced." She grinned. "I can get free."

"I'm glad. I don't think I could pull this off without you."

"I'm working for you. Not for Carrington."

"All right."

"Where is the great man, anyway? Scuba diving in the bathtub?"

"No," came a quiet voice from the doorway. "I've been sky-diving in the lobby."

His wheelchair was a mobile throne. He wore a four-hundred-dollar suit the color of strawberry ice cream, a powder blue turtleneck, and one gold earring. The shoes were genuine leather. The watch was that newfangled bandless kind that literally tells you the time. He wasn't tall enough for her, and his shoulders were absurdly broad, although the suit tried hard to deny both. His eyes were like twin blueberries. His smile was that of a shark wondering which part will taste best. I wanted to crush his head between two boulders.

Shara was on her feet. "Bryce, this is Charles Armstead. I told you . . ."

"Oh, yes. The video chap." He rolled forward and extended an impeccably manicured hand. "I'm Bryce Carrington, Armstead."

I remained seated, hands in my lap. "Oh yes. The rich chap."

One eyebrow rose an urbane quarter-inch. "Oh, my. Another rude one. Well, if you're as good as Shara says you are, you're entitled."

"I'm rotten."

The smile faded. "Let's stop fencing, Armstead. I don't expect manners from creative people, but I have far more significant contempt than yours available if I need any. Now I'm tired of this damned gravity and I've had a rotten day testifying for a friend and it looks like they're going to recall me tomorrow. Do you want the job or don't you?"

He had me there. I did. "Yeah."

"All right, then. Your room is 2772. We'll be going up to Skyfac in two days. Be here at eight A.M."

"I'll want to talk with you about what you'll be needing, Charlie," Shara said. "Give me a call tomorrow."

I whirled to face her, and she flinched from my eyes.

Carrington failed to notice. "Yes, make a list of your requirements by tomorrow, so it can go up with us. Don't scrimp—if you don't fetch it, you'll do without. Good night, Armstead."

I faced him. "Good night, Mr. Carrington." Suh.

He turned toward the narghile, and Shara hurried to refill the chamber and bowl. I turned away hastily and made for the door. My leg hurt so much I nearly fell on the way, but I set my jaw and made it. When I reached the door I said to myself, you will now open the door and go through it, and then I spun on my heel. "Carrington!"

He blinked, surprised to discover I still existed. "Yes?"

"Are you *aware* that she doesn't love you in the slightest? Does that matter to you in any way?" My voice was high, and my fists were surely clenched.

"Oh," he said, and then again, "Oh. So that's what it is. I didn't *think* success alone merited that much contempt." He put down the mouthpiece and folded his fingers together. "Let me tell you something, Armstead. No one has ever loved me, to my knowledge. This suite does not love me." His voice took on human feeling for the first time. "But it *is mine*. Now get out."

I opened my mouth to tell him where to put his job, and then I saw Shara's face, and the pain in it suddenly made me deeply ashamed. I left at once, and when the door closed behind me I vomited on a rug that was worth slightly less than a Hamilton Masterchrome board. I was sorry then that I'd worn a necktie.

The trip to Pike's Peak Spaceport, at least, was aesthetically pleasurable. I enjoy air travel, gliding among stately clouds, watching the rolling procession of mountains and plains, vast jigsaws of farmland, and intricate mosaics of suburbia unfolding below.

But the Jump to Skyfac in Carrington's personal shuttle, *That First Step*, might as well have been an old Space Commando rerun. I *know* they can't put portholes in spaceships—but dammit, a shipboard video relay conveys no better resolution, color values, or presence than you get on your living room tube. The only differences are that the stars don't "move" to give the illusion of travel, and there's no director editing the POV to give you dramatically interesting shots.

Aesthetically speaking. The *experiential* difference is that they do not, while you are watching the Space Commando, sell hemorrhoid remedies, strap you into a couch, batter you with thunders, make you weigh better than half a ton for an unreasonably long time, and then drop you off the edge of the world into weightlessness. I had been half expecting nausea, but what I got was even more shocking: the sudden, unprecedented, total absence of pain in my leg. At that, Shara was hit worse than I was, barely managing to deploy her dropsickness bag in time. Carrington unstrapped and administered an anti-nausea injection with sure movements. It seemed to take forever to hit her, but when it did there was an enormous change— color and strength returned rapidly, and she was apparently fully recovered by the time the pilot announced that we were commencing docking and would everyone please strap in and shut up. I half expected Carrington to bark manners into him, but apparently the industrial magnate was not that sort of fool. He shut up and strapped himself down.

My leg didn't hurt in the slightest. Not at all.

The Skyfac complex looked like a disorderly heap of bicycle tires and beach balls of various sizes. The one our pilot made for was more like a tractor tire. We matched course, became its axle, and matched spin, and the damned thing grew a spoke that caught us square in the airlock. The airlock was "overhead" of our couches, but we entered and left it feet first. A few yards into the spoke, the direction we traveled became "down," and handholds became a ladder. Weight increased with every step, but even when we had emerged in a rather large cubical compartment it was far less than Earth-normal. Nonetheless, my leg resumed biting me.

The room tried to be a classic reception room, high level ("Please be seated. His Majesty will see you shortly."), but the low gee and the p-suits racked along two walls spoiled the effect. Unlike the Space Commando's armor, a real pressure suit looks like nothing so much as a people-shaped baggie, and they look particularly silly in repose. A young dark-haired man in tweed rose from behind a splendidly gadgeted desk and smiled. "Good to see you, Mr. Carrington, I hope you had a pleasant jump."

"Fine thanks, Tom. You remember Shara, of course. This is Charles Armstead. Tom McGillicuddy." We both displayed our teeth and said we were delighted to meet one another. I could see that beneath the pleasantries, McGillicuddy was upset about something.

"Nils and Mr. Longmire are waiting in your office, sir. There's . . . there's been another sighting."

"God *damn* it," Carrington began and cut himself off. I stared at him. The full force of my best sarcasm had failed to anger this man. "All right. Take care of my guests while I go hear what Longmire has to say." He started for the door, moving like a beach ball in slow motion but under his own power. "Oh yes—the *Step* is loaded to the gun'ls with bulky equipment, Tom. Have her brought around to the cargo bays. Store the equipment in Six. He left, looking worried. McGillicuddy activated his desk and gave the necessary orders.

"What's going on, Tom?" Shara asked when he was through.

He looked at me before replying. "Pardon my asking, Mr. Armstead, but—are you a newsman?"

"Charlie. No, I'm not. I am a video man, but I work for Shara."

"Mmmm. Well, you'll hear about it sooner or later. About two weeks ago, an object appeared on radar within the orbit of Neptune, just appeared out of nowhere. There were . . . certain other anomalies. It stayed put for half a day and then vanished again. The Space Command slapped a hush on it, but it's common knowledge on board Skyfac."

"And the thing has been sighted again?" Shara asked.

"Just beyond the orbit of Jupiter."

I was only mildly interested. No doubt there was an explanation for the phenomenon, and since Isaac Asimov wasn't around I would doubtless never understand a word of it. Most of us gave up on intelligent nonhuman life when the last intersystem probe came back empty. "Little green men, I suppose. Can you show us the Lounge, Tom? I understand it's just like the one we'll be working in."

He seemed to welcome the change of subject. "Sure thing."

McGillicuddy led us through a p-door opposite the one Carrington had used, through long halls whose floors curved up ahead of and behind us. Each was outfitted differently, each was full of busy, purposeful people, and each reminded me somehow of the lobby of the New Age, or perhaps of the old movie *2001.* Futuristic Opulence, so understated as to fairly shriek. Wall Street lifted bodily into orbit —the *clocks* were on Wall Street time. I tried to make myself believe that cold, empty space lay a short distance away in any direction, but it was impossible. I decided it was a good thing spacecraft didn't have portholes—once he got used to the low gravity, a man might forget and open one to throw out a cigar.

I studied McGillicuddy as we walked. He was immaculate in every respect, from necktie down to nail polish, and he wore no jewelry at all. His hair was short and black, his beard inhibited, and his eyes surprisingly warm in a professionally sterile face. I wondered what he had sold his soul for. I hoped he had gotten his price.

We had to descend two levels to get to the Lounge. The gravity on the upper level was kept at one-sixth normal, partly for the convenience of the Lunar personnel who were Skyfac's only regular commuters, and mostly (of course) for the convenience of Carrington. But descending brought a subtle increase in weight, to nearly a quarter normal. My leg complained bitterly, but I found to my surprise that I preferred the pain to its absence. Its a little scary when an old friend goes away like that.

The Lounge was a larger room than I had expected, quite big enough for our purposes. It encompassed all three levels, and one whole wall was an immense video screen across which stars wheeled dizzily, joined with occasional regularity by a slice of mother Terra. The floor was crowded with chairs and tables in various groupings, but I could see that, stripped, it would provide Shara with entirely adequate room to dance; equally important, my feet told me that it would make a splendid dancing surface. Then I remembered how little use the floor was liable to get.

"Well," Shara said to me with a smile, "this is what home will look like for the next six months. The Ring Two Lounge is identical to this one.

"Six?" McGillicuddy said. "Not a chance."

"What do you mean?" Shara and I said together.

He blinked at our combined volume. "Well, *you* might be good for that long, Charlie. But Shara's already had over a year of low gee, while she was in the typing pool."

"So what?"

"Look, you expect to be in free fall for long periods of time, if I understand this correctly?"

"Twelve hours a day," Shara agreed.

He grimaced. "Shara, I hate to say this . . . but I'll be surprised if you last a month. A body designed for a one-gee environment doesn't work properly in zero gee."

"But it will adapt, won't it?"

He laughed mirthlessly. "Sure. That's why we rotate all personnel Earthside every fourteen months. Your body will adapt. One way. No return. Once you've fully adapted, returning to Earth will stop your heart—if some other major systemic failure doesn't occur first. Look, you were just Earthside for three days—did you have any chest pains? Dizziness? Bowel trouble? Dropsickness on the way up?"

"All of the above," she admitted.

"There you go. You were close to the nominal fourteen-month limit when you left. And your body will adapt even faster under no gravity at all. The free-fall endurance record is ninety days, by the first Skylab crew—and *they* hadn't spent a year in one-sixth gee first, *and* they weren't straining their hearts the way you will be. Hell, there are four men on Luna now, from the original dozen in the first mining team, who will never see Earth again. Eight of their teammates tried. Don't you two know *any*thing about space?"

"But I've got to have at least four months. Four months of solid work, every day. I *must*." She was dismayed but fighting hard for control.

McGillicuddy started to shake his head and then thought better of it. His warm eyes were studying Shara's face. I knew exactly what he was thinking, and I liked him for it.

He was thinking, *How to tell a lovely lady her dearest dream is hopeless?*

He didn't know the half of it. I *knew* how much Shara had already —irrevocably—invested in this dream and something in me screamed. And then I saw her jaw ripple and I dared to hope.

Doctor Panzarella was a wiry old man with eyebrows like two fuzzy caterpillars. He wore a tight-fitting jumpsuit which would not foul a p-suit's seals should he have to get into one in a hurry. His shoulder-length hair, which should have been a mane on the great skull, was tied tightly back against a sudden absence of gravity. A cautious man. To employ an obsolete metaphor, he was a suspenders-*and*-belt type. He looked Shara over, ran tests, and gave her just under a month and a half. Shara said some things. I said some things. McGillicuddy said some things. Panzarella shrugged, made further, very careful tests, and reluctantly cut loose of the suspenders. Two months. Not a day over. Possibly less, depending on subsequent monitoring of her body's reactions to extended weightlessness. Then a year Earthside before risking it again. Shara seemed satisfied.

I didn't see how we could do it.

McGillicuddy had assured us that it would take Shara at least a month simply to learn to handle herself competently in zero gee, much less dance. Her familiarity with one-sixth gee would, he predicted, be a liability rather than an asset. Then figure three weeks of choreography and rehearsal, a week of taping and just maybe we could broadcast one dance before Shara had to return to Earth. Not good enough. She and I had calculated that we would need three successive shows, each well received, to make a big enough dent in the dance world for Shara to squeeze into it. A year was far too big a spacing—and *who knew how soon Carrington would tire of her?* So I hollered at Panzarella.

"Mister Armstead," he said hotly, "I am specifically contractually forbidden to allow this young lady to commit suicide." He grimaced sourly. "I'm told it's terrible public relations."

"Charlie, it's okay." Shara insisted. "I can fit in three dances. We may lose some sleep, but we can do it."

"I once told a man nothing was impossible. He asked me if I could ski through a revolving door. You haven't got. . . ."

My brain slammed into hyperdrive, thought about things, kicked itself in the ass a few times, and returned to realtime in time to hear my mouth finish without a break: ". . . much choice, though. Okay, Tom, have that damned Ring Two Lounge cleaned out, I want it naked and spotless, and have somebody paint over that damned video wall, the same shade as the other three and I mean *the same*. Shara, get out of those clothes and into your leotard. Doctor, we'll be seeing you in twelve hours. Quit gaping and *go,* Tom—we'll be going over there at once; *where the hell are my cameras?*"

McGillicuddy sputtered.

"Get me a torch crew—I'll want holes cut through the walls, cameras behind them, one-way glass, six locations, a room adjacent to the Lounge for a mixer console the size of a jetliner cockpit, and bolt a coffee machine next to the chair. I'll need another room for editing, complete privacy, and total darkness, size of an efficiency kitchen, another coffee machine."

McGillicuddy finally drowned me out. "Mister *Armstead,* this is the Main Ring of the Skyfac One complex, the administrative offices of one of the wealthiest corporations in existence. If you think this whole Ring is going to stand on its head for you . . ."

So we brought the problem to Carrington. He told McGillicuddy

that henceforth, Ring Two was *ours,* as well as any assistance whatso-
ever that we requested. He looked rather distracted. McGillicuddy
started to tell him by how many weeks all this would put off the opening of the Skyfac Two complex. Carrington replied very quietly that
he could add and subtract quite well, thank you, and McGillicuddy
got white and quiet.

I'll give Carrington that much. He gave us a free hand.

Panzarella ferried over to Skyfac Two with us. We were chauffeured
by lean-jawed astronaut types, on vehicles looking, for all the world,
like pregnant broomsticks. It was as well that we had the doctor with
us—Shara fainted on the way over. I nearly did myself, and I'm sure
that broomstick has my thigh-prints on it yet—falling through space
is a scary experience the first time. Shara responded splendidly once
we had her inboard again, and fortunately her dropsickness did not
return—nausea can be a nuisance in free fall, a disaster in a p-suit.
By the time my cameras and mixer had arrived, she was on her feet
and sheepish. And while I browbeat a sweating crew of borrowed
techs into installing them faster than was humanly possible, Shara
began learning how to move in zero gee.

We were ready for the first taping in three weeks.

Living quarters and minimal life support were rigged for us in Ring
Two so that we could work around the clock if we chose, but we spent
nearly half of our nominal "off hours" in Skyfac One. Shara was
required to spend half of three days a week there with Carrington, and
spent a sizable portion of her remaining putative sack time out in
space, in a p-suit. At first it was a conscious attempt to overcome her
gut-level fear of all that emptiness. Soon it became her meditation, her
retreat, her artistic reverie, and attempt to gain from contemplation
of the cold black depths enough insight into the meaning of extrater-
restrial existence to dance of it.

I spent my own time arguing with engineers and electricians and
technicians and a damn fool union legate who insisted that the second
Lounge, finished or not, belonged to the hypothetical future crew and
administrative personnel. Securing his permission to work there wore
the lining off my throat and the insulation off my nerves. Far too many
nights I spent slugging instead of sleeping. Minor example: every interior wall in the whole damned second Ring was painted the identical
shade of turquoise—and they couldn't duplicate it to cover that god-
forsaken video wall in the Lounge. It was McGillicuddy who saved me
from gibbering apoplexy—at his suggestion I washed off the third latex
job, unshipped the outboard camera that fed the wall screen, brought
it inboard and fixed it to scan an interior wall in an adjoining room.
That made us friends again.

It was all like that: jury-rig, improvise, file to fit, and paint to cover.
If a camera broke down, I spent sleep time talking with off-shift engineers, finding out what parts in stock could be adapted. It was sim-

ply too expensive to have anything shipped up from Earth's immense gravity well, and Luna didn't have what I needed.

At that, Shara worked harder than I did. A body must totally re-coordinate itself to function in the absence of weight—she had to forget literally everything she had ever known or learned about dancing and acquire a whole new set of skills. This turned out to be even harder than we had expected. McGillicuddy had been right: what Shara had learned in her year of one-sixth gee was an exaggerated attempt to *retain* terrestrial patterns of coordination—rejecting them altogether was actually easier for *me*.

But I couldn't keep up with her—I had to abandon any thought of handheld camera work and base my plans solely on the six fixed cameras. Fortunately GLX-5000s have a ball-and-socket mount: even behind that damned one-way glass I had about forty degrees of traverse on each one. Learning to coordinate all six simultaneously on the Hamilton Board did a truly extraordinary thing to me—it lifted me that one last step to unity with my art. I found that I could learn to be aware of all six monitors with my mind's eye, to perceive almost spherically, to—not share my attention among the six—to *encompass* them all, seeing like a six-eyed creature from many angles at once. My mind's eye became holographic, my awareness multilayered. I began to really understand, for the first time, three-dimensionality.

It was that fourth dimension that was the kicker. It took Shara two days to decide that she could not possibly become proficient enough in free-fall maneuvering to sustain a half-hour piece in the time required. So she rethought her work plan too, adapting her choreography to the demands of exigency. She put in six hard days under normal Earth weight.

And for her, too, the effort brought her that one last step toward apotheosis.

On Monday of the fourth week we began taping *Liberation*.

Establishing shot:

A great turquoise box, seen from within. Dimensions unknown, but the color somehow lends an impression of immensity, of vast distances. Against the far wall, a swinging pendulum attests that this is a standard-gravity environment; but the pendulum swings so slowly and is so featureless in construction that it is impossible to estimate its size and so extrapolate that of the room.

Because of this trompe l'oeil effect, the room seems rather smaller than it really is when the camera pulls back and we are wrenched into proper perspective by the appearance of Shara, prone, inert, face down on the floor, facing us.

She wears beige leotard and tights. Hair the color of fine mahogany is pulled back into a loose ponytail which fans across one shoulder blade. She does not appear to breathe. She does not appear to be alive.

Music begins. The aging Mahavishnu, on obsolete nylon acoustic, establishes a minor E in no hurry at all. A pair of small candles in simple brass holders appear, inset on either side of the room. They are larger than life, though small beside Shara. Both are unlit.

Her body . . . there is no word. It does not move, in the sense of motor activity. One might say that a ripple passes through it, save that the motion is clearly all outward from her center. She *swells,* as if the first breath of life was being taken by her whole body at once. She lives.

The twin wicks begin to glow, oh, softly. The music takes on quiet urgency.

Shara raises her head to us. Her eyes focus somewhere beyond the camera yet short of infinity. Her body writhes, undulates, and the glowing wicks are coals (that this brightening takes place in slow motion is not apparent).

A violent contraction raises her to a crouch, spilling the ponytail across her shoulder. Mahavishnu begins a cyclical cascade of runs, in increasing tempo. Long, questing tongues of yellow-orange flame begin to blossom *downward* from the twin wicks, whose coals are turning to blue.

The contraction's release flings her to her feet. The twin skirts of flame about the wicks curl up over themselves, writhing furiously, to become conventional candle flames, flickering now in normal time. Tablas, tambouras, and a bowed string bass join the guitar, and they segue into an energetic interplay around a minor seventh that keeps trying, fruitlessly, to find resolution in the sixth. The candles stay in perspective but dwindle in size until they vanish.

Shara begins to explore the possibilities of motion. First she moves only perpendicular to the camera's line of sight, exploring that dimension. Every motion of arms or legs or head is clearly seen to be a defiance of gravity, of a force as inexorable as radioactive decay, as entropy itself. The most violent surges of energy succeed only for a time—the outflung leg falls, the outthrust arm drops. She must struggle or fall. She pauses in thought.

Her hands and arms reach out toward the camera, and at the instant they do we cut to a view from the left-hand wall. Seen from the right side, she reaches out into this new dimension and soon begins to move in it. (As she moves backward out of the camera's field, its entire image shifts right on our screen, butted out of the way by the incoming image of a second camera, which picks her up as the first loses her without a visible seam.)

The new dimension too fails to fulfill Shara's desire for freedom from gravity. Combining the two, however, presents so many permutations of movement that for a while, intoxicated, she flings herself into experimentation. In the next fifteen minutes, Shara's entire background and history in dance are recapitulated in a blinding tour de force that incorporates elements of jazz, modern, and the more graceful aspects of Olympic-level, mat gymnastics. Five cameras come into play, singly and in pairs on split-screen, as the "bag of tricks" amassed in a lifetime of study and improvisation are rediscovered and performed by a superbly trained and versatile body, in a pyrotechnic display that would shout of joy if her expression did not remain aloof, almost arrogant. *This is the offering,* she seems to say, *which you would not accept. This, by itself, was not good enough.*

And it is not. Even in its raging energy and total control, her body returns again and again to the final compromise of mere erectness, that last simple refusal to fall.

Clamping her jaw, she works into a series of leaps, ever longer, ever higher. She seems at last to hang suspended for full seconds, straining to fly. When, inevitably, she falls, she falls reluctantly, only at the last possible instant tucking and rolling back onto her feet. The musicians are in a crescendoing frenzy. We see her now only with the single original camera, and the twin candles have returned, small but burning fiercely.

The leaps begin to diminish in intensity and height, and she takes longer to build to each one. She has been dancing flat out for nearly twenty minutes: as the candle flames begin to wane, so does her strength. At last she retreats to a place beneath the indifferent pendulum, gathers herself with a final desperation, and races forward toward us. She reaches incredible speed in a short space, hurls herself into a double roll and bounds up into the air off one foot, seeming a full second later to push off against empty air for a few more inches of height. Her body goes rigid, her eyes and mouth gape wide, the flames reach maximum brilliance, the music peaks with the tortured wail of an electric guitar, and—she falls, barely snapping into a roll in time, rising only as far as a crouch. She holds there for a long moment, and gradually her head and shoulders slump, defeated, toward the floor. The candle flames draw in upon themselves in a curious way and appear to go out. The string bass saws on, modulating down to D.

Muscle by muscle, Shara's body gives up the struggle. The air seems to tremble around the wicks of the candles, which have now grown nearly as tall as her crouching form.

Shara lifts her face to the camera with evident effort. Her face is anguished, her eyes nearly shut. A long beat.

All at once she opens her eyes wide, squares her shoulders, and contracts. It is the most exquisite and total contraction ever dreamed of, filmed in realtime but seeming almost to be in slow motion. She holds it. Mahavishnu comes back in on guitar, building in increasing tempo from a downtuned bass string to a D with a flatted fourth. Shara holds.

We shift for the first time to an overhead camera, looking down on her from a great height. As Mahavishnu's picking increases to the point where the chord seems a sustained drone, Shara slowly lifts her head, still holding the contraction, until she is staring directly up at us. She poises there for an eternity, like a spring wound to the bursting point. . . .

. . . and explodes upward toward us, rising higher and faster than she possibly can in a soaring flight that *is* slow motion now, coming closer and closer until her hands disappear off either side and her face fills the screen, flanked by two candles which have bloomed into gouts of yellow flame in an instant. The guitar and bass are submerged in an orchestra.

Almost at once she whirls away from us, and the POV switches to the original camera, on which we see her fling herself down ten meters to the floor, reversing her attitude in midflight and twisting. She comes out of her roll in an absolutely flat trajectory that takes her the length of the room. She hits the far wall with a crash audible even over the music, shattering the still pendulum. Her thighs soak up the kinetic energy and then release it, and once again she is racing toward us, hair streaming straight out behind her, a broad smile of triumph growing larger in the screen.

In the next five minutes all six cameras vainly try to track her as she caroms around the immense room like a hummingbird. trying to batter its way out of a cage, using the walls, floor, and ceiling the way a jai alai master does, *existing in three dimensions.* Gravity is defeated. The basic assumption of all dance is transcended.

Shara is transformed.

She comes to rest at last at vertical center in the forefront of the turquoise cube, arms-legs-fingers-toes-face straining *outward,* turning gently end over end. All four cameras that bear on her join in a four-way split-screen, the orchestra resolves into its final E major, and—fadeout.

I had neither the time nor the equipment to create the special effects that Shara wanted. So I figured out ways to warp reality to my need. The first candle segment was a twinned shot of a candle being blown out from above—in ultraslow motion, and in reverse. The second segment was a simple recording of reality. I had lit the candle, started taping—and had the Ring's spin killed. A candle behaves oddly in zero gee. The low-density combustion gases do not rise up from the flame, allowing air to reach it from beneath. The flame does not go out: it becomes dormant. Restore gravity within a minute or so, and it blooms back to life again. All I did was monkey with speeds a bit to match in with the music and Shara's dance. I got the idea from the foreman of the metal shop where we were designing things Shara would need for the next dance.

I set up a screen in the Ring One Lounge, and everyone in Skyfac who could cut work crowded in for the broadcast. They saw exactly what was being sent out over worldwide satellite hookup (Carrington had sufficient pull to arrange twenty-five minutes without commercial interruption) almost a full half-second before the world did.

I spent the broadcast in the Communications Room, chewing my fingernails. But it went without a hitch, and I slapped my board dead and made it to the Lounge in time to see the last half of the standing ovation. Shara stood before the screen, Carrington sitting beside her, and I found the difference in their expressions instructive. Her face showed no surprise or modesty. She had had faith in herself throughout, had approved this tape for broadcast—she was aware, with that incredible detachment of which so few artists are capable, that the wild applause was only what she deserved. But her face showed that she was deeply surprised—and deeply grateful— to be given what she deserved.

Carrington, on the other hand, registered a triumph strangely mingled with relief. He too had faith in Shara, backing it with a large investment—but his faith was that of a businessman in a gamble he believes will pay off, and as I watched his eyes and the glisten of sweat on his forehead, I realized that no businessman ever takes an expensive gamble without worrying that it may be the fiasco that will begin the loss of his only essential commodity: face.

Seeing his kind of triumph next to hers spoiled the moment for me, and instead of thrilling for Shara I found myself almost hating her. She spotted me and waved me to join her before the cheering crowd, but I turned and literally flung myself from the room. I borrowed a bottle from the metal-shop foreman and got stinking.

The next morning my head felt like a fifteen-amp fuse on a forty-amp circuit, and I seemed to be held together only by surface tension. Sudden movements frightened me. It's a long fall off that wagon, even at one-sixth gee.

The phone chimed—I hadn't had time to rewire it—and a young man I didn't know politely announced that Mr. Carrington wished to see me in his office. At once. I spoke of a barbed-wire suppository, and what Mr. Carrington might do with it, at once. Without changing expression, he repeated his message and disconnected.

So I crawled into my clothes, decided to grow a beard, and left. Along the way I wondered what I had traded my independence for, and why?

Carrington's office was oppressively tasteful, but at least the lighting was subdued. Best of all, its filter system would handle smoke— the sweet musk of pot lay on the air. I accepted a macrojoint of "Maoi-Zowie" from Carrington with something approaching gratitude and began melting my hangover.

Shara sat next to his desk, wearing a leotard and a layer of sweat. She had obviously spent the morning rehearsing for the next dance.

I felt ashamed, and consequently snappish, avoiding her eyes and her hello. Panzarella and McGillicuddy came in on my heels, chattering about the latest sighting of the mysterious object from deep space, which had appeared this time in the neighborhood of Mercury. They were arguing over whether it displayed signs of sentience or not, and I wished they'd shut up.

Carrington waited until we had all seated ourselves and lit up, then rested a hip on his desk and smiled. "Well, Tom?"

McGillicuddy beamed. "Better than we expected, sir. All the ratings agree we had about 74 percent of the world audience. . . .

"The hell with the Nielsens," I snapped. "*What did the critics say?*"

McGillicuddy blinked. "Well, the general reaction so far is that Shara was a smash. The *Times* . . ."

I cut him off again. "What was the less than general reaction?"

"Well, nothing is ever unanimous."

"Specifics. The dance press? Liz Zimmer? Migdalski?"

"Uh. Not as good. Praise, yes—only a blindman could've panned that show. But guarded praise. Uh, Zimmer called it a magnificent dance spoiled by a gimmicky ending."

"And Migdalski?" I insisted.

"He headed his review, 'But What Do You Do For An Encore?' " McGillicuddy admitted. "His basic thesis was that it was a charming one-shot. But the *Times* . . ."

"Thank you, Tom," Carrington said quietly. "About what we expected, isn't it, my dear? A big splash, but no one's willing to call it a tidal wave yet."

She nodded. "But they will, Bryce. The next two dances will sew it up."

Panzarella spoke up. "Ms. Drummond, may I ask why you played it the way you did? Using the null-gee interlude only as a brief adjunct to conventional dance—surely you must have expected the critics to call it gimmickry."

Shara smiled and answered: "To be honest, Doctor, I had no choice. I'm learning to use my body in free fall, but it's still a conscious effort, almost a pantomime. I need another few weeks to make it second nature, and it *has* to be if I'm to sustain a whole piece in it. So I dug a conventional dance out of the trunk, tacked on a five-minute ending that used every zero-gee move I knew, and found to my extreme relief that they made thematic sense together. I told Charlie my notion, and he made it work visually and dramatically—that whole business of the candles was his, and it underlined what I was trying to say better than any set we could have built."

"So you have not yet completed what you came here to do?" Panzarella asked Shara.

"Oh, no. Not by any means. The next dance will show the world that dance is more than controlled falling. And the third . . . the third will be what this has all been for." Her face lit, became animated. "The third dance will be the one I have wanted to dance all my life. I can't entirely picture it, yet—but I know that when I become capable of dancing it, I will create it, and it will be my greatest dance."

Panzarella cleared his throat. "How long will it take you?"

"Not long," she said. "I'll be ready to tape the next dance in two weeks, and I can start on the last one almost at once. With luck, I'll have it in the can before my month is up."

"Ms. Drummond," Panzarella said gravely, "I'm afraid you don't have another month."

Shara went white as snow, and I half rose from my seat. Carrington looked intrigued.

"How much time?" Shara asked.

"Your latest tests have not been encouraging. I had assumed that the sustained exercise of rehearsal and practice would tend to slow your system's adaptation. But most of your work has been in total weightlessness, and I failed to realize the extent to which your body is accustomed to sustained exertion—in a terrestrial environment."

"*How much time?*"

"Two weeks. Possibly three, if you spend three separate hours a day at hard exercise in two gravities."

"That's ridiculous," I burst out. "We can't start and stop the Ring six times a day, and even if we could she could break a leg in two gees."

"I've got to have four weeks," Shara said.

"Ms. Drummond, I am sorry."

"I've got to have four weeks."

Panzarella had that same look of helpless sorrow that McGillicuddy and I had had in our turn, and I was suddenly sick to death of a universe in which people had to keep looking at Shara that way. "Dammit," I roared, "she needs four weeks."

Panzarella shook his shaggy head. "If she stays in zero gee for four working weeks, she may die."

Shara sprang from her chair. "Then I'll die," she cried. "I'll take that chance. I *have* to."

Carrington coughed. "I'm afraid I can't permit you to, darling."

She whirled on him furiously.

"This dance of yours is excellent PR for Skyfac," he said calmly, "but if it were to kill you it might boomerang, don't you think?"

Her mouth worked, and she fought desperately for control. My own head whirled. Die? Shara?

"Besides," he added, "I've grown quite fond of you."

"Then I'll stay up here in low-gee," she burst out.

"Where? The only areas of sustained weightlessness are factories, and you're not qualified to work in one."

"Then for God's sake give me one of the new pods, the small

spheres. Bryce, I'll give you a higher return on your investment than a factory pod, and I'll . . ." Her voice changed. "I'll be available to you always."

He smiled lazily. "Yes, but I might not *want* you always, darling. My mother warned me strongly against making irrevocable decisions about women. Especially informal ones. Besides, I find zero-gee sex rather too exhausting as a steady diet."

I had almost found my voice and now I lost it again. I was glad Carrington was turning her down—but the way he did it made me yearn to drink his blood.

Shara too was speechless for a time. When she spoke, her voice was low, intense, almost pleading. "Bryce, it's a matter of timing. If I broadcast two more dances in the next four weeks, I'll have a world to return to. If I have to go Earthside and wait a year or two, that third dance will sink without a trace—no one'll be looking, and they won't have the memory of the first two. This is my only option, Bryce—*let me take the chance*. Panzarella can't guarantee four weeks will kill me."

"I can't guarantee your survival," the doctor said.

"You can't guarantee that any one of us will live out the day," she snapped. She whirled back to Carrington, held him with her eyes. "Bryce, *let me risk it*." Her face underwent a massive effort, produced a smile that put a knife through my heart. "I'll make it worth your while."

Carrington savored that smile and the utter surrender in her voice like a man enjoying a fine claret. I wanted to slay him with my hands and teeth, and I prayed that he would add the final cruelty of turning her down. But I had underestimated his true capacity for cruelty.

"Go ahead with your rehearsal, my dear," he said at last. "We'll make a final decision when the time comes. I shall have to think about it."

I don't think I've ever felt so hopeless, so . . . impotent in my life. Knowing it was futile, I said, "Shara, I can't let you risk your life. . . ."

"I'm going to do this, Charlie," she cut me off, "with or without you. No one else knows my work well enough to tape it properly, but if you want out I can't stop you." Carrington watched me with detached interest. "Well?"

I said a filthy word. "You know the answer."

"Then let's get to work."

Tyros are transported on the pregnant broomsticks. Old hands hang outside the airlock, dangling from handholds on the outer surface of the spinning Ring. They face in the direction of the spin, and when their destination comes under the horizon, they just drop off. Thruster units built into gloves and boots supply the necessary course corrections. The distances involved are small. Shara and I, having spent more weightless hours than some technicians who'd been in Skyfac for years, were old hands. We made scant and efficient use of our thrusters, chiefly in canceling the energy imparted to us by the spin of the Ring we left. We had throat mikes and hearing-aid-size receivers, but there was no conversation on the way across the void. I spent the journey appreciating the starry emptiness through which I fell—I had come, perforce, to understand the attraction of sky-diving—and wondering whether I would ever get used to the cessation of pain in my leg. It even seemed to hurt less under spin those days.

We grounded, with much less force than a sky-diver does, on the surface of the new studio. It was an enormous steel globe, studded with sunpower screens and heat-losers, tethered to three more spheres in various stages of construction on which p-suited figures were even now working. McGillicuddy had told me that the complex when completed would be used for "controlled density processing," and when I said, "How nice," he added, "Dispersion foaming and variable density casting," as if that explained everything. Perhaps it did. Right at the moment, it was Shara's studio.

The airlock led to a rather small working space around a smaller interior sphere some fifty meters in diameter. It too was pressurized, intended to contain a vacuum, but its locks stood open. We removed our p-suits, and Shara unstrapped her thruster bracelets from a bracing strut and put them on, hanging by her ankles from the strut while she did so. The anklets went on next. As jewelry they were a shade bulky—but they had twenty minutes' continuous use each, and their operation was not visible in normal atmosphere and lighting. Zero-gee dance without them would have been enormously more difficult.

As she was fastening the last strap I drifted over in front of her and grabbed the strut. "Shara. . . ."

"Charlie, I can beat it. I'll exercise in *three* gravities, and I'll sleep in two, and I'll make this body last. I know I can."

"You could skip *Mass Is a Verb* and go right to the *Stardance*."

She shook her head. "I'm not ready yet—and neither is the audience. I've got to lead myself and them through dance in a sphere first—in a contained space—before I'll be ready to dance in empty space, or for them to appreciate it. I have to free my mind, and theirs, from just about every preconception of dance, change the postulates. Even two stages is too few—but it's the irreducible minimum." Her eyes softened. "Charlie—I must."

"I know," I said gruffly and turned away. Tears are a nuisance in free fall—they don't *go* anywhere. I began hauling myself around the surface of the inner sphere toward the camera emplacement I was working on, and Shara entered the inner sphere to begin rehearsal.

I prayed as I worked on my equipment, snaking cables among the bracing struts and connecting them to drifting terminals. For the first time in years I prayed, prayed that Shara would make it. That we both would.

The next twelve days were the toughest of my life. Shara worked twice as hard as I did. She spent half of every day working in the studio, half of the rest in exercise under two and a quarter gravities (the most Dr. Panzarella would permit), and half of the rest in Carrington's bed, trying to make him contented enough to let her stretch her time limit. Perhaps she slept in the few hours left over. I only know that she never looked tired, never lost her composure or her dogged determination. Stubbornly, reluctantly, her body lost its awkwardness, took on grace even in an environment where grace required enormous concentration. Like a child learning to walk, Shara learned how to fly.

I even began to get used to the absence of pain in my leg.

What can I tell you of *Mass* if you have not seen it? It cannot be described, even badly, in mechanistic terms, the way a symphony could be written out in words. Conventional dance terminology is, by its built-in assumptions, worse than useless, and if you are at all familiar with the new nomenclature you *must* be familiar with *Mass Is a Verb,* from which it draws *its* built-in assumptions.

Nor is there much I can say about the technical aspects of *Mass.* There were no special effects, not even music. Brindle's superb score was composed *from the dance* and added to the tape with my permission two years later, but it was for the original, silent version that I was given the Emmy. My entire contribution, aside from editing, and installing the two trampolines, was to camouflage batteries of wide-dispersion light sources in clusters around each camera eye and wire them so that they energized only when they were out of frame with respect to whichever camera was on at the time—ensuring that Shara was always lit from the front, presenting two (not always congruent) shadows. I made no attempt to employ flashy camera work; I simply recorded what Shara danced, changing POV only as she did.

No, *Mass Is a Verb* can be described only in symbolic terms, and then poorly. I can say that Shara demonstrated that mass and inertia are as able as gravity to supply the dynamic conflict essential to dance. I can tell you that from them she distilled a kind of dance that could only have been imagined by a group-head consisting of an acrobat, a stunt-diver, a sky-writer, and an underwater ballerina. I can tell you that she dismantled the last interface between herself and utter freedom of motion, subduing her body to her will and space itself to her need.

And still I will have told you next to nothing. For Shara sought more than freedom—she sought meaning. *Mass* was, above all, a spiritual event—its title pun paralleling its thematic ambiguity between the technological and the theological. Shara made the human confrontation with existence a transitive act, literally meeting God halfway. I do not mean to imply that her dance at any time addressed an exterior God, a discrete entity with or without white beard. Her dance addressed reality, gave successive expression to the Three Eternal Questions asked by every human being who ever lived.

Her dance observed her *self*, and asked, *"How have I come to be here?"*

Her dance observed the universe in which self existed, and asked, *"How did all this come to be here with me?"*

And at last, observing her self in relation to its universe, *"Why am I so alone?"*

And having asked these questions, having earnestly asked them with every muscle and sinew she possessed, she paused, hung suspended in the center of the sphere, her body and soul open to the universe, and when no answer came, she contracted. Not in a dramatic, ceiling-spring sense, as she had in *Liberation*, a compressing of energy and tension. This was physically similar, but an utterly different phenomenon. It was a focusing inward, an act of introspection, a turning of the mind's (soul's?) eye in upon itself, to seek answers that lay nowhere else. Her body too, therefore, seemed to fold in upon itself, compacting her mass so evenly that her position in space was not disturbed.

And reaching within herself, she closed on emptiness. The camera faded out, leaving her alone, rigid, encapsulated, yearning. The dance ended, leaving her three questions unanswered, the tension of their asking unresolved. Only the expression of patient waiting on her face blunted the shocking edge of the non-ending, made it bearable, a small, blessed sign whispering, "To be continued."

By the eighteenth day we had it in the can in rough form. Shara put it immediately out of her mind and began choreographing *Stardance*, but I spent two hard days of editing before I was ready to release the tape for broadcast. I had four days until the half hour of prime time Carrington had purchased—but that wasn't the deadline I felt breathing down the back of my neck.

McGillicuddy came into my workroom while I was editing, and although he saw the tears running down my face he said no word. I let the tape run, and he watched in silence, and soon his face was wet, too. When the tape had been over for a long time he said, very softly, "One of these days I'm going to have to quit this stinking job."

I said nothing.

"I used to be a karate instructor. I was pretty good. I could teach again, maybe do exhibition work, make ten percent of what I do now."

I said nothing.

"The whole damned Ring's bugged, Charlie. The desk in my office can activate and tap any vidphone in Skyfac. Four at a time, actually."

I said nothing.

"I saw you both in the airlock, when you came back the last time. I saw her collapse. I saw you bringing her around. I heard her make you promise not to tell Dr. Panzarella."

I waited. Hope stirred.

He dried his face. "I came in here to tell you I was going to Panzarella, to tell him what I saw. He'd bully Carrington into sending her home right away."

"And now?" I said.

"I've seen that tape."

"And you know the *Stardance* will probably kill her?"

"Yes."

"And you know we have to let her do it?"

"Yes."

Hope died. I nodded. "Then get out of here and let me work."

He left.

On Wall Street and aboard Skyfac it was late afternoon when I finally had the tape edited to my satisfaction. I called Carrington, told him to expect me in half an hour, showered, shaved, dressed, and left.

A major of the Space Command was there with him when I arrived, but he was not introduced and so I ignored him. Shara was there too, wearing a thing made of orange smoke that left her breasts bare. Carrington had obviously made her wear it, as an urchin writes filthy words on an altar, but she wore it with a perverse and curious dignity that I sensed annoyed him. I looked her in the eye and smiled. "Hi, kid. It's a good tape."

"Let's see." Carrington said. He and the major took seats behind the desk, and Shara sat beside it.

I fed the tape into the video rig built into the office wall, dimmed the lights, and sat across from Shara. It ran twenty minutes, uninterrupted, no soundtrack, stark naked.

It was terrific.

Aghast is a funny word. To make you aghast, a thing must hit you in a place you haven't armored over with cynicism yet. I seem to have been born cynical; I have been aghast three times that I can remember. The first was when I learned, at the age of three, that there were people who could deliberately hurt kittens. The second was when I learned, at age seventeen, that there were people who could actually take LSD and then hurt other people for fun. The third was when *Mass Is a Verb* ended and Carrington said in perfectly conversational tones, "Very pleasant; very graceful. I like it," then I learned, at age forty-five, that there were men, not fools or cretins but intelligent men, who could watch Shara Drummond dance and fail to *see*. We all, even the most cynical of us, always have some illusion which we cherish.

Shara simply let it bounce off her somehow, but I could see that the major was as aghast as I, controlling his features with a visible effort.

Suddenly welcoming a distraction from my horror and dismay, I studied him more closely, wondering for the first time what he was doing here. He was my age, lean and more hard-bitten than I am, with silver fuzz on top of his skull and an extremely tidy mustache on the front. I'd taken him for a crony of Carrington's, but three things changed my mind. Something indefinable about his eyes told me that he was a military man of long combat experience. Something equally indefinable about his carriage told me that he was on duty at the moment. And something quite definable about the line his mouth made told me that he was disgusted with the duty he had drawn.

When Carrington went on, "What do you think, Major?" in polite tones, the man paused for a moment, gathering his thoughts and choosing his words. When he did speak, it was not to Carrington.

"Ms. Drummond," he said quietly, "I am Major William Cox, commander of *S.C. Champion*, and I am honored to meet you. That was the most profoundly moving thing I have ever seen."

Shara thanked him most gravely. "This is Charles Armstead, Major Cox. He made the tape."

Cox regarded me with new respect. "A magnificent job, Mister Armstead." He stuck out his hand and I shook it.

Carrington was beginning to understand that we three shared a thing which excluded him. "I'm glad you enjoyed it, Major," he said with no visible trace of sincerity. "You can see it again on your television tomorrow night, if you chance to be off duty. And eventually, of course, cassettes will be made available. Now perhaps we can get to the matter at hand."

Cox's face closed as if it had been zippered up, became stiffly formal. "As you wish, sir."

Puzzled, I began what I thought was the matter at hand. "I'd like your own Comm Chief to supervise the actual transmission this time, Mr. Carrington. Shara and I will be too busy to . . ."

"My Comm Chief will supervise the broadcast, Armstead," Carrington interrupted, "but I don't think you'll be particularly busy."

I was groggy from lack of sleep; my uptake was rather slow.

He touched his desk delicately. "McGillicuddy, report at once," he said, and released it. "You see, Armstead, you and Shara are both returning to Earth. At once."

"*What?*"

"Bryce, you *can't*," Shara cried. "You *promised*."

"I promised I would think about it, my dear," he corrected.

"The hell you say. That was weeks ago. Last night you *promised*."

"Did I? My dear, there were no witnesses present last night. Altogether for the best, don't you agree?"

I was speechless with rage.

McGillicuddy entered. "Hello, Tom," Carrington said pleasantly. "You're fired. You'll be returning to Earth at once, with Ms. Drummond and Mr. Armstead, aboard Major Cox's vessel. Departure in one hour, and don't leave anything you're fond of." He glanced from McGillicuddy to me. "From Tom's desk you can tap any vidphone in Skyfac. From my desk you can tap Tom's desk."

Shara's voice was low. "Bryce, two days. God damn you, name your price."

He smiled slightly. "I'm sorry, darling. When informed of your collapse, Dr. Panzarella became most specific. Not even one more day. Alive you are a distinct plus for Skyfac's image—you are my gift to the world. Dead you are an albatross around my neck. I cannot allow you to die on my property. I anticipated that you might resist leaving, and so I spoke to a friend in the," he glanced at Cox, "*higher* echelons of the Space Command, who was good enough to send the major here to escort you home. You are not under arrest in the legal sense—but I assure you that you have no choice. Something like protective custody applies. Goodbye, Shara." He reached for a stack of reports on his desk, and I surprised myself considerably.

I cleared the desk entirely, tucked head catching him squarely in the sternum. His chair was belted to the deck and so it snapped clean. I recovered so well that I had time for one glorious right. Do you know how, if you punch a basketball squarely, it will bounce up from the floor? That's what his head did, in low-gee slow motion.

Then Cox had hauled me to my feet and shoved me into the far corner of the room. "Don't," he said to me, and his voice must have held a lot of that "habit of command" they talk about because it stopped me cold. I stood breathing in great gasps while Cox helped Carrington to his feet.

The millionaire felt his smashed nose, examined the blood on his fingers, and looked at me with raw hatred. "You'll never work in video again, Armstead. You're through. Finished. Un-employed, you get that?"

Cox tapped him on the shoulder, and Carrington spun on him. "What the hell do you want?" he barked.

Cox smiled. "Carrington, my late father once said, 'Bill, make your enemies by choice, not by accident.' Over the years I have found that to be excellent advice. You suck."

"And not particularly well," Shara agreed.

Carrington blinked. Then his absurdly broad shoulders swelled and he roared, "Out, all of you! *Off my property at once!*"

By unspoken consent, we waited for McGillicuddy, who knew his cue. "Mister Carrington, it is a rare privilege and a great honor to have been fired by you. I shall think of it always as a Pyrrhic defeat." And he half bowed and we left, each buoyed by a juvenile feeling of triumph that must have lasted ten seconds.

The sensation of falling that comes with zero gee is literal truth, but your body quickly learns to treat it as an illusion. Now, in zero gee for the last time, for the half hour before I would be back in Earth's own gravitational field, I felt I was falling. Plummeting into some bottomless gravity well, dragged down by the anvil that was my heart, the scraps of a dream that should have held me aloft fluttering over-head.

The *Champion* was three times the size of Carrington's yacht, which childishly pleased me until I recalled that he had summoned it here without paying for either fuel or crew. A guard at the airlock saluted as we entered. Cox led us to a compartment aft of the airlock where we were to strap in. He noticed along the way that I used only my left hand to pull myself along, and when we stopped, he said. "Mr. Armstead, my late father also told me, 'Hit the soft parts with your hand. Hit the hard parts with a utensil.' Otherwise I can find no fault with your technique. I wish I could shake your hand."

I tried to smile, but I didn't have it in me. "I admire your taste in enemies, Major."

"A man can't ask for more. I'm afraid I can't spare time to have your hand looked at until we've grounded. We begin re-entry immediately."

"Forget it."

He bowed to Shara, did *not* tell her how deeply sorry he was to, et cetera, wished us all a comfortable journey, and left. We strapped into our acceleration couches to await ignition. There ensued a long and heavy silence, compounded of a mutual sadness that bravado could only have underlined. We did not look at each other, as though our combined sorrow might achieve some kind of critical mass. Grief struck us dumb, and I believe that remarkably little of it was self-pity.

But then a whole lot of time seemed to have gone by. Quite a bit of intercom chatter came faintly from the next compartment, but ours was not in circuit. At last we began to talk, desultorily, discussing the probable critical reaction to *Mass Is a Verb,* whether analysis was worthwhile or the theater really dead, anything at all except future plans. Eventually there was nothing else to talk about, so we shut up again. I guess I'd say we were in shock.

For some reason I came out of it first. "What in hell is taking them so long?" I barked irritably.

McGillicuddy started to say something soothing, then glanced at his watch and yelped. "You're right. It's been nearly an hour."

I looked at the wall clock, got hopelessly confused until I realized it was on Greenwich time rather than Wall Street, and realized he was correct. "Chrissakes," I shouted, "the whole bloody *point* of this exercise is to protect Shara from overexposure to free fall! I'm going forward."

"Charlie, hold it." McGillicuddy, with two good hands, unstrapped faster than I. "Dammit, stay right there and cool off. I'll go find out what the holdup is."

He was back in a few minutes, and his face was slack. "We're not going anywhere. Cox has orders to sit tight."

"What? Tom, what the *hell* are you talking about?"

His voice was all funny. "Red fireflies. More like bees, actually. In a balloon."

He simply *could not* be joking with me, which meant he flat out *had* to have gone completely round the bend, which meant that somehow I had blundered into my favorite nightmare where everyone but me goes crazy and begins gibbering at me. So I lowered my head like an enraged bull and charged out of the room so fast the door barely had time to get out of my way.

It just got worse. When I reached the door to the bridge I was going much too fast to be stopped by anything short of a body block, and the crewmen present were caught flatfooted. There was a brief flurry at the door, and then I was on the bridge, and then I decided that I had gone crazy too, which somehow made everything all right.

The forward wall of the bridge was one enormous video tank—and just enough off center to faintly irritate me. Standing out against the black deep as clearly as cigarettes in a darkroom, there truly did swarm a multitude of red fireflies.

The conviction of unreality made it okay. But then Cox snapped me back to reality with a bellowed, *"Off this bridge, Mister."* If I'd been in a normal frame of mind it would have blown me out the door and into the farthest corner of the ship; in my current state it managed to jolt me into acceptance of the impossible situation. I shivered like a wet dog and turned to him.

"Major," I said desperately, "what is going on?"

As a king may be amused by an insolent varlet who refuses to kneel, he was bemused by the phenomenon of someone failing to obey him. It bought me an answer. "We are confronting intelligent alien life," he said concisely. "I believe them to be sentient plasmoids."

I had never for a moment believed that the mysterious object which had been leap-frogging around the solar system since I came to Skyfac was *alive*. I tried to take it in, then abandoned the task and went back to my main priority. "I don't care if they're eight tiny reindeer; you've got to get this can back to Earth *now*."

"Sir, this vessel is on Emergency Red Alert and on Combat Standby. At this moment the suppers of everyone in North America are getting cold. I will consider myself fortunate if I ever see Earth again. Now get off my bridge."

"But you don't *understand*. Sustained free fall might kill Shara. That's what you came up here to prevent, dammit. . . ."

"MISTER ARMSTEAD! This is a military vessel. We are facing nearly a dozen intelligent beings who appeared out of hyperspace near here twenty minutes ago, beings who therefore use a drive beyond my conception with no visible parts. If it makes you feel any better I am aware that I have a passenger aboard of greater intrinsic value to my species than this ship and everyone else on her, and if it is any comfort to you this knowledge already provides a distraction I need like an auxiliary anus, and I can no more leave this orbit than I can grow horns. Now will you get off this bridge or will you be dragged?"

I didn't get a chance to decide; they dragged me.

On the other hand, by the time I got back to our compartment, Cox had put our vidphone screen in circuit with the tank on the bridge. Shara and McGillicuddy were studying it with rapt attention. Having nothing better to do, I did too.

McGillicuddy had been right. They *did* act more like bees, in the swarming rapidity of their movement. I couldn't get an accurate count: forty or so. And they *were* in a balloon—a faint, barely tangible thing on the fine line between transparency and translucence. Though they darted like furious red gnats, it was only within the confines of the spheroid balloon—they never left it or seemed to touch its inner surface.

As I watched, the last of the adrenalin rinsed out of my kidneys, but it left a sense of frustrated urgency. I tried to grapple with the fact that these Space Commando special effects represented something that was more important than Shara. It was a primevally disturbing notion, but I could not reject it.

In my mind were two voices, each hollering questions at the top of their lungs, each ignoring the other's questions. One yelled: *Are those things friendly? Or hostile? Or do they even use those concepts? How big are they? How far away? From where?* The other voice was less ambitious but just as loud; all it said, over and over again, was: *How much longer can Shara remain in free fall without dooming herself?*

Shara's voice was full of wonder. "They're . . . they're *dancing*."

I looked closer. If there was a pattern to the flies-on-garbage swarm they made, I couldn't detect it. "Looks random to me."

"Charlie, look. All that furious activity, and they never bump into each other or the walls of that envelope they're in. They must be in orbits as carefully choreographed as those of electrons."

"Do atoms dance?"

She gave me an odd look. "Don't they, Charlie?"

"Laser beam," McGillicuddy said.

We looked at him.

"Those things have to be plasmoids—the man I talked to said they were first spotted on radar. That means they're ionized gases of some kind—the kind of thing that used to cause UFO reports." He giggled, then caught himself. "If you could slice through that envelope with a laser, I'll bet you could deionize them pretty good—besides, that envelope has to hold their life support, whatever it is they metabolize."

I was dizzy. "Then we're not defenseless?"

"You're both talking like soldiers," Shara burst out. "I tell you they're dancing. Dancers aren't fighters."

"Come on, Shara," I barked. "Even if those things happen to be remotely like us, that's not true. Samurai, karate, kung fu—they're dance." I nodded to the screen. "All we know about these animated embers is that they travel interstellar space. That's enough to scare me."

"Charlie, look at them," she commanded.

I did.

By God, they didn't look threatening. They did, the more I watched, seem to move in a dancelike way, whirling in mad adagios just too fast for the eye to follow. Not like conventional dance—more analogous to what Shara had begun with *Mass Is a Verb*. I found myself wanting to switch to another camera for contrast of perspective, and that made my mind start to wake up at last. Two ideas surfaced, the second one necessary in order to sell Cox the first.

"How far do you suppose we are from Skyfac?" I asked McGillicuddy.

He pursed his lips. "Not far. There hasn't been much more than maneuvering acceleration. The damn things were probably attracted to Skyfac in the first place—it must be the most easily visible sign of intelligent life in this system." He grimaced. "Maybe they don't *use* planets."

I reached forward and punched the audio circuit. "Major Cox."

"Get off this circuit."

"How would you like a closer view of those things?"

"We're staying put. Now stop jiggling my elbow and get off this circuit or I'll . . ."

"Will you listen to me? I have four mobile cameras in space, remote control, self-contained power source and light, and better resolution than you've got. They were set up to tape Shara's next dance."

He shifted gears at once. "Can you patch them into my ship?"

"I think so. But I'll have to get back to the master board in Ring One."

"No good, then. I can't tie myself to a top—what if I have to fight or run?"

"Major—how far a walk is it?"

It startled him a bit. "A mile or two, as the crow flies. But you're a ground-lubber."

"I've been in free fall for most of two months. Give me a portable radar and I can ground on Phobos."

"Mmmm. You're a civilian—but dammit, I need better video. Permission granted."

Now for the first idea. "Wait—one thing more. Shara and Tom must come with me."

"Nuts. This isn't a field trip."

"Major Cox—Shara *must* return to a gravity field as quickly as possible. Ring One'll do—in fact, it'd be ideal, if we enter through the 'spoke' in the center. She can descend very slowly and acclimatize gradually, the way a diver decompresses in stages, but in reverse. McGillicuddy will have to come along to stay with her—if she passes out and falls down the tube, she could break a leg even in one-sixth gee. Besides, he's better at EVA than either of us."

He thought it over. "Go."

We went.

The trip back to Ring One was far longer than any Shara or I had ever made, but under McGillicuddy's guidance we made it with minimal maneuvering. Ring, *Champion,* and aliens formed an equiangular triangle about a mile and a half on a side. Seen in perspective, the aliens took up about as much volume as Shea Stadium. They did not pause or slacken in their mad gyration, but somehow they seemed to watch us across the gap to Skyfac. I got an impression of a biologist studying the strange antics of a new species. We kept our suit radios off to avoid distraction, and it made me just a little bit more susceptible to suggestion.

I left McGillicuddy with Shara and dropped down the tube six rings at a time. Carrington was waiting for me in the reception room, with two flunkies. It was plain to see that he was scared silly and trying to cover it with anger. "God damn it, Armstead, those are my bloody cameras."

"Shut up, Carrington. If you put those cameras in the hands of the best technician available—me—and if I put their data in the hands of the best strategic mind in space—Cox—we *might* be able to save your damned factory for you. And the human race for the rest of us." I moved forward, and he got out of my way. It figured. Putting all humanity in danger might just be bad PR.

After all the practicing I'd done, it wasn't hard to direct four mobile cameras through space simultaneously by eye. The aliens ignored their approach. The Skyfac comm crew fed my signals to the *Champion* and patched me in to Cox on audio. At his direction I bracketed the balloon with the cameras, shifting POV at his command. Space Command Headquarters must have recorded the video, but I couldn't hear their conversation with Cox, for which I was grateful. I gave him slow-motion replay, close-ups, split screen—everything at my disposal. The movements of individual fireflies did not appear particularly symmetrical, but patterns began to repeat. In slow motion they looked more than ever as though they were dancing, and although I couldn't be sure, it seemed to me that they were increasing their tempo. Somehow the dramatic tension of their dance seemed to build.

And then I shifted POV to the camera which included Skyfac in the background, and my heart turned to hard vacuum and I screamed in pure primal terror—halfway between Ring One and the swarm of aliens, coming up on them slowly but inexorably, was a p-suited figure that had to be Shara.

With theatrical timing, McGillicuddy appeared in the doorway, leaning heavily on the chief engineer, his face drawn with pain. He stood on one foot, the other leg plainly broken.

"Guess I can't . . . go back to exhibition work . . . after all," he gasped. "Said . . . 'I'm sorry, Tom' . . . knew she was going to swing on me . . . wiped me out anyhow. Oh dammit, Charlie, I'm sorry." He sank into an empty chair.

Cox's voice came urgently. "What the hell is going on? Who is that?"

She *had* to be on our frequency. "Shara!" I screamed. "Get your ass back in here!"

"I can't, Charlie." Her voice was startlingly loud, and very calm. "Halfway down the tube my chest started to hurt like hell."

"Ms. Drummond," Cox rapped, "if you approach any closer to the aliens I will destroy you."

She laughed, a merry sound that froze my blood. "Bullshit, Major. You aren't about to get gay with laser beams near those things. Besides, you need me as much as you do Charlie."

"What do you mean?"

"These creatures communicate by dance. It's their equivalent of speech; it has to be a sophisticated kind of sign language, like hula."

"You can't know that."

"I *feel* it. I know it. Hell, how else do you communicate in airless space? Major Cox, I am the only qualified interpreter the human race has at the moment. Now will you kindly shut up so I can try to learn their 'language'?"

"I have no authority to . . ."

I said an extraordinary thing. I should have been gibbering, pleading with Shara to come back, even racing for a p-suit to *bring* her back. Instead I said, "She's right. Shut up, Cox."

"What are you trying to do?"

"Damn you, *don't waste her last effort.*"

He shut up.

Panzarella came in, shot McGillicuddy full of painkiller, and set his leg right there in the room, but I was oblivious. For over an hour I watched Shara watch the aliens. I watched them myself, in the silence of utter despair, and for the life of me I could not follow their dance. I strained my mind, trying to suck meaning from their crazy whirling, and failed. The best I could do to aid Shara was to record everything that happened, for a hypothetical posterity. Several times she cried out softly, small muffled exclamations, and I ached to call out to her in reply, but did not. With the last exclamation, she used her thrusters to bring her closer to the alien swarm, and hung there for a long time.

At last her voice came over the speaker, thick and slurred at first, as though she were talking in her sleep. "God, Charlie. Strange. So strange. I'm beginning to read them."

"How?"

"Every time I begin to understand a part of the dance, it . . . it brings us closer. Not telepathy, exactly. I just . . . know them better. Maybe it is telepathy, I don't know. By dancing what they feel, they give it enough intensity to make me understand. I'm getting about one concept in three. It's stronger up close."

Cox's voice was gentle but firm. "What have you learned, Shara?"

"That Tom and Charlie were right. They are warlike. At least, there's a flavor of arrogance to them—conviction of superiority. Their dance is a challenging, a dare. Tell Tom they *do* use planets."

"What?"

"I think at one stage of their development they're corporeal, planet-bound. Then when they have matured sufficiently, they . . . become these fireflies, like caterpillars becoming butterflies, and head out into space."

"Why?" from Cox.

"To find spawning grounds. They want Earth."

There was a silence lasting perhaps ten seconds. Then Cox spoke up quietly. "Back away, Shara. I'm going to see what lasers will do to them."

"No!" she cried, loud enough to make a really first-rate speaker distort.

"Shara, as Charlie pointed out to me, you are not only expendable, you are for all practical purposes expended."

"No!" This time it was me shouting.

"Major," Shara said urgently, "that's not the way. Believe me, they can dodge or withstand anything you or Earth can throw at them. I *know*."

"Hell and damnation, woman," Cox said, "what do you want me to do? Let them have the first shot? There are vessels from four countries on their way right now."

"Major, wait. Give me time."

He began to swear, then cut off. "How much time?"

She made no direct reply. "If only this telepathy thing works in reverse . . . it must. I'm no more strange to them than they are to me. Probably less so; I get the idea they've been around. Charlie?"

"Yeah."

"This is a take."

I knew. I had known since I first saw her in open space on my monitor. And I knew what she needed now, from the faint trembling of her voice. It took everything I had, and I was only glad I had it to give. With extremely realistic good cheer, I said, "Break a leg, kid," and killed my mike before she could hear the sob that followed.

And she danced.

It began slowly, the equivalent of one-finger exercises, as she sought to establish a vocabulary of motion that the creatures could comprehend. *Can you see,* she seemed to say, *that* this *movement is a reaching, a yearning? Do you see that* this *is a spurning,* this *an unfolding,* that *a graduated elision of energy? Do you feel the ambiguity in the way I distort this arabesque, or that the tension can be resolved* so?

And it seemed that Shara was right, that they had infinitely more experience with disparate cultures than we, for they were superb linguists of motion. It occurred to me later that perhaps they had selected motion for communication because of its very universality. At any rate as Shara's dance began to build, their own began to slow down perceptibly in speed and intensity, until at last they hung motionless in space, watching her.

Soon after that Shara must have decided that she had sufficiently defined her terms, at least well enough for pidgin communication— for now she began to dance in earnest. Before she had used only her own muscles and the shifting masses of her limbs. Now she added thrusters, singly and in combination, moving within as well as in space. Her dance became a true dance: more than a collection of motions, a thing of substance and meaning. It was unquestionably the *Stardance,* just as she had prechoreographed it, as she had always intended to dance it. That it had something to say to utterly alien creatures, of man and his nature, was not at all a coincidence: it was the essential and ultimate statement of the greatest artist of her age, and it had something to say to God himself.

The camera lights struck silver from her p-suit, gold from the twin airtanks on her shoulders. To and fro against the black backdrop of space, she wove the intricacies of her dance, a leisurely movement that seemed somehow to leave echoes behind it. And the meaning of those great loops and whirls slowly became clear, drying my throat and clamping my teeth.

For her dance spoke of nothing more and nothing less than the tragedy of being alive, and being human. It spoke, most eloquently, of pain. It spoke, most knowingly, of despair. It spoke of the cruel humor of limitless ambition yoked to limited ability, of eternal hope invested in an ephemeral lifetime, of the driving need to try and create an inexorably predetermined future. It spoke of fear, and of hunger, and, most clearly, of the basic loneliness and alienation of the human animal. It described the universe through the eyes of man: a hostile environment, the embodiment of entropy, into which we are all thrown alone, forbidden by our nature to touch another mind save second-hand, by proxy. It spoke of the blind perversity which forces man to strive hugely for a peace which, once attained, becomes boredom. And it spoke of folly, of the terrible paradox by which man is simultaneously capable of reason and unreason, forever unable to cooperate even with himself.

It spoke of Shara and her life.

Again and again, cyclical statements of hope began, only to collapse into confusion and ruin. Again and again, cascades of energy strove for resolution, and found only frustration. All at once she launched into a pattern that seemed familiar, and in moments I recognized it: the closing movement of *Mass Is a Verb* recapitulated—not repeated but reprised, echoed, the Three Questions given a more terrible urgency by this new altar on which they were piled. And as before, it segued into that final relentless contraction, that ultimate drawing inward of all energies. Her body became derelict, abandoned, drifting in space, the essence of her being withdrawn to her center and invisible.

The quiescent aliens stirred for the first time.

And suddenly she exploded, blossoming from her contraction not as a spring uncoils, but as a flower bursts from a seed. The force of her release flung her through the void as though she were tossed like a gull in a hurricane by galactic winds. Her center appeared to hurl itself through space and time, yanking her body into a new dance.

And the new dance said, *This is what it is to be human: to see the essential existential futility of all action, all striving—and to act, to strive. This is what it is to be human: to reach forever beyond your grasp. This is what it is to be human: to live forever or die trying. This is what it is to be human: to perpetually ask the unanswerable questions, in the hope that the asking of them will somehow hasten the day when they will be answered. This is what it is to be human: to strive in the face of the certainty of failure.*

This is what it is to be human: to persist.

It said all this with a soaring series of cyclical movements that held all the rolling majesty of grand symphony, as uniquely different from each other as snowflakes, and as similar. And the new dance *laughed,* and it laughed as much at tomorrow as it did at yesterday, and it laughed most of all at today.

For this is what it means to be human: to laugh at what another would call tragedy.

The aliens seemed to recoil from the ferocious energy, startled, awed, and faintly terrified by Shara's indomitable spirit. They seemed to wait for her dance to wane, for her to exhaust herself, and her laughter sounded on my speaker as she redoubled her efforts, became a pinwheel, a Catherine wheel. She changed the focus of her dance, began to dance *around* them, in pyrotechnic spatters of motion that came ever closer to the intangible spheroid which contained them. They cringed inward from her, huddling together in the center of the envelope, not so much physically threatened as cowed.

This, said her body, *is what it means to be human: to commit harakiri, with a smile, if it becomes needful.*

And before that terrible assurance, the aliens broke. Without warning, fireflies and balloon vanished, gone, *elsewhere.*

I know that Cox and McGillicuddy were still alive, because I saw them afterward, and that means they were probably saying and doing things in my hearing and presence, but I neither heard nor saw them then; they were as dead to me as everything except Shara. I called out her name, and she approached the camera that was lit, until I could make out her face behind the plastic hood of her p-suit.

"We may be puny, Charlie," she puffed, gasping for breath. "But by Jesus, we're tough."

"Shara—come on in now."

"You know I can't."

"Carrington'll *have* to give you a free-fall place to live now."

"A life of exile? For what? To dance? Charlie, *I haven't got any thing more to say.*"

"Then I'll come out there."

"Don't be silly. Why? So you can hug a p-suit? Tenderly bump hoods one last time? Balls. It's a good exit so far—let's not blow it."

"*Shara!*" I broke completely, just caved in on myself and collapsed into great racking sobs.

"Charlie, listen now," she said softly, but with an urgency that reached me even in my despair. "Listen now, for I haven't much time. I have something to give you. I hoped you'd find it for yourself, but . . . will you listen?"

"Y—yes."

"Charlie, zero-gee dance is going to get awful popular all of a sudden. I've opened the door. But you know how fads are, they'll bitch it all up unless you move fast. I'm leaving it in your hands."

"What . . . what are you talking about?"

"About you, Charlie. You're going to dance again."

Oxygen starvation, I thought. But she can't be that low on air already. "Okay. Sure thing."

"For God's sake stop humoring me—I'm straight, I tell you. You'd have seen it yourself if you weren't so damned stupid. Don't you understand? *There's nothing wrong with your leg in free fall!*"

My jaw dropped.

"Do you hear me, Charlie? You can dance again!"

"No," I said, and searched for a reason why not. "I . . . you can't . . . it's . . . dammit, the leg's not strong enough for inside work."

"Forget for the moment that inside work'll be less than half of what you do. Forget it and remember that smack in the nose you gave Carrington. Charlie, when you leaped over the desk: *you pushed off with your right leg.*"

I sputtered for a while and shut up.

"There you go, Charlie. My farewell gift. You know I've never been in love with you . . . but you must know that I've always loved you. Still do."

"I love you, Shara."

"So long, Charlie. Do it right."

And all four thrusters went off at once. I watched her go down. A while after she was too far to see, there was a long golden flame that arced above the face of the globe, waned, and then flared again as the airtanks went up.

There's a tired old hack plot about the threat of alien invasion unifying mankind overnight. It's about as realistic as Love Will Find A Way —if those damned fireflies ever come back, they'll find us just as disorganized as we were the last time. There you go.

Carrington, of course, tried to grab all the tapes and all the money —but neither Shara nor I had ever signed a contract, and her will was most explicit. So he tried to buy the judge, and he picked the wrong judge, and when it hit the papers and he saw how public and private opinion were going, he left Skyfac in a p-suit with no thrusters. I think he wanted to go the same way she had, but he was unused to EVA and let go too late. He was last seen heading in the general direction of Betelgeuse. The Skyfac board of directors picked a new man who was most anxious to wash off the stains, and he offered me continued use of all facilities.

And so I talked it over with Norrey, and she was free, and that's how the Shara Drummond Company of New Modern Dance was formed. We specialize in good dancers who couldn't cut it on Earth for one reason or another, and there are a surprising hell of a lot of them.

I enjoy dancing with Norrey. Together we're not as good as Shara was alone—but we mesh well. In spite of the obvious contraindications, I think our marriage is going to work.

That's the thing about us humans: we persist.

Honorable Mentions—1977

ALDISS, BRIAN W., "Where the Lines Converge," *Galileo 3*.

ALLEN, WOODY, "The Kugelmass Episode," *F & SF*, December.

ATTANASIO, A. A., "The Blood's Horizon," *New Dimensions 7*.

BEAR, GREG, "Sun-Planet," *Galaxy*, April.

BENFORD, GREGORY, "A Snark in the Night," *F & SF*, August.

BISHOP, MICHAEL, "At the Dixie-Apple," *Cosmos 4*.

——, "Leaps of Faith," *F & SF*, October.

BROXON, MILDRED DOWNEY, "The Book of Padraig," *Stellar 3*.

BRUNNER, JOHN, "The Taste of the Dish and the Savor of the Day," *F & SF*, August.

BRYANT, EDWARD, "The Hibakusha Gallery," *Penthouse,* June.

CADIGAN, PAT, "Last Chance for Angina Pectoris at Miss Sadie's Saloon, Dry Gulch," *Chacal 2*.

CHILSON, ROBERT, "People Reviews," *Universe 7*.

DANN, JACK, "Among the Mountains," *A World Named Cleopatra*.

——, "The Islands of Time," *Fantastic*, September.

DAVIDSON, AVRAM, "Manatee Gal Ain't You Coming Out Tonight," *F & SF*, April.

DE CAMP, L. SPRAGUE, "Heretic in a Balloon," *IASFM*, Winter.

——, "Spider Love," *F & SF*, November.

DRAKE, DAVID, "The Hunting Ground," *Superhorror*.

EFFINGER, GEORGE ALEC, "From Downtown at the Buzzer," *F & SF,* November.

——, "Ibid." *Universe 7*.

EISENSTEIN, ALEX, and EISENSTEIN, PHYLLIS, "You Are Here," *New Dimensions 7*.

EISENSTEIN, PHYLLIS, "The Land of Sorrow," *F & SF,* September.

ELLISON, HARLAN, "Eggsucker," *Ariel 2*.

——, "The Other Eye of Polyphemus," *Cosmos 4*.

FELICE, CYNTHIA, "Longshanks," *Galileo 2*.

FREDE, RICHARD, "Oh Lovelee Appearance of the Lass from the North Countree," *Graven Images*.

GIBSON, WILLIAM, "Fragments of a Hologram Rose," *Unearth 3*.

GOTSCHALK, FELIX C., "Home Sweet Geriatric Dome," *New Dimensions 7*.

——, "The Veil Over the River," *Orbit 19*.

GRANT, CHARLES L., "A Glow of Candles, A Unicorn's Eye," *Graven Images*.

——, "Red River Lies Drowning," *Fantastic*, February.

GUTHRIDGE, GEORGE, "The Exiled, the Hunted," *F & SF*, June.

HALDEMAN, JACK C., "Vector Analysis," *Analog,* May.
HALDEMAN, JOE, "A Time to Live," *Analog,* May.
KILLOUGH, LEE, "Tropic of Eden," *F & SF,* August.
LEIBER, FRITZ, "A Rite of Spring," *Universe 7.*
————, "Dark Wings," *Superhorror.*
LUPOFF, RICHARD, "The Child's Story," *Cosmos 3.*
LYNN, ELIZABETH A., "I Dream of a Fish, I Dream of a Bird," *IASFM,* Summer.
MALZBERG, BARRY N., "Choral," *Graven Images.*
MARTIN, GEORGE R. R., "The Stone City," *New Voices in SF.*
MC CLINTOCK, MICHAEL W., "Under Jupiter," *Orbit 19.*
MC INTYRE, VONDA N., "Aztecs," *2076: The American Tricentennial.*
MONTELEONE, THOMAS F., "Camera Obscura," *The Arts and Beyond.*
NIVEN, LARRY, "Three Vignettes," *Cosmos 1.*
PRENTICE, PATRICK HENRY, "Welcome to the Tricentennial," *2076: The American Tricentennial.*
REAMY, TOM, "The Detweiler Boy," *F & SF,* April.
REAVES, J. MICHAEL, "Shadetree," *F & SF,* September.
ROBERTS, KEITH, "The Big Fans," *F & SF,* May.
ROBINSON, KIM STANLEY, "The Disguise," *Orbit 19.*
RUSS, JOANNA, "How Dorothy Kept Away the Spring," *F & SF,* February.
SCHENCK, HILBERT, "Three Days at the End of the World," *F & SF,* September.
SCHOLZ, CARTER, "The Ninth Symphony of Ludwig Van Beethoven and Other Lost Songs," *Universe 7.*
SIMAK, CLIFFORD D., "Auk House," *Stellar 3.*
SPINRAD, NORMAN, "Blackout," *Cosmos 3.*
STRUGATSKY, ARKADY, and STRUGATSKY, BORIS, "Roadside Picnic," *Roadside Picnic.*
STURGEON, THEODORE, "Harry's Note," *Chrysalis.*
THURSTON, ROBERT, "The Mars Ship," *F & SF,* June.
————, "Wheels Westward," *Cosmos 4.*
TIPTREE, JAMES, JR., "Time-Sharing Angel," *F & SF,* October.
TUTTLE, LISA, "Kin to Kaspar Hauser," *Galaxy,* April.
————, "The Family Monkey," *New Voices in SF.*
UTLEY, STEVEN, "Time and Hagakure," *IASFM,* Winter.
————, "Upstart," *F & SF,* June.
VANCE, JACK, "The Bagful of Dreams," *Flashing Swords! 4.*
VARLEY, JOHN, "Equinoctial," *Ascents of Wonder.*
————, "Lollipop and the Tar Baby," *Orbit 19.*
VINGE, JOAN, "Eyes of Amber," *Analog,* June.
WALDROP, HOWARD, "The Adventure of the Grinder's Whistle," *Chacal 2.*
WOLFE, GENE, "Many Mansions," *Orbit 19.*
————, "The Marvelous Brass Chessplaying Automaton," *Universe 7.*